DEVIL OF A DUKE

KATHLEEN AYERS

Nicholas Tremaine, Viscount Lindley, heir to the most cursed title in England, hummed a merry tune and pretended to trip over his feet. The alley behind the Green Parrot was dark and quiet, the perfect spot to stage a robbery of a drunken soul, newly arrived to the islands of Bermuda. Which was likely what the pair of dirty nitwits stalking him assumed.

The dirty nitwits were quite wrong.

Nick had much more experience in stalking prey than the fools behind him, though he supposed he did not look dangerous at the moment. They thought him half blind and drunk.

A footstep shuffled behind him. A stone rolled past the toe of his boot and settled in the dirt.

Nick sighed, flicking an ash off his cheroot. *Best to get on with this*. He forced his feet into a shuffle, tangling his long legs as if he couldn't walk properly.

The footsteps at his back quickened in anticipation.

A bead of sweat slid down Nick's forehead to settle behind the eye-patch covering his left eye. He resisted the urge to tear the damn bit of leather off his face. Hot and uncomfortable, the eye-patch was a necessary evil, and he had no wish to allow anyone, even his assailants, see him without it. The risk was simply too great. One look at his mismatched eyes and the jig would be up. His eyes, one brown, the other a brilliant blue, marked him immediately. No one but the Devil of Dunbar sported eyes like that in all of England. The mark, the *ton* gossiped, of the Dunbars' continued pact with Old Scratch himself.

Nick itched at the flesh behind the eye patch as a rusty cough erupted over his shoulder.

He might be damned, but he was certainly healthier than *that*. The man's deep hacking, sounding as if he breathed through swamp water, belied his future fate. Nick would be doing his assailant a favor if he snapped his neck tonight.

"Damn! My blasted head hurts!" Nick groaned mournfully, slurring the words. He wobbled, then stumbled and fell against the thorny vines covering the brick wall of the Green Parrot. The thorns tore at his clothes and fluttered about his broad shoulders.

The footsteps hesitated.

Nick gave a drunken sounding snort. He should have taken a fork from the tavern to defend himself, but he supposed his bare hands would have to do. He'd snapped a man's neck before, but not lately. He was given a wide berth in London, most footpads and pickpockets in the city aware of what Nick was. Being damned had few advantages, but not being set upon by thieves while wandering the London wharves was one of them.

Nick's ears picked up the sound of hands fumbling at clothing and a knife being brought out. He took a deep breath and waited, wishing he had gone straight to the Governor's instead of deciding to have a tankard of ale. He had only wanted a bit of cool ale served to him by an attractive woman, who preferably was possessed of lovely tits. Attractive women, and indeed, the viewing of lovely tits, had been in short supply during the ocean crossing. The captain's wife, Mrs. Warren, reminded Nick of a wizened apple one found left from the previous fall. If Mrs. Warren ever suckled anyone from her shriveled bosom, it had to have been a lifetime ago. The woman detested Nick on sight, even though he'd made every effort to be charming. The only other female to make the crossing was a minister's wife. Nick never did find out her name. Mousy and timid, she barely came out of her cabin the entire trip. He passed her once and gave her a smile, which promptly sent her scurrying off to the depths of the ship as if the devil himself were after her. The little mouse did have some sense, apparently.

More whispers. Nick nearly turned to give them instruction on just how to accost him. He was trying to avoid drawing attention, which was why he deliberately chose to draw them into the alley and not the main road leading to the Governor's. He wanted neither questions nor anyone to come upon him dispatching two of Bermuda's thieves. Damn that barmaid.

The Green Parrot's barmaid, Drusilla, was a buxom lass who upon spying Nick, immediately put down a large tankard as well as a plate of cheese and bread. And, Drusilla *was* possessed of a lovely pair of tits. Unfortunately, the rest of Drusilla did not quite measure up to Nick's standards.

Nick admired the large orbs thrust at him but found the rest of Drusilla a bit worn for his tastes, even after his monkish existence of the last few months.

"Will there be anything else?" She smiled broadly enough to show her missing teeth.

"No." Nick lifted the tankard. He preferred a clean lass who had more than five teeth in her head.

Drusilla brushed a large breast against him and moved

back behind the bar, her annoyance at his rejection plain. Two men slid down in front of the bar and spoke to her in hushed tones. The first man, with the sallow looking skin of a corpse, stared particularly hard at the buttons on Nick's coat. His friend, a bit older with a fringe of greasy red hair around the edges of his scalp, chewed sporadically on the dirty nail of one hand. After speaking to Drusilla, the two men sauntered out, barely glancing at Nick.

Now, Nick surmised, the pair from the bar were behind him, intent on theft and possibly murder.

Drusilla herself had tipped Nick off. She'd brought him another ale, one he hadn't asked for. Planting a hand on her hip, she'd leaned over until he could smell the garlic on her breath. "On the house. You look parched, milord."

As Nick took a sip of the cool liquid, he did not swallow, instead the drugged ale stayed in his mouth until Drusilla turned. Then he immediately spat the mouthful into the sawdust beneath the table. Dru had slipped something into the ale, he was sure. It was an old trick, one that many taverns used in the islands to rob an unsuspecting gentleman. The idea was for Nick to wander away, drugged, and simply pass out so to be easily relieved of his purse. Once, when Nick was much younger, he'd fallen for the ruse on a trip to Jamaica. Never again.

So he'd left the tavern, pretending to be unsteady and decided to allow himself to be followed out into the alley. What else could he do? The men would likely not be put off, and he did not want to be followed to the Governor's. So Nick picked the alley and told himself he was performing a public service ridding the world of the two miscreants.

The point of a sword suddenly poked him below his left shoulder disturbing his reverie. *Finally!* Nick gave a muffled sound of distress.

"Stand right where you are, toff. I've got a sword and will

run you through in a thrice!" The words dissolved into a moist gurgle.

"Please! Don't ruin my coat," Nick slurred. "I've not much but I do so love this coat. I've only just arrived, and I fear I've had too much to drink." Nick bit his lip to keep from laughing. This whole affair was becoming most amusing.

The sword pressed harder, but the blade was so dull Nick could barely feel the tip. "Stop your blubbering, toff." The man laughed. "You've only got one eye, and for a big man you're a bit of a coward."

Nick decided he would break the man's nose. Possibly, a wrist or the man's forearm before killing him.

"Where's yer purse? I seen it in the tavern. Throw it down on the ground."

"Purse?" Nick whined. "I have no purse."

"Just gut 'im, Bobo. Dru put enough in his drink to take down two men at least." The other man slid out from behind a brilliantly blooming bougainvillea in front of Nick.

Ah! The admirer of my buttons! Part of the man's form remained in the lengthening shadows, but Nick recognized him all the same.

"Take off the coat, toff," the man coveting Nick's buttons announced to the alley. "Don't want to be getting blood on it."

Obviously, these two did not have Nick's vast experience in gutting a man. Blood got on everything. The coat would most assuredly be ruined. Nick changed his mind and decided to kill Admirer of Buttons first.

"Are ye deaf? I said take off the coat. Wren wants it." Bobo's irritated whisper came to Nick accompanied by another shaky push from the sword.

Wren. Nick watched the man in front of him. Yes, he'd have to teach Wren not to covet thy toff's buttons. Falling to one knee, he spread the long fingers of his hands, feeling the assurance of the Devil's ring on his thumb. He could twist easily from this position and kick Bobo, breaking the man's leg.

"Knew this would be easy as pie with him being one-eyed and all. Wren," Bobo addressed the younger man, "find you a big rock over there to hit him with. Dru's potion is doing our work for us. He can't even stand."

"Big man like that," Wren mused with a snicker. "Thought he'd be more of a challenge." He picked up a large rock, hefting the weight of the stone in his hand. "This will be an easy day's work."

"Am I just to lounge here quietly then and allow you to beat me over the head?" Nick tried to keep the sarcasm out of his voice and failed. He'd had quite enough of these two idiots. He planned to be at the Governor's in time for tea.

"Shut up, ye one-eyed bugger," Wren snarled.

"Yes, terribly inconvenient, being one-eyed. But I am hardly a Cyclops and you, my friend are no Odysseus." Nick turned slightly, lifting his head.

"Who's that?" Bobo sounded dumbfounded.

"Ah. You are decidedly uneducated and know nothing of mythology. What a pity. Well, I've no time to tell you the tale now."

Wren strode confidently forward, the rock clutched in his hand. "I'm sick of listening to him talk. He shouldn't even be *able* to talk with what Dru gave 'im." Wren stopped halfway to where Nick sat sniffing the air like a rodent who has sighted a mousetrap but still wishes the cheese.

"Ah! The barmaid with the fabulous pair of tits. Lovely girl," Nick said thoughtfully. "Thought about fucking her, but she's a bit, well, *used* for my tastes. I'm sure most of the Royal Navy's had a go."

"You *bastard*!" Wren spat. "That's my sister you're talking about." The rock fell from his hand to the ground. "Don't care no more about the damned coat. I'm just going to shoot you and leave you here to bleed." He pulled an ancient pistol from his coat and cocked the weapon. "No one will hear the shot. The Parrot's got thick walls."

Nick changed his position slightly, in light of the fact he had a pistol pointed at him. He'd turn and grab Bobo, throw the red-haired man over his shoulder like a filthy rag doll, snapping Bobo's neck as he did so. Wren's shot would go through Bobo and not Nick. Nick would then snap Wren's neck. He knew there was quicksand in the mangrove swamps. He could drag the bodies through there and—

A shot broke the silence of the alley followed by the smell of gunpowder.

Nick winced and grabbed his midsection, expecting the impatient Wren had fired.

Instead, Wren fell to the ground with a small thump.

Blood shot out like a spigot. "You!" Wren screamed at someone barely discernible in the shadows. "You shot my bloody knee!" Dropping his unfired pistol, he writhed on the ground in pain. Blood spurted from between his clasped fingers, splattering the grass and dirt around him.

"Drop the sword." The sound of another pistol being cocked sounded from the depths of the mangrove swamp. "Now."

The sword fell away from Nick's back.

"Don't shoot!" Bobo's frantic cry came from behind Nick.

A slight figure materialized at the edge of a line of mangroves, a slim lad holding a pistol. While he couldn't have been but a year or two out of the schoolroom, he walked with authority and little fear as he neared Nick and the two thieves. Obscured by the large, broad brimmed hat he wore, Nick couldn't make out the boy's face. Shells crunched under the soles of the boy's well worn leather boots as he approached. Nick did not miss the glimmer of the hilt of a knife tucked into the top of the left boot, nor a third pistol hanging from his belted waist.

As he approached Bobo and Wren, the boy acted as if he shot at men everyday in dark alleys, for he showed not the slightest hesitation or fear. He put his pistol even with Bobo's temple.

"I beg you drop the sword."

Bobo complied immediately and the sword fell to the ground, landing against Nick's boots. The lad nodded towards the bleeding Wren. "Collect your friend and go."

The aroma of chocolate filled the air as the boy moved closer to Nick. The scent certainly didn't come from Bobo who reeked of grease and onions. Had the lad eaten a chocolate tart or other sweet before appearing to rescue Nick? The image of the boy with a cache of desserts hidden in the mangrove swamp would have made Nick smile if the current circumstances didn't require him to be serious.

"We weren't gonna hurt 'im!" Wren screeched at the lad. "You shot out my knee! I'll likely not walk again without a crutch. High and mighty, aren't you?" Wren's free hand crawled towards his unfired pistol lying in the grass. "I know who you are, don't think for a minute I don't." Wren gave another cry. "I'm crippled because of you!"

"Don't." The boy sounded blasé and a bit annoyed. "Just *don't*. I'll be forced to shoot you again, perhaps in your other knee. Or maybe your stomach. That's a painful death I'm told. You'll suffer for days before expiring with your guts in your hands."

Wren paled. His blood-stained hand retreated from the pistol and returned to his knee, where he rocked in pain.

Bobo's mouth hung open in shock, a bit of drool dangling from his lips.

What a gruesome little lad he was. While Nick was grateful his time in Bermuda would not start with a bloody hole in *his* stomach, he found he was a bit irritated he'd been needlessly rescued. And that Bobo and Wren would not meet their deserved demise at his hands. *I'm the bloody Devil of Dunbar. Saved by a boy from incompetent thieves no less.*

"Go on." The boy said, lifting the pistol a bit higher, prodding Bobo to move.

Bobo nodded, eyes wide, his chin quivering in fear. Slowly, his hands in the air, he made his way to Wren. Hooking his beefy arms around the younger man, he turned away from the boy as if afraid to look the lad in the eye and scooped up his friend.

Wren's cheeks puffed out as he tried to stand on his injured leg. He glared at the boy, his eyes narrowing into slits. "I'll not be forgetting this." He winced. "Your name won't protect you." He spit into the grass and leaned his body against Bobo.

The boy didn't flinch or even acknowledge the implied threat. His arm remained steady, pistol aimed at the two men until they hobbled off around the corner. A trail of blood from Wren's shattered knee wound through the dirt and grass, marking their passage.

The boy lowered his pistol to his waist but kept the weapon cocked. He turned towards Nick, his arm taut, ready to shoot Nick at a moment's notice.

Nick rather thought the boy's suspicion a bit unwarranted, given the circumstances. He unraveled his tall form slowly until he stood, towering over the lad. He held up his large hands in supplication and took a careful step towards his savior.

The pistol came up in a flash.

Nick raised a brow in question but put some distance between himself and the pistol. *Distrustful little shit.* "Nice hat." Nick gave the lad a polite smile. "You smell of chocolate. Do you have a horde of it stockpiled in the mangrove swamp?"

"Funny." The boy didn't lower the pistol.

A bit of wind gusted up and blew against the boy's oversized shirt. The cotton billowed about his slight frame.

Nick struggled again to make out the lad's face beneath the hat, but the brim was too large, ridiculously so. Almost, Nick thought, as if the lad was concerned about getting too much sun on his cheeks.

Wind whistled again through the alley, this time causing the fronds of a large palm to sway to and fro.

The boy's shirt puffed about him like a sail around his form, threatening to pull the well-worn cotton out of the lad's waistband. A light brown lock of hair fell from beneath his hat, landing neatly on his shoulder.

The boy cursed under his breath.

Nick lifted a brow in surprise. *What a salty vocabulary the boy had.* No doubt he was the bane of his tutor. He lowered his hands and slowly moved forward.

"That's far enough," his rescuer snapped. "You may have noticed that I am an excellent shot."

"I did, indeed," Nick admitted. "You are a most excellent shot. I wonder what you could do with a knife?" His gaze flickered down to the bit of silver protruding from the top of a boot.

"And at this close range." The pistol turned to point directly at Nick's chest. "I would do far worse than ruin your coat."

"Agreed. I am quite partial to this coat." Nick swept a hand down one tailored sleeve. "I'll behave."

"Newly arrived?" The boy lowered his pistol but did not put it down. He walked over to Wren's discarded pistol and bent to pick up the weapon. "Only the newly arrived are stupid enough to venture into the Green Parrot. I'm betting

Drusilla served you." The tone was clipped and decidedly upper class.

Nick took objection to being called stupid. "I was not stupid enough to drink Dru's concoction," he countered. "And yes, my ship docked mere hours ago. I've received such a charming introduction to your little island and its citizens that I am considering settling here."

"Oh, I doubt you'd like it." The boy snorted. "I've seen many an English gent come to these islands and leave within a month."

"I disagree." Nick threw out the story he'd concocted for himself. "I am here to purchase land and start my life afresh. I have a wealthy patroness, the Dowager Marchioness of Cambourne. Perhaps you've heard of her?"

"I didn't ask for your life history, though I'm sure I'd find it endlessly entertaining." The boy shook his head. "You'd do better to take the next ship back to London and ask your 'patroness' for her assistance there. While Hamilton, and indeed all of Bermuda abounds with opportunity, I'm not sure you are suited to the climate." The brim of the hat pointed towards Nick's brow, now dripping with sweat.

He'd been nearly robbed, killed, and now his reputation as a gentleman was being insulted all in one afternoon! Nick was having a glorious time. The current situation was the most amusing thing that had happened to him in ages. "Bermuda and it's 'climate' do not concern me in the least." He wiped his brow. "I'll get used to the heat as well as the citizenry."

"You nearly got yourself killed and by your own admission, you are newly arrived. Despite your size you aren't very menacing." The boy shrugged. "And you're half blind."

"Yes." Nick waved to the eye-patch. "I suppose they thought I'd be an easy mark."

"And the fact you didn't even try to fight back." The patrician voice mocked him. "Man as big as you and no weapon?

Not even a knife? I thought all you London dandies kept at least a small pistol up your sleeve."

Not in the whole of his life had Nick *ever* been accused of being a dandy. Ever.

"Good thing I came along. Saved you. Else you'd be dead. I don't suppose your patroness would appreciate that?"

His rescuer's smug attitude started to grate on Nick's nerves, though he wasn't about to correct it. "Indeed. I am in your debt. You saved me," Nick said softly. He bowed low as if meeting royalty. "Nick Shepherd, lately of London, at your service."

"Well, Nick Shepherd, lately of London. Take my advice and take the next ship right back to England where you'll be more at home. I might not be around the next time you find yourself in trouble." The words were tinged with dislike and scorn.

Interesting. Usually one had to know Nick for at least an hour before a negative opinion was formed. He thought his savior's quick assessment to be totally unfair. "Indeed, I am quite terrified to view the island without you by my side," Nick said, not bothering to hide his sarcasm. "I quiver with fear at the mere thought."

The figure before him stiffened. "You are quite ungrateful."

"Quite," Nick agreed with a shrug before leaning back against the wall of the Green Parrot. He pulled a cheroot from his pocket and lit it, tossing the match down on the ground where it landed at his savior's well-booted feet.

"Well, it's been delightful getting to know you," Nick said into the late afternoon air, pretending to be totally immersed in his cheroot. "I shall be sure to call out for you if I am in need of assistance. What *is* the name of my *savior?*" He was determined to goad the figure before him. "I shall include you in my prayers."

"Jem." The name came out choked and angry. "Though I sincerely doubt you pray, Mr. Shepherd."

"Jem? An interesting name. Short for Jeremiah?"

"Truly," the voice tightened. "I should have let them shoot you." The brim of the hat shook in agitation. "I wish I *had* let them shoot you." The pistol was uncocked and tucked into the waistband. "And by the way, if you recall, the Cyclops ended up blinded and his brother dead."

Nick bit the end of his cheroot. "I see you know your Greek myths, Jem. How did you come by such an education in the wilds of Bermuda?"

The loose curl danced in the soft breeze and bounced against the boy's shoulder. "Good day to you Mr. Shepherd. Have a care for your favorite coat. Your charming personality will no doubt cause you to pawn those buttons for food within a fortnight, if you don't get killed first."

Nick opened his mouth to reply, but at that very moment a group of drunken sailors burst into the alley. The sailors were singing a delightful tune about mermaids as they stumbled about in the dirt. Nick stepped aside quickly to let them pass and dropped his cheroot in the process. He straightened after picking it up, only to find that his savior had fled and quietly melted back into the mangrove swap.

2

"**D**ear God, Mercy. I wish to actually breathe tonight." Jane Emily Manning grasped the solid mahogany post of the bed and felt wood bite into her fingers. She held on for dear life as her maid pulled the stays of her corset tight.

"Miss Jemma," Mercy used her childhood nickname, "if I don't pull, you won't fit into your gown. Don't you want Mr. Augustus to think you beautiful? You have to—"

"Yes, of course," Jemma cut her off. "By all means we should make sure that I am properly coiffed—" She winced as the stays cut into her waist. "For Augie's sake. Though I imagine he would prefer that I don't faint into the fish course."

Mercy frowned, her coffee colored skin wrinkling across her broad brow, giving her the appearance of a worried tortoise. "You're not too old for me to put over my knee, missy." The maid gave one final tug, grunting in satisfaction as she nearly pulled Jemma off her feet. "Mr. Augie is a *good* man. He's handsome and has nice manners. He's the son of the Governor." Mercy tied off the stays. "And he's mad in love with you."

"Mad in love with me? Mad in love with Sea Cliff," Jemma muttered under her breath, referring to her home.

Mercy strode over to the dressmaker's model where Jemma's gown hung and tossed the layers of frothy, cream colored taffeta over a muscular arm. "Most women would kill to have a man like Mr. Augie. Every girl on the island wishes he were courting *her*. So what if he loves Sea Cliff as much as you? It's gonna be his when you marry. You don't want him to sell it like Joanna Parson's husband did. Now that was a bit of a shock to us all. She married a fortune hunter and no sooner did they wed than he sold her inheritance and took her to London."

"I remember."

"Well, Mr. Augie won't never sell Sea Cliff. He won't leave Bermuda. He's not some man coming here to make his fortune."

Not like Mr. Shepherd. Mercy's words conjured up the image of the large, dark man with the eye-patch, bringing to mind their meeting of little more than a week ago. *He* certainly was just another gentleman hoping to make his fortune in Bermuda by wedding an heiress. Bermuda, situated amongst multiple trade routes, bred wealthy merchants by the dozens. The islands were also a major source of salt for the British Empire. Jemma's father himself owned several salt operations. The island saw a fresh crop of fortune hunters every year or so. A well connected man could marry his wealth rather than work for it.

"I suppose that's true." But Mr. Shepherd hadn't struck her as the typical fortune hunter either. She obediently stood, arms out, to step into her gown.

Mercy gave a snort. "It *is* true. Besides, I don't know any other man that allows his betrothed to run around in breeches shooting skinks."

"Future betrothed." Jemma frowned. What else was she supposed to use for target practice if not the large lizards that dotted the island?

"You two have an understanding. Everyone knows it. Mr. Augie puts up with your nonsense, is all I mean."

"I prefer to call it an eccentricity," Jemma countered at Mercy's reference to her preference for wearing breeches in order to hunt. She was proud of the fact that she could shoot as well as any man. She could even hit a quickly moving skink with a thrown knife. Not an easy feat.

Mercy buttoned up the gown and said nothing.

"So what if I like to do a bit of hunting and fishing?"

Mercy smoothed down the silk around the buttons. "You promised your father you would stop now that you're grown and about to be married."

"I'm not about to be married. Yet. And I can't go sneaking behind a skink in a dress, wearing gloves. Honestly Mercy," Jemma cajoled. "I know you don't like it. But no one sees me. I promise."

The maid adjusted the fit, tugging down the bodice until the tops of Jemma's breasts were partially exposed. "Oh they see you, they just pretend not to. I hear about it. We servants talk, you know. Best you not let Lady Corbett find out."

Looking down at her exposed bosom, Jemma sighed at the mention of her future mother-in-law. "Why must you do that, Mercy?" Jemma tugged the bodice up. "You find my hunting attire to be scandalous but baring my chest to all of Bermuda is acceptable? I look quite wanton."

Mercy clucked her tongue. "Now Miss Jemma, they aren't big." She nodded towards Jemma's breasts and pulled the bodice down again. "But most men still want to see a bit of them. That's not being wanton. That's just showing what the

Lord gave you." Mercy held Jemma's chin, looking at her charge's face intently. "Told you to put some lemon juice on your arms and face. Told you to wear a hat."

"I did. I swear. The brim covered the whole of my face. Not a bit of sun touched my cheeks."

Mercy dropped her hand. "Why, you're nearly as dark as I am. That won't do. And look at those freckles." She shook her head. "I suppose there's no help for it now."

"No, there isn't." Jemma turned about, the layers of fabric swishing about her ankles. The dress was a creamy confection, sewn through with brilliants in a diamond pattern across the skirt and bodice. The gown was incredibly beautiful and had cost her father a fortune, but it *did* draw attention to the honeyed tone of Jemma's tanned skin. Lady Corbett, Augie's mother, *was* apt to have a fit when she saw the march of freckles across Jemma's cheeks. Honestly, Jemma *tried* to stay out of the sun. Truly. But it was incredibly difficult to shoot a pistol while carrying a parasol in the other hand.

"It's not that bad. Stop exaggerating." Jemma pursed her lips in rebuke and turned her head to the side to study her cheeks.

Mercy raised one dark brow and started to work Jemma's light brown hair into an elegant chignon.

"Stop being so disapproving." When the maid didn't respond, Jemma continued, "Fine. I'll let you put lemon juice all over me tomorrow. I promise."

Jemma glanced into the mirror again, noting the folds of silk piled around her hips. *Dear God, I appear to be sitting in a bowl of whipped cream.*

Mercy twisted Jemma's hair expertly, arranging it so that a small wisp of curls caught at the base of her neck. "And Lady Corbett will have something to say about those freckles. If you'd just put that paste on your skin like I've asked."

"You mean that horrible smelling concoction Lady

Corbett raves about? No, thank you." Jemma wrinkled her nose. "It smells terrible. Like seaweed and lemon. Besides, one day freckles will be all the rage. I'm sure of it."

Mercy's lips pressed together, but her eyes were merry. "You are the *most* contrary child." She kissed Jemma's cheek. "Always have been. Wait until Mr. Augie sees you in this dress. Why, he'll go down on one knee and propose I bet."

Jemma sincerely hoped not. She realized she was the only one not anticipating the marriage of Augustus Corbett and herself. The entire population of Hamilton, and indeed all of Bermuda, seemed poised for the event. The marriage of William Manning's daughter to the son of the Governor was akin to royalty being wed—at least on Bermuda. Everyone wished the marriage, except Jemma herself. She adored Augie, truly. But she felt not the slightest hint of passion for him. Shouldn't she feel passion? Shouldn't there be more? He didn't make her heart leap or her palms sweat.

Not like Nick Shepherd.

The image of *that* man popped into her head again. How unnerving their brief meeting had been. And it wasn't because she'd shot a man defending Mr. Shepherd. It was Mr. Shepherd himself.

Large, *handsome* gentlemen sporting eye-patches weren't all that common in Bermuda, unless you counted the retired pirates who diced and drank in seedy environs at Hamilton's wharf. But Mr. Shepherd was no retired pirate.

He was certainly a gentleman, for his clothes and accent marked him as such. And he was no dandy. Few dandies that passed through Bermuda sported a crooked nose like a prize-fighter. Fewer still bore scars across their knuckles as if they'd fought often with their hands. The sheer size of him also left her in awe. He was at least a head taller than Augie and broad of shoulder. A man like that could easily defend himself. She supposed he'd really not needed her assistance. "And arrogant," Jemma murmured under her breath. "So full of himself."

"Miss Jemma?" Mercy's eyes watched her closely, her hands still on Jemma's hair. "You're blushing."

"I'm just a bit warm," Jemma stuttered, feeling the heat in her cheeks at the thought of Mr. Shepherd's mocking smile across his full lips. He had made her feel warm that day in the alley as well, and now the mere thought of the man set her cheeks to flame. "I should have shot him."

"Miss Jemma?" Mercy placed a hand on Jemma's arm. "Who should you shoot? You look strange. Are you ill?"

"I missed a wild pig just the other day. I waited too long to shoot," she said automatically. *Mr. Shepherd. Arrogant man.* What would it be like to kiss him? To have that brilliant blue eye look down at her while he pressed his lips to hers? The thought unsettled her.

"Mmm." Mercy answered as her hands flew back over a stray curl, pushing a final pin into place. "You should be thinking about babies and not hunting pigs. Lord! What will your father and Mr. Augie do with you?"

Jemma lifted her chin and regarded her cream-colored reflection in the mirror. She wondered if Mr. Shepherd realized she was a woman that day and not a lad and if he would recognize her if their paths crossed. Why had she given him her name? "Jem" had popped out of her lips without thinking.

"What does it matter?" she answered Mercy, not really thinking of her father or Augie, but of Nick Shepherd. It didn't matter, for Jemma doubted she'd see Mr. Shepherd again.

3

Nick surveyed the group of what constituted Hamilton's society from his seat next to his hostess, Lady Corbett. As the capital city of Bermuda, Hamilton was the Governor's seat and the populace tried desperately to keep up appearances so far from home.

The table, a long, carved affair made of heavy dark wood, stretched nearly the entire length of the cavernous dining room, easily seating the twenty or so people present. The women were all dressed in bright colors—pinks, greens and yellows. Hibiscus and orchids were placed strategically in several of the lady's coiffures, no doubt plucked from their very own gardens.

The men, many of them round and plump, sat sweating in clothes made for a much colder climate. Their faces were red and blustering, both from the heat and too much rum. Rum punch, Nick noted, was being poured as much as wine at the Governor's table, not unusual considering Hamilton was a port of call in the rum trade. Nick lifted a glass of punch to his lips.

"Mr. Shepherd?" The women to his right twittered his name

Nick struggled to remember who she was, though he'd been introduced to her just before dinner. "Miss Sinclair," he recalled with relief.

Miss Sinclair's homely face beamed back at him.

"I fear you've not heard a word I've said, Mr. Shepherd. Perhaps I am boring you with my tale?" Miss Sinclair pouted, making her even more homely, if that were possible.

"My apologies, wool gathering," Nick said smoothly. "You were saying?"

Miss Sinclair giggled, showing a bit of discolored teeth. "I was just wondering how long you planned on being in Bermuda?" She cut into her fish, forking a bit of the white flesh, and reaching out with her tongue to take the fish into her mouth. She chewed slowly and seductively, watching Nick with eager eyes.

Dear God but the woman was forward. Nick hadn't blushed since he was a lad, but he nearly did now. Clearly, the ladies of Bermuda wished to be caught by any male, fortune hunter or not.

"Now Bertha," Lady Corbett intoned from Nick's other side. "Stop peppering Mr. Shepherd with questions. He's only just arrived to our fair isle. I'd venture he's made no plans to leave just yet. Have you Mr. Shepherd?"

Lady Corbett winked at Nick as if they were co-conspirators.

He smiled politely at his hostess. Lady Corbett was nothing if not ambitious. When Nick appeared on the Governor's doorstep nearly a week ago, with his letter of introduction clutched in his hand, she'd welcomed him as if he were a long lost relative. Just as he suspected she would. The Governor's wife, the avarice clear as she clutched his letter of introduction from the Dowager Marchioness of

Cambourne, could not *wait* to invite him to stay at their estate. In fact, she practically begged to install him in the guest wing. Apparently Dorthea, the Corbett's daughter, had married the second son of Lord Jennings. The pursing of Lady Corbett's lips told Nick that Dorthea's marriage did not meet her mother's expectations. Desperate to further her daughter's social standing, she was asking him to write to the Dowager Marchioness on Dorthea's behalf before Nick's tea went cold. Governor Lord Corbett, however, was more restrained in his welcome.

Nick's host sat at the opposite end of the dinner table stuffing oysters into his mouth, a stray wisp of gray hair flopping over his forehead. He laughed loudly at something the man to his right said and caught Nick observing him.

The Governor frowned slightly, drawing the deep wrinkles surrounding his mouth into a look of distaste. He chewed the oysters slowly, the jowls around his cheeks wiggling wildly as if a small animal were trapped within the folds. He regarded Nick coldly before taking another sip of punch. Turning his attention back to the table he proceeded to ignore his unwanted guest but continued to watch Nick beneath hooded eyes.

No, Nick decided, Governor Lord Corbett did not particularly like Nick Shepherd. Not a bit.

Nick didn't care.

Lady Corbett's need to curry the favor of one of London's premiere hostesses for her daughter overruled any of her husband's objections in regards to their houseguest. Nick could stay with the Corbett's as long as he liked, which suited his purposes completely.

The man to the Governor's right stopped laughing once he saw the direction of his host's gaze. An older, slightly balding man, his face florid with drink, barely gave Nick a glance before taking a sip of his rum punch. The cup trembled against his lips as his eyes slid away from Nick's face.

A stocking-clad feminine foot ran up his calf. Nick jerked suddenly in surprise, nearly knocking his chair over.

Agnes Sinclair, twin sister to the woman next to him shot him a seductive look from across the table. "Mr. Shepherd, are you all right? Do you find it warm in here?" Agnes leaned forward. "I certainly do." She strived to contort her homely face, identical to her sister's, into seduction.

A lone gazelle pinned down by two lionesses would have been more comfortable than Nick was in that moment. As practiced as he was in the art of seduction, being stalked by the Sinclair sisters was something he wasn't accustomed to.

Someone giggled at his discomfort. The feminine giggle was followed by a brief, unladylike snort.

No one but Nick seemed to notice. He swung his one-eyed gaze down the table and spotted a girl sitting next to Augustus Corbett, his host's son. Brilliants danced in her golden-brown hair as her slender shoulders shook with barely contained laughter.

Nick's lips drew together. His plight apparently held amusement for one of Lady Corbett's dinner guests.

Without looking up at him, she quickly pulled herself back behind Corbett's shoulder, hiding all but one slender forearm.

Not many people, and certainly *no* young ladies, ever mocked Nick. He'd been gossiped about all his life, had a few bibles thrown at him and Lady Withers, a Catholic, had discreetly sprinkled his jacket with holy water once, but no one made fun of the Devil of Dunbar.

Except the lad that rescued him outside the Green Parrot.

Nick turned his attention back to his dinner companions, two of Bermuda's most determined spinsters, identical twin sisters. He'd always imagined a pair of twins fighting for his affections, though the twins in his fantasies didn't even remotely resemble the plain and quite homely Sinclair sisters. "The weather, Miss Sinclair, is quite unlike what I am used to. I suppose it is a bit warm for me."

"Perhaps it's not the weather," Agnes Sinclair whispered from across the table, her pronounced lisp ruining any chance to sound remotely seductive.

No, it was definitely the weather since it was most assuredly *not* the roaming foot of Agnes Sinclair, which even now was inching back up his leg. Dear God. She put the whores in London to shame. "I suppose," he said flirtatiously hoping to draw out the giggling girl again, "that it could be something else."

Agnes Sinclair's cheeks pinked immediately. She batted her eyelashes at him and sat, arching her back so that the small bit of bosom she possessed thrust forward at him. Her sister, Bertha, ran a hand down his thigh.

Nick shifted in his chair, a false smile pasted on his face as he wondered if the twins would attempt to molest him through the meat course.

He heard it again, even over a loud discussion about the salt trade taking place to his left. Nick didn't turn his head, he merely slid his glance down the table. This time, he saw her clearly as she seemed to be so overcome with hilarity, she neglected to hide herself.

The girl bit her lip to keep from laughing out loud, but every so often an amused snort escaped her lips. Obviously, she found his plight humorous beyond belief. Her shoulders continued to rock as she attempted to contain herself. A lock of light brown hair loosened and bounced to her shoulder.

That stray lock seemed familiar.

Augustus Corbett leaned in and shushed the girl, no doubt voicing his disapproval at her antics.

Nick had several encounters with Augustus Corbett

during his brief stay at the Governor's mansion and thought the younger man a terrible stick in the mud.

The girl promptly sat back again, her laughter silenced.

"Tell me, Mr. Shepherd." Governor Lord Corbett's voice boomed from the far end of the room. "How you came to land on our fair shores. Surely with a connection to the esteemed Dowager Marchioness of Cambourne, opportunities would abound closer to home."

Twenty pairs of eyes turned to Nick as the table grew quiet in anticipation of his answer.

Agnes Sinclair's foot ceased its roving.

Lady Corbett frowned at her husband and stabbed at her fish.

"True, true," Nick stated nonchalantly in a respectful tone. "I wish, my lord to thank you first for your enormous generosity."

"Hear, hear!" The entire table lifted their goblets in toast.

Lord Corbett didn't flinch or acknowledge the compliment. He narrowed his eyes at Nick, waiting for a response.

Nick drained his glass and regarded his host. "The Dowager Marchioness is a distant cousin on my mother's side," Nick lied glibly. "My parents, God rest their souls, died when I was only a lad. The Dowager was kind enough to offer me assistance."

Well, at least that's true. Donata Reynolds, the Dowager Marchioness of Cambourne, *had* offered him assistance as a lad. She often gave him a place to stay when Nick was on the outs with Henry, his grandfather. She knew him quite well, Nick being the closest friend of her grandson, Sutton. Only she knew of his purpose in coming to Bermuda and wrote Nick his false introduction letter without a qualm.

"Indeed?" Lord Corbett speared a bit of plantain on his fork.

"The Dowager was quite generous with me. She insisted

that perhaps I should go on an adventure and make a name for myself. Be my own man."

The Sinclair twins glowed with rapt attention.

Lady Corbett smiled.

Lord Corbett merely raised a brow. "I see. Related on your father's side are you?"

The Governor sought to trip Nick up. "Sorry, sir. The Dowager Marchioness and I are related on my mother's side," Nick said smoothly. "She loved my mother dearly and despaired at her death. Lady Cambourne, knowing that I wished to be my own man and not live at her largesse, directed me to Bermuda. She spent some time here as a young woman and remembered the people of Hamilton quite fondly."

Lady Corbett gasped in happy surprise at Nick's comment and clapped her pudgy hands together. Her desire to become an acquaintance of the Dowager's was akin to a thirsty man's want of water.

Several people at the table nodded in approval at Nick's words.

The sisters Sinclair both looked at Nick greedily, he could almost hear their minds whirling with scenarios in which they could compromise themselves at his expense.

"Interesting, no doubt that dear lady visited long ago." Governor Lord Corbett bit into a roll. "Before my time."

"Yes, my lord. The Dowager is quite elderly. I don't believe she travels out of London much these days."

"Of course," the Governor intoned.

Lady Corbett pursed her lips and stared down the long table with admonishment at her husband. She clutched her knife so tightly, Nick worried that she was poised to fling it down the table into her spouse's chest.

Nick nodded to a passing servant to refill his glass. "She suggested I look into purchasing property in Bermuda, perhaps an estate whose owners wished to return to London. I feel certain I could prosper here. Her ladyship was very generous with me." He annunciated the word *generous,* which elicited another sigh from Agnes Sinclair.

The man next to Governor Lord Corbett smiled, reminding Nick of a drunken elf.

Lord Corbett did *not* smile, instead he raised his glass to his lips and continued to regard Nick over the rim of fine crystal.

"You shall stay as long as you like, Mr. Shepherd." Lady Corbett shot her husband a quelling glance.

"The Dowager will be most appreciative of your kindness to me, my lady. I thank you." Nick bowed his head and considered the man sitting next to Governor Corbett. He assumed Governor Lord Corbett to be his quarry, but perhaps Nick was mistaken, for Lord Corbett's friend appeared to listen to Nick's speech with more than polite interest and his hand continued to tremble as he popped a piece of bread into his mouth.

The expensive cut of the man's clothes and the rubies winking at his wrists marked him as wealthy. The laugh lines around his mouth and the plumpness of his face suggested he was happy, well fed and had not a care in the world. His manner with Lord Corbett was relaxed and lacking in artifice, so the two men were close friends.

Nick was perceptive, sometimes so perceptive that his observations were taken to be a form of mind reading or witchcraft. Neither was true, but given Nick's status as the Devil of Dunbar, it seemed convenient to allow the *ton* to believe it for their misconception instilled a healthy dose of respect for the his family.

The man stared back at Nick and drained his glass of drink. The goblet came back down to the table slowly and the man's eyes widened, a smile frozen on his lips as if something important to him had just been remembered.

He recognizes me. Even with the eye-patch, somehow he knows me.

Nick had come to Bermuda to find the traitorous bastard who dared to steal a packet of papers from the Duke of Dunbar's home during a house party when Nick was barely a lad. The documents were the property of the duke and contained a list of English spies embedded in France. Locations and names were noted. Treason, apparently not enough of a heinous crime for the thief, also arranged the evidence of the theft so that blame would fall on an innocent man, Nick's father, the duke's heir. Whoever the true mastermind was, he had much to answer for—the death of loyal Englishmen, Nick's parents and of course the taint of treason which sullied his family.

The last offense nearly trumped the other two as the loyalty of the Duke of Dunbar and his family had never fallen into question. The Duke of Dunbar served the Crown. *Always.*

Nick focused his attention on the man sitting next to the Governor. Who was he?

Every guest who attended that ill fated party, every man who had dealings with Nick's father had been carefully tracked down and questioned by Nick. None proved to be the man he sought. Frustrated at not finding the true culprit, Nick's search returned to one man. Lord Corbett. A man who he originally disregarded because Corbett sent a note of regret that he couldn't attend the party. He was leaving London immediately to assume the Governorship of Bermuda.

The man sitting next to Governor Lord Corbett looked up at Nick, then quickly looked away.

Nick's sixth sense tingled. The Governor's friend fairly

reeked of fear. Perhaps Corbett was not the person he sought after all.

❦

JEMMA RESISTED THE URGE TO YAWN AS SHE LISTENED TO Augie chatter on about the latest news from his sister Dorthea. Composing her features into a look of attentiveness, she nodded and interjected at the appropriate times, feigning interest. She couldn't care less what Lady Whatshername wore to Lord WhoCares' fete in the country. Or how Dorthea adored the creamed truffles that Lady Something served at the one dinner party Dorthea attended in London. Augie, his face a bit red from drink, and his dark brown hair flopping over a brow, cheerfully described every detail to her.

Lady Corbett ushered the remainder of her guests into the drawing room after dinner, disregarding the custom of the gentlemen having brandy and cigars, to announce a game of charades. She clung to Nick Shepherd's arm, leading him about the room and introducing him to the dinner guests.

What in the world was *that* man doing at the Governor's?

Jemma and her father arrived a bit late, in time only to be ushered in for dinner. Nodding her head in greeting to several of the guests, her breath caught as she saw the large form of Mr. Nick Shepherd seated next to Lady Corbett at the far end of the table.

Good Lord! Her heart beat faster and she felt giddy at the sight of him, seated amongst Lady Corbett and the Sinclair sisters. During the soup course she admired him as the glint of red in his hair caught in the candlelight and his coat stretched across the breadth of his shoulders. A warmth spilled through her as she attempted to concentrate on her soup even as she reminded herself of the man's arrogance. When the Sinclair sisters began to flirt madly with him, she smiled, thinking how appropriate that a fortune hunter should fall prey to Agnes and Bertie. When Agnes Sinclair, true to form, nearly attacked him over the fish course, Jemma simply couldn't contain her mirth.

Now he circled the room with the Governor's wife, greeting wealthy merchants and their wives cordially and with the grace and manners of the upper class. The limited society of Hamilton swirled about Nick Shepherd, the attractive, well connected stranger in their midst. Every woman present either approached the man for an introduction or forced her husband into Nick Shepherd's orbit. Connections to those in the *ton* were highly sought, and Nick Shepherd, according to the letter of introduction, had them. He never once looked her way.

Jemma was relieved. *Wasn't she?*

"There is Mother, leading about our house guest." Augie frowned, his brown eyes narrowed with dislike. "I don't know why mother is so *fascinated* with the man. I suppose she hopes that if she treats him well, the Dowager will invite Dorthea to tea in London. Dottie's husband is only a barrister in Yorkshire. He needs all the assistance Mother can provide."

"Even the vicar's wife is behaving like a silly school girl." Jemma nodded towards a portly woman who extended her beefy hand to Nick Shepherd, giggling as she did so. "I find this entire display a bit ridiculous. Bertie Sinclair nearly wedged herself into the man's lap while the chocolate tarts were served. Agnes leaned so far across the table her bodice nearly burst apart on the cheese tray. Why didn't you mention you had a houseguest?"

Augie shrugged. "I find him of no import. He's common."

"Common?" Jemma questioned, thinking that was the last word she would use to describe Nick Shepherd. He seemed the most uncommon man she'd ever met. "He's a bit too self assured. He—" Augie twisted his lips, "acts as if we are below him somehow. I don't suppose I like it. Not one bit. My father's the Governor, after all. Ah. Here they come. Mother and her new pet."

Jemma thought Augie sounded more than a little put out that all of his mother's attention wasn't focused on him.

Augie wrapped his fingers about Jemma's arm possessively. "Behave yourself and do not antagonize Mother."

Jemma stiffened at the mention of Lady Corbett. A woman she could not please no matter what she did.

Lady Corbett beamed as she pranced about on Nick Shepherd's arm as if she were the belle of the ball.

Mr. Shepherd appeared enchanted with the Governor's wife. Towering over his petite, plump hostess, he allowed her to lead him around, matching his longer strides to her practiced, mincing steps.

An unexpected jolt of anticipation slid up Jemma's spine as Mr. Shepherd neared.

"My dear Augustus," Lady Corbett's face beamed with pride as she lifted a plump cheek for his kiss.

Augie obediently pecked his mother's cheek and nodded in greeting to Shepherd but did not release his hold on Jemma. "Mr. Shepherd. Did you enjoy dinner?"

"Magnificent." The deep voice rumbled as the brilliant blue gaze fell on Jemma.

"And this is our dear Jane Emily, daughter of our great friend William Manning." Lady Corbett lay a gloved hand on Jemma's arm while pressing her cheek to Jemma's. "My dear," she whispered in Jemma's ear. "I will have my maid send over some of my special lotion for those *hideous* freckles tomorrow. I did not realize how out of hand they had become."

Jemma barely heard her. All she saw was Nick Shepherd.

Mr. Shepherd bowed, but not before his incredibly inappropriate gaze slid over the whole of Jemma's form, lingering on her bosom.

Bits of fire lit her skin where his eye touched her body. Her skin tingled and prickled with warmth.

"Miss Manning, a pleasure." He took Jemma's hand in his own, his touch causing a flame of sensation to run up her arm. He pressed a seemingly polite kiss across the knuckles of her outstretched hand, his lips lingering a bit too long before reluctantly releasing her.

Augie blew out a small puff of annoyance and clutched Jemma's arm tighter.

She ignored Augie. Indeed, Augie and his anxious puffing, as well as everyone in the room, faded into insignificance until only Nick Shepherd remained. Was that the tip of his tongue that glanced against her knuckles?

Shepherd straightened, and inclining his head politely he said, "Your servant, Miss Manning." The brilliant blue gaze again lingered on her bodice, seeming to dip down into the valley between her breasts.

Dumfounded at his attention, she swayed a bit on her feet and her pulse raced. The hammering of her heart was so loud she wondered if he could hear it. His presence caused her world to tip, threatening to upend her, just as it had that day behind the Green Parrot.

"Mr. Shepherd." She nodded, pulling her hand from his grasp to hide her burning knuckles in the fold of her skirts. She told her heart to slow. "A pleasure."

"How did you find dinner, Miss Manning?" The full lips quirked into a half smile as he tilted his head slightly.

The voices of the other guests receded into the background, becoming no more than a distant hum. What would happen if she reached out to run her fingers over that mocking grin? Or touched the dark hair that curled about his shoulders, the red highlights glinting like copper. Jemma's hand twitched in response to her thoughts, and she had to forcibly restrain herself.

"Delicious." The words left her mouth in a seductive whisper. What in the world was wrong with her? "I found dinner, delicious."

Augie stopped talking to his mother and turned to look at her, his mouth hardening in disapproval as he heard her tone. He pulled her against him.

Lady Corbett thankfully, didn't notice the exchange. She was far too busy inspecting the Sinclair sisters as the pair drew close. Agnes, in particular, seemed the focus of her attention.

"Ah," Nick Shepherd said softy. "I would have thought you found it," he hesitated briefly, the whiskey notes of his voice purring over her body, "amusing."

"Indeed?" Jemma did not look away from that brilliant blue gaze. She was entranced, enthralled at the way he regarded her.

"There you are Mr. Shepherd." Agnes ignored Lady Corbett's frown of disapproval and marched over. Sparing Jemma a nod of victory, she and her sister came about him on either side, each winding about him like an ivy plant gone mad. Agnes batted her eyelashes wildly while Bertha got as close as she could, fitting against him like a barnacle.

Jemma blinked, the shrill voice of Agnes bringing her abruptly back to reality.

"Have you heard, Jemma," Agnes said, her voice high like an excited child. "About Mr. Shepherd's nearly being robbed of his purse when he first arrived? How brave he was.' A hand flew to her meager bosom dramatically.

"*Jemma?*" Shepherd raised a dark brow, his look intent upon her.

"Well, *yes*," Agnes tweeted. "Forgive me, Mr. Shepherd. We are so much less formal in Bermuda. I meant to say Miss Manning." She giggled, tightening her hold on his arm.

"Jemma is a nickname." She lifted her chin defiantly. "Short for Jane Emily."

"I see." He seemed obscenely pleased with himself.

Jemma tilted her head in acknowledgement, knowing at that moment he did indeed recognize her as Jem, the boy outside the Green Parrot.

"An unusual name to be sure. Not common." His gaze flickered again to the tops of her breasts. "I've met only one other with a name similar." The wide mouth broke into a smug smile.

Jemma stood her ground, refusing to look away. Must he look so pleased? The dark head inclined again. "A pleasure."

"Come, Mr. Shepherd, we wish you to be on our side for charades." Bertha cooed.

"Yes," Agnes parroted her sister. "Come Mr. Shepherd." She ran her fingers over his forearm and batted her lashes at the man.

Someone really must tell Agnes she looks most unattractive when she flutters her lashes, like she's having a fit of apoplexy.

Jemma nodded politely, somehow disappointed that Mr. Shepherd hadn't made more of their previous meeting. Ridiculous, of course. As the trio turned away, the sound of the Sinclair sisters giggling forced Jemma to grit her teeth in annoyance.

Augie waited until the Sinclairs and Mr. Shepherd were out of earshot. "I don't like him." Raising his glass to his lips, he drained down the wine in one swallow and waved down a passing servant for another.

"Yes," Jemma agreed automatically as she watched Mr. Shepherd walk away. "You find him common."

A mean look crossed Augie's boyish features. "Yes, common. Perhaps, even a bit vulgar. Only his connections make him remotely appealing. What woman finds an eye-patch attractive? I suppose." His voice was peevish. "The

Sinclair sisters are just pleased to find a suitor, even one as ill-bred as Mr. Shepherd."

Jemma seemed fixated on the messy bit of dark curl that brushed against his shoulders as he led the Sinclair sisters confidently around the room. *Did all London gentlemen wear their hair so unfashionably long?*

"And his audacity." Augie continued. "I did not care for the way he admired you. Why, we are practically engaged." Augie thrust out his chest as if about to do battle. His hair, a dull shade of brown when compared to Mr. Shepherd's, flopped over his forehead and he pushed it away in agitation.

"We are not yet betrothed," she said, her attention drawn away from her thoughts of Mr. Shepherd. "I have not given my consent." Everyone assumed she would marry Augie, and she likely would, but just now, the notion of marrying the man who stood next to her fairly bristling with petulance, filled her with annoyance.

Augie took back her hand, squeezing gently. "Cease with this nonsense, Jemma. This is what we both want. What everyone wants." He spoke to her as if she were a wayward child. "It's been decided."

Jemma snatched her hand away. "Not by me."

Augie shook his head sadly. "Your father has overindulged you and allowed you too much freedom. This headstrong attitude will change once we are married. No more riding about shooting pistols and the like. It's made you much too opinionated. Mother says—"

"I don't care what your mother says," Jemma said in a heated whisper, not wishing to draw attention. "Nor do I care for your highhandedness."

Augie sputtered a bit, acting as if she'd doused him with icy water.

"My father has said I may decide. Not you. Not Lady Corbett."

"Don't be upset, my love," Augie said in a soothing tone "We have been promised to each other since we were barely out of the nursery. Must you be so stubborn?" He gave her an adoring smile, stroking her forearm with the tip of his finger. "We are meant to be together."

Annoyance. Irritation. Those were the feelings Augie inspired in her, especially at this moment. Shouldn't she feel more than annoyance towards the man she was to wed? Augie was sweet, kind and *boring.* "I need some air." She put her hand up to stop Augie as he moved closer. "Alone."

"You are behaving poorly. Mother will no doubt—"

Jemma spun on her heel as he mentioned Lady Corbett again and walked swiftly out of the drawing room before Augie could protest further.

❧ 4 ❧

Jemma stopped ten paces out of the drawing room and sniffed the air. A delicious, most welcome aroma filled her nostrils.

Oh my. That's chocolate. Simply loads of it.

Lady Corbett's cook outdid herself this evening, serving a wide array of desserts for the enjoyment of the Governor's guests, the foremost of which, were individual chocolate tarts. A favorite of Jemma's.

Actually, Jemma adored *anything* chocolate, she had since she tried her first bite of the dark, sweet treat when still a toddler. Her father insisted she stay active, recommending long walks and a most demanding regimen of dancing and piano lessons as protection against stoutness. She did well with dancing, but the piano lessons she found dull, so instead she begged Tally, her father's man, to allow her to tag along with him as he fished or practiced with his pistols. Her father was most displeased when he realized she couldn't play a simple tune and voiced his objections to her unladylike hobbies. He relented when he found out what a good shot she was. The piano collected dust in the Sea Cliff drawing room.

Jemma pushed aside all thoughts of the piano and regarded the sideboard before her. Silver trays still held a number of desserts as the servants had not finished cleaning the dining room. Lady Corbett, her mouth grim, had nodded in disapproval when Jemma asked for another dessert after dinner.

"Well, she's not here now, is she?" Jemma spotted her quarry. A trio of lovely, round tarts of dark chocolate, powdered with sugar, shining like a beacon in the candlelight. She sniffed the air in appreciation and stepped closer.

"I feel better already," Jemma said out loud to the empty room.

Approaching the tray of chocolate tarts as a hunter stalks its prey, Jemma took her time deciding exactly *which t*reat would follow her outside to the gardens.

A stack of linen napkins, neatly folded, sat next to the tray. Jemma grabbed a chocolate tart, wrapping it tightly in a linen napkin.

A bit of chocolate and some fresh air will clear my head.

She held the napkin lightly in her hand, hoping she wouldn't see anyone as she made her way outside. She thought of the Sinclair sisters throwing themselves at Mr. Shepherd, and she clutched the tart tighter. "I only wish," she said to out loud, "that Agnes and Bertie wouldn't make such cows of themselves in public." *Liar, a* voice whispered in her ear.

Jemma hurried down the hallway, towards the large French doors leading to the terrace and the gardens beyond. A male servant, headed to the dining room with an empty tray, quirked a brow at her but said nothing as she sailed past him, her treasure held firmly in her hand.

The doors to the Corbett gardens were slightly ajar. Torches lit the portion of the gardens closest to the house, though the paths remained in shadow. Jemma disregarded the darkened paths and instead slid towards the left where she knew a small bench sat facing an atrocious statue of a cupid. She often thought the statue an odd addition to the gardens as everything else, plants, fountains and other statuary was of exquisite taste.

Damn and blast! She could feel the chocolate seeping through the napkin. She looked down at her dress, praying none of the dark sticky sweetness marred the cream-colored taffeta. She'd never be able to explain the stain away.

"Oh bloody hell." Her foot slipped over an uneven brick. The chocolate tart flew out of her hands, landing with a small smacking sound on the terrace. The cupid stared at her, seeming to chastise her clumsiness.

Jemma shot the ugly cherub a beleaguered glance, wondering where her treasure had landed. "I shall blame you. You are most ridiculous looking."

"But you are not," a whiskey-laden voice murmured from the shadows.

"Mr. Shepherd?" she whispered into a dark corner of the terrace as her heart skipped a beat. "What are you doing lurking about? I thought you were happily ensconced inside with the sisters Sinclair. Why you could be accosted again."

A husky laugh came from in front of her, followed by a large, dark form. "Hello Jem." He held aloft the napkin wrapped chocolate tart.

Jemma glanced at her treat and reached out, hoping he would hand her the chocolate and excuse himself. Hoping he would not.

"May I have that, Mr. Shepherd?" She nodded to the chocolate tart.

"Possibly. I too enjoy chocolate."

He said chocolate in a most sinful way. In fact, every word the man spoke sounded sinful.

"Does your father know you traipse about dressed as a boy, shooting pistols and saving visitors to your fair island from thieves?" He tossed the chocolate tart up with his hand and deftly caught it. "I can't imagine he approves. Nor your Mr. Corbett."

"My father's approval is none of your business." She watched him fling her dessert up in the air again. "And he knows, as does Mr. Corbett," she said glibly. "If you seek to discredit me you will be disappointed, Mr. Shepherd. My eccentricity is well known." The terrace suddenly felt very warm. She couldn't breathe and thought the reason likely the tightness of her stays.

"Discredit you? Perish the thought." Torchlight lit the side of his face, illuminating the pretended look of shock upon his handsome features.

"I'm curious, Mr. Shepherd," she said, ignoring his sarcasm. "Why are *you* in Bermuda?"

He tossed her poor abused chocolate tart between his large hands as he spoke. "I believe the entire dinner conversation was dedicated to my reasons for being in Bermuda. Lady Corbett *interrogated* me at length as to my connections, my financial status and my relation to the Cambournes. That lady would put the Spanish Inquisitors to shame. The sisters Sinclair displayed all the delicacy of the king's solicitors as they questioned every detail of my life to determine my suitability as a husband." He peered down at her with a serious expression. "Were you not paying attention Jem? I could have sworn you were. Perhaps, I'm mistaken." He tossed up the tart again.

"Arrogant dandy," she scoffed. "You must think all women are as *enthralled* by you as the Sinclair sisters. I'm afraid I paid not a bit of attention to your conversation at the end of the table. I was much more interested in the soup course."

"I'm sure you were," he agreed.

"You are nothing more than a fortune hunter, a man with nothing to recommend him but a letter from one of England's famous families. Why, who even knows if it's real?" Jemma taunted.

"An excellent point. However, I assure you, I know the Dowager Marchioness quite well." He dangled the tart in the air before her.

Jemma grabbed for it, frowning in frustration when he pulled it out of her reach. "The sisters Sinclair are fairly well off and their brother desires them out of the house. I'm sure either one would suit your purposes."

"My purposes?"

"If the Sinclairs are not to your liking, you would do well to make sure that neither Agnes nor Bertie traps you in a compromising position. You'll find them much more dangerous than those two inept thieves I saved you from," she shot back. "And I still don't believe you are properly grateful."

"I appreciate the warning in regards to the sisters. But I am in no danger from the delightful Sinclairs, nor was I in danger behind the Green Parrot."

Jemma bit her lip, fuming. He really was a most *annoying, attractive man*. "Truly, you are the most smug, full of himself, prancing—"

"I prance?" he stated in horror.

"—*mincing*,"

"Dear God, I also *mince*? You should have allowed Bobo and Wren to shoot me."

"—ungrateful man I've ever met. I *saved* you." She stressed the word. "From being stuck like a pig. Will your pride not let you admit it?"

The large man before her laughed quietly, a deep, rumbling that caused Jemma's stomach to flutter in the most pleasant way.

"You are priceless, Jem." He shook his head. "Forgive me for not being properly *appreciative* of your talents. I see this is most important to you." He held out the chocolate tart. "I gladly give you your just desserts." He laughed again, a bit louder, proud of his joke.

"You are not nearly as witty as you seem to believe. Your puns are awful." She snatched the seeping bit of napkin from his hand, knowing her dessert was ruined. "Please go and leave me in peace."

"Why Jem, you speak as if you wish to be alone with a lover."

She nearly dropped the poor ruined chocolate tart at his words, mindful of the way she tingled every time he called her Jem.

"Stop calling me that." She tried to sound determined and haughty as Lady Corbett did when giving someone a set down. "My name is Jane Emily, or Jemma if you prefer, though I've not given you leave to call me anything but Miss Manning."

"*I* prefer Jem. It suits you." He moved towards her.

Jemma backed up in response, bumping into the edge of a garden trellis. *I should not be out here alone, not with this man.*

"No, you should not."

The huskiness of his voice cascaded down her spine, causing her to shiver deliciously. How could he know what she was thinking? "Can you read minds then?" Her hands pressed against the edge of the trellis, holding on to it for dear life. Wishing she were more worldly, to better deal with such a man.

A gust of wind blew the dark strands of his hair about his

shoulders, making him appear dark and demonic, a virtual Hades, before her.

"Just yours, Jem." This time her name fell as an endearment from his lips.

Warm honey pooled between her thighs, a most disturbing and pleasurable sensation. She dropped the chocolate tart again to the brick of the terrace, not caring what happened to her treat. Inhaling she tried to take a deep breath and found she couldn't. It was akin to being in the eye of a hurricane.

"Tsk tsk, Jem. It's a good thing you are not so careless with a pistol." He bent, assessing the chocolate tart at her feet. "It appears ruined, and I did so want a taste." The last part came out in a growl as he snatched her hand still hovering in the air. "No matter, I believe there is a bit left." He brought her hand to his lips, "*Here.*"

Warmth engulfed her index finger as nearly the whole of it found its way into his mouth. He gently sucked the chocolate off her finger, his tongue swirling and caressing the extended digit.

Fascinated, she watched as her finger disappeared into his mouth, aghast that she allowed him to do such a thing to her. She slid down the length of the trellis, praying a stray thorn wouldn't tear her gown.

He ran his tongue down the inside of her hand before stopping to press a kiss in the center of her palm.

"Delicious," he whispered.

Jemma thought she would faint, and she had never fainted, not in the whole of her life.

"No you won't." He gave her a wolfish grin.

"Stop doing that." Jemma snatched back her hand and braced herself against the trellis, welcoming its meager support.

"Kissing your hand?"

"Reading my thoughts," she sputtered.

"Ah." A wry smile appeared across the full lips. "Thank goodness. I thought you wished me to cease in my seduction of your person."

"Seduction?" She nearly choked on the word.

"And that...won't do at all." Grabbing her wrists in one fluid move, he pulled her arms over her head and pinned her against the trellis, effectively trapping her with his larger form.

He smelled of the cheroot, the sea and powerful male. As much as she objected to his pinning of her wrists, the sensation of being held captive by Nick Shepherd was not displeasing. In fact, it was quite the opposite.

"Your impropriety towards me is unseemly." She pushed up at him, and her voice caught at the sensation of her breasts against his coat. "Release me now or I shall scream for help." Her tongue tripped over the words.

"So determined to be waspish. Shush." His mouth descended over hers.

Jemma did not realize until that very moment, that there was a distinct difference between the barely amorous press of lips from a *boy* and being kissed, really kissed, by a *man*. This was no prim peck, no courtly gesture of affection. No kiss she would willingly break from. She sagged, her body giving in to the feeling of his lips on hers.

Nick transferred both her wrists to one large hand, freeing his other hand to roam, unhindered, across the tops of her breasts. His finger dipped into the valley between them as if searching for something.

"I am an admirer of your bosom. Small and delightfully shaped, fitting perfectly." He cupped a breast. "You bind them? When you wander about in breeches?"

"Sometimes," Jemma panted, lightheaded from his kiss. She could not allow him any further liberties. What if someone came out? Dear God, what if Augie found her pinned to the trellis by Nick Shepherd? She moved her body to slip away. Futile as the gesture only served to bring her already sensitive body in touch with the hardness that was Nick Shepherd.

"Stop," he said against her mouth, his tongue lingering at the corner of her lips. "You do not really wish to get away."

And she didn't. Not really. She wanted to experience what he offered. Her body gave a deep sigh, recognizing the truth of his words. Jemma's legs fell open of their own accord, wantonly, spreading open to him beneath her skirts. She thought perhaps this was a dream.

He wedged his body between her legs, nudging the apex between her thighs. Jemma's breath caught in her throat. She moaned softly, submitting to him, her mind going blank to anything except the man before her.

He nipped her lips gently. "Open to me, Jem."

Obediently, she opened her mouth, feeling the tip of his tongue touch her lips first, then twine around her own tongue.

He pulled away to nip softly at the nape of her neck. "Kiss me back."

She complied, shyly pressing her lips to his, fitting her body to his larger form.

Carefully, he tugged at the edging of brilliants and lace at her bodice until the small mound of one breast popped free. He murmured something against her neck while his thumb found her nipple and brushed against the sensitive tip.

Jemma moaned softly and struggled to push herself closer as he toyed with her nipple, pinching and circling it with his thumb and forefinger, kissing her deeply.

Abruptly his mouth left hers.

"No, don't—" she gasped as the wet heat of his mouth descended over the peak of her nipple. Waves of sensation rolled from her nipple, down her breasts and stomach to center between her thighs.

Dear God. This is why women allow themselves to be ruined. This is why they keep young girls away from men like Nick Shepherd, otherwise we would line up in droves to offer him our virtue.

He nibbled, making his way slowly around her engorged nipple. He suckled leisurely, licking around the areola. Releasing her wrists, he sighed in satisfaction. "I told you that you did not really wish to get away."

Her hands reached up to touch his shoulders, feeling the press of his muscles against her palms, the silkiness of his dark hair as it touched her fingertips. A pressure built between her legs—painful and needful. She wanted something but didn't know what it was or how to ask for it. The heat of Nick seeped through her skirts, winding around the aching apex between her thighs. She wished desperately for him to touch her. *There.*

His knee pressed into her skirts and the ache intensified.

"In time," he whispered, pulling his mouth from her throbbing breast. Peering down into her face, he took a deep breath and pressed a kiss to her erect nipple before carefully pulling up her bodice.

The enormity of what had just passed between them, the liberties she'd allowed this man, a virtual stranger, shocked her to her core. "Are you a witch then, that you can read my thoughts, cause me to behave in such a way?"

A coldness descended suddenly, as if someone thrust a block of ice between them, and Jemma sensed she'd offended him in some way.

"Perhaps." He adjusted her bodice, laying the lace back, minding the brilliants that dotted the edging. He did so efficiently as if he'd had much practice. Which, she thought with alarm, he likely had.

"What," she stuttered, confused at the intimacy that just transpired. "Is this?"

"Wanting," he said, digging a cheroot from his pocket and lighting it as if her flushed trembling body was of no import.

She winced at his nonchalance. Perhaps intimacies such as this happened all the time in London at the parties of the *ton*. "I should go," she said unsteadily as shame replaced her wanton feelings of only a moment ago. "Augie will likely be looking for me to play charades." She tried to match his casual tone and failed. Miserably. If only she could say something witty and stroll off as if he hadn't just kissed her breast and ravished her against a garden trellis, leaving her wanting. But for what?

"Charades?" Laughing, he flicked the ash of the cheroot. "The irony does not escape me."

Confused, she waited for him to say more, but he only watched her as he smoked. "You'll excuse me." Jemma smoothed down her gown, determined to appear as unaffected as he. "I am returning to the party."

He said nothing, merely nodding to her in dismissal.

"Good evening, Mr. Shepherd." The sting of tears filled her eyes as humiliation blossomed and took root within her chest. What had come over her to allow this man to take such liberties? She felt so foolish. So stupid. So reckless.

He stepped aside to let her pass, giving her no more attention than he would a servant. "Yes, you should go inside."

Jemma tried to reply and found she couldn't. Years of careful coaching by Mercy and Lady Corbett on a lady's behavior proved useless when tested against a man like Nick Shepherd. How she failed those two women and their teachings. Her morals flew apart in the face of a practiced seducer of women, which Mr. Shepherd clearly was. He would joke about her attraction to him over drinks with his cronies in

London no doubt. A feather in his cap, nothing more. If she had her pistols, she *would* shoot him.

"Move," Jemma commanded, raising her chin and daring him to speak.

He stepped out of her way, the cheroot clamped firmly between his teeth. A smile played about his lips.

That smile stoked the flame of her anger. Jemma spun about, grabbed the skirt of her gown and turned her back on the arrogant and jaded Mr. Shepherd. Proudly and with purpose, she strode towards the lighted safety of the mansion. Glancing down at her bodice, she was grateful that only a slight flush across her breasts betrayed her actions in the garden.

I shall tell them I felt a bit unwell. Augie will feel so guilty for upsetting me earlier he'll likely not question me too much.

"Jem." The voice lingered over the stone terrace.

She halted, her skirts swirled about her ankles, but she did not turn around.

"I've found something I desire much more than a chocolate tart. Have you?"

Jemma's heart thudded madly, and she swayed a bit but forced herself to move forward, away from the dark lure of Nick Shepherd.

5

W *hat an unexpected evening.*
Nick stretched out on the mattress in his guest room and felt the quake of the bed beneath him. He struggled to get comfortable, sighing in frustration as the frame creaked loudly, protesting his weight. His feet hung over the edge, the bed being built for someone of lesser stature. Governor Lord Corbett struck Nick as a bit of an ass, in addition to his other sins. While Lady Corbett considered Nick an honored guest, Lord Corbett probably instructed the staff to find the shortest bed available. No matter. Nick wasn't sleepy.

He blinked both eyes, relieved to be rid of the eye-patch if only for the night. He hated the heat on this island, detested the bugs, in fact, there wasn't much he liked in Bermuda. But he made a promise. A promise to his grandfather, Henry. A promise that lay upon Nick's broad shoulders like the heaviest of weights.

"I would know the name of the man who dared to steal documents from the Duke of Dunbar."

Nick wondered, in his youth, why his grandfather would have a secret list of English spies tucked into a false bottomed drawer of the desk in his study. He knew now, of course, and wished he did not. He could still see Henry pounding on the long, wooden table that graced the dining room, startling the servants and causing Nick's sister to flee the room.

"The taint of treason. Your parents are dead because of some sniveling coward. I would have that man's name!"

Actually, Nick thought his parents weren't dead because of the traitor, they were dead because of being drunk and stupid. Phillip and Charlotte were both given to drink and gambling and shared an appetite for handsome stable boys. His parents' debts were enormous before Henry cut them off from the Dunbar fortune. Nick had been sailing a toy boat in the park with his nanny when Phillip *accidentally* shot Charlotte, then himself, with a hunting rifle.

Henry took the news of his son's death much better than he did the slur against the Dunbar name. He extracted a promise from Nick. *"Find the man before I die. I would curse him and his descendants. I would take all from him that he took from me."*

"William Manning. Though I doubt that was the name he was born with." Nick scratched at a bite on his arm. How *did* one live in Bermuda with the incessant biting insects?

Manning proved to be polite, charming and nothing more than a content, wealthy, merchant. Full of rum punch, Manning nervously regaled Nick with small talk of his years in the salt trade, which made him wealthy beyond comprehension. He mentioned his delightful daughter, Jane Emily. Jane Emily who was the future betrothed of Augustus Corbett. But, Nick noticed, Manning's eyes looked to the side as he spoke and his hand trembled.

Nick shifted on the bed, rubbing his left eye.

Jane Emily Manning. The girl who found his pursuit by the Sinclair sisters to be so amusing. She could be useful.

Then he saw her.

Slender and willowy, she stood across the drawing room from him, Augustus Corbett's fingers wrapped possessively about her elbow. She had a reckless, stubborn look to her, which Nick immediately seized upon. The cream of her gown enhanced the unfashionable tan of her skin, a color not unlike molten honey. He saw the spray of freckles dancing across her cheeks and the sparkle of green in her hazel eyes. Dozens of brilliants danced across her bodice and in her light brown hair. She held a glass carelessly in one hand.

The sight of her, standing thus, sent a bolt of lust through Nick the likes of which he'd never felt before.

Lady Corbett, clinging to Nick's arm, stopped in front of the pair and made introductions.

Jane Emily's eyes widened at the sight of him.

The spark, unexpected and intense, as he touched her hand, caused a curious sensation in Nick. He likened it to a *craving,* an instant need for the girl. The revelation that followed, that Jane Emily Manning was also *Jem*, only intensified Nick's lust. He'd had many beautiful, sensuous partners, but none that he might have to disarm in order to bed. He thought of nothing but those long legs, clad in breeches, while the Sinclair sisters swirled about him in the drawing room. He behaved badly. Instead of flirting with her as he meant to do on the Governor's terrace, he'd nearly thrown up her skirts and taken her against a garden trellis.

The future ruination of Jane Emily, for he'd already decided he'd have her, would certainly qualify as revenge. If indeed Manning was the man he sought. And Nick thought he was.

Manning was not a name Nick knew from searching his

grandfather's papers, only the name Corbett. But perhaps he should be looking for two men instead of one.

Nick laced his hands behind his head. He needed to be sure. Absolutely, sure. The Crown had promised to look the other way were the traitor to disappear, even if that man proved to be the Governor of Bermuda. Of course, there was the possibility that Manning and Corbett would try to have him killed.

Nick rubbed the Devil's ring on his thumb. The pewter, worn and pitted with age, felt cool against his skin. He nearly didn't wear it to Bermuda, but the ring had not been seen in over thirty years, and it was unlikely anyone would recognize it. Besides, the ring gave him an odd sense of comfort. He'd received the token just prior to leaving for Bermuda, upon the death of an elderly aunt, the last Devil of Dunbar. She died insane and hidden away at a distant estate.

"I will likely suffer a similar fate," Nick said as he squashed another mosquito. "We Dunbars are cursed, though only I am truly damned."

Damned. Even the gypsy knew of his fate. Three boys, drunk on whisky Colin stole from his father. The bullying never ended at Eton, but that day had been particularly bad. Colin and Cam each bore the bruises to prove it. The head-master did not care to intervene on either boy's behalf. Nick himself, was taunted daily, only his size keeping the other boys at bay.

They say your mother screamed when she saw your eyes. My mother says she started drinking that very day and never stopped. Your father was a traitor, sold out his own country to pay his gambling debts.

Poor Colin, the smallest of the three, had been kicked into a mud puddle and pelted with refuse before all three ran into the woods, Colin drunkenly leading the way.

Who saw the gypsy first?

The gypsy read Cam's palm and the fortune she gave him was so near the truth of his life, he remained white-faced and terrified until they left the old hag's camp. Colin, drunk on what couldn't have been more than a thimbleful of whisky, lay in the grass. Colin was given a fortune, though Nick doubted his friend remembered the words the gypsy spoke.

Nick's fortune came last.

"We share an ancestor." The gypsy, shriveled and old, smelling of horses and garlic, winked at Nick. She turned his head back and forth between her withered hands. "The Devil's curse still lives."

Nick pushed her filthy hands from his face. "Nothing you can say will frighten me. I am already damned." Full of the arrogance and assurance of youth he lifted his head and looked the crone right in the eye.

The gypsy laughed, a deep hacking sound that left spittle on her cracked lips. Her mouth twisted into an evil grin. "Yes, yes. But not until your relative dies and the curse is passed."

"How do you know about us?" Nick asked, his voice shaking.

"Oh, my Wicked." Her eyes took on a dreamy quality as she took his hand and forced it open to gaze at his palm. "You will kill the very thing you love most in this world. That is why you are damned."

Cam, frightened after his own fortune, took the bottle of whisky from Colin and drank deeply. He wiped his mouth with the back of his hand and jerked his head towards the school. "Nick lets just go. We'll carry Colin. Let's just go."

But Nick was not leaving. He would hear it all. "Your prophecy doesn't frighten me, for I already know it."

"But you do not, my Wicked." Her eyes, bright like dark bits of glass were cold. Nick felt the creep of her yellowed nails against his thigh. "The sins of the fathers will revisit upon the children. You will know unimaginable grief. Grief so unbearable you will wish to die from it. Grief of your own making."

Nick's eyes snapped open, the clearing in the deep woods and the smell of the gypsy's fire still stinging his nostrils.

Sweat trickled down his armpits and stomach. He thought of Jem, and the need to have her, a need not entirely motivated by revenge. The traitor's daughter. Nick, unlike his friends, *did* believe in prophecy. Prophecy and witchcraft were woven into the very fabric of his family. He rubbed the Devil's ring on his thumb and closed his eyes.

But sleep did not come for a very long time.

6

"Tally," William Manning said to his best friend and manservant. "Stop fussing and do as I ask." William lay on his bed under the mosquito netting. He wiggled his toes, glad to be free of his stockings and boots. He'd felt excessively tired after the dinner at Corbett's house. Something he ate hadn't agreed with him. Or rather, someone he *met* did not agree with him.

"Aye, Willie. The armoire you say?" Tally addressed him in private by his first name as if they were still the children they once were, and not the wealthy gentleman and servant all of Bermuda took them to be. Tall and lean, with a thatch of stark white hair, William thought Tally had begun to resemble a stork or perhaps a crane.

"Something funny, Willie?" Tally's hand touched the side of the tall cherry armoire in the corner of the room. He opened the armoire door and waited patiently, plucking absently at a loose bit of thread on his breeches.

"The panel. Feel for it with your fingers. It's all the way in the back. There's a latch on the left you'll trigger, and it will slide open." William made a motion with his hand, almost too exhausted to keep his arm aloft. His hand quivered as he instructed Tally. Unable to keep his arm up, William let his hand drop to his chest just as he felt another sharp pain.

The pains in his chest along with the sensation of being suffocated occurred nearly every day. His stomach troubled him after his meals. He tossed and turned nightly, never really resting. That's when he saw Maureen.

His dead wife haunted his dreams—her round, pretty face wreathed in disappointment. The same way she'd looked after he confessed how they came to be in Bermuda. How he'd paid for the finery she wore and the large house they lived in.

"Foolish," he muttered under his breath. "So foolish."

"What's that, Willie?" Tally's head was deep inside the armoire.

"Nothing." William winced, thinking of his stupidity. He should have gone to a minister or spoken to God himself if he wished absolution. Not his pregnant wife. The confession of his sins did not absolve him as he hoped, instead Maureen went into early labor, killing both she and the son she carried. There had been so much blood. The bed and mattress had been soaked with it. He took Maureen's hand in his, holding it to his heart, willing her to live.

She didn't of course. Maureen, his lovely Irish lass, who he'd given up everything to have, never opened her eyes again. Prostrate with guilt and grief, William decided he must confess to the authorities. He must pay for his crimes. Maureen would wish him to. He explained this all to George Corbett.

But George would have none of it. He sat William down, poured rum for the both of them and looked William square in the eye.

"I am sorry, truly sorry about Maureen, but you cannot confess. It is too late. I have a wife and two children. Your family, in England, believes you dead. If you will not keep your mouth shut for yourself,

think of what your confession will do to me, to your family, and to Jane Emily. The Dunbars will destroy us. They will destroy your family in England. You can do nothing now but repent in silence. To do otherwise will doom us all."

William, sobbing, had agreed. George was right. He was always right. George and William were bound together for the remainder of their days, tied by the horrible crime committed. It was George who arranged Maureen's funeral while William grieved. June Corbett tended Jane Emily and allowed William to cry on her shoulder. He devoted himself to becoming even more prosperous and raising Jane Emily while George Corbett grew fat from his partnership with William. They spoke no more of treason. William pushed aside all thoughts of the Devils of Dunbar, choosing not to think of his crime or the innocents who suffered.

Until now.

"Maureen," he whispered.

God, how he missed his wife. He felt her loss just as keenly now as he had nearly twenty years ago. But he would see Maureen soon. He was unwell, and William knew he would not see another Christmas. The guilt he carried surfaced, bubbling up to poison him. Worry, not for himself, but for his only child, made him anxious. He once thought that giving Jane Emily and Sea Cliff to Augustus Corbett would bring him peace, but the decision brought only more worry. He did not insist she set a date to wed Augustus, thinking that the young man's affections were more for Sea Cliff than Jane Emily. Then, the final harbinger of William's impending demise arrived in the form of Nick Shepherd.

When he saw the man at the end of George Corbett's dinner table, William felt a surge of dread unlike any he'd ever known since Maureen's death.

"George," he whispered to Lord Corbett. "Who is that man?"

George shoved a bit of cheese in his mouth and shrugged. "Who,

Willie? You mean June's newest pet? Some failed gentleman with a proper letter of introduction. June's invited him to stay." George rolled his eyes. "As she does them all. She seeks to further Dorthea's fortunes though I must remind her endlessly that Dorthea is quite happy in Yorkshire with her barrister. God help Dorthea if her husband's elder brother dies and he inherits. June will have us on their doorstep in a thrice."

"It's him. The Devil of Dunbar. They have finally found us."

"Don't be ridiculous. I'll admit there's something I don't like about the man, but he calls himself Nick Shepherd." George tore into a piece of bread. "It's been twenty years, Willie. The Dunbars have forgotten about us. Why the current duke must be near eighty if he's a day."

"They won't have forgotten, George." William swallowed the lump down that formed in his throat as he watched the Sinclair sisters throw themselves at the man. "That cursed family never forgets."

Just then, Shepherd turned his head towards William, striking him with an assessing, brilliant blue gaze.

"It's him. I know it," William said.

George pursed his lips and waved for more rum punch while he chewed on an oyster. "We'll see."

"Are you sure there's something back here Willie? Perhaps you only thought there was."

"Yes." Tally's voice snapped William back to the moment. "Must I come help?" William winced at the pain lancing through his chest. Time was of the essence, he knew. Tally must be convinced of the rightness of William's decision. William trusted no one else with Jane Emily.

Tally shooed him away with a hand and went back to reaching through shirts and underclothes in the armoire, the sounds of his fumbling the only noise in the room.

I am tired. Tired of living with my guilt. Tired of waiting to be discovered.

William remembered the Duke of Dunbar, the Old

Spider, a man who terrified nearly everyone at that doomed house party, *especially* William. Stealing from the Tremaine family was the act of a desperate man, which William had been. He'd only stolen the papers, it was George who sold them to the French. He didn't even know what the papers actually contained, until later.

Yet I stayed silent, even after I knew that George made it look like the duke's wastrel of a son committed the crime. Even after I knew that men died because of me. That the heir to Dunbar killed himself because of me.

"But I need not stay silent much longer," William whispered.

He reached to his nightstand to clutch at the miniature of Maureen he kept there. "He's found me, Maureen, just as I always thought he would." William saw the bit of pewter Nick Shepherd wore on his thumb and knew what the ring meant, even if George did not. Nick Shepherd was the heir to Dunbar, the son of the unfortunate viscount who killed himself over the scandal of treason. George wasn't ready to accept the truth, that the Devil of Dunbar was on Bermuda. But William knew. He would make his own preparations.

A popping sound in the room, along with Tally's exclamation of surprise, heralded the discovery of the hidden drawer in the armoire.

William watched as Tally removed a small leather packet, holding it carefully out to William.

"This what yer lookin' for Willie?"

William nodded wearily and rubbed at his chest again. "It is, indeed." He waved Tally forward. "Bring it here."

William cared not what would happen to him, he deserved the wrath of the Dunbar family, but Jane Emily was innocent. He must take measures to protect her from the Devil of Dunbar. And, George Corbett.

"I need to show you what's inside." He waved at Tally again. "I'm tired, do hurry."

Tally nodded solemnly and placed the packet on the bed. "You've decided then? You're sure?"

William smiled. Tally was his dearest, closest friend in all the world. Growing up together, Tally the son of the head groom, William the second son of an earl, they were inseparable. Tally loved Jane Emily as if she were his own. William counted on that.

"It's all there?" Tally nodded towards the packet on the bed, the trepidation on his craggy features clear even in the dim light of the room.

"Yes. Bring me a quill and ink." William sat up. "There is something I need you to do."

⚜

GOVERNOR LORD CORBETT WIPED A NAPKIN ACROSS THE bacon grease on his lips and waved for a servant to bring more tea. Not typically an early riser, he had been unable to sleep last night. His hand shook slightly as he sipped at his tea, the hot liquid searing the tip of his tongue.

That man. William seemed certain Nick Shepherd was not some fortune hunter but the heir to Dunbar, come to Bermuda to punish them both. George was not quite convinced. Twenty years was a very long time for anyone, even the Duke of Dunbar to wait out his revenge. He thought it much more likely that William's regret and guilt had mushroomed over the years causing his imagination to run wild. Sometimes, he claimed to see his dead wife.

But William seemed sure.

Lady Corbett insisted Shepherd stay at the Governor's home until he purchased property of his own, chattering on about the man's connections and how those connections could help Dorthea. George, for once, agreed with his wife, though not for the reasons she assumed. If the man was indeed the spawn of Dunbar, George thought it best to keep Shepherd nearby. If he wasn't, well, he could not afford to anger a relation of the Marquess of Cambourne.

"Good morning, husband." Lady Corbett strolled into the breakfast room, a brief smile for him about her thin lips. He found it the only thin thing about her. She sat her plump form across the table from him and asked a servant for toast and tea.

George's stomach soured. He wished to be left in peace to finish his meal. If his wife appeared, it meant she wanted something.

Once the servants left, Lady Corbett took a small bite of toast. "We must impress upon William the urgency to announce Augustus and Jemma's betrothal."

His wife rarely minced words, unlike most women who refused to state their concerns plainly. His annoyance grew. She constantly harped on the impending marriage of Augustus to Jane Emily. It seemed all she thought of.

"How do you propose we do that, my pet?" George spat sullenly, not pleased that his breakfast would go cold while she tried to force him to go again to William and set a date for the betrothal. He detested the nagging litany his wife forced on him. Regarding her across his breakfast plate, he supposed they got on well enough. Better than most. But on mornings like this, he was hard pressed to remember why he'd married her to begin with, except that his parents told him she possessed a fat dowry.

She raised a brow at him, making her forehead wrinkle in a most unattractive manner. Her hair once a glorious red, now hung in dull, faded curls about her temples.

The hair.

I once could not think of anything but the red of her hair. I thought the color magnificent, like newly minted copper.

"George?" She took another bite of toast. "Do you hear me?"

"I cannot help but hear you, June. As I told you, William does not wish to force Jane Emily. I personally think he has allowed the girl too much latitude in her opinions. Think where we would be if we had allowed Dorthea such freedom." He took a bite of bacon. "The girl is temperamental and could do something reckless if forced. There is an *understanding,* June. We must be patient, pet."

Lady Corbett said nothing. She took a sip of tea then proceeded to crunch her toast so forcefully crumbs flew from her mouth.

"Stop that, June. The sound grates on my ears and you're getting bits of toast all over the table." As if it were a gauntlet, George threw down his napkin in disgust. "You are ruining my breakfast."

"I do understand, George. Really I do." Lady Corbett ceased destroying her toast and placed the remains carefully on her plate. "But I do *worry*." Her eyes widened in a silent plea for understanding. "Our dear William isn't well. He could barely finish his plate at our dinner party earlier this week. I fear he is ill. What if something, something *terrible,* were to happen to William before Augustus and Jane Emily are officially betrothed? Why, she could fall victim to a fortune hunter or worse. Then what would happen to Sea Cliff? What would happen to her? She is like my own daughter. I promised Maureen I would care for her." Tears formed in June's eyes. "I cannot break that promise."

George sighed. He'd forgotten how close Maureen Manning and June had been. June was there when her friend died. Of course, June felt responsible for Jane Emily. "I would never allow that. I, rather *we*, are her guardians should anything happen."

Lady Corbett sat back, lips pursed, wiping at her eyes with a napkin. "Truly?" She dabbed at her eyes again. "If anything were to happen to William, Jane Emily shall come to us?"

"Of course, June. I impressed upon William the need that provision be made for Jane Emily long ago. He saw the wisdom of establishing us as her guardians should something happen to him." George must have forgotten to tell June, feeling it wasn't something she needed to know until necessary. "I thought I had mentioned this to you. An oversight on my part, I'm afraid." He patted her hand clumsily. "Please don't give it another thought my dear, we shall take care of Jane Emily if need be."

"Thank you, husband." Lady Corbett stood. "You don't know how much that eases my mind. I have worried overmuch it seems. You have it all in hand." She stood and walked over to where he sat. Leaning over, she pecked him on the cheek. "I should never have doubted you."

"No indeed," George sputtered under his breath, wishing her gone so he could finally breakfast in peace.

Lady Corbett walked sedately from his side to the open doors of the morning room. "I'll have Cook prepare something special for dinner this evening." She inclined her head. "Enjoy your day, husband."

He gave her a brittle smile and waited until the sound of her footsteps faded. "More eggs," George yelled. "Mine have gone cold."

A footman popped his head through the door. "Immediately, my lord."

"And more tea." George grabbed another piece of bacon. He snorted in agitation. "Tedious woman." Jane Emily would marry Augustus. More pressing matters required George's attention, namely the true identity of his unwanted houseguest.

❧ 7 ❧

ugie steered the open brougham expertly through
Hamilton, swerving to avoid the potholes that
dotted the main street with a flick of his wrist. He
tipped his hat to a group of gaily clad women.

The women giggled and waved in return.

Jemma frowned as the brougham sank a bit into a rut.

"Sorry." Augie smiled apologetically, though Jemma
doubted he *was* sorry. He adored being fawned over, and
Jemma was sparse with her affection.

I shouldn't begrudge him the admiration of others.

She gripped the edge of the leather seat with one hand
while desperately attempting to keep her parasol over her
head, Mercy's threats ringing in her ears.

*"If you intend on going to that fair, then you must take a parasol,
and I expect you to use it! I will scrub you raw with lemons if I must.
Lady Corbett sent a note just yesterday. She is distressed you have
ruined your complexion and the freckles are unseemly and I'm to make
a special paste for you to use."*

"I will break another wheel on this road." Augie flicked
the reins. "I thought Father had all the holes filled."

"Your attention wandered." Jemma adjusted the angle of the parasol.

Augie shot her an apologetic glance tinged with satisfaction. "Don't be jealous, Jemma."

"I'm not. I would just rather you not tip over the carriage, and me with it."

Augie leaned closer to her. "My goodness. I was just being polite." His chest puffed out a bit. "And it is *you* I escort to the festival."

Jemma gave him a wane smile. Truly, she didn't care who Augie smiled at. That was the problem. A rather large problem.

The day was warm, and the sun strong, so that for once, Jemma was glad of the parasol's meager protection. A breeze sifted through the streets bringing the cooling relief of the ocean. She closed her eyes in contentment as the air pulled at her parasol and tickled the strands of her hair. She sniffed in appreciation at the aroma of fried conch fritters wafting towards her from the festival. Her stomach gave an unladylike grumble.

"I'm so glad you are heeding Mother's wisdom." Augie nodded towards the parasol. "Not that I mind," he assured her. "But Mother is quite concerned. She can be a bit forceful on such things." He pushed the end of the parasol with the tip of his finger so that Jemma's cheeks were more firmly covered.

Yes, I'd hate to give Lady Corbett any cause for concern. Jemma bit her lip to keep from voicing the thought out loud. Augie rarely went against his mother's wishes. A trait of his Jemma never paid heed to, until recently. *He's such a little boy, constantly striving for Lady Corbett's approval.* "Yes, I would hate to disappoint your mother."

Augie either ignored or didn't notice the sarcasm in her tone. "Since you are following Mother's advice," he continued cheerfully, "I hope that you will follow her direction on other things?"

The bloody betrothal.

Jemma turned away to stare at the expanse of ocean visible between the apothecary shop and the dressmakers. Not a day went by that Augie or someone else didn't mention the upcoming engagement. Her father turned a deaf ear to her questions on the subject, no doubt not wishing to hear her continued reasons for delaying her marriage.

"Isn't this just the most glorious day?" Jemma ignored Augie's question regarding the betrothal and instead lay a gloved hand on his arm. The urge to flee Augie, and indeed all of Bermuda, threatened to choke her. She literally crossed her ankles to keep from leaping over the side of the brougham. "I've so been looking forward to coming today. Can't you smell the conch fritters?" She closed her eyes and sat back, allowing Augie a decent view of her bosom. "I'm terribly hungry." Jemma opened her eyes and batted her lashes as she'd seen other women do. "I'll let you win me a trifle. I should so enjoy that."

Augie took the bait. "Well of course I'll win you a trinket. I'm rather good at the bottle toss. Perhaps a ribbon for your hair? Or some earbobs?"

"Oh, that would be lovely," Jemma said with false enthusiasm. In truth, she was much better at the bottle toss than Augie, but her suggestion seemed to steer him away from more discussion of their betrothal.

Studying Augie as he steered the brougham between two trees a short distance from the King Square where the festival was being held, Jemma wondered what was wrong with her. Every woman in Bermuda envied her relationship with Augustus Corbett, the handsome son of the Governor. Educated and possessed of boyish charm, he was considered the catch of the islands. She should be counting the days until they posted the banns. Instead, talk of marriage gave Jemma the most horrible feeling as if she were trapped in a pit of quicksand and struggled futilely against being sucked into its waiting depths.

"I'm so sorry your father was not up to joining us, though from last night's adventure, I can easily see why not. We played cards well into the night with our houseguest, Mr. Shepherd." Augie's lips curled as he said the name. "He's quite a poker player."

Jemma raised an eyebrow at Augie's revelation. Her father had never mentioned his playing cards last night. She thought of her father's ashen skin this morning as they breakfasted, so unlike his usual ruddy complexion.

"Yes, I expect you all had a bit too much to drink as well. I didn't realize Mr. Shepherd was still in residence." Just the thought of Nick Shepherd, brought a delicious chill to Jemma's flesh, though she hadn't spoken to him since the night he accosted her against the Governor's trellis. She had seen him though, just last week. He'd been watching her, his tall form leaning against a tree as she exited the dressmaker's. The full mouth twitching in amusement at the sight of her as if she and he shared a private joke.

"Jemma?" Augie nudged her with his elbow, none too gently. "What in the world are you daydreaming about?" He jumped from the brougham and wound the reins around a small tree. "You have the oddest look on your face, as if you've been eating chocolate." He frowned at her. "You haven't, have you?"

"Haven't what?" Good Lord! Must Augie question every bit of her life?

"Eating chocolate. You must try to tame that desire of yours. Mother says you'll become so stout you won't be able to sit a horse." He eyed her slim figure in concern.

"Lady Corbett should worry about her own stoutness," Jemma muttered under her breath.

Augie's nostrils flared. "What did you say about Mother?"

"I said your mother was kind to worry about my future stoutness. I shall take her guidance to heart." Jemma took his hand as he helped her down from the brougham, careful not to hit him with her parasol, though she longed to do so. She found Augie unbelievably annoying today and...*boring*. When did being in his company become such a chore?

After I rescued a one-eyed stranger from a pair of thieves and I was nearly ruined against a garden trellis.

"Mother thinks I should start to take over some of the pressing needs at Sea Cliff. Your father could certainly use the assistance, I think. I will be running the estate one day, after all."

Jemma stifled the urge to kick him in the shin. Instead, she took a deep breath. "I must thank your mother for the cakes she sends to Papa." Jemma continued. "He adores them. I believe she used to make them for my mother as well."

"Yes, Mother claims it is a secret family recipe. I don't know that she's ever made them for anyone but your parents." His brow wrinkled. "She's never made them for me, certainly."

"Perhaps she'll teach me to make them," Jemma said hoping Lady Corbett would never wish to share the particulars of cake making with her as Jemma had little interest in learning such a thing.

Pleased with her answer, Augie pressed a kiss to her knuckles. "How delightful that would be." He tucked her hand into his waiting arm and led her towards the festival.

Paper lanterns in bright reds and yellows dotted the branches of the trees that surrounded King Square. Streamers woven through the shorter brush around the area, fluttered in the ocean breeze. Former slaves, sailors, servants from the various estates, shipbuilders as well as merchants and their families, all mixed together in a cacophony of accents, gossip and frivolity. A group of young boys played hide and seek, darting back and forth amongst the tents, while several older men sat on a log with their pipes and ale.

"Hello Jemma." Mrs. Stanhope, the vicar's wife waved. Her plump figure waddled next to her husband's. "Bring that darling young man over here and have some cider." Mrs. Stanhope laughed merrily, wiggling her fingers at Augie as she stood by a brightly colored tent.

"Oh my," Augie said, hearing Mrs. Stanhope's flirtation. "I do hope Mr. Stanhope isn't the jealous type. He may challenge me to a duel of bible verses."

Jemma giggled. That was the first truly funny thing Augie had said in ages. Her heart warmed with sudden affection. The appearance of Nick Shepherd and her interactions with him had unsettled her and caused her to perhaps judge Augie and his intentions a bit harshly. She squeezed Augie's arm, feeling a bit more light-hearted than she had earlier. Perhaps she was being a bit too hard on him.

As they moved in the direction of the Stanhopes, Jemma's eyes discerned a tall form walking away from one of the booths, a Sinclair sister clinging to each arm.

Nick Shepherd.

Jemma's pulse leapt, and she could feel again the press of his lips and body against hers.

The Sinclair sisters each sported a clutch of colorful ribbons. Agnes giggled loudly at some comment Shepherd made while Bertie stroked his arm.

Jemma willed her racing heart to calm down. After all, Nick Shepherd was only a handsome fortune hunter, and clearly, the Sinclair sisters were more than willing to be his prey. *I hope he ruins them both. What a scandal that will cause, when he can only marry one.*

"What *is* wrong with you?" Augie hissed. "Stop pointing that parasol as if you are brandishing a sword." He followed her gaze to where Nick Shepherd walked with the Sinclair sisters. "Oh, yes. There's mother's houseguest and the unfortunate Sinclair sisters."

"Unfortunate?" Jemma smoothed her features lest Augie guess her interest in the trio. "How so?"

"Well, it's clear the man is only after a rich heiress, isn't it? He'll likely marry one of them, then abscond with her dowry to points unknown. Their brother is simply desperate to marry at least one of the two off, even if it's to a scoundrel like Mr. Shepherd. Why, we don't even know if his connection to the Cambourne family is a real one. Mother insists I'm wrong. I daresay she's just being hopeful."

"Oh?" Jemma pretended disinterest. "Did he reveal nothing of himself while you played cards?" Nick Shepherd probably made advances to half the women on Bermuda by now, an incredibly disappointing thought.

"No." Augie's face took on an ugly cast. "He tells quite a tale about his relation to the Dowager Marchioness, but I don't believe him. Neither does my father. Or yours." Augie shrugged and his features relaxed. "The Sinclair sisters keep coming by for tea in hopes of seeing our houseguest. Mother is at wits end with their visits."

Jemma clutched her parasol tighter. *Mr. Shepherd does not concern me. He is of no import.* "I'm sure you are right, Augie. I feel pity for Agnes and Bertie, to be so taken in."

Liar. Her own voiced mocked. *You dream of his mouth against your breast, of the way his hair felt against your fingertips. You are sorely disappointed he's not sought you out, even to kiss you again.*

"Bloody hell." Jemma said without thinking.

Augie's lips tightened in disapproval at her outburst. "Jemma, you *must* watch your tongue. I allow you latitude when we are alone, but not in public. You are quite improper."

The warm feelings towards Augie of a moment ago evaporated at his chastisement of her behavior, especially since he had no idea how incredibly improper she really was.

"My apologies, I must have stepped on a bit of shell," she said, trying to sound duly contrite, though she didn't feel sorry at all. She simply wished to avoid the inevitable argument that would follow, with Augie listing her eccentric behaviors. She thought briefly of pleading a headache in order to return home, but had no wish to leave the festival. So instead, Jemma took Augie's arm and smiled brilliantly. "I blame my lack of decorum on the fact I am starving." Jemma lifted her nose and sniffed the air. "Can't you smell the conch?"

Mollified by her response, Augie stroked her fingers. "You are forgiven, minx, and I know you cannot resist fried conch."

He led her into the tent, regaling her with the latest gossip about the Latimers' daughter who fled to America with a ship's captain, and Horatio Caldwell, the magistrate who was busy romancing the widow who ran Hamilton's boarding house.

Holding on to her tightly, he neatly dodged two elderly men wobbling drunkenly about the stalls as they argued over some past grievance with each other. Augie expertly maneuvered her towards the far side of the tent where it opened up to a copse of trees. Rows of tables and benches sat amongst the tall grass where groups of people sat enjoying a cool drink or munching on fried conch. Stalls flanked either side of the opening, offering a variety of delights.

Mr. Brixton, a large, heavy-set man and a close neighbor of Jemma's, stood at one of the stalls between two large barrels. A servant girl, her dark hair woven with flowers and ribbons, filled mugs from one of the two barrels at Mr. Brixton's direction while the merchant collected the coin.

Next to Mr. Brixton, the Downey family, the best fishermen in Hamilton, sold conch fritters. The six Downey sons formed an assembly line of sorts with their mother at the head, taking each customer's order, down to their father at the end who handed out the finished product. The delicacy, dipped in cornmeal and fried until crunchy, were Jemma's favorite. Scores of people floated through the tents laughing, their mugs raised in merriment.

Augie collected two mugs from Mr. Brixton, cider for her and ale for himself.

"And where's Mr. Manning today, Miss Jane Emily?" Mr. Brixton, his round face red and shiny with the heat of the day, smiled down at her.

"Busy, I'm afraid Mr. Brixton, but I shall tell him you asked after him."

"Tell him," he deftly collected several coins from Augie's outstretched hand. "That he missed the best cider on the island. Now you." He pointed a finger at Augie. "Need to quit dilly dallying and marry this lovely girl." Mr. Brixton took out a handkerchief and mopped the sweat from his brow.

Jemma forced a polite smile to her lips and said nothing.

"Soon enough, Mr. Brixton. I'll expect a large barrel of your ale as a wedding gift!" Augie laughed and held his mug aloft, toasting the older man. "And you to be our honored guest."

"Yes of course." Mr. Brixton laughed, pleased at the compliment. "And a dance with the bride." He nodded towards Jemma.

She kept her lips frozen into a smile, not wishing to hurt Mr. Brixton's feelings, for he meant well. He was only giving voice to what the entire island assumed would come to fruition. The urge to drop her mug of cider at poor Mr. Brixton's feet and run as fast as she could caused her feet to dance beneath her skirts.

Leading Jemma down the row of stalls, Augie lifted his mug once more in farewell to Mr. Brixton. "Really, Jemma," he hissed in her ear, "we must set a date. I tire of everyone assuming it is me who delays our betrothal." He waved at Mr. and Mrs. Reckitt who waved merrily back. "Mother is positively in fits over having the wedding before the next rainy season. She says we may honeymoon in London and visit Dorthea. Doesn't that sound lovely? Our houseguest," a derisive note entered his voice, "has told Mother he'll write us a letter of introduction to the Dowager Marchioness of Cambourne as a wedding gift."

Jemma stopped cold. "Well that's certainly kind of him." The thought of Nick Shepherd's acceptance of her marriage left her feeling betrayed, a silly notion. They'd shared a kiss and nothing more. *Well, a bit more than a kiss*, she thought, feeling a blaze of warmth on her cheeks. "I think I need to eat something. I've rather a headache."

"I should say so," Augie agreed. "You've been quite ill tempered today."

Jemma bit her lip. She hadn't planned on being so *off* today, but thinking of Nick Shepherd gave her such an *unsettled* feeling, as if the earth moved beneath her feet and she couldn't find her balance. "I just don't believe that someone like Mr. Shepherd has such a connection and your mother's hopes will be dashed. Why, he probably cheats at cards." She smoothed down her skirts. "Shall we have our fried conch now?"

Augie stopped abruptly, his features carefully blank, but a curious light glowed in his eyes. "Why would you say that?" The muscles of his arm went taut beneath her fingers.

"Well, a man like him, if his connections are false, must

need to make a living somehow. Gambling would seem to be the obvious choice. Aren't most gamblers accused of cheating at one time or another?" She took a step towards the Downey family and their fried conch, but Augie didn't budge. "What of it?" Jemma spun to face Augie. "You played cards with him last night, didn't you?"

"A hand or two. And it was only a friendly game. You know I don't gamble." He didn't meet her eyes and his fingers drummed against his thigh.

Jemma thought Augie a terrible liar. Every time he stole a sweet or punched another boy as a child, and lied about it, he drummed his fingers. All of Hamilton whispered that Augie gambled, though no one had said so to her face. She'd put it down to gossip and nothing more. Her eyes flew to his fingers beating against his thigh.

Apparently, she'd been wrong.

"Why are you so interested in what Mr. Shepherd does?" He put his hand in his waistcoat pocket and changed the subject.

"Mr. Shepherd? I thought we were discussing *your* playing cards?" Jemma replied evenly.

"I did not miss his interest in you the other night." He ignored her question and pouted childishly.

"Don't be silly." Afraid that her attraction had been evident, she shrugged carelessly. "He may have shown an interest in me, but I'm afraid if he did, I found him to be rather arrogant and crude. My only concern is that he'll hurt either Agnes or Bertie. Or even your mother. I fear her hopes are misplaced in his having any connections, and I should hate it if she is taken advantage of." She let the topic of Augie's gambling slide, for now. She would ask her father later if he'd heard the rumors.

His stance softened at her words. "I stand corrected, Jemma, and I apologize. It's just that you don't seem in any hurry to marry, and I've noticed that half the women on the island seem to find him appealing." He ran a hand through his hair and gave her a sideways glance. "I suppose next to him I appear a bit boring."

"Mr. Shepherd does not hold any appeal for me." She squeezed Augie's arm, feeling guilty. "Not a bit." Jemma hoped that would satisfy him, for she did not wish to discuss Nick Shepherd any longer.

Augie pushed a lock of brown hair off his forehead. "Forgive me for being a jealous dolt. I am just anxious for us to become man and wife. Come, let's walk a bit then we'll find you something to eat?"

Jemma kept her features bland as Augie proceeded to parade her about the festival, a smug expression on his boyish face. He made sure everyone saw them together, clutching her possessively to his side to solidify his claim on her. How many times had he paraded her about in such a fashion? She thought the number very high, and she had never really taken note. Until today. The Governor's son and the prize catch of Hamilton, the richest heiress in all of Bermuda.

He whirled her about, speaking to nearly everyone, while she smiled automatically as if she hadn't a care in the world. Augie's grip on her elbow never lessened, his hold akin to that of warden with a prisoner. And that's what she was.

How naïve I have been. There was no choice about her marriage. Not really. Augie was not a choice—he was the *only* choice. Their parents had decided years ago that she and Augie would wed. No other man dared to approach her, the understanding between the Mannings and the Corbetts dissuading all other suitors. If she didn't marry Augie, who, *exactly,* would she marry?

Her gaze wandered over the clustered groups at the festival, noting the lack of eligible bachelors. She thought of her friend, Martha Covington. A lovely girl who'd been married off to a man old enough to be her grandfather. Martha now spent her days playing nurse, wiping drool from his chin. She thought of her papa's business associates from America. Mr. Morley and his son, the father a widower and the son a bachelor. The pair eyed Jemma as if she were a fat goose ripe for roasting. She'd been grateful for Augie's claim on her at the time.

I have only been delaying the inevitable. Father will only indulge me for so long. I would wish to have the love my parents did, but I shall have to settle for familiarity.

The idea made her incredibly sad.

"Why hello there, Corbett." A beefy ginger-haired man clapped Augie on the shoulder, interrupting Jemma's self-pitying thoughts. He shot Jemma a toothy grin. "Good day, Miss Manning."

"Jones!" Augie gave the man a wan smile, clearly not happy at all to see Mr. Jones. "What an unexpected pleasure to see you here."

Preston Jones wobbled a bit but held steady as he shook Augie's hand forcefully. Mr. Preston Jones was short and round and clothed in a jacket of green and gold plaid. The waistcoat stretched snugly across his belly. An oval shaped sticky looking red stain spotted the waistcoat with several small crumbs stuck to it.

Cherry tart, Jemma surmised, thinking that Preston Jones looked like a large leprechaun. She sniffed the air. *A leprechaun that fairly reeks of rum.*

Wealthy and spoiled, Preston Jones was known to be a bit of drunkard. And a gambler. Though he was married, his wife, Susan, was constantly pregnant and rarely left their estate.

Jemma gave a small sigh. Augie really was the best Bermuda had to offer.

"Glad to see you here, Corbett. I've some business to

settle with you from the other night." A meaty hand clapped Augie on the shoulder.

Augie stumbled in the dirt, and his arm fell from Jemma's elbow.

Surprised, she raised a brow in question. She'd not known that he and Preston Jones did business together. Or were even friends.

"I'm a bit busy, Jones. Now is not a good time." He gave Jones a pointed look. "Can't you see I am escorting Miss Manning today?"

Mr. Jones laughed, though his eyes remained hard, all trace of amiable drunkenness gone. "Well, now. Miss Manning wouldn't mind if I borrowed you for a moment, would you Miss Manning? Just a bit of business." He winked at Jemma. "Won't take more than a moment."

Augie moved back and forth on the balls of his feet, nervous as a rabbit after scenting a hunter. "If you insist."

Jones smiled but his response was curt. "I do."

"You don't mind, do you?" Augie's voice wavered.

"Of course not." She was actually relieved to be free of Augie under the circumstances, no matter that her salvation took the form of Preston Jones. "If you and Mr. Jones have business to discuss I'll leave you to it. I believe I'll have another cup of cider and I am rather hungry. I'll have a twist of conch with Mrs. Stanhope." She nodded to Augie. "Find me when your business is concluded."

"I won't be long." Augie took her hand, squeezing softly. "I promise."

Clapping Augie on the shoulder, Jones pushed him towards the other side of the festival where a carriage sat waiting. Turning, he doffed his hat to Jemma. "I'll make sure he stays out of trouble, Miss Manning. I wouldn't let anything happen to your *betrothed*."

Jemma inclined her head politely and turned towards the

main tents. She did not care for the way in which Preston Jones looked at her, nor the highhanded way in which he strolled away with Augie. She swung her parasol, swatting at the long grass somewhat viciously, thinking how trapped she felt. A month ago there had been no such discontent about her future. What had changed?

Nick Shepherd.

She found Mrs. Stanhope and finally sat down to enjoy a twist of fried conch with the vicar's wife but caught herself reluctantly searching the tents for a tall, dark form. Appalled at her actions, she turned back to Mrs. Stanhope and the conch fritter and allowed herself to be peppered with questions about Augie. After nearly an hour, Jemma excused herself. Where in the world had Augie gone?

Wandering idly through the aisles of stalls, she took in the display of wares displayed by the local artisans of Hamilton. She visited Mr. Brixton again, accepting another mug of cider before she made her way to one of the stalls displaying jewelry made from shells.

A pair of earrings caught her eye. The shell was cut into small circles and burnished until it shone with several rings of color. As she was admiring the way the sun reflected off the colored rings of a shell, a large shadow fell over her, blocking the sunlight. She didn't need to turn around. The skin on her arms and neck tingled immediately as the scent of a cheroot and citrus tickled her nostrils, and a husky whisper murmured her name against her neck.

"Hello Jem."

8

Jemma told her body to cease the sudden longing that burned through her the moment he spoke her name in that dark voice that conjured up a certain wildness within her. She'd prepared a speech of course, a massive set-down meant to put him in his place after their last meeting. Not a word of it did she remember now.

"Mr. Shepherd," Jemma said crisply, determined to maintain her composure. She made a show of examining each of his arms as if searching for something. "But where are Agnes and Bertie? Have they tired of your company so soon? A difficult decision to decide which one to assault on a dark terrace, Mr. Shepherd."

"Assault?" A half-smile crossed his lips. "I need a trellis in order to assault a female properly. Alas, there are none to be had here."

"What a difficult decision you have before you," Jemma continued, ignoring the glorious ache stretching across her body as she thought of him pressing her against that trellis. "You can't marry both, but they each have large dowries."

"Jealous Jem?"

"Of being courted by a fortune hunter? Hardly." She turned her back on him, afraid of losing her resolve.

Shepherd leaned down and said against her ear. "Where's young Mister Corbett? Did he leave you to wander about by yourself?" His breath tickled the hairs against her neck.

Jemma reached behind her, swatting at him as if he were a mosquito.

"Oh, that's right," he said, his tone smug. "I believe I saw him get into a carriage with Preston Jones. I'm sure they'll have a delightful ride about town."

"I'm not sure the whereabouts of Mr. Corbett is any of your concern," Jemma retorted, annoyed that he knew Augie left her alone.

"Oh, it isn't. My interest in Mr. Corbett is purely tied to my interest in you."

Jemma took a deep breath, willing her heart to stop thudding so hard in her chest, and turned to face him.

"You should know." He sighed as if disinclined to give her bad news. "Your man's a gambler, and not a good one. He's terrible, in fact." Shepherd nodded knowingly.

"Augie doesn't gamble." She could still see Augie's expression earlier, and his dismay at seeing Preston Jones, and knew she was wrong and Shepherd right.

He shrugged. "Your father's much better at playing his cards close to his chest, but Augustus couldn't bluff a child." The brilliant blue eye sparkled down at her.

"Why are you telling me this, Mr. Shepherd? I am well aware that you were playing cards with my father and the Governor last night. I find it possible you cheated them. I expected no less."

"What makes you think I cheat at cards?" An incredulous look came across the handsome face. "I'm rather good. I've no need to cheat. In fact—" He stepped closer.

"That's far enough." Jemma brandished the parasol, the

tip pointed directly at his midsection. "Our conversation is over, Mr. Shepherd. Good day." She tried to turn gracefully but caught her heel in the back of her skirt instead. She swung the parasol wildly in one hand while trying not to spill the mug of cider clasped in her other hand.

"Good lord." He took her elbow to steady her. "Stop swinging that thing about." Shepherd sidestepped the parasol, but not before it hit him on the leg. "You're going to hurt someone, namely me."

The press of his hand against her elbow caused the most delicious sensation to run down her arm. She shook his hand off even as she peered up at him.

Shepherd's hair, shaggy and carelessly cut, hung in a haphazard dark mass to brush against his shoulders. She could see the shadow of his beard and the little knot in his crooked nose and wondered if he broke it in a fight. The eye-patch was as crooked as his nose, and she resisted the urge to reach up and straighten it. The finely cut coat he wore stretched tight across the breath of his shoulders, testament to either the bulk of muscles bunched underneath the fabric or perhaps the man just needed a good tailor.

Jemma thought the former.

Mr. Shepherd wore an odd-looking ring on his thumb, dull and worn with age. It shone like old silver. Had she noticed that before?

"Are you quite done with your assessment of me?" The full mouth drew up into a boyish grin.

"I was wondering about your nose," Jemma retorted, irritated he'd caught her looking at him so thoroughly. "I was not *assessing* you."

A deep rumble of amusement sounded from his chest. "My *nose?*"

"Yes," she said, ignoring the skipping of her heart against her ribs. "You've broken it, at least twice." She cocked her head. "You'd be surprised at the number of fistfights one witnesses as a boy. I've seen literally dozens of broken noses."

"Have you indeed? I forget that you have more experience in such things than other women." A large hand waved at a mosquito that hovered in the air about his head.

"Did it hurt?" Jemma raised a finger up, then just as quickly put it down, unnerved by her own actions.

"A bit." The deep voice murmured. "Walk with me?" He crooked his arm, meaning for her to take it.

Jemma looked away and ignored his offer. The man's allure was greater than an entire tray of chocolate tarts.

"I promise," he said, "to keep you in full sight of the festival and all of your curious neighbors. As I said, since the current festivities lack a garden trellis, your virtue shall remain quite safe, Miss Manning."

"As you wish." She shrugged her shoulders carelessly, but her body hummed as a bee when it nears honey. *Damn him*.

"And close the parasol Jem." His tone became overly familiar once again. "You're likely to put out my other eye the way you wave that thing about. Clearly, you are unaccustomed to using a parasol properly as most young ladies are wont to do." He took the parasol from her and folded it up neatly. "I'll carry it." He placed it under his arm. "Your dress is quite fetching."

Jemma looked down at her muslin day dress of light green. She doubted seriously he gave a fig for her gown. "I'm told the color brings out the green in my eyes and downplays the fact that I am not as pale as porcelain."

Mr. Shepherd nodded. "It does indeed. Yet, I sense you prefer to run about in your breeches and boots."

"I do." Jemma tilted her chin. "Some find it eccentric. Odd. Reckless."

"Not odd. Different." He gave her a crooked smile. "Reckless? Perhaps a bit. But, think how boring the world would be if we all followed rules."

"I have never been very good at following the rules." Jemma picked up her skirt in her free hand.

"Nor have I," he said in a thoughtful voice, leading her forward.

Before Jemma could think of how improper her behavior was, she found herself strolling in the sun beside the tall form of Nick Shepherd. He took a path that bordered King Square, far enough not to be overheard, but close enough so they stayed in plain sight of the food and beverage booths. The grass scrunched under his large booted feet as they walked towards the shelter of a large tree. He took great care to match his longer strides to her shorter ones, pointing out a stray branch or rock so that she didn't trip.

"Certainly, your father did not teach you to shoot?" Shepherd leaned towards her.

Jemma shook her head. "No."

"You're quite a good shot. Better than most men. So who was it? That dour man who accompanied your father to the Governor's last night?"

"You mean Tally. He's been my father's man since before I was a child. I think of him as an uncle, of sorts. He taught me to shoot, use a knife, and I even fence a bit, though not well." She waited for Mr. Shepherd to react with scorn as most men would at her list of unladylike accomplishments.

"Go on," the whiskey laced voice encouraged her. "Why would your father allow such an unorthodox upbringing?"

"Papa wanted to keep me occupied, I think." Before she could wonder why Mr. Shepherd cared to know such things or why she felt the need to tell him, she told him more. "He grieved deeply and for many years after my mother's death. I suppose it was a way to keep me from being underfoot. And, Tally didn't mind." She shrugged. "There is also the matter of my sweet tooth. It is hard to become stout when one is always running around outside chasing skinks and such."

"Skinks?"

"Lizards. Big ones. They're everywhere." She lifted her skirt away from a bramble. "Tally surmised that following him about in a skirt would be problematic, so he brought me breeches and boots. No one cared for the longest time. Except Lady Corbett. If she knew I still wore my breeches the knowledge would give her fits. She worries overmuch for my complexion as well."

"I did wonder about the hat." Mr. Shepherd twirled the parasol about in the grass.

"The hat?" Jemma puzzled, not sure what he meant.

"I thought it odd a boy would wear a hat with such a large brim, and I was correct." His gaze roved over her body. "You are not a boy."

"Would that I were as then there would be no lemon juice on my face," Jemma retorted.

"I for one am happy that you are not." He stopped in front of a juniper tree and leaned against the trunk.

Jemma inhaled sharply at the soft tone of his words. Once again that odd feeling overtook her, as if she and Nick Shepherd were the only two people in the world.

"Your complexion will be safe here," he waved up at the thick canopy of green above their heads," though I happen to be overly fond of freckles."

Jemma grasped the mug of cider tighter. She'd forgotten she held the cup entirely. Taking a deep breath, she said, "If I asked you a question, Mr. Shepherd, would you reply honestly?" She brushed one foot over the grass, enjoying the feel of it against her shoes.

He didn't answer for the longest time. "Will you call me Nick?"

Jemma stopped waving her foot and looked at him

"That is my price for your interrogation," he countered. "And I must be allowed to ask a question in turn. One for one. Agreed?"

"As you wish, Mr.—I mean Nick." His name flowed smoothly from her lips. She cleared her throat. "Do you not have the use of a valet? You are nearly always in need of a shave."

"You wonder about my crooked nose and whether I have a valet? Those are certainly," his mouth quivered, and she could see he was trying not to laugh, "probing questions." He crossed his long legs in front of him. "I do not currently have a valet, I am borrowing the Governor's man, who finds minding me a bit of a chore. The man's dislike is quite apparent. I've no desire to have my cheeks and chin covered with cuts, so I've resorted to the distasteful task of shaving myself, apparently with mixed results. Are you applying for the position? You could stand on a box or something."

Jemma ignored his outlandish comment. "Is that your question to me?" she said boldly, taking a sip of cider. "Then I shall answer."

"No. I retract the question." He grinned wickedly down at her, looking like a child about to cause trouble. "Though I do wonder what my shaving habits discern about me."

"That you are used to having a valet because you do such a poor job. A man of lesser fortune would have learned to shave himself by now. Which begs the question of whether you were raised with wealth and lost it, or you are just mimicking your betters," Jemma stated tartly.

"Clever girl." Nick bowed.

"Will you answer?"

"No. That's two more questions, *Jem.*"

The way he said *Jem* caused her toes to curl. The breeze lifted a dark curl against his cheek. She wished to pull it back behind his ear.

"Now it's my turn," the dark voice whispered.

Jemma looked towards the festival and noticed Mrs. Stanhope had caught sight of them. The vicar's wife held her hand up to shield her eyes from the sun and watched their every move.

"Mr. Corbett will be back soon. I should go." What a ruckus it would cause if Mrs. Stanhope took it upon herself to march out across the grass and lead Jemma away.

"Doubtful. Mr. Jones has quite a lot to say to your Mr. Corbett. I know that because Mr. Jones mentioned as such when I told him where to find young Augustus." Nick proceeded to twirl the parasol about. "Silly bit of fluff and quite useless. I *adore* freckles, by the way."

"Yes, you've mentioned your affinity for them." A languid heat wrapped itself around her, even as her mind urged her to flee. What if he tried to kiss her? In full view of Mrs. Stanhope?

"Now." He stroked his chin. "It's my turn." He must have sensed her urge to leave because he said, "You did promise to answer a question." The whiskey of his voice seeped into her skin, warming her all the way down her spine. "Did you like the way I touched you?" The brilliant blue eye bored into her. "You must answer honestly."

Jemma trembled, but not with fear, something far more dangerous, desire. A consuming need to know what this man offered her. "Yes." She clutched her mug of cider tighter, unable to look away from Nick.

"You've lovely breasts, by the way," he murmured, sliding up from the tree to step closer to her. The brilliant blue gaze flicked down her bodice.

A burst of warmth spread down her neck and around her breasts. "You are incredibly forward and possibly depraved, Mr. Shepherd," she whispered.

"Nick. And yes, I suppose I am. Next question." His voice

became gravelly. "Would you like me to kiss you again, and *where?*"

Jemma blinked at his outrageous, inappropriate question. "That's two questions, Mr. Shepherd."

"Nick." He gave her a wolfish smile.

"I will answer the first." Would he kiss her again if she goaded him? Suddenly she cared little that Mrs. Stanhope watched. "Yes." She hesitated before continuing, "Under this tree." Boldly, she named the location and did not look away.

Nick shook his head and moved to stand in front of her. "No, I meant—" a long slim finger reached out to trail against the line of her bodice. "Where?"

Jemma dropped the mug of cider, the contents spilling across Nick's boots. "You *are* depraved." A trickle of perspiration fell between her breasts, the nipples becoming taut as she remembered his mouth on the sensitive peak. "Are you deliberately trying to shock me?" Frozen in place, she feared if she moved it would be into Nick's arms.

"Yes. Did I mention my predilection for your freckles?"

"Several times. But they are unfashionable," she said stupidly.

"Are they?" Nick bent over, picking up her now empty mug. "First the chocolate tart, and now your cider. I find it utterly amazing you ever manage to put a forkful of food your mouth." He stood, leaning over her. He cocked his head, his lips grazing over the base of her ear. "I wish to kiss every freckle, *Jem*, that marches across your nose. And anywhere else you may have them."

"I—" She snatched the cider mug out of his hand. "You —" She panted helplessly as her body tingled from the brief touch of his lips. "You are forward, *Mr. Shepherd.*" Jemma took a deep breath, causing her breasts to push across her bodice.

Nick's gaze flicked down immediately.

"Do not." He gave her a hungry look. "Pretend ignorance of what lies between us."

"There is nothing between us." Jemma tried desperately to compose herself. "You are a bloody horrible man," she spat weakly.

"Yes. I am the very Devil himself." His forefinger lingered against her arm.

Heat seared into her skin from his touch. She must get away from him, though she longed to have him strip the clothes from her body. Lay her down in the tall grass around the tree. Show her the things her body yearned for. A host of wildly provocative thoughts ran through her mind none of them appropriate for a virginal, nearly betrothed young lady.

"If you'll excuse me, I must find Mr. Corbett." The words were shaky, skittish. "I have lost my taste for the festival and wish to go home." She shied away from him, terrified of the feelings he invoked in her. "Please give me my parasol."

He held out the much-abused accessory. "Jem."

Jemma's heart stopped. Why must he call her that? Why speak as if it were an endearment?

"You must stop calling me that," she said firmly, though her knees were wobbly, and her legs quivered like a bowl of jelly. Afraid he'd see how her eyes filled with tears, she turned away. "Please stop this senseless baiting of me."

"It is not senseless, and it is not baiting. It is something else entirely. Were you not so innocent, you would know the difference."

Jemma jerked the parasol from his hands, his words shaking her to the very core of her being. Because he was right.

Nick bowed to her, his glorious hair twinkling with hints of red. "Good day, Miss Manning. I am sorry if I caused you any distress."

He didn't mean it. He wished to distress her endlessly.

Jemma could tell by the quirk of his lips. She wished to ask him what there was between the two of them but wasn't sure she should hear the answer. Nodding to him politely she headed back in the direction of the festival, wishing again she'd shot *him* instead of Wren that day behind the Green Parrot.

❧

NICK DID NOT RETURN TO THE FESTIVAL, INSTEAD HE walked around the perimeter to his horse in order to avoid Jem. He'd no wish to see her with Augie. Particularly now.

Marching back to Corbett's brougham, her skirts swinging from her long unladylike strides, she did not look back at him. Thank God, she did not, for he might have run to her and kissed her senseless.

He'd *planned* to meet her today. He wished all of Hamilton to see them. He'd even thought that he would seduce her under this very tree, hoping the vicar's wife or some other upstanding citizen would discover them. That had been his plan at any rate. Only when the chance had come, he found himself unable to act, or at least act with most of Hamilton in plain view.

If *only* Jem were empty headed, dull and *common*. Lovely but stupid, as so many women he met were. If only he didn't actually *like* her. Whatever transpired now between he and Jem would not be done for revenge. He had not thought he would want her so much. Or have a care if he hurt her.

I will hurt her whether I wish it or not.

He thought back to last night at the Governor's mansion and the game of cards he'd played with Augie, Manning, and Corbett. Manning's hands shook so badly his cards kept fluttering to the table top, though the man tried to keep his voice even. He grimaced every so often in pain that led him to reach up and rub his chest with his free hand. Manning's eyes were bloodshot, and his skin held a grayish hue. The man was not well and would likely die soon, whether at Nick's hands or not.

Corbett the elder regarded Nick with the assessing gaze of a cautious alligator who wonders the price if he leaves the water to eat a tasty pig on shore. The Governor drank heavily, his words to Nick rife with meaning and innuendo. He was uncertain whether Corbett knew who he was but suspected he did.

Augustus, unaware of the undercurrents swirling about the table played poorly and stupidly, allowing the others to win nearly every hand. Nick assumed Augustus played dice the same way, which was why Preston Jones wished to speak to young Corbett. Nearly half the men in Bermuda held Augie's markers. Just how in debt was he?

Nick had gone to his room after the last hand, wondering how much more subterfuge he could tolerate. He wished to make both men suffer, and to do that he needed to ruin the traitor's daughter. He would force Manning to confess his sins and leave the man to die on this island, his daughter ruined. Nick thought he would just strangle Corbett outright. Perhaps make sure he had an accident on the stairs or something.

At least that *had* been Nick's plan when he left the Governor's mansion this morning. And it had seemed a solid plan, one in which he would relish torturing the men who had dared injure the Dunbars.

"Please stop this senseless baiting of me."

"Bloody hell." Nick spat and climbed his waiting horse.

The more I speak to her, touch her, the more I desire her. Her father destroyed mine. This should be simple. Ruin her and delight in my revenge.

Nick gripped the reins of his horse tightly, causing the

animal to dance beneath him. A fierce longing rose up in him for Jem.

He would fulfill his promise to his grandfather, but not at Jem's expense. Not after today. Not now, after he knew that what was between them was more than attraction, more than a flirtation. Now that he knew he had the power to break her heart.

❧ 9 ☙

J emma slowed her horse, eyes squinted to discern the trail which wound around a cluster of mangroves. Quicksand abounded on both sides and more than one less cautious rider had found himself and his horse trapped in the quagmire that was the swamp.

Carefully she wound Ajax around a large dead stump. The fetid odor of vegetation and stagnant water made its way to her nostrils and she grimaced. The trail was the quickest way to get to her favorite fishing spot, but she didn't enjoy the sensation of being trapped that the darkness of the swamp gave her. Or the smell.

"Almost there, Ajax." Jemma ran her hand over the stallion's thick gray mane. Ajax had been a gift from her father on her 15th birthday. While she clapped her hands in delight, Lady Corbett had shaken her head in consternation, admonishing William Manning for giving his daughter a *stallion* and not some docile, dappled mare. The stallion as a gift for a girl was *unseemly*, Lady Corbett said. Thankfully, Jemma's father ignored her.

"I don't find you unseemly in the least," Jemma said out

loud, and Ajax snickered back as if he understood and agreed with her.

"I do hope I find some tasty crabs. I would so like crab chowder for dinner." Patting the basket hanging from her saddle horn, she stifled a yawn and checked the basket to make sure she'd brought enough bait. "I think I am in need of a nap, Ajax." Sleep had eluded her since the encounter with Nick at the festival. Though she'd been in his company for less than an hour, that short time changed her view on all manner of things. The dreaded betrothal hung over her like a hangman's noose now, and the familiar sense of complacency she'd felt about marrying Augie had vanished. Now the thought of marrying him seemed almost abhorrent. Wrong.

I belong with Nick.

Jerking back on the reins at the truth of her thoughts, she pulled too tight on the bit, and Ajax shook his head in agitation.

I want him, even though I should not.

Her sleepless nights were testament to his effect on her. She dreamt of him, of lying naked with him. She would awake with a start, a painful ache between her thighs and the taste of him on her lips. Why she would want a one-eyed man of dubious character and background instead of the Lord Governor's son, she didn't know. Did it matter?

Jemma had not seen Nick in Hamilton, nor had he sought her out. She sensed his avoidance of her and was hurt by it. Wishing to see him, she even resorted to having tea with Lady Corbett, hoping to catch a glimpse of him, but to no avail. He seemed to have vanished, and Jemma was too embarrassed to ask Lady Corbett or Augie of his where-abouts. For all she knew, he'd left the islands.

"Perhaps he's romancing one of the Sinclair sisters. I can't blame him, really. After all, I am nearly betrothed." Jemma shrugged, feeling as if a great weight sat on her shoulders. "He makes me feel things I should not. Makes me want things. I fear it best I never cross paths with him again."

Ajax snorted and lifted his head.

"Yes." She reached down and ran her fingers through the horse's mane. "I should stay well clear of Nick Shepherd. But I don't really wish to, you see. That's the rub."

The heat of the sun warmed Jemma's cheeks and she quickly adjusted the brim of her hat. It was early, and still cool, but Jemma didn't dare go home with her nose burnt.

Morning sunlight touched the top of her shoulders as she made her way out of the dark pit of the swamp. She led Ajax down a narrow path between to boulders. The path ended on a small, sanded inlet with a tidal pool. Fish, crab, and occasionally a spiny lobster found their way into the tidal pool and couldn't get back out.

A large outcropping of rock jutted out over the pool, creating a shaded area next to the water. The sand here was still cool and the breeze gentle. No one knew of this place, not even Tally. Jemma found the spot years ago and returned here often. She would not be bothered she thought, stifling another yawn. "Goodness Ajax, it is a miracle I made it here without falling asleep in the saddle."

Dismounting in one graceful motion, she looped the reins around a small bush that struggled to burst through the rock. Digging into her saddlebag, she pulled out a ragged quilt and a napkin filled with a fresh mango and some cheese. A leather flask of water hung from the saddle horn as did her fishing basket.

Tossing the quilt onto the pink sand, she placed her lunch on top, throwing a stone on each corner of the quilt to ensure it would stay flat. She deftly grabbed a grub from the hamper and stuck it through the small barb dangling off her pole. The grub wiggled around the hook, trying to escape its fate. "I feel rather the same way." She flung the line out into the pool then tossed her hat aside with a sigh.

"I don't give a fig if my skin looks like burnt toast, and I'd rather fish than play the pianoforte. I don't wish to give up my eccentric behavior to sit and sew and gossip while listening to Lady Corbett instruct me on how to be a proper wife."

Ajax shook his large head in agreement.

"Mr. Shepherd doesn't seem to find my behavior too odd. He complimented my shooting."

The stallion snorted and pawed at the sand.

She braced the pole against a small boulder next to her. "I don't love Augie. I won't ever love him, except as a brother. I should marry him, though, shouldn't I? What other choice do I have?" Lying down on the quilt, she looked up at the clouds dotting the sky above her. "I think I may love Nick Shepherd, which is ridiculous, since I barely know him. Well, that's not exactly true. I feel as if I *do* know him. It's very complicated and I don't know that I'll ever see him again."

Ajax whinnied in response.

"I do appreciate your council, my friend." Jemma blew a kiss to Ajax. She rolled over and grabbed at her discarded hat. She squished the quilt into the sand with her shoulders to get comfortable and put the hat over her face. Contemplating her feelings for Nick Shepherd was best done with her eyes shut.

NICK SLOWED HIS HORSE TO A WALK NOW THAT HE WAS well out of sight of the Sinclairs' home. He wished desperately that he'd absconded with a bottle of Abel Sinclair's rum to fortify him after the "Sinclair Assault," of yesterday evening and his subsequent discussion with Abel. Had it not been so late, and had he somewhere else to go, Nick would have fled the Sinclair estate last night, but he found he was averse to sleeping out of doors under a cloud of mosquitos. He was quite used to women throwing themselves at him, after all he was heir to a dukedom, albeit a cursed one, but the Sinclair sisters put even the most determined spinsters in London to shame.

Nick stayed with the Sinclairs', at Abel's invitation, for nearly a week after the festival in Hamilton. During his stay, Agnes and Bertie each plead their case for marriage. Afternoon tea became a battleground of sorts as each twin fought for Nick's affections. Agnes attempted to sit herself on Nick's lap yesterday, under the guise of pouring him tea. This enraged Bertie so, that she flung a teacake at her sister's head. The two nearly came to fisticuffs over who would put jam on Nick's scone. Dinner became all out war. Bertie tried to feed Nick a bit of fish off her fork while Agnes and her roving foot caused Nick to push his chair back from the table to deter her.

Abel Sinclair was not amused.

After advising his sisters to retire early, Abel asked Nick to join him for a brandy in the study. He instructed the servants to keep the twins away from the study door.

Abel sat, his pale grey eyes watery and exhausted with the antics of his sisters. He regarded Nick with one bushy gray brow raised. "Well?"

Nick thanked Abel for his hospitality but informed the man, in the most polite way possible, that both Agnes and Bertie would stay unmarried. At least to Nick.

Abel nodded, giving Nick a beleaguered look. "If you'll forgive my honesty, Mr. Shepherd, I did not think you would suit either Agnes nor Bertie, though they both feel otherwise." He'd pursed his lips, hesitating as if he wasn't sure he should continue. "If you don't mind, I'd like to give you a bit of advice. You'd best consider leaving Hamilton, for your own safety, of course."

"I shall heed your warning in regards to your sisters." Nick stood, bowing slightly. "I will retire and leave you on the morrow." The eye-patch itched furiously, and he longed to be free of the bit of leather. He'd been afraid to take it off, even at night, lest one of the sisters burst in on him as he slept.

"I wasn't speaking of my sisters, Mr. Shepherd." Abel gave Nick a level look, his meaning clear. "I've warned you. Take my advice or not."

Nick thought the advice a bit late though he was sure Abel meant well.

After the festival in Hamilton, Nick arrived at the Governor's mansion to find his room neatly put in order, just not the order Nick left it in. The Governor, or rather someone in Corbett's employ, had been very careful. A less observant man wouldn't have noticed a shirt folded, *not quite right*. Or Nick's traveling trunk, moved just a bit, the lid not shut tightly.

He'd taken one look around the room and suspected he'd worn out his welcome. Unsure where to go, Nick took what he needed and decided to accept the hospitality of Abel Sinclair. The Corbetts did not inquire about Nick's whereabouts, but they likely knew he was at the Sinclairs'.

George Corbett would come looking for Nick soon.

The *Pegasus*, a ship from the Dunbars' fleet, was due to arrive in the next week, but Nick's sixth sense told him not to wait. After several discrete inquiries, Nick found the *Artemis*, bound for England, on the morning tide. He planned to board as soon as he confronted William Manning, which he meant to do tonight.

I cannot bed her in anger or revenge.

Nick would honor his grandfather's wishes. He would ask Manning for his confession, possibly even threaten the man's life in order to receive the truth of his identity. Jem need never know. Would she wonder what became of Nick Shepherd?

"I've finally become an honorable man. How horrified London would be." Nick wiped the sweat off his brow and nudged his horse into a trot.

Jem.

He would leave her to live her life, though he wished nothing more than to stay near her. Touch her. Bury himself in her softness. His grandfather would need to be content with the knowledge of the traitors, if not the traitors themselves. While it pained Nick to think of Manning living out his days peacefully in Bermuda, he did not think the man had many days left to him. George Corbett, however, Nick would take care of later.

Jem will marry Augustus Corbett. She'll share his bed and bear his children. Lady Corbett will destroy Jem's glorious, reckless nature. Augustus will never appreciate her or how unique she is. He will never know her as I do.

A mosquito landed on his arm and he swatted at it. "I hate this fucking island." Nick wiped the sweat running down his face with his sleeve. Even the stench of London would be most welcome, as horrible as the smell was, because it would *not* be Bermuda. *Not Bermuda, where there is a constant reminder of what I cannot have.*

He stopped his horse angrily. "I am tired," he tugged off his coat, nearly tearing the sleeves "of this bloody heat." He balled up the garment, shoving it into his saddlebag as a vision of Jem lying in Augie Corbett's arms filled his mind. Pummeling the coat, he finally managed to shove the whole of it away. Satisfied, he looked up from his abused coat and glanced at the rutted road ahead of him.

A small, slight figure wearing an overly large hat popped into view, then just as quickly disappeared again.

Jem.

Nick took a deep breath, mindful of what he *should* do and not caring.

"I am not as honorable as all that." He nudged his horse forward, his resolve to leave the island without seeing her again fading into nothingness.

Where was she going?

A path, barely discernible through the thickness of the trees led into a marshy area. Patches of quicksand dotted either side of the trail, and Nick carefully picked his way through the thick weeds and dense vegetation. Gnats swirled in clumps before him and mosquitos buzzed his ears. The light dimmed and Nick nearly turned back, sure he'd never find her.

A flash of white darted through the trees and a horse whinnied. The sound came from his left.

Determined now, Nick dismounted to walk his horse along the narrow trail. He slowed and matched his path to Jem's, suspecting that if he deviated from her footsteps, he and his mount would find themselves sucked into a bed of quicksand.

"I've no desire to do that treacherous shit Corbett any favors," he said to himself quietly.

A breeze stirred the stagnant air of the swamp, the sharp tang of salt reached Nick's nostrils and the roar of the ocean crashing against the cliffs reached his ears. Sunlight broke through the trees, and he found himself on a small cliff overlooking the pink sands below.

Jem seemed to have vanished.

"Bloody hell." Nick walked back and forth in the tall grass for nearly a half hour before his horse gave a cry as a lizard ran across the path.

The faint sound of another horse answered.

He walked to the edge of the grass and saw a pile of shells marking the start of another, incredibly narrow path, which stretched down the rocky side of the cliff to the sand below.

"The lass has no fear." Nick tied his horse to graze and cautiously approached the path. The shell strewn trail declined sharply before opening on to a beautiful pink, sandy cove that held a small tidal pool. A fishing pole, its line bobbing gently in the pool, lay wedged into a crevice of rock. He looked across the brilliant expanse of sand, sparkling in the morning sun and saw no one.

Where was she?

A small unladylike snore sounded from behind a boulder.

Nick approached slowly, peering over the boulder into a shaded area. He didn't see her immediately, hidden as she was under a cropping of rock.

Jem lay on her back, her head pillowed by one arm, the other lying across her stomach. Her hat sat atop her face. A pair of boots sat discarded in the sand, and he was immediately drawn to the sight of her exposed calves and feet.

Jem made another soft snorting sound and curled back against the sand.

A strange fluttering started in Nick's chest, crossing the region of his heart. Hunger for Jem spooled within him, despite his formerly honorable intentions.

Carefully, he knelt down into the sparkling sand next to her and gently pulled the hat from her face. He didn't wish her awake. Not yet. The fluttering in his chest grew in intensity as he looked down at her. Nick's gaze ran from the beautiful lines of her jaw, admiring the honey color of her skin and the light spray of freckles across her nose.

Augustus Corbett would never appreciate those freckles.

Jem's chest rose softly as she dozed, drawing Nick's attention to the small, rounded mounds of her breasts. He remembered the feel of her in his mouth that night on the Governor's terrace. Unable to stop himself, he ran a finger against the tiny peak of her left breast, delighting when the nub hardened beneath his questing touch.

Jem stirred but did not wake. Her lips pursed and her brow wrinkled as if she were contemplating something, then she smiled.

"Are you dreaming of chocolate?" Nick whispered as he brushed his lips against hers. He tasted salt and sunshine, with just a bit of chocolate.

She kissed him back, her lips moving in time with his. Her eyes flickered open slowly, widening in wonder as she gazed up at him.

"Nick." Jem stretched a bit like a kitten after taking a nap. One hand ran up his arm, then stopped. The sleepy look left her eyes. "Nick?"

The flutter in his chest became stronger as if a dozen butterflies were trapped above his heart. Joy, an emotion Nick never thought to feel, surged through him as he took in the loveliness of her features in the morning light.

Rubbing his thumb and the Devil's ring against her plump lower lip, he marveled at the softness of her mouth.

"Hello, Jem."

৩১৯

SHE'D BEEN DREAMING OF NICK.

He was kissing her under a tall tree at the festival in King Square while his hand stole wickedly up her skirts. The other hand cupped her breast. She urged him on while all of Hamilton watched. He was about to lay her down in the winding grass, in truth, she was begging him to do so, when he stopped and merely brushed his lips against hers and smiled.

Her eyes opened to see Nick's face above her, the soft smile on his lips as real as in her dream. Unbidden, her hand slid to touch the eye-patch lying crookedly against his cheek. She sighed as she felt the rasp of his beard against her fingertips.

I find him so beautiful.

The dark, shaggy hair curled about his ears in the early morning heat. The fine lawn of his shirt, heavy with moisture, clung to the sculpted muscles of his shoulders and arms. The top button of his shirt opened, revealing a spill of dark hair. His thumb ran across her bottom lip again.

"You are forever assessing me," he whispered. "If you look for flaws I have many and would be happy to list them for you. It would save time, time that should be spent on other, more delightful, pursuits. Don't you agree?" A finger ran down her arm.

"How did you get here?" She shivered deliciously as he touched her.

"I followed you."

"But, where's your horse?" She came up on her elbows and looked behind him. "And you have no coat." A throbbing ache started between her thighs, a sudden and immediate response to being close to Nick.

"Coat?" Nick scoffed. "I've come to loath my coat, a useless garment in this heat. Were I not sure it would cause Lady Corbett to have fits I would walk about shirtless." A half-smile crossed his lips.

The ache became stronger at the thought of Nick nearly unclothed.

"You followed me through the swamp? Why would you do such a thing?" she asked. "Not only is it improper, had you gone off the path you could have—"

"I wanted to see you. I—" he cut her off and stared at her with a strange intensity. The deep baritone lowered to a growl. "I wanted to see *you*."

"Why?" She knew the answer, of course. The warmth

running up her body told her. Wanting. Nick wanted her, and she wanted him. The thread of that wanting tugged at her, pulling her to him.

A gull cried in the open air above them while the surf roared and Ajax stomped in the sand. The sounds came to her muted and faded as all of her senses came into sharp focus around the man kneeling before her.

Nick reached out and took the thick braid of her hair in his hand. "I wish to see your hair down, about your shoulders." Before she could object, he untied the thong holding her braid, pulling apart the strands of her hair. He ran his hands through the weight of it before winding the thickness around his wrist and pulling her to him. "I wanted to see you," he said again before his mouth descended on hers.

Sinking into his kiss, her lips softened and opened beneath his questing tongue. She placed her hands against his chest and felt the coiled strength of his body beneath her fingertips. The flame of her desire for Nick flickered until it roared with heat, threatening to consume her.

"Jem." He sat back on his heels, a small smile playing at the corner of his lips. "Mmm." He let go of her hair. "I must admit, I prefer you without stockings." A hand ran down her calf.

Jemma trembled.

Fingers danced across the top of her toes then ran down the sole of her foot.

"Stop." She jumped back at his touch, wondering how tickling the bottom of her foot could possibly be so *erotic*. "You shouldn't."

"I should." He cocked his head, studying her bare feet intently.

Self-consciously, she twisted her feet, wondering what it was about them that merited his attention. Were her feet objectionable in some way? Nick did not seem to be bound by propriety, but perhaps her current state was a bit more than even he appreciated. Certainly, most men would find the sight of bare feet slightly indecent. "I'm not very proper, am I?"

"No," he said in a solemn tone, still looking at her feet. "Definitely not."

Jemma frowned at his quick agreement.

"It is a failing of mine."

"I have to agree." His hand inched up her thigh to her waist.

Annoyed she tried to pull away, but the feel of Nick's fingers holding the waist of her breeches held her fast.

"Now, the sisters Sinclair," the whiskey voice lectured, "they are *truly* proper ladies." The hand at her waist floated across her stomach towards her breasts.

The heaviness pressed against the cotton of her shirt almost painfully. Her breath caught in her throat at the featherlight touch of his fingers moving across her waist.

"Quite interested in pleasing a man, I might add. Agnes," a finger trailed up, to circle the outline of Jemma's breast, "made me a tart, just the other day. The berries a bit sour, but I appreciated the effort."

"I'm," Jemma gasped as Nick's finger brushed against the nipple, "certain you did."

"Quite." He toyed with the top of her nipple until it hardened into a peak. "Bertie, now, she *truly* will make a fine wife. She sings like a lark and plays the piano. Why, she even monogrammed a handkerchief for me."

"How lovely of her." Jemma panted and tried to remain still as Nick moved on to her other breast.

"Yes." Nick growled as his hand descended between her legs, rubbing gently but insistently. "Well, I suppose if you caught me a fish for dinner, or perhaps a rabbit?" His hand hovered over the apex between her thighs. "That would be something."

"There are no rabbits in Bermuda." Her entire body throbbed with an ache she could not put words to. "You bloody arrogant man. I'd like to see Agnes hold a pistol. Tart making. Embroidery. I should despise doing either." She stifled a moan as his hand came back to the waist of her breeches.

"Do not distress yourself, Jem." Nick stretched out next to her on the quilt and propped himself up on one elbow. "You have other attributes I admire far more." The top of her breeches came apart and his hand descended down the bare skin of her stomach. The long fingers wove themselves into the down of her womanhood. "So like you, Jem, not to wear any underthings with your breeches."

"They don't—" She moaned as his fingers slipped between the moist folds, "fit under my breeches." Jemma clasped his forearm with her hand as his thumb rubbed against the nub nestled between the folds.

Nick pressed a kiss to her neck, his mouth moving down across the top of her breasts. "I wish to see these," he breathed roughly, his hand moving up from her breeches to cup one breast. As he sat up, he cupped one side of her face, kissing her roughly. "Now. I would see them now."

The rough cotton of her shirt suddenly slid up before she could protest. Not that she was *capable* of protesting. This was wrong. Wicked even. But, oh how she wanted Nick, wanted *this*.

The string holding her chemise loosened, and that garment too flew off her body, the wispy material caught by a gust of air and landing on her boots. She should be horrified, even embarrassed. Instead she was elated, her body taut with excitement. Still, she looked away from Nick.

"So lovely, like sweet cherries."

A jolt of intense pleasure caused Jemma to arch her back as Nick sucked one sensitive peak into his mouth. Reaching up to clutch at his head, she cried softly, "Do not stop, Nick, I do not wish you to stop."

He lifted his mouth from her breast and regarded her solemnly. "Then, we are in agreement." His tongue flicked against her nipple as he watched her. "Aren't we?"

Jemma paused for a moment, but only a moment. There was nothing she wanted so much as to be with this man. This moment had been destined since he first touched her. She was no worldly woman of the *ton*, nor was she a girl who idly discarded her virtue, but Nick was the desire of her heart. "Yes. I am certain." Marriage to Augie and her father's disappointment paled in comparison to the *rightness* of Nick. Jemma ran her fingers through his hair. "I am *very* sure."

"As you wish, Jem." Slowly, he pulled the breeches from her body, kissing each newly exposed bit of skin until she lay naked and quivering on the quilt. She turned her face to the ocean, too unsure to meet the eyes of the man above her. Would he find her wanting?

"You are so lovely," Nick said in a hushed voice. "Look at me."

"I cannot. I——" She shut her eyes. The confidence she'd had in all things her entire life deserted her. Fear and longing caused her to tremble.

"If you don't open your eyes, you won't be able to see what I will do next." The strands of his hair trailed against the skin of her stomach. He pressed a kiss just below her belly button.

Jemma's eyes shot open.

Nick grinned wickedly at her. "Now, stay still." His hand splayed across her stomach, holding her. He ran one hand down her leg. "I've thought of your legs often, dreamt of them, in fact. They are just as I imagined." He pushed them apart, looking at her all the while as he brushed the hair atop the mound of her womanhood with his fingers. He blew gently, tickling the hairs with his breath.

The most delicious sensations spread out across Jemma's thighs. Her legs quivered. She'd heard about such things of course, of what a man might do to a woman.

Nick's nose nudged at the inside of her thigh.

"Oh God." The tip of his tongue flicked out and Jemma's hips lifted off the blanket. That tiny nub, that spot which tingled sometimes if she rode astride, was now the focus of all of her pleasure.

"Yes?" He pushed a finger inside of her.

"Nick." She pressed her body up, wanting more.

"You're already wet, Jem." His tongue leapt out to flick at the nub while his finger moved in and out slowly. "It's like lightning in a bottle," he moved his body between her splayed legs, "when we touch. Isn't it?"

"Yes," she stuttered, barely able to form the words. Her mind became numb, her thoughts incoherent, blank to everything but the intensity of sensation created by Nick's mouth.

"You don't feel this when Corbett touches you." He breathed against the flesh of her thighs. "Do you?"

Unable to answer, she shook her head in denial against the quilt as another finger joined the first.

"I thought not." Pulling one leg over his shoulder, he pushed the other to the side until they were spread wide. His mouth sucked at her tender flesh while his fingers pressed into her.

Jemma twisted on the quilt as a delicious pressure built inside of her. There was a mountain she climbed, a wave she sought to break through. Glancing down, to see Nick's dark head, nestled between her thighs, her legs falling wantonly about his broad shoulders, intensified the pleasure she felt.

"Please." She heard herself beg.

Clumsily she pushed against his moving hand, wanting his fingers deeper as his tongue laved against her taut nub.

"Be still love," he murmured against her thighs. "Just wait."

Slowly Nick sucked the tiny, sensitive nub into his mouth and simultaneously his fingers pushed deeper.

Jemma screamed out loud. She couldn't help it. Her body exploded, ripped apart in such a tide of primal pleasure, she felt as if her heart would stop. The sensations would subside, only to begin anew as Nick's mouth and hands forced her body over each peak again and again until she lay drained and exhausted, her legs hanging limply across Nick's shoulders.

"Jem?" The whiskey voice sounded both concerned and amused.

"Oh." Exhausted from the last few moments, she could not say more. Words could not describe the experience.

"I've never killed a woman before by making her climax, but I suppose there is a first time for everything." He pressed a kiss to her thigh.

Jemma said nothing, his words reminding her there must have been other women before her, she would be foolish to think otherwise, but still, the thought hurt her.

"Jem."

Unable to look at him just yet, she shut her eyes.

"Do not think of what came before, for none of them compare to you."

AND HE MEANT IT.

There had been many women, more than he could count, the first had been when he was no more than fifteen. He enjoyed them, pleasured them, used them, and put them aside. But no woman, no courtesan, no talented widow, nor skilled lady of the *ton* remotely compared to this reckless girl from Bermuda. The traitor's daughter. The attachment to Jem was more than sexual, his desire for her would not be slaked in an afternoon, he did not believe it would ever cease, nor did he wish it to. He remembered something his grandfather once told him of Nick's deceased grandmother.

"I desired her even when she grew old and wrinkled, when she grew withered and sick. Every part of me longs to be reunited with her still."

Jem smiled shyly then and pulled Nick to her, kissing him lightly on the lips, and he could sense her uncertainty. "That was quite marvelous," she said, her face lovely and flushed. "I did not realize. I—" She bit her lip.

"That such was possible?"

"I did not know it would be like that." The intensity of her gaze caused the bits of green in her hazel eyes to sparkle like emeralds.

"It is not always."

"But it is for us," she said softly, her fingers running to the buttons of his shirt.

"Yes." He sat back and unbuttoned his shirt, hesitating at the last button. Ruination of this girl was something he promised he would not do, yet here he was, about to compromise her. He pulled off his shirt and tossed it to lay over her boots.

Her hands reached out to him, running over his chest and shoulders, through the thick mat of hair to linger at his stomach. The light touch paused over a particularly nasty scar that ran between his ribs. Puckered and purple, it was a reminder of the blade that nearly killed him years ago. He waited for her questions. Most women assumed the scars to be the result of duels, a terribly romantic notion, or they thought them a result of his family's rumored servitude to the Crown. In either case, the women he bedded didn't care to ask.

"Who has hurt you so?" Her genuine concern for him and the wounds he bore surprised Nick, as her lips pressed against the rough edges of that scar.

His heart, which up until now only fluttered in Jem's presence, burst wide open. The pain, as if a door nailed shut had been forced open, caused him to pause. Nick's conscience, absent for most of his life, chose now to make itself known.

"Jem, are you certain? If we stop now, you will still be a virgin. Your virtue will remain intact. There is much we can do without—"

She kissed his chest again in response.

Nick swallowed, grabbing her, forcing her to look up at him. "Once done, it cannot be undone. You are certain?"

Jem nodded, her eyes never leaving his face. "I am sure."

"Then my lot will be yours." He did not say such a thing lightly. Indeed, no member of the Tremaine family would say such a thing unless they meant it. What the Devils of Dunbar *claimed*, they *kept*. Jem may not realize the import of his words, but Nick did.

His mind made up, he stood in one fluid movement and looked down at Jem, naked and waiting at his feet. He prayed she wouldn't run from him once he took his breeches off. He could feel his arousal, hard and swollen, about to burst forth. Nick was a big man—*everywhere*.

Pulling off his boots, he tossed them to flop in the sand. Then he rolled his breeches down over his hips as Jem watched, seemingly mesmerized by his actions. As his arousal sprung forth, her bravery seemed to desert her, for she looked down only sparing a glance at his naked body from beneath her lashes.

"Don't be afraid."

"I'm not."

But he could see she was.

She bit her lower lip. "I didn't think it would be quite so large. I mean, I've seen horses and such but—"

Nick laughed softly. "There is an expression—but now is not the time. I just don't wish you to be afraid."

"I'm not. I am never afraid of you, even when I should be."

He came to her on all fours. Hovering over her, he leaned down to graze her lips with his own.

She kissed him back fiercely as her hand trailed along his chest to wrap her fingers around the length of him.

"Jesus," he growled.

"I'm sorry—" she stuttered, her hand falling back, "I—I thought I should touch you as you touched me? Should I not? Should—"

"You may touch me anywhere you like," his voice shook with desire, "but I think we will save the exploring for later. I'm not sure I can wait much longer." He kissed her neck before pushing her legs further apart.

Jem's body shivered beneath him.

Reaching between her legs, he found her slick and warm. He rolled his thumb back and forth through her folds.

"Ahh." Jem sighed softly and wrapped her arms about his neck. Her hips twisted beneath his fingers. "I want you, Nick."

And she did, he realized, want *him*. Not the Devil of Dunbar, not the heir to a fortune, not a man that so many considered damned. She thought him to be Nick Shepherd, a man with few prospects, one eye and possibly a fortune hunter. Yet, she still wanted *him*.

He took away his hand and pressed his arousal between her thighs, the tip hovering just outside of her entrance. Gently, he pushed into her, watching her face for any signs of distress, worried that he would cause her pain. "It will hurt, the first time."

Jem cupped his face, her lips twisting into a small smile. "I've ridden horses all my life. I'm told that may make it easier."

Nick returned her smile and kissed the tip of her nose. He wrapped one arm beneath her bottom, holding her and thrust slowly but firmly into her, feeling the small obstruction give way.

Jem tensed beneath him, her legs tightening. A small cry of pain escaped her lips.

Nick didn't move, allowing her body time to become accustomed to his. Beads of sweat hovered about his upper lip as he resisted the urge to push further. As her body softened against him, he brushed his lips against hers, gently nipping at her mouth. "Jem."

She moved her hips as he said her name, pushing up, so that he sunk deeper inside her.

"Tell me what I need to do"" She moaned and her hands clung to his waist, pulling him close to her. "Like this?"

"Yes. Like that." Nick struggled to maintain his control lest he spill himself like an untried lad. He thrust into her again and again, swiveling his hips so that his body caught against her sensitive flesh.

The most delightful little noises emanated from her lips as she moved beneath him, trying to match his movements. "Harder." She nipped his chest. "Oh God, please, harder. You won't hurt me." Her nails bit into his buttocks. "I promise."

Jem found his rhythm and matched him thrust for thrust, her hips lifting and turning against him. The tightening of her body beneath his, caused him to pause and slow, wanting to prolong the pleasure for them both as long as possible. He wished this moment never to end.

"Nick." Jem said, her breath coming in short bursts.

"Wait, love." He lifted one of her legs up, hooking it over his arm. "Wait for me."

Her body tightened around him, pulling him deeper as she climaxed.

Nick rocked forward, burying his face in Jem's neck, the intensity of his own release shocking him with the ferocity of it. He whispered his want, his longing for only her, his lips pressing against the softness of her skin.

They lay there while the sun moved across the sky and the gulls flew over their heads. Their bodies remained joined as if it had always been so.

When at last Nick came to his senses, he pulled from her, ignoring her small sound of disappointment. One leg thrown over hers possessively, he lay next to her, allowing the gentle ocean breeze cool their bodies.

They talked then, speaking of nothing and yet of everything. He did not tell her the truth of who he was, he couldn't. He would have to concoct some fabricated tale to skirt the true reason for his presence in Hamilton. But, not yet. In spite of that lie between them, Nick felt light of heart for the first time since he was a child, before his parents died and he wore the mantle of the Devil of Dunbar.

Later, he made love to her again slowly, trying to tell her with his body what he could not yet say. He could not explain, even to himself, the depth of his need for her. Why it should be Jem, the daughter of the very man he sought revenge against, remained a mystery. The haunting prophecy of the gypsy whispered in his mind, but he pushed the thought back.

Jem rained kisses upon his face and lips, cradling Nick's head against her heart. In a low voice, she spoke of her love for him, whispering the words into his hair to keep him from hearing.

But he did.

Jem, the traitor's daughter. A rare and precious gift he

thought never to have. He held her for a long time, still wanting her, knowing he must leave her, for now.

Tonight, he would confront William Manning, no longer able to postpone the inevitable. He would ask for his identity and confession. Nick's grandfather would have to be content with only that and not the man himself. Nick would not destroy Manning for the sake of the woman who lay in his arms. He wished Jem never to know what brought him here. Or what her father was.

A choice, a chance, had been bestowed upon Nick. The Devil it seemed, had a sense of irony. The Dunbars kept what they claimed, and he claimed this lovely, eccentric girl who lay next to him. His lot would be Jem's, whether she willed it or not.

When Nick left this cursed island tomorrow, Jem would be going with him.

❧ 10 ❧

William Manning rubbed at the ache in his chest, willing the pain to go away, knowing it would not. "I'm coming Maureen," he said softly to his dead wife's portrait. "Soon."

Maureen said nothing, of course, only staring at him, a gentle smile on her lips from her perch above the mantle in his study.

His sweet Maureen. Dead for so many years, but always alive still in his heart. Dead because of *him*. He'd paid dearly for his part in the betrayal of the Dunbars, his punishment, a lifetime without Maureen.

"I'm sorry, my love. I have done the best I could." He turned from the portrait to the pages of his confession lying atop his desk.

George Corbett, his greatest friend and his accomplice in treason and duplicity for twenty years. George, who told William to attend that damned house party at the Duke of Dunbar's. George, who knew exactly where those papers were hidden and knew exactly who to sell them to for the greatest amount of money. George, who arranged William's *death*. George, who was content to allow William to shoulder the blame for all of it.

William looked back up at Maureen's portrait. She was posed with her hair down, one hand protectively over the gentle swelling of her belly where his son lay. "You're dead because of me." William dabbed at one eye, his voice breaking in the empty study. "I only did it because I was young and stupid. Father cut me off, but I wouldn't set you aside. I should have trusted that we could find our own way, but I was a coward then," William muttered to himself. "And I am now."

Maureen continued to smile serenely down at him, encouraging him to speak. "I'm very frightened, my love. The Devil has come to Hamilton. Finally. I have made arrangements to keep Jane Emily safe, in case George means to do her harm. And I think he does. Or she doesn't wish to wed Augustus, which I am certain she does not." He stopped and ran his fingers through his hair. "I don't wish her to know I am a traitor, my love, unless there's no other way. Selfish of me, I'll admit."

It took several weeks of convincing on William's part for George to come around and realize that the Devil was in their midst. "*Why does he not just declare himself?*" George mused after cards the other night. "*What do you think he wants Willie?*"

"*I think, George,*" he'd said "*that he wishes to toy with us, as a cat does a mouse.*"

George had shaken his head, so arrogant and full of his own self importance. *'The Crown would never allow him to hurt me. I'm the Governor of Bermuda. I think we should wait, Willie, and let him approach us.*"

William thought George a great fool. "A great fool," he whispered.

No one *ever* crossed that cursed family and expected not

to pay. William would pay the price, gladly, as long as Jane Emily was safe.

Rubbing his eyes, he walked over to the sideboard and poured himself a brandy. If not for Jane Emily, he would have confessed his crimes long ago. It would be such a relief to finally be free of the past. George claimed to have not seen his erstwhile houseguest for several days and thought perhaps the heir to Dunbar left of his own accord, but William knew the man wasn't gone, only waiting. He wanted something, and he imagined it was a signed confession. Perhaps, he even meant to take William back to England in chains. Truthfully, he no longer cared. He was ready.

A soft knock at the door interrupted his thoughts.

"Sir?" Gladdings, the head butler of Sea Cliff, poked his head into the study.

"Yes?" William took another sip of the brandy. His head ached as dreadfully as his chest. "It's not time for dinner yet Gladdings, is it? And where is Jane Emily? I haven't seen her all day."

Gladdings, a tidy man who arrived on Bermuda a bond servant and ended up at Sea Cliff, bowed slightly. "Dinner will be ready at half past seven, sir. Miss Jane Emily is upstairs and should be down shortly."

"Where's she been all day? Fishing, I suppose?"

Gladdings nodded. "I believe she left a basket with Cook."

William smiled. Jane Emily was the joy of his life. He adored her eccentric habits, though he never encouraged them.

"Sir?"

"Yes, Gladdings, is there more?"

"Governor Lord Corbett and Lady Corbett sent word that they will be here promptly at seven."

William frowned. "Did I invite them?" He couldn't seem to remember. "I don't recall."

"I assumed you did, sir." Gladdings sounded confused.

William shook his head. His memory failed him. "I'm sure I did. Why wouldn't I? Will Augustus be joining us?"

"I don't believe so, sir. Only Lord and Lady Corbett."

William waved Gladdings out. "Tell the Governor to indulge me in a drink before dinner. Please direct Lady Corbett to the drawing room. Jane Emily can keep her company before we dine."

"Very good, sir." Gladdings quietly shut the door behind him.

He planned to tell George tomorrow but would now tell him tonight. William had already written out his confession, admitting to all he had done, leaving out George Corbett's part in the theft. He planned to trade his confession and life, if necessary, for the guaranteed safety of Jane Emily and William's family in England. The confession lay on his desk now, the lines of words proclaiming his sins standing out starkly against the creamy paper.

Another knock sounded at the door.

Gladdings' head popped in again. "I'm sorry sir, but you have a visitor. I've explained that you are not available, but he insists and threatens to come in uninvited. Mr. Nick Shepherd."

William took a deep breath. The Devil meant to have his due tonight it seemed. So be it. His pulse beat his temple, with fear, though he also felt an odd sense of relief. No more playing games.

"Show him in." William drained the brandy and poured himself another glass. He was in dire need of courage just now.

Heavy footsteps sounded in the hall and made their way

to William's study. Gladdings opened the door wide, ushering Mr. Shepherd through the wide doors.

William didn't look up. His hands trembled against the brandy snifter.

"Good evening, Manning." The dark voice floated towards him.

"Shepherd." William looked up, determined to see this through. He tried to keep his features serene and polite. "I mean, my lord." William nodded. "Would you care for a drink?"

Nick Shepherd, or rather the man who presented himself as Nick Shepherd, strolled into the study to stand before William's desk. Dressed all in black, except for the snowy white of his shirt, the man certainly looked like the devil he was purported to be. The heir to Dunbar smiled cheerfully at William. "Shepherd will do."

William looked into the odd mismatched eyes, determined to keep his voice even, though he felt like screaming. "Brandy or rum?"

"Whisky, actually. If you have it." The deep baritone was polite. "You've suspected who I was since that dinner party at Corbett's, haven't you? You knew I would eventually come to you."

William nodded. "Yes." He could hear the frightened beat of his own heart pulsing in his ears.

"I thought as much. Corbett didn't believe you, did he?" Shepherd's lips twisted into a wry smile.

"No." He'd tossed and turned at night, wondering how his meeting with the Devil of Dunbar would present itself, but he never imagined having drinks with the man. William found a bottle of whisky hidden behind the decanter of brandy on the sideboard. Dusting off the top he said, "I don't drink whisky." He held up a bottle. "Will this do?"

"Indeed, it will."

William poured out a glass of the dark amber liquid and held it out to Shepherd's waiting hand, telling himself not to stare at the man's eyes. Impossible, of course. The contrast of one brown eye and one brilliant blue was so pronounced one could not look away. "I see you've finally done away with the eye-patch," William said stupidly, stating the obvious.

"I saw no point in continuing with the charade. An eye-patch is horribly uncomfortable, especially in this God awful heat. I suppose that is why pirates grow to be so ill tempered. However do you grow accustomed to the weather?" He took a sip of whisky and nodded in approval. "Quite good."

"Time," William answered. "One's blood grows thin over the years and you become used to the heat. I suppose I should freeze in London. Are you taking me there?" He shuddered slightly at seeing the dull wink of pewter on the man's thumb. The ring. Even as a child he'd heard about the ring and the stories about the Devils of Dunbar.

Shepherd made his way over to a chair facing William's desk, seeming to assess the piece of furniture. Apparently satisfied, he sat, the chair creaking in protest as the big man settled himself.

Shepherd rolled his eyes in resignation and muttered something under his breath.

"You don't look like your father, if I may say." The words tumbled from William's mouth.

"You may."

Emboldened, he continued, lest he lose his nerve. "I recall that your father was leaner, and his hair lighter." You resemble your grandsire. The duke. I assume he is still alive? Or should I address you as Your Grace? I'm afraid I'm not sure what to call you," William rambled.

"As I said, Shepherd will do for now. I prefer to leave this island as I arrived. Minus the eye-patch. And what should I call you?"

William cleared his throat and ignored the pointed question of his identity. "Then you will be leaving?"

"Yes." Shepherd sipped his whisky, smiling as he did so. "Of course. There is no reason for me to stay any longer. I have found what I sought."

A trickle of sweat dripped down the side of William's face. "Me." He wiped the sweat away with the back of his hand. "I assume, my lord, that you wish me to confess my sins to you?"

"Yes," the husky voice murmured. "I would have it from your own lips."

"If it matters, my lord," he started shakily. "I didn't mean to hurt anyone nor did I wish ill to your family."

The broad shoulders gave a small shrug. "Ill wished or not, my family was harmed."

William cleared his throat again and tugged at his cravat. He felt as if he were strangling. He held up the pages he'd written out so carefully only this morning, in preparation for this meeting. "Confession is good for the soul, I'm told. If there's any saving of my soul. It's all here." His eyes watered and he looked away. "I did not know your father would be blamed. The death of your parents weighs heavily upon me."

"Not so heavily," Shepherd said, waving a hand about the room, "that you didn't enjoy the fruits of your deceit. You fled England and allowed all that happened, to happen."

He winced, knowing Shepherd spoke the truth.

"How did you know about the papers? The list? How did you know to steal them?" Shepherd swirled his whisky as if admiring the dark liquid in his glass. "Who told you?"

"George. I'm not sure if your father told him or—" he shook his head. "I take full blame for the entire affair. I am the traitor."

"Indeed you are, but you certainly had help becoming one. Manning is not your real name. I have read the guest list of my grandfather's house party at least a dozen times. George

Corbett sent regrets, three of the men I've cleared and the other two are dead. Manning is not a name in either my father's correspondence nor my grandfather's." Shepherd's odd eyes glinted. "Who are you?"

William grew very still. "My family believes me dead, and I wish to stay dead. I would not bring my disgrace upon them. You may take me away in chains if you must or kill me on the spot. I no longer care. But I will not give them up, for you would destroy them all without a qualm."

Shepherd merely cocked his head. "You are of noble birth. Perhaps, the second or third son, aren't you?"

William could feel the blood leave his face.

"Why did you do it?" Shepherd said softly. "You caused the death of three men whose names were on that list. The French garroted two and had the third tortured."

William swayed back and gripped the desk for support. Would the demon before him not shut up?

"You purposefully allowed the taint of treason to attach itself to an innocent man. Granted, my father was of no high moral standing, but still, to allow anyone, especially a member of my family to bear the taint of treason, is a most hideous crime."

"They could never prove anything, my lord," William whispered, his mouth dry as dust.

"No." Shepherd growled. "My father did not hang, instead he and my mother became pariah's within the *ton*. My family bore the taint of treason and added to it the scandal of suicide. How bold you and Corbett were to do such a thing to *my* family. And, the men who died. Two of them left wives and children. How do you sleep at night, *Manning*?"

"George...he never told me—" Dear God. He'd known about this man's parents but not about the men whose lives he helped end. *George never told me all of it—the sum of my evil.*

"Did you sell out the lives of three men and ruin another's

life, just so you could have all of this?" Shepherd flung out his arm to include the fine furnishings of the study. "I would have your name." The words came out clipped and cold.

"I didn't know!" William tried to remain calm but found he couldn't. "I didn't even look at those damned papers. George never told me exactly what was in them." William wiped at his eyes. "I didn't *know*! I didn't know your father would be blamed or that men would die. Oh, Dear God."

"I'm sure Corbett knew exactly what would happen." Shepherd tossed back the rest of the whisky in one swallow.

"What does it matter now?" William's voice shook with fear and emotion. "You've found me. I am guilty. You have your confession."

"Why?" Shepherd demanded. "I wish to hear from your own lips why a man does such a thing."

William spun away from him, tears rolling down his cheeks. The horror of what he'd done, what he'd caused, made him sick to the core of his being. He no longer cared if Shepherd saw his weakness. He wished the man would just run him through and end this horrible conversation.

"Do you see her?" William said wildly, his hand shaking as he pointed to Maureen's portrait. "I did it for want of *her*. I got her with child, willingly, I might add. But she was Irish, a maid, and Catholic to boot. I refused to put her aside and my family disowned me. My father sent me packing. I had no skill, no trade." He turned back to Shepherd and said savagely, "Have you ever been in love, my lord?"

The big man looked away, refusing to meet William's eyes.

William nodded. "Yes, well, then possibly you understand. She died, by the way, only a few years after I came to Bermuda. Childbirth. I told her, confessed to her what I had done and the shock and disappointment caused early labor. She wouldn't look at me, even as she bled to death upstairs, struggling to bring my son into the world. She and my boy died," his voice broke, "in my arms. She never spoke to me again, my wife died *disgusted* with me and what I'd done." His voice raised an octave and he thanked God that Jemma was still upstairs. "So, you see, my lord, I have been well and duly *punished*. I have lived an *eternity* without her. I killed the very thing I loved most. A far worse punishment than even the infamous Devil of Dunbar can mete out." William took a great heaving breath.

"You have my confession, and you may take me to hang if you wish. I would have your word that if I hand you this paper, give you my name, that you will leave my family, and particularly my daughter, alone. You will leave the Corbetts alone." William held up the paper. "It's all there, Devil. Your family's honor will be restored. I will go with you tonight and you may kill me at your convenience."

⚜

NICK LISTENED TO MANNING'S SPEECH AND WISHED HE could do as the poor, pathetic man before him asked, for surely killing Manning would be doing him a great service. But he found he could not.

"Have you ever been in love, my lord?"

Nick looked up at the portrait of Maureen Manning and saw Jem.

"I killed the thing I loved most."

The words, so like the gypsy's prophecy spoken to Nick on that long ago night sent a prickling, a foreboding through him, and he squashed it down. He glanced back at Maureen Manning again and cursed himself for feeling sorry for the woeful man before him. Nick had his confession. He was taking Jem. Manning he would leave to the fates.

"I have no intention of killing you, nor taking you to London in chains." Nick put down his glass. "You have my word that your family will not be harmed. Now, I would have your confession," Nick nodded to the paper Manning held, "and your true name."

Suddenly, the door to the study burst open, to reveal the corpulent form of Governor Lord Corbett.

"Pardon my interruption." Lord Corbett sneered as he strolled into the study, an ugly look on his florid features. "I knew if I left you alone, Willie, for a minute," he raised a finger to emphasize his point, "that you'd fall on your knees whining and sobbing like a virgin on her wedding night. I told you I would handle *this*." Corbett waved a be-ringed hand towards Nick.

"George." Manning's face turned red as he faced his friend, his eyes popping in agitation. He laid his hand on the desk, concealing the written confession from Corbett's wondering glance.

Corbett, sweat clinging to his forehead, walked to the sideboard and poured himself a brandy. "Thank goodness I got here before you did something stupid," he spat.

"I'm not sure what you mean, George." Manning's fingers crawled over the paper containing his confession to the edge of the large desk. His eyes flitted to the side.

"Good evening Governor Lord Corbett." Nick flexed his large fingers, wanting to snap the man's neck like a bit of kindling. Corbett deserved to die, but that chore would need to wait. He wanted nothing of this evening to hurt Jem, especially not the duplicity of her father and her father's best friend. Once he and Jem were well away, Corbett would be dealt with. There were other ways to destroy the Lord Governor and in light of Corbett's sins, Nick thought killing too quick.

Corbett turned to Nick, lips curled in distaste. "Good Lord, your eyes are as ghastly as they say. No wonder your mother screamed as you were first placed in her arms."

Nick flinched. Everyone in London knew the tale of his birth, it was no great secret, but hearing Corbett say the words out loud still caused a twinge across Nick's chest. "I would be mindful, Corbett, of what you say to me."

Corbett's eyes flickered with a hint of fear before narrowing once again. He lifted his chin and replied, his words thick with arrogance, "*You* should be careful of what you say to *me*." He wiped his upper lip. "You are on my island. My domain. All answer to me."

"Yes," Nick said softly. "All commanded by a traitor. One wonders what the Crown will think about *that*."

Corbett paled a bit but otherwise maintained his composure. "Traitor?" He sipped his brandy. "You've no proof of anything. The ramblings of your drunken sire are not enough to hang a man. Certainly, they weren't enough to convince anyone of his complete innocence, though I suppose your grandsire kept him from being thrown into prison.

Nick raised his glass in a mock salute to Corbett. "Indeed."

"Did I tell you," Corbett's mouth turned into a malicious grin, "that I played cards with your father? What an incredible waste of title and privilege. He drank like a fish. He found himself so in debt once during a card game that he tore the buckles off his shoes. How we laughed at him."

Nick said nothing. He wished only to leave, not stay and be baited by the likes of George Corbett. His eyes ran to the piece of paper that Manning now clenched in his hand. *I've given my word.*

"And, let's not forget your dear mother, Charlotte. A more silly, frivolous woman I've yet to meet. I'm told she was so drunk she thought your father was joking with the gun and actually put the end of the weapon in her mouth." Corbett shook his head. "She loathed you. Simply, loathed you."

"George," Manning's face had grown ashen. "Please, don't

say more. His lordship was just leaving." Manning shot Nick a nervous look.

"Oh, please don't fuss, Willie. We're just catching up, aren't we?" Corbett sipped his drink and regarded Nick carefully. "I wonder that you didn't just rip off that eye-patch and declare yourself the other night."

"I wonder that you didn't dispose of me, when you realized who I was." Nick's temper flared at the man's pompous arrogance. "Oh, but then you aren't sure who will come looking for me. And, it's a dangerous thing, to attempt to murder the heir to Dunbar. You got lucky with my father, I'll grant you that, but my grandsire and myself," Nick scratched his chin, "we are not quite so weak."

Corbett's hand trembled slightly as he took another small sip of his brandy, but his face remained frozen, hatred for Nick stamped across his features.

"And there is Dorthea, your daughter, to think about." Nick dipped his head. "Who knows what could happen to *her* if I don't return. What instructions I may have left?"

Corbett's nostrils flared. "Don't threaten me, my lord, you are not off my island, *yet*."

"Stop it! Stop!" Manning cried, setting his glass down on the desk. "There is no reason for threats," he held his hand up in supplication. "The past is to stay buried." Manning shot Nick a sideways glance. "Please," Manning lowered his voice, "for Jane Emily's sake."

"Oh, yes. Dear Jane Emily. My son's betrothed. The soiled bride to be."

Nick's stomach twisted. Damn Corbett. How could he know what transpired that afternoon? "I should take my leave." He set down his glass and held out a hand for Manning's confession.

"What do you mean?" A dark purple flush crept up

Manning's cheeks and his mouth hardened. He clutched the papers to his chest with one hand.

"Revenge." Corbett said cheerfully, lowering his eyes and raising a brow at the papers Manning clutched. "Revenge, my dear friend. Why do you think he disguised himself and walked among us? He was looking for your weak spot. Your Achilles' heel. I believe he found it, or rather, *her*." Corbett lifted his glass in a mock toast to Nick. "Tell him about Jane Emily."

Nick stood and reached out for Manning's confession.

Manning's cheeks puffed and his face took on a horrible purple hue. He slid back behind the desk to collapse in the large leather chair that sat there, still clutching the sheaf of papers to his heart. "What," he gasped, ignoring Nick, "are you implying George?"

"Oh, I think you know, don't you?" Corbett sipped his brandy. "I can't believe you meant to give him that," he nodded to the now crumpled paper in Manning's hands, "after what he's done. He's defiled her. Fucked your precious daughter like some common whore." He reached across the desk and easily took the papers out of Manning's hands. He held them up, briefly scanning Manning's words before tossing the pages into the fire. "I'll have to speak to Augustus about Jemma's indiscretion, of course."

Nick's chest hurt. "Damn you." Nothing had gone as planned since he set foot on Bermuda.

"Agnes Sinclair was quite distraught over your rejection." Corbett smirked. "She wished to persuade you to take her back to England, so she followed you. Agnes painted quite a vivid picture for her brother. She's no fan of Jane Emily's, I'll warrant. Her brother was absolutely horrified. Distraught. He came straight to me." Corbett patted Manning on the shoulder. "Don't worry, Willie, I paid him well not to repeat the story. We can't have my son's future wife be known as a slut."

Manning panted, like a dying dog, behind the desk. "I meant to do the right thing." He lifted a shaking finger towards Nick. "And you ruined my daughter?"

Corbett lifted a brow at Nick. "Why, she could be carrying his bastard right now!"

Nick watched the last wisps of Manning's confession blacken and burn in the fireplace and cursed George Corbett. Years of planning and searching for the man who betrayed England and framed Nick's father became ashes before his eyes. He told himself it didn't matter. All that mattered now, was leaving this island, alive, with Jem. He would need to take her now. "Move." He snarled at Corbett.

Corbett didn't budge. "Tell us all what happened on the beach with Jane Emily."

Manning stood on shaky legs and approached Nick. His skin had turned greenish gray and his eyes were crazed. "You defiled my daughter. You filthy bounder." Manning lurched forward.

"Deny it. Deny you ruined her." Corbett's eyes flitted to the open doorway.

"I do not deny it." Nick walked deftly past Corbett.

"I thought not. You didn't get what you came for, and you've sullied Jane Emily. You'll get not a farthing here. Now, get out," Corbett said, his voice rising loudly. "Get out I say!" Corbett looked past Nick into the hall as if he saw someone there.

Nick puzzled for only a moment over Corbett's odd comment before walking from the room. He didn't think that Corbett would have the audacity to try to kill him, but he didn't intend to stay long enough in Bermuda to find out. Nick felt the reassuring weight of his knife in his boot and hoped he could find Jem quickly.

As it turned out, Nick didn't need to look for Jem at all.

She stood just outside the study door, her hands trembling

against the folds of her skirts, looking for all the world like a wounded animal. Her eyes widened as she took him in, though he doubted she could see his face clearly in the dim light.

He knew from her stance that she'd heard every vile word George Corbett spoke. "Jem."

"You ruined me for money?" She swayed and reached for the wall to steady herself. "Why?" Pain and betrayal etched the lovely planes of her face.

A thud, of a body falling to the floor, came from inside the study.

Jem jumped at the sound, her eyes flying to the open study doors.

"God's blood!" Corbett shouted. "William. Shepherd's killed him."

She turned from him and ran into the study, falling to her knees before the collapsed form of her father.

George Corbett regarded Nick over Jem's shoulder, his eyes flickering with triumph. "Oh no!" His eyes never left Nick's face. "William has collapsed from the shock. Money in return for your reputation. Blackmail."

Nick turned and walked as quickly as he could out of Sea Cliff, his mind racing. He brushed past the shocked butler who had let him in barely an hour before.

The house erupted into a frenzy as the butler screamed out an order to send for the doctor while Lady Corbett burst from the drawing room.

No one stopped Nick on his way out the door. He quickly counted the number of servants, the location of the stairs and wished he knew the exact location of Jem's bedroom.

His boots crunched across the gravel drive as he moved towards his horse. Jem would fight him now, every step of the way, thanks to George Corbett. He would have to find a place to hide, then break into Sea Cliff once everyone was abed.

Kidnapping would now be added to the list of his crimes, for Jem was going with him, whether she willed it or not.

The first blow hit him across his face, and he felt his nose break. The second blow, from a cudgel, hit him in the temple and drove him to his knees.

"Hello toff," Wren whispered as Nick struggled to get to his feet. "Governor Lord Corbett sends his regards."

He felt something heavy against the back of his head and knew nothing else.

11

The wind whistled across the clearing, moving the bared branches of a dying mulberry tree and filling Jemma's nose with the smell of the sea. She reached up to brush a stray strand of hair from her cheek.

I miss you so much, Papa.

Her hands ran over the hump of earth, not caring for the condition of her gloves. Grief, sharp and painful, caused her to clutch at the earth under her fingers.

At least, he's finally with my mother. Her eyes misted with tears and she tried to blink them away. Her father spoke of his deceased wife often, as if she were still roaming the halls of Sea Cliff, but Jemma barely remembered her mother. A vague recollection of a lilting Irish voice and a warm embrace smelling of tea roses were all Jemma had of Maureen Manning. She wiped bitterly at a lone tear that ran down her cheek. Now, all Jemma had were memories of her father to sustain her. Memories and guilt.

I am responsible.

Jemma stood, the force of the wind whipping the skirt of her mourning dress about her ankles. She could see the ocean just over the rise and the profusion of hibiscus encircling the tiny graveyard at the edge of Sea Cliff. A beautiful spot for her parents to spend all of eternity. She was alone now.

Firm hands grabbed her shoulders. *Augie*. She'd not even heard him come up behind her.

"Come, my dear." He pulled her to him, clutching her hands in his. He turned his head towards her father's resting place. "I loved him as well, you know." The pain of the loss Jemma felt was reflected in Augie's drawn features. "He was as much a father to me as my own."

"I know." And, Jemma *did* know. Augie Corbett learned well from Jemma's father how to run a vast enterprise, and the two had spent many evenings together discussing trade ventures, the salt industry and the price of rum. Augie *had* loved her father, but he also coveted Sea Cliff. She suspected that Augie's affection towards her had less to do with her person than it did with the vast Manning empire of which Sea Cliff was the seat. In the week following her father's death, Jemma saw lust in Augustus Corbett's eyes, but it wasn't for her. Nor did she feel an ounce of desire for him.

I am being uncharitable.

Augie had been her rock, a steady shoulder for her during the days when Jemma's father lay ill and dying. Apoplexy, Doctor Wade called her father's affliction, brought on by a sudden shock.

The shock of being blackmailed by the very man who ruined me.

Jemma nursed her father, refusing to leave him, even though he never spoke and barely opened his eyes. Mrs. Stanhope arrived to stay at Sea Cliff, and Augie handled her father's affairs. Two weeks after that horrible night while Jemma mopped his brow, William Manning simply expelled a deep breath and went silent.

Numb with grief and guilt, Jemma sat in a daze while the Corbetts handled the arrangements of the funeral and the running of Sea Cliff. She moved through those days in a fog, so full of sorrow she barely acknowledged those around her. Her thoughts remained chaotic, disjointed, as if not wishing to believe that her entire world was suddenly changed.

Nick.

How did one still long for a man who caused such a tragedy? Hours upon hours she berated herself for her stupidity while her heart still ached for him.

Lord Corbett had told her the truth of Nick Shepherd. How the man planned to ruin the richest heiress on the island and blackmail her father to stay silent. Money. That was all Nick ever wanted. All else was a lie. He'd fled Bermuda the moment her father collapsed, else Lord Corbett would have had him put in chains. She cursed herself a thousand times over for being so blind. But nothing would bring back her father.

"Come, Jemma. You must not walk out here alone, along the cliffs," Augie said quietly. "I was worried when I came to call, and Mrs. Stanhope said you were out here again. Mother says it's not safe."

At the mention of Lady Corbett, Jemma stiffened and attempted to pull away from Augie. Grateful though she was for Lady Corbett's assistance immediately following her father's death, the older woman's concern was quickly beginning to feel more like suffocation.

"While I appreciate," Jemma struggled to keep the irritation out of her voice, "your mother's concern for my welfare, she does not dictate my actions." Jemma wrenched her arm from Augie. "She will not even allow my own coachman to take me into Hamilton with Mrs. Stanhope. I am not some fragile flower that need be coddled."

Augie took her elbow again, his fingers digging into her skin. "Stop behaving like a child." His mouth drew into a grim line and his eyes darkened. "You know very well why you cannot go to town. Mrs. Stanhope is poor protection for such an endeavor." He raised a brow and his words were tinged with distaste. "Mother is not to blame for your lack of discretion."

Jemma's cheeks grew warm. Augie was right, though it pained her to admit it. Abel Sinclair had not breathed a word of Jemma's affair with Nick, but his sister, Agnes, did not keep quiet. The stares of her neighbors at her father's funeral had told Jemma as much. Still, she refused to believe that she had become a pariah. "I cannot believe the people of Hamilton would treat me so unkindly. Your father has assured me that—"

Augie snorted and dropped her arm, his manner making clear his annoyance. "You spoiled little brat." A strand of hair fell over his brow and he pushed it back sharply. "What about me? What about the humiliation I have suffered? Do you not think I must endure the whispers of your indiscretion as well?" He held up his hands as if seeking agreement from the gulls that flew overhead. "Had you any sense of humility you would do exactly as Mother asks until the gossip dies down. If it dies down. My parents have done all they can do to quell the likes of Agnes Sinclair. All you must do is stay at home and show some remorse for your scandalous actions. You are so selfish you cannot even do *that*."

Jemma stopped and clasped her hands across her stomach. She shut her eyes against Augie's harsh words.

"That I am willing to overlook your indiscretion and still marry you," Augie's voice raised an octave, "is a testament to the esteem in which I held your father."

"How honorable of you. I'm sure Sea Cliff has nothing to do with your sense of duty," Jemma said without thinking, her eyes snapping open to glare at him.

Augie took her arm again in a painful grip. "You are my betrothed, soon to be my wife. I will brook no further disobedience on your part. My mother says you are willful and reckless, traits which I will not tolerate once we are married."

Jemma opened her mouth, then quickly shut it. She'd learned in the last few weeks that arguing with Augie did nothing but antagonize him further. The man who practically dragged her down the slope back to Sea Cliff was not her childhood friend, nor the gentle suitor of just a month ago.

She stumbled, her toe hitting a small stone jutting up in the path and used it as an excuse to pull her arm away from his grasp.

He let her go, shaking his head. "Do you really think you have a choice? Now? After everything that has happened? Does my touch offend you? Oh, I know," he mocked. "You're still pining for Shepherd, aren't you? The very man who ruined you so he could extort money from your father. Betrayed by a fortune hunter.

A sob caught in Jemma's throat at the mention of Nick and his betrayal. She stumbled again and this time Augie let her struggle to stand. He laughed sharply, stepping back as she reached out to steady herself against him.

Jemma swayed, catching herself. The skirt of her dress spun furiously about her ankles as her footsteps quickened. Keeping her eye on the peaked roof of Sea Cliff, she hurried, determined to get far from Augie and his hateful words. She had no wish to endure another moment of his taunting.

He caught her just at bottom of the hill, grabbing her by one shoulder and twisting her around so she was forced to look up at him. "I am the *best* offer you will ever have, Jemma. At least outside of a brothel. You should be *grateful*, instead you insult me with your insolence. You wish to go to Hamilton?"

"I do not care to discuss this matter further with you, Augie."

He let go of her abruptly, pushing her from him.

This time, she did fall to the ground, the shells that littered the path cutting into her palms, even through the gloves she wore. Clutching at the shells, she wanted to weep, but held back tears.

"Don't delude yourself, Jemma. My mother has put it out that the rumors about you and Shepherd are nothing more than the rant of a jealous Agnes Sinclair. But without the support of my family, without your status as the betrothed or wife of the Governor's son..." Augie's words hung in the humid air. "You are just the sullied daughter whose indiscretion killed her father." He leaned down to look at her. "What? No sharp retort? No witty comment?" He gave a snort of amusement. "I thought not."

He stood, turning his back on her and walked down the path to Sea Cliff, his steps confident and sure. The notes of the jaunty tune he whistled filled the air merrily as if he'd not just ground her into dirt with his words.

What am I to do? The words thudded in her mind as she sat, not yet ready to stand and face the future. *I could run, but this is my home. And, I have nowhere to go. No one to go to.* Nick's features swam before her eyes and again the pain of his betrayal pierced her.

"Jemma?" Augie stopped but didn't look back at her. "Are you coming? Mother wishes to discuss our wedding plans over tea." He tapped his foot. "Hurry along. You know Mother doesn't like to be kept waiting."

12

"**W**ife, do quit pacing, you will wear a hole in the carpet." Lord Corbett slurped his tea. "And we cannot replace the carpet. Not yet, at any rate."

Lady Corbett stopped and glared at her husband. "She is still being most disagreeable in regards to the wedding. I've had tea with her twice and she refuses to discuss any details or even to feign interest. She drags Mrs. Stanhope to every meeting, brandishing the woman at me like a shield." Lady Corbett swatted at the air with her fan. "I've told everyone that it was William's deathbed request that they not mourn him and marry posthaste. I've no doubt we will have to drag her to the altar with a gun pressed to her back to recite her vows. Think what a stir that will cause, and I'll have no more scandal, George." Lady Corbett stomped her foot. "No more. Bad enough we must contend with the fact that she is damaged goods. If not for her fortune, I'd never allow Augustus to wed her." The faded red curls of her hair batted against her cheeks as she shook in agitation. "But, I want Sea Cliff. God's truth, we need Sea Cliff."

George Corbett took another sip of his tea, savoring the taste of the Earl Grey. June had worked herself into a fine fiddle over Jane Emily. The girl had always been a bit wild, to no one's surprise. George blamed Willie for Jane Emily's shortcomings. Allowing the girl to wear breeches and shoot a gun was beyond the pale. So contrary. The fact that Jane Emily hadn't disgraced herself before now was actually a bit of a miracle.

"Do sit down, June, and calm yourself." George pinched his nose between his fingers. "You are causing my head to ache with your rantings."

His wife sputtered at his comment but seated herself, arms crossed, in the chair across from him.

He bit into a biscuit and ignored her combative demeanor. Jane Emily would marry Augie. She had no other choice. He supposed she could try to leave the island, but her efforts would prove fruitless. June had already put out the story that Jane Emily was quite *unhinged* over her father's death. Her questionable sanity coupled with the story of William's "deathbed request" led not one person to object to the immediacy of the marriage. No one would assist Jane Emily if she tried to seek passage off the island. "You worry needlessly, wife."

"I will not lose Sea Cliff, husband. I've waited too long."

"And we won't, my dear. The girl displayed outlandish behavior even before William's death. None will gainsay our claim that she is a bit mad if she doesn't marry Augie willingly."

Lady Corbett chewed at her bottom lip. "What if she tries to flee or enlist the Stanhope's aid?"

"June," George sighed in frustration, "we are her guardians as decreed by William in his will, years ago. All of Bermuda, including the Stanhope's, think her eccentric behavior a sign of mental illness which allowed her to fall prey to a man like Shepherd. None will stop us if we force her to marry Augie, for her own good, of course. None will aid her."

"Shepherd? Must we still call him that? I cannot believe I did not see through his disguise immediately." Lady Corbett's cheeks puffed in agitation. "How silly you must think me not to have suspected what he was."

"Perhaps next time, you will heed me, wife. Do not blame yourself. I didn't see through him at first either. I never suspected that family would ever find William."

June bowed her head and smoothed her skirts. "Still, I should have listened."

"Think of it no more. Besides, we are free of the Devil of Dunbar." Lord Corbett held his tea cup up in toast to his wife.

"You are certain?" Lady Corbett stopped fidgeting and regarded her husband coldly.

George shivered at the look on his spouse's face. Sometimes, June could be quite *bloodthirsty*. "Very. I made sure to tell the captain to be leagues from Bermuda before *Nick Shepherd*." George winked "Meets his demise between the jaws of a shark. Can't have bits of him washing up on shore, can we?"

TALLY O'DELL STOOD WAITING, HIS HAND RAISED TO knock on the door of Governor Lord Corbett's morning room. He hesitated upon hearing the way in which Corbett decided Jemma's future and lowered his hand. The name Dunbar meant nothing to him, and he wasn't surprised that Lord Corbett was having Shepherd fed to the sharks. The man deserved it after what he'd done. His only concern was Jemma and the promise he'd made to his friend, Willie.

When Willie asked Tally to retrieve that packet of papers

from the armoire, Tally knew this day would come. Willie did not trust George or June Corbett, at least not in the last six months of his life. He outlined for Tally exactly what must be done for Jemma. The packet, along with a bag of coins, Willie entrusted to Tally as well as a sealed envelope. Willie's instructions were very specific, particularly in regards to Lord and Lady Corbett. *"Do not trust the Corbetts, Tally, no matter what they tell you."*

That was fine by Tally. He'd never cared for George Corbett, his meddling wife nor their son, Augustus. Dorthea, their daughter had been a lovely lass, but she was long gone from Bermuda and unlikely to return. Not that it mattered.

Do not trust the Corbetts.

Tally wasn't an educated man, though Willie had taught him to read, but he was smart. Smart enough to know that Augie Corbett's IOU's fairly littered Bermuda and that the Corbetts were in debt up to their eyeballs. The amount of money Willie loaned to the Corbetts in the last two years alone staggered the imagination. The Governor could never repay the debt to his friend, nor could the Corbetts ever cover Augie's expenses. Their only hope was to access the wealth of Sea Cliff, and the only way to do that was for Augustus to marry Jemma.

Tally's heart ached for the girl he considered a substitute daughter. Had she given the slightest inclination that she wished to marry young Corbett, Tally would have thrown that packet of Willie's into the ocean. He cursed under his breath as he thought of that scoundrel who'd taken her innocence. Tally failed Willie in that. He would not fail his dearest friend now.

Counting to five, he knocked lightly at the door.

"Come." Lord Corbett's command answered.

He opened the door, determined to play the obliging manservant. Not that Corbett would ever expect anything but total obedience from Tally. Governor Lord Corbett considered him to be of little importance, and Tally meant to keep it that way. "My lord." He doffed his hat and bowed. "Your ladyship."

"Tally, my good man." When Lord Corbett smiled, as he did now, he reminded Tally of an alligator.

Lady Corbett clasped her be-ringed hands on her lap and acknowledged Tally with a brief nod.

"Lady Corbett and I require your assistance."

"I am at your service." Tally clutched his hat in both hands.

"Thank you, dear man." Lady Corbett raised a handkerchief to her eyes and dabbed. "We are so concerned about Jane Emily."

Tally thought Lady Corbett's true calling should have been the stage.

"She is so overwrought with grief. I fear it has," Lady Corbett hesitated as if finding it difficult to voice such painful thoughts, "*broken* her." She gave a small sob.

"Broken her?" Tally asked, knowing full well where the conversation was headed. He thought of Willie's packet and instructions, safely hidden along with the Sea Cliff account books under a loose brick in the stables.

"Yes." Governor Lord Corbett interjected, his features drawn down into a mask of paternal concern. "Her childish indiscretion with Nick Shepherd combined with the death of William have brought about a *breakdown*, I fear, of her mental state. She has become quite fragile."

Jemma was the least fragile female Tally had ever known, but he wrinkled his brow in concern at Lord Corbett's words just the same.

"I see from your expression," Lord Corbett continued, "that you share our concern and affection for Jane Emily."

"Indeed, my lord," Tally answered, wishing he could

punch the self-satisfied look off of Lord Corbett's face with his fist. *I will enjoy getting the better of the Corbetts.*

"I fear she has become addled." Lady Corbett shook her shoulders and stuck her nose in her handkerchief.

Tally shifted back on the balls of his feet and nodded in agreement, though he didn't agree. Not in the least.

"I know that Sea Cliff is Jane Emily's home, but William's funeral was weeks ago, and it is time for Mrs. Stanhope to return to her husband and the vicarage. Jane Emily, an unmarried young woman, can certainly not remain alone in that house with only servants around her. She needs a proper chaperone. You understand? We are worried that she may *injure* herself. She would be far better with her family," Lady Corbett waved to herself and Lord Corbett, "to watch after her. After all, she and Augustus will soon be married. She must be brought here."

And there it was, just as Willie predicted.

"You understand, don't you Tally?" Lord Corbett snapped the top of a biscuit and began to chew with gusto, daring Tally to disagree.

"Of course, my lord." Tally understood only too well. He'd heard the gossip himself just yesterday in Hamilton while making his own discreet inquiries. Half of Bermuda thought Jemma driven mad by her father's death, the other half thought her a woman of no moral standing. Tally knew full well who stoked the fires of those lies.

Lady Corbett fluttered her fan and waved at a servant for more tea. "Augie has already ridden to Sea Cliff for luncheon and to gather the pertinent estate information. I would hate for our dear William's personal papers to fall into the wrong hands." She exchanged a knowing look with her husband. "I think it is best that today you bring Jane Emily to us. Remember, her mental state is quite delicate, poor dear, from all she has endured. She may behave erratically. I pray you will not need to force her." Lady Corbett pursed her lips.

Tally nodded politely. There would be no account books for Augie to find nor William's deeds to property in Virginia and Newport. The papers detailing Willie's vast holdings were in the packet to be given to a London solicitor. The Corbetts might be able to take Sea Cliff, after a time, but they would get none of Willie's wealth and especially not his daughter. He would make sure of it.

"Please see to it immediately, Tally. I wish Jane Emily here in time for tea." Lord Corbett took another bite of biscuit, dismissing Tally with barely a wave of his fingers.

Tally placed his hat on his head, bowing low, anxious to leave the presence of these blue-blooded parasites as soon as he could. He had no intention of delivering Jemma or Sea Cliff to the Corbetts. Tally had something else planned entirely.

13

"Jemma? Are you listening to me?" Augie stabbed a piece of melon and pointed it towards her. "Day-dreaming again, I expect. I hope it isn't about Nick Shepherd. You know, flights of fancy, such as you seem to have, are a sign of mental impairment."

Jemma focused her gaze on a brilliant pink bougainvillea blooming outside the breakfast room window. She *had* been thinking of Nick, asking herself again how she could have been so wrong. Why she still felt the pain of his absence nearly as much as the absence of her father.

"I'm sorry, Augie." Jemma looked back to the table, replying as evenly as possible so as not to set him off. "And I am not simple minded, pray do not treat me as such." She wished Augie would leave. The delicious luncheon that Cook prepared still lay untouched on her plate.

"I'm sorry, Augie." He mimicked rudely, pulling his lips into an ugly sneer. "Good Lord." He nodded at her uneaten food. "Eat something. I've no wish to marry a skeleton."

Her temper flared at his words and suddenly she didn't

care if she angered him. "Good," she retorted, throwing her napkin down. "I've no wish to marry a childish boor." How she detested his endless baiting of her, his insults, his condescending attitude, and most of all, he and his parents' arrogant assurance that Jemma's only hope was to marry *him*. Truth be told, the pain of being a social pariah was no worse than facing a future with a man she was rapidly growing to detest. Her father had been wealthy, surely she could use some of that wealth and leave Bermuda behind.

Augie drained his glass. "I tire of your mooning over a man who used you for money." He poured more wine for himself. "I held my tongue and my hand," he raised his palm, "out of respect for your father. But perhaps that is my mistake, for I think a good beating is exactly what you need to keep you in line."

His words caused a trickle of apprehension down her spine. What had happened to Augie? Dislike and fear of her former friend rose up in Jemma until she thought it would spill out of her and flood the table. Enough was enough. Surely if she explained to Lady Corbett that she could not marry Augie under such circumstances, she would understand. "How dare you speak to me in such a way. I want you to leave."

"Leave?" He put his elbows on the table and glared at her. "You wish me to leave so that you can pine for that one-eyed fortune hunter? Is that it? Perhaps you have the foolish notion he will return."

"You're drunk." The fumes of the wine he drank wafted towards her as he spoke. "Please see yourself out."

"I still can't believe you wallowed in the sand with him like some common slut. I had the whole story from Agnes Sinclair. I gave you respect, affection, tolerated your oddities—"

"Stop." Jemma stood determined, shaking from his

constant barrage of insults. "This is my house, and I bid you leave before I have you thrown out."

"He only wanted Sea Cliff, or rather the wealth of Sea Cliff. Not you. Never you." Augie picked up his fork again and stabbed at a bit of poached chicken lying next to his melon.

"Then you and he are much alike," Jemma spat, her words echoing harshly in the morning room. "Get out." She wished fervently she had a pistol handy or some other weapon. Her eyes flew to the cheese knife lying in the middle of the table.

Augie followed her glance and smirked. "Not likely." He placed the chicken in his mouth and chewed slowly, his eyes never leaving her face. "Where did you hide your father's account books, Jemma?"

She tried not to let her surprise show on her face that the account books had gone missing. If Augie didn't have them, then they were safe with Tally. "I don't know what you're talking about and even if I did—the accounts of Sea Cliff are none of your business. I will inform your parents myself that our ill-fated betrothal is off. I would rather stay here at Sea Cliff, an outcast, or a withered old maid than marry you, Augustus."

"What did you say?" Augie carefully dabbed at the corners of his mouth with a linen napkin.

"I believe you heard me," Jemma retorted. "For the sake of the friendship and affection I once bore you, I tell you that I am deeply and truly sorry I have hurt you. But I have apologized and tried to make amends. I thank you for all your kindness during the last few weeks—"

"Whore."

Jemma grabbed at the edge of the table, shocked to hear him call her such, sickened that his opinion of her came of her own foolishness.

"Another man would toss you aside without a thought."

He returned his attention to his food, "But then," he annunciated each word, "you've already been tossed aside. Like an overripe peach that sits too long in the sun."

"I cannot believe your parents would allow you to treat me this way." Lord and Lady Corbett had many faults, but she refused to believe they would sanction Augie's harsh treatment of her. After all, they were her father's dearest friends.

The sound of his laughter made her skin crawl. "Now that," he pointed a finger at her, "is amusing."

"Get out of my house!" She choked out, trying to sound brave.

"Your house?" Augie snorted and pounded the table drunkenly. "Your house?" Wine dribbled down his chin and he wiped it away with the back of his hand. "It will be mine soon enough." Standing unsteadily, he moved towards her. "Mine, along with everything in it. You are much like the furniture. You come with the estate."

Jemma inched back slowly from the look of loathing on Augie's face.

"I've courted you for years! You've barely let me kiss your hand. I've tolerated your ridiculous habits. You've always assumed you were so much smarter than I, you overeducated, overindulged, trollop."

My God, how he hates me. Jemma had suspected his anger, possibly his dislike, but never this virulent hatred that seeped out of him. He would beat her, should they marry. Sucking in her breath, she realized with a growing sense of horror that the Corbetts would certainly not come to her aid, for they surely knew of his feelings for her. She could see the meanness in him, the delight he would take in hurting her. *Dear God, they must despise me as well.*

"Mother says I may have you locked in a room since there are no institutions for the insane on Bermuda."

Her worst fears confirmed, she raised a shaking hand to the servants' bell, praying Tally was nearby and would answer her summons. Augie's next words dashed all hope of rescue.

"Oh, don't bother ringing for Tally. He'll be my father's man now, not yours. Nor will Mercy come, nor Gladdings. I've already instructed them all that to interfere would terminate their employment immediately, and I'll ensure that they will have to resort to begging in the streets. Who would go against the Governor's son?" A drunken giggle escaped his lips. "That would be me, I am the Governor's son."

"Mrs. Stanhope!" Surely the vicar's wife would not allow Jemma to be torn from her home. "Mrs. Stanhope will not tolerate your treatment of me nor your highhandedness in ordering about my servants."

"I've already sent that good woman on her way home along with a generous donation to the vicarage. She is most distressed that you have become addled. Let me assure you, she did mention that in her experience with you she saw not one whit of insanity, but I've assured her that you are always on your best behavior around her. That you are, in fact, deeply distressed."

Jemma quickly placed a hand over her mouth to stop a sob from escaping her lips.

"We will not be disturbed, which is just as well. I've a notion to sample the wares, well-used though they may be." He leered at her, his gaze lingering on the modest neckline of her mourning dress.

Jemma shook her head and glanced hopefully towards the door. "Mrs. Stanhope wouldn't leave without telling me goodbye."

"But, yet she did, my contribution to the vicarage clutched in her greedy plump fist. She did tell me how noble she thought I was, to marry you in spite of what you've done.

Good Mrs. Stanhope despairs for your soul, fallen woman that you are. Her husband will marry us." He pointed at her, the wine glass dangling from his hand. "I'm not sure what you think you can do? All of Hamilton believes you addled and ruined." He set the glass down on the table. "Have you forgotten that my parents are your legal guardians? They have conveniently signed the betrothal agreement in your father's stead. Come, now. Do not make this more difficult than it needs to be." Licking his lips, he waved her towards him. "Come now."

Jemma wanted to scream in horror at the grim picture Augie and his parents planned for her. All her life, she had thought of the Corbetts as her family, indeed she had believed all of Hamilton her family. She had never been so terrified in her life. No one would help her, she realized that now. She must save herself.

"Better to submit, don't you think?" He grabbed her, pressing his wet, questing lips against her mouth.

Jemma bit his lip, causing him to curse and give her time to twist out of his grasp. "Don't you touch me." She slapped him so hard the mark of her handprint stood out against his cheek.

Then he hit her. Before Jemma had time to think or react, the balled up fist of Augie's right hand landed on the side of her face with such force she thought at first her cheekbone had been shattered. The blow knocked her to the floor, her legs moving back and forth to tangle in her skirts as she fell. Panting and trembling she watched Augie, tasting the blood in her mouth from his blow.

"See what you made me do?" A clucking noise, as if she were an errant child, came from his lips. We'll have to tell everyone you fell off your horse. Mother will suspect the truth, of course, but she'll not say a word. Ajax is not a horse for a woman, so she'll be thrilled to finally have an excuse to get rid of the animal. I'll use Ajax to settle my debt to Preston Jones." Augie nodded, pleased with his resolution. Holding out a hand to her, he said, "I am sorry, Jemma. You'll have to watch your mouth."

She swatted his hand away.

"Now Jemma," he chastised her. "We've had enough of that. Let's go upstairs and pack some of your things. Tally should be here soon and can bring over the rest."

Jemma got to her feet, her legs shaking so badly she could barely stand. Backing further away from him, she pressed one hand to her aching cheek. *My God. I don't know him at all.*

He shot her a look of confused irritation, as if he hadn't just hit her. "Pray don't be difficult, darling."

Her feet moved back tentatively, until she reached the sideboard. Leaning against the mahogany cabinet, she steadied herself. Her head ached dreadfully and the room tilted for a moment. She blinked. Something hard pressed against her back—a pewter water pitcher. Nearly swooning with relief at finding a weapon within reach, she stayed still, willing Augie to come closer.

"Come, Jemma. I'm finding this all very tiresome."

Turning quickly before he could react, she wrapped her hands around the handle of the pitcher. "I'm not going anywhere with you." Mustering every bit of strength, she slammed the pitcher hard against Augie's temple, knocking him to his knees.

Water spewed across them both.

Augie shook his head and struggled to stand, but fell back, the look on his face incredulous. "Wait until Mother finds out," he slurred as he placed his hands on the floor to steady himself. Blood ran down the side of his face as he shook his head. "Bitch. Mother is going to be very angry with you." He lifted one hand, fingers fluttering madly about in the air as he made a grab for her skirt.

Jemma stepped back, grabbing her skirts to her sides. She didn't wait to see if he would get up. She didn't call for help. She ran.

❧ 14 ❧

Nicholas Tremaine, the 11th Duke of Dunbar, was tired of waiting. He paced impatiently before the large window in his study, moving about like a tiger, caged and ready to pounce.

Damn! What was taking so long!

The ship bearing Nick's solicitor, and hopefully Jem, docked no more than an hour ago. A young boy, whose job it was to watch the harbor, ran from the docks to Nick's home bearing the news of the ship's arrival.

Jem.

She would have had the entire voyage to be furious, and he thought it unlikely she would be pleased to see him. If she could get over her anger at having been kidnapped, it would give her time to focus on the fact that he'd deserted her after ruining her.

As I originally set out to do.

Nick winced with guilt, both at hurting Jem and for disappointing his grandfather. He'd tossed his family's honor aside for want of one slender girl from Bermuda, a fact that displeased his grandfather, Henry. So much so that Henry had died almost immediately after Nick's arrival in London.

The death and subsequent burial of Henry Tremaine, 10th Duke of Dunbar required all of Nick's attention, as did the mantle of responsibility for the vast properties and wealth of the Dunbars. He could not leave London to return to Bermuda to fetch Jem, even though every fiber in his being instructed Nick to do so without haste. Instead, he'd dispatched Hotchkins, his most trusted solicitor, in his place. Hotchkins was a resourceful, discreet man who promised Nick he'd bring back Jem. Nick pressed his nose against the glass of the window as if he were a child staring into a candy shop, his stomach churning with frustration and worry. *I should never have left her that day on the beach. Damn George Corbett.*

Nick awoke after his unexpected meeting with Wren that ill-fated night with a knot the size of a hen's egg on his temple. The floor on which he lay moved softly beneath him and the smell of the ocean reached his nose. A dull ache thudded in his temples and one eye was swollen completely shut. When he wiped at the crusted blood on his cheeks, he found he was limited by the heaviness of manacles about his wrists. He was chained aboard a ship.

Several days went by, but no one came to see him. No food was left for him, nor water. He assumed that he would die slowly from starvation and thirst.

"I should have killed Corbett that night," Nick said out loud, his words fogging the window.

He awoke one day to find the sun streaming through the small porthole above his head. The creak of the door sounded loudly in the dim light of the tiny cabin.

"Whatever it was you did to the Governor of Bermuda, he's making damn sure you don't visit him again." A small, neat man, sporting an enormous beard reaching nearly to the middle of

his chest, approached Nick's shackled body. Two beefy sailors stood on either side of the man whom he took to be the captain. *"Make your peace with God, man, before you are food for the sharks."*

Nick found himself quite opposed to becoming someone's dinner. *"I am worth far more alive to you than dead,"* he whispered, lifting his head so that he could stare directly into the face of the man who spoke. His face had healed enough so that he could finally open both eyes.

The effect on the trio was immediate and not unexpected. The captain quickly made the sign of the cross. He waved for the two sailors accompanying him to move back, well out of Nick's reach.

Lifting his lips in a mocking smile, Nick kept his eyes on the captain. He absolutely adored Catholics, for they held the deepest respect for the devil. If only he could have convinced the captain to return to Bermuda.

"Your Grace?" A firm wrap of knuckles on the study door brought Nick back to the present.

"Yes." Nick bellowed, hoping it was his solicitor being announced.

Only Peabody, the butler of the Dunbar town house entered and bowed as low as his elderly body allowed.

Nick hissed in annoyance at the butler's appearance. "Well?"

Peabody had served the Dunbar family for many years, and like any servant who knew he'd never be sacked, made known his displeasure at Nick's mood with a mere raise of one eyebrow.

Nick didn't mind. Serving the Dunbars, particularly Nick's grandfather, was not for the weak of heart. He appreciated Peabody's courage, to say the least, as a lesser man would have fled years ago.

"Your Grace." Peabody held out a silver tray on which lay a missive.

Nick recognized the scrawl of his solicitor, Hotchkins, across the creamy vellum. He looked over Peabody's shoulder to the hallway beyond.

"I am sorry Your Grace." Peabody's lined face continued to remain bland, but the butler's voice held genuine concern. "Mr. Hotchkins is not here. A messenger dropped this off. I'm feeding him for his trouble, and he'll wait for a reply."

"Where's Hotchkins?" Nick growled.

"I fear," Peabody's face creased a bit as he frowned, "that he has not returned from his errand." The silver tray was thrust at Nick.

Nick grabbed at the note, annoyed to find his hand trembled. A chill descended over him as if the sun had suddenly gone behind a cloud. "Leave me." Moving towards the sidebar, he clutched the note in one hand. He needed a drink. Jem was not here, which likely meant she'd married Corbett, and Nick would now find it necessary to make her a widow.

Peabody stood frozen at the door and cleared his throat.

"What is *it?*" Nick snarled at the butler. "I am capable of pouring my own drink." Nick poured out the dark amber fluid into a glass. He set down the decanter, then picked it up again. He might well need more than a glass.

"Lady Arabella wishes to know if she should expect you at dinner."

"Yes, yes." Nick waved Peabody away. Something was terribly wrong. His sixth sense sounded alarms as he shooed out Peabody. *Very wrong.* After locking the study door, he tore into the envelope.

HAMILTON, BERMUDA
  To His Grace, the Duke of Dunbar,

I apologize, Your Grace, for not attending you in person. In consideration of your instructions, I am staying on Bermuda to gather all the pertinent facts as I know Your Grace would wish me to be thorough.

Nick expected nothing less of Hotchkins. He crossed to a leather chair and sat. A fire blazed in the hearth before him, but Nick shivered all the same.

I arrived in Hamilton and made discreet inquiries. William Manning died shortly after your departure from Bermuda.

So Manning died. He should have felt a sense of satisfaction, but he found no real pleasure in Manning's death for it meant that Jem was alone and unprotected in her grief.

I admit to feeling some relief at the knowledge of Manning's death as Miss Manning could not have married Mr. Corbett while in mourning. My task would thus be easier to accomplish if she were not another man's wife. I proceeded to Sea Cliff in order to seek out Miss Manning. I bore Your Grace's letter confident that she would see reason, prepared should she not.

Nick made a mental note to give Hotchkins a bonus. The man had absolutely no reservations about kidnapping a woman for his employer.

I arrived to find the entire house in deep mourning, not unexpected given Manning's death. I inquired at the door after Miss Manning only to have the servant who answered burst into tears and run from me.

Why was his chest tight? A knot formed in his throat. The awful sense of dread felt earlier at the letter's arrival, intensified. He carefully turned to the next page.

I waited on the step, unsure what to do, when an older woman came to the door. She introduced herself as the vicar's wife, Mrs. Stanhope.

Nick's hands started shaking. He imagined Mrs. Stanhope's plump form at the door of Sea Cliff.

Mrs. Stanhope, tears streaming down her face, asked what I wanted Miss Manning for, as Miss Manning was gone. When I asked the good lady where, Mrs. Stanhope sobbed in earnest. She asked why I wished to see Miss Manning?

Nick gulped in air and tried to catch his breath. He pressed one hand against his chest and felt his heart race beneath his palm.

I have a letter for her, I explained, holding out your envelope. Mrs. Stanhope swayed against the doorjamb, and I feared she would fall at my feet. "I cannot help you, sir. Jane Emily is gone". She gave a great sob. "Poor lamb, she has thrown herself from the cliffs."

"What do you mean?" I said.

"Grief, sir. Her father's death did something to her mind. She's gone. Dead. Poor lamb."

Nick blinked at the words, quite sure he'd read them wrong. The paper crumpled as he gripped the pages tighter.

I decided to investigate, Your Grace. Miss Manning apparently took off suddenly during a luncheon with Augustus Corbett and ran towards the cliffs. He claims she was irrational during the meal, speaking of her father and blaming herself for his death. Mr. Corbett pursued her, but she disappeared. After a search of the area, Miss Manning could not be found. A group of men, led by a Mr. Tally O'Dell searched the area, but found nothing, only a scrap of cloth from Miss Manning's dress.

Nick looked up from the page, imagining the rocky trails that surrounded Sea Cliff. The color of the dress, Jem wore that day. The arrogant smirk of Augie Corbett. He reached out to take the glass of whisky from the table next to him and watched as the glass fell from his trembling hands and the dark amber liquid spilled onto the floor. He tried to stand and couldn't.

The consensus is, Your Grace, that Miss Manning threw herself from the cliffs in her grief over her father. I continue to investigate, as there is no body, but I believe, as does all of Hamilton, that Miss Manning is dead. My deepest sympathies, Your Grace.

A horrible sound, the sound of a soul dying, or a banshee being released, echoed through the study. Nick put his hands over his mouth in an effort to quell the horrific noise.

Peabody knocked urgently at the door. "Your Grace!" The doorknob rattled.

The letter fell from Nick's hands, that creamy wisp of paper that destroyed him. The note fluttered to the rug beneath his feet. If the captain had just turned the ship back to Bermuda as Nick begged him to do. If only Henry hadn't passed away so soon after Nick's arrival. *If only.*

He grabbed the decanter of whisky and brought it to his lips. Drinking deeply, he prayed that the liquor would blot out the awful words of the letter. He wished this were a nightmare, and he would awake with Jem in his arms. "I should never have left her on the beach. I should have taken her then."

Nick slid to the floor, the decanter, now empty, slipping from his grasp. He pulled his knees to his chest, rocking back and forth like a terrified child who sought to comfort himself.

"This is my fault."

The ghost of the gypsy hag, from that day in the woods so long ago, whispered in his ear.

"You will destroy the thing you love most, that is why you are damned. You will know unimaginable grief. Grief of your own making."

"Not Jem, please." His eyes flew to those awful words standing out clearly in Hotchkin's letter. "No. Please, anything but this."

The click of a woman's heels sounded outside the study door.

"Nick." Arabella, his sister, beat her palm against the door. The knob twisted and turned. He heard her order Peabody to find the key. "Nick! What is it? What has happened? You must let me in."

"Go away!" Nick cried. "Go away! You must all go away!"

Then the Devil of Dunbar did something he'd never done before, not at the death of his parents, nor as his grandfather was buried.

He wept.

❧ 15 ❧

L ondon, One year later

"THAT'LL DO I BELIEVE, MY LADY." ANNA'S REFLECTION smiled at Jemma in the mirror.

Jemma watched as her lady's maid tucked a stray lock of hair into the simple bun that graced Jemma's neck. Her vision blurred, and for just a moment she saw Mercy, her maid at Sea Cliff.

"Thank you, Anna." The familiar wave of pain, of being homesick for Bermuda made her blink furiously lest she begin to weep. Mercy thought Jemma dead, indeed everyone in Hamilton assumed such, and they must continue to do so. Tally had been very clear.

"My lady? Do you not like your hair?" The maid bit her lip. "Lady Marsh said my styling was much improved."

"No, you've done a wonderful job." Jemma patted the

maid's arm. "I look lovely and have you to thank for it. It was a long journey from Essex, I'm just a bit tired."

Anna's long face wrinkled in concern. "Yes, and you've come so far already." Jemma managed a small smile and nodded politely to the maid. She'd come much farther than Anna knew.

Nearly a year ago, Jemma arrived on the shores of England, still in shock, her thoughts confused and uncertain, her entire world turned upside down with the knowledge that she was not at all who she thought she was. Scared and shaken, carrying only a small bag that Tally had packed in secret for her and clutching the worn leather packet to her chest, she silently repeated the instructions he'd recited to her before he kissed her goodbye in Hamilton. Just as he instructed, she hailed a passing hack upon her arrival in London and directed the coachman take her to Meecham and Sons, one of the city's finest solicitors. She paid the man in silver from the small pouch Tally gave her that day on the cliffs.

"Go to the docks, lass," Tally had instructed her as he'd wiped the blood from her lip and cursed Augustus Corbett. *"Keep your head down lest someone recognize you. There's passage booked for a widow, Sarah Soakes, aboard the Red Rose, and the ship leaves on the evening tide. I've left a small bag for you on board. Don't speak to anyone until Bermuda is but a speck in the distance. There's a note from your father."* Then Tally lifted his head sniffing at the air just as the sound of Augie, stumbling amongst the bramble met her ears. Tearing a scrap of cloth from her dress, Tally put a finger to his lips to stop her questions and motioned for her to take off her shoes. *"He's coming. Godspeed my girl. Go!"*

The stench of the London streets, the press of hundreds of bodies hurrying to and fro, so unlike the quiet of Hamilton, unnerved her. Sailors winked at her and beggars plucked at her skirts as she waved down a passing coach. The hack lurched forward, bouncing back and forth as it traversed the cobbled streets, forcing Jemma to hang on to the door for dear life. The damp of England permeated the coach and she wrapped her thin shawl about her shoulders, wondering again how she found herself here, how her father could have kept such a secret from her.

Arriving at Meechum & Sons, she approached a young clerk who was scribbling furiously at a stack of papers. He looked up at her, his eyes running over the frayed edges of her dress, lingering on the well-worn bag in her hand.

"Can I help you?" His tone implied he couldn't.

Jemma lifted her chin and addressed the young clerk with the speech she had rehearsed in her cabin all the way from Bermuda.

"I am Jane Emily Grantly, niece of the Earl of Marsh. I need to be taken to my uncle. Immediately."

The door to Jemma's room burst open, pushing aside the memory of her first day in London.

"Are you nearly ready, Cousin?" Lady Petra Grantly fluttered towards her in a flurry of pink taffeta and trailing ribbons. "Mother insists we be in the drawing room when His Grace arrives. We are to engage Lady Arabella and His Grace's aunt, Lady Cupps-Foster, in conversation until Papa deems it time to present me to His Grace like a sacrificial lamb." Petra frowned dramatically, her eyes dark with self-pity. Sighing, she flounced on the chair next to Jemma. "That will be all Anna." She waved the maid out.

Anna, quite used to Petra's theatrics, merely nodded, but not before catching Jemma's eye in the mirror with a knowing look.

She waited to respond until she heard the click of the latch behind the maid. "A sacrificial lamb? I would think it a great honor to be a duchess."

Petra lowered her voice to a whisper, and her eyes

widened. "A *cursed* duke. The Devil of Dunbar. He's a witch, they say, and so is his sister."

"Ridiculous," Jemma stated firmly. "There's no such thing as a witch." An image of Nick Shepherd on the Governor's terrace shimmered before her. She'd accused him that night of bewitching her. *Go away, Nick.*

Petra twisted her fan about her wrist, toying with the delicate silk. "The first duke made a deal with the Devil for his family's power and influence. The *ton* whispers about the activities of His Grace. He is said to have," Petra lowered her voice even more, "killed men." She looked towards the door as if someone would hear her. "Did I not tell you about his eyes?"

"A thousand times, Petra. His Grace has a rare hereditary condition. He likely had an ancestor with a similar affliction."

"The first duchess. She was nearly burned at the stake. They say her portrait hangs at The Egg."

A fit of giggles burst from Jemma's lips. "The Egg? There is an estate in England called The Egg? Really, Petra, you're joking."

Petra pursed her lips. "Stop making fun, Jemma. I swear it's true."

Her cousin was a dear girl, and Jemma adored her, but Petra was more than a bit dramatic. She reached out and took her cousin's hands in her own, biting her lip so as not to laugh and injure Petra's feelings more.

"I'm sorry, Petra. I didn't mean to poke fun. But, why would a mysterious cursed duke have an estate named The Egg? Even you must admit it sounds a bit silly."

"I suppose it does," Petra agreed. "Perhaps he won't like me."

"Unlikely. You are pretty as a picture." Jemma didn't lie, Petra *was* lovely. Her pink taffeta gown fit her petite body to perfection with the modest neckline drawing discreet attention to Petra's full bosom. Pink satin ribbons wound through her dark golden hair and tiny pink diamond earrings danced from her ears. Petra's complexion was like cream, not one freckle or blemish marred it, unlike Jemma's own. Her cousin could dance exceedingly well, play the pianoforte, sing, embroider and speak perfect French. How in the world could the duke *not* find Petra suitable?

"Perhaps if you caught me a fish, or a rabbit for supper, now that would be something."

"Stop it." At the oddest times, she would hear Nick's voice, teasing her, making her ache with loss and the memory of her own foolishness.

Petra took back her hands, her eyes filled with hurt. "You do not need to chastise me, Jemma. I am not nearly as brave as you are."

"I didn't mean you. I was speaking to myself. I am nervous, you see, to meet a duke. London fairly terrifies me after the quiet of Bermuda and your father's home in Essex," Jemma lied smoothly, squeezing Petra's hand in apology.

Mollified, Petra flashed a brilliant smile. "It is rather *exciting*, though I don't at all wish to marry him. I've only seen him once and he's never spoken to me. He is quite handsome, in a rough sort of way, and very tall."

Jemma took a deep breath, thinking again of Nick. "See? Not all bad then is it?"

"Well, there is his sister, Lady Arabella. She's a holy terror. I heard Mother whispering about it to one of her friends at tea. I shouldn't like having *her* as my sister-in-law," Petra confided. "She's quite formidable."

A knock came at the door and Anna poked in her head. "Lady Petra, Miss Jane Emily, I beg your pardon, but Lady Marsh requests your presence in the drawing room straightaway. His Grace will be here any moment."

Petra sighed in resignation. "I suppose it is time for the lamb to go down."

"Perhaps the duke will decide he doesn't care for lamb." Jemma winked and linked arms with Petra, leading her cousin down the large curving staircase to the drawing room. She hugged Petra tightly to her, determined to help her cousin navigate the evening. It was the least she could do, for hadn't her uncle welcomed her into his home?

"I shall escort you myself, my lady. Your uncle has been in London for the last month on business, but is due to return to Essex. Hopefully we shall catch him before he departs," Mr. Meechum, a bit flustered by her appearance in his offices, had taken a few moments to read the contents of a letter addressed to him in William Manning's own hand. He'd pulled a handkerchief from his pocket and handed it to Jemma, smiled kindly as he did so. *"You look as if you are about to weep, child. Don't fear, for if Lord Marsh has left for the country, I will take you myself to Essex."* Mr. Meechum need not have worried for they were informed upon their arrival at the Marsh town home that Lord Marsh was still in residence.

The solicitor and she were settled in the drawing room to await Lord Marsh. Jemma dabbed repeatedly at her eyes, grateful for the handkerchief, not wishing to meet her family for the first time in tears. What if her uncle threw her out? Declined to acknowledge her? She need not have worried.

Lord Marsh entered the drawing room, the suspicion clear in his manner as he greeted Mr. Meechum and took the proffered letter from the solicitor. Jemma watched as her uncle regarded her with a shocked look. "Willie. You are Willie's daughter?" Her uncle's voice broke as he stood before her. "You look like Maureen." Shaking his head in disbelief he wrapped his arms around her in a fierce paternal embrace. "Do not worry, niece," he said as he pressed a kiss to the top of her head, *"you are home now and safe."*

"Jemma." Petra admonished as Jemma tripped on a step.

"You very nearly took a tumble." Petra held on to Jemma's arm firmly. "I fear you are a bit melancholy tonight, and I think your mind is elsewhere. You are missing Uncle William, aren't you?"

Jemma righted herself, grateful for her cousin's hold on her.

"It's all right," Petra said softly. "It is hard to come out of mourning I expect, after wearing black for so long. Tonight is the first night you've been allowed some color and it's brought back your memories." Her cousin pressed a kiss on her cheek. "You don't have to stay, of course, for the sacrificing."

Hearing her cousin's joke, Jemma couldn't help but laugh. "Oh, Petra. What would I do without you?"

"You will have to make do with me, I expect, after we've married Petra off to her cursed duke." Rowan, Petra's older brother, announced from the bottom of the stairs. "What a pretty pair you two are. I shall have to fight suitors off of you, cousin, when I escort you about this Season." He winked mischievously up at Jemma, his hazel eyes twinkling in delight. "But not Petra, of course, she'll likely be married before the Season starts and miss all the fun. She'll be busy having tea with Lady Dobson and her cronies while we're out dancing."

"I do not find you amusing, Rowan." Petra stuck out her tongue at her brother. "Lady Dobson is a horrid woman who I would not have tea with even were I married."

Rowan flicked back a lock of dark brown hair absently as he held out both arms for she and Petra. "Perhaps the duke will simply turn you into a newt or something," Rowan stated solemnly to his sister. "I'm told Lady Arabella can cast a spell with a crook of her pinky finger."

Petra's fan lashed out, neatly smacking her brother on the arm. "Stop Rowan."

"Rowan, leave Petra be." Aunt Mary, her plump form clothed in dark blue silk, rushed forward. "Come, let us have a sherry in the drawing room while we wait for His Grace." She pulled Petra away from Jemma and towards the seat before the pianoforte, "let's have you sit right here." She patted the plump cushion. "Play something."

Petra thumped down on the bench, annoyance stamped on her pretty features. "I don't feel inspired."

Jemma's aunt arranged Petra's pink skirts to drape fetchingly over the pianoforte's bench. She pinched her daughter's cheeks.

"Ow." Petra's gloved hand flew to her injured cheek. "Really, Mother."

"Just tinkle the keys with your fingers, pet. Turn your face from the door so the duke can see your lovely profile."

"Now, my dear, let me look at *you*." She ran her eyes down Jemma's slim form. "The dark green suits you, I'm so thrilled to see you out of black and gray. The duke has many connections, niece, so you must make an impression as well. Think of yourself as a complement to your cousin until you are the centerpiece."

Aunt Mary lifted her cheek to Rowan. "Thank you for being on time, scamp."

Rowan pecked his mother's proffered cheek obediently. "Of course, Mother. I wouldn't miss Petra's big night." He winked at his sister.

Petra hit a sour note on the pianoforte. "Do shut up, Rowan."

Aunt Mary gave both her children a pained smile. "Rowan, why don't you and Jemma start a game of chess before dinner?" She commanded with a firm press of her lips.

Rowan walked Jemma across the drawing room to the family chess table while Petra half-heartedly plucked at the pianoforte's keys.

"Mother is a tyrant, isn't she?" Rowan whispered, taking care not to be overheard.

"No. Well a bit," Jemma acknowledged with a grin.

"Wait until she decides to marry you off, Cousin. You may not find it so amusing," Rowan cautioned her. "She'll have all manner of eligible men presented to you, after checking their pedigrees, of course."

She thought of Nick and his questionable background. Would that Aunt Mary, Lady Marsh, had been able to *research* his connections. She could still feel his hands and the brush of his legs twisted about hers. Grieving over her father and the loss of her home these last months, she'd tried desperately to forget Nick Shepherd. Forgetting had been easier at her uncle's estate in Essex. But her arrival in London seemed to remind her all over again of her flight from Bermuda and the reasons for it. Today had been particularly difficult and she struggled to push thoughts of him aside. Perhaps it was the thought of the Season and that some of the *ton* might actually know Nick. Could he be here, in London? Or had that been a lie as well?

"Jemma? Have I upset you?" Rowan signaled to a waiting servant for refreshments.

"No, of course not."

"The feel of your nails through the fabric of my coat would lead me to think otherwise." He pulled out her chair and waited for her to answer. When she didn't, he moved to the other side of the table.

"Who was he?" Rowan placed the pieces neatly on the chessboard.

"I'm afraid I don't know what you mean." Jemma busied herself with settling her skirts about her.

"Your secret is safe with me, Cousin. Just don't ever tell Petra, she'll blab to Mother. Did you love him?"

Jemma lowered her eyes lest she give herself away.

Yes, I loved him. I still do, even after all he has done.

Rowan moved his pawn, watching her with a curious look.

Would she ever truly get over Nick? Each morning she awoke to the vague sense of loss, not just of her father and her life in Bermuda, but for Nick. As Anna dressed her for the day, she would tell herself how lucky she was that her indiscretion had not brought her a bastard to raise. Fortunate indeed that she had managed to escape Hamilton and the machinations of the Corbetts. As she sat at dinner, she would ignore the gnawing ache in her heart, discounting the loneliness and utter desolation that would bubble up before dessert was served. Lying in her bed at night she would finally allow herself to think of the day on the beach, then curse herself for still caring for the scoundrel.

"Perhaps there is hope?" her cousin said softly, nodding for her to take her turn.

"No." She lifted her chin, steeling herself against the sense of loss and anger. "I'll never see him again and it's better I don't."

"I see." His eyes darkened with concern. "I would not wish to meet him then, for I would take offense to anyone who has hurt you so. We will speak of it no more."

Jemma moved her knight. "Thank you, Rowan."

"I've met His Grace," he deftly changed the subject. "In fact, I've played cards with him at White's."

"Have you?" Thankfully, her cousin decided to not question her further. "And how do you find him? I understand he's quite frightening."

"You must stop listening to Petra. She's afraid of her own shadow." Rowan stroked his chin in thought. "I would say that he is not a man you should cross and those that have, rarely live to tell the tale. He is reputed to be a wicked, damned man, capable of horrible things."

"What sorts of wicked, horrible things?" Jemma was

rather looking forward to meeting him. "That he's a witch?" At Rowan's frown she said, "And I didn't hear that only from Petra."

"He's no witch, he just allows others to believe it. I think he finds it amusing for he is possessed of a dry wit and a sense of irony. As for his being damned, well *that* tale goes back to the time of Henry VII. The first duke allegedly married a witch—"

"Yes, Petra did tell me that part." Jemma frowned as Rowan took her rook.

"—and together they supposedly made a pact with the Devil. The Dukes of Dunbar were to always retain their influence in court, but in return, they must always serve the Crown."

"Serve the Crown? In what way? You mean as administrators of some sort?"

Rowan said nothing for a moment, then he gave her a pointed look. "That is a question better for all not to ask." He relaxed and shrugged his broad shoulders. "The marked one forfeits his or her soul. The Dunbars' loyalty has never been questioned, save that one time."

"And what happened?" Jemma found the entire tale to be quite diverting and scandalous. While she didn't wish Petra to be unhappy, the Duke of Dunbar certainly sounded mysterious and exciting.

"His Grace's father was suspected of treason, but the crime, or his innocence, has never been proven, though it matters little now."

"Why?"

Rowan pursed his lips. "I should say no more, but," he looked up at Lady Marsh who patrolled the door lest she hear him. "His parents died suddenly shortly after the entire affair."

"How terrible."

"Yes. You've heard about his," Rowan waved his fingers before his eyes, "affliction? That's the sign, of course, of his damnation."

"Hogwash." Jemma bit her lip and observed the board.

"I would have to agree, for His Grace has no shortage of female companions, is possessed of an enormous fortune, is a grand wit and can out box any man in London. He's also very lucky at cards. I wish I was so cursed."

Jemma looked up at her cousin as she took his knight. "So he won't turn us all into toads then? Perhaps hex us if the quail is not to his liking?"

"I should think not," Rowan pretended affront, but his eyes twinkled, "though his sister, Lady Arabella, is another story. A more contentious, ill-tempered woman I have yet to meet. It is not her brother nor the old allegations of treason that keep her unmarried." Rowan snorted. "Her dowry is the largest in London, yet any man who attempts to converse with her is cut to the quick by her tongue. I wish good luck to any man unfortunate enough to win her favor, though I can't imagine she is possessed of any affection."

"Really?" Jemma thought Rowan protested a bit too much. He'd already said more about Lady Arabella than she'd heard him say about any girl, including Lady Gwendolyn, the woman her uncle hoped Rowan would marry. "How unattractive she must be as well. Poor thing, she will likely never find a husband if that is the case."

"On the contrary, she's quite beautiful, but she never smiles. Never." Rowan's brow wrinkled in thought. "One would think she didn't know how."

Jemma could not wait to meet the girl who caused her rakish cousin such concern. She opened her mouth to ask about Lady Arabella further, but the drawing room door opened suddenly. Startled, she dropped the chess piece she'd been about to play.

"His Grace, the Duke of Dunbar, Lady Arabella, and Lady Cupps-Foster," Jacobs, the Marsh butler intoned.

Jemma leaned down to reach for the chess piece where it lay beneath the table. Stretching her arm, her fingers ran over the floor for the piece.

"Jemma." Rowan stood. "Get out from beneath there. His Grace has arrived. He's greeting my parents and Petra."

Jemma grabbed the chess piece, smiling in satisfaction. "I've got you." She tried to discreetly make her way out but succeeded only in butting her head against the bottom of the table. "Bloody hell that hurts."

"Your Grace, Lady Arabella," she heard Rowan say. "May I present my cousin—"

Jemma did not straighten, instead she gracefully dipped into an immediate curtsy and lowered her eyes, pasting a polite smile on her lips. She hid the chess piece in the folds of her skirt and ignored her throbbing head as she slowly stood to greet His Grace, the Duke of Dunbar.

"—Miss Jane Emily Grantly," Rowan said solemnly, bowing slightly to the duke and his sister.

Jemma looked up at the duke. The chess piece fell from her fingers and scuttled under the sofa. Her vision dimmed as if she were viewing the duke through a long tunnel, and she couldn't seem to take a breath. The room tilted, as did she, her knees buckling and her feet sliding across the floor.

His Grace reached for her, as did Rowan. The last thought Jemma had before she fainted for the first time in her life was that Nick wasn't wearing his eye-patch.

❧ 16 ❧

Nick stood, his hand outstretched, mind struggling to comprehend that Jem stood before him in the drawing room of the Earl of Marsh. Automatically he reached for her as her eyes widened at the sight of him before she toppled over in a most ungraceful, but not *dead*, way. He thought he hallucinated, but surely, a ghost would not faint in such a manner.

Immediately, without any thought for propriety, he moved forward and fell to his knees. Cradling her, he stroked the top of her head, feeling the solidity of her body and the silk of her hair. He ignored the startled gasps of surprise at his improper actions and concentrated only on the fact that he held that which he thought lost to him forever.

Jem. She was not *dead*. The impish spray of freckles across her nose and the slight scent of chocolate assured him she was real. *Not dead, yet everyone in Hamilton believes she is.* His mind raced, trying to piece together exactly why and how Jem could be in England. How she could be the niece of the Earl of Marsh, the very man whose daughter he thought he might marry.

Her eyes fluttered open slowly as she tried to focus. "I must have fainted, which I never do. I'm sorry, Your Grace, I thought—" The hazel orbs narrowed. "Dear God, no wonder I fainted," she hissed, struggling to sit up. "Bloody hell, what are *you* doing here?"

"Jane Emily?" Lady Marsh questioned in a horrified tone.

A throat cleared behind Nick. "Your Grace," Lord Marsh began, stepping forward. "I beg your apology. I fear my niece has hit her head."

"Yes," Lady Marsh chimed in brightly, nodding her agreement. "Bring the smelling salts." she ordered the butler, a nervous smile on her face.

"My deepest apologies, I'll just—" Lord Marsh moved into Nick's line of sight, meaning to assist his niece in getting up.

"No," Nick snarled before he could think, tightening his arms and ignoring the stiffening of Jem's body.

Lord Marsh stepped back immediately, his face contorted in surprised confusion, his mouth bent into disapproval at Nick's improper regard towards his niece.

Nick didn't care if he was rude. He didn't care if the Earl of Marsh thought him crazed and in the habit of accosting barely conscious females. He ran a finger down Jem's cheek. Nothing mattered. He had the disgusting urge to rain kisses across her face like a delighted puppy.

The slender girl in his arms swatted his hand away. "What are you doing here pretending to be a duke?"

"Oh," Lady Marsh uttered. "It is apparent my niece *has* hit her head and quite forgot herself. Where are those smelling salts? I'll have one of the footmen carry her upstairs, shall I?"

Nick didn't spare Lady Marsh an answer. He cared only for Jem, who was studying him closely, especially his eyes.

A hand cautiously patted his shoulder.

"Your Grace," Nick's aunt said in a hushed tone. "I do not know what has come over you, but this is *unseemly*. Even for you. You cannot sit in our host's drawing room with your hands on his niece. I'm not sure what has caused such impropriety. Have you been drinking?" She sniffed the air.

Nick shut his eyes and willed his aunt and everyone else away. No one in this room could understand the overwhelming joy he felt. The loss he awakened with each day, no matter the amount of alcohol he used to blot it out, was suddenly gone.

Lord Marsh cleared his throat again.

"*Nick.*" Aunt Maisy leaned over and hissed in his ear. "You must let Miss Grantly's family see to her. The girl merely fainted at the sight of your eyes." She turned and addressed the group in a polite tone. "Please, do not be distressed. This is not the first time such has happened. His Grace's features can cause quite a stir at first. Your niece is not to blame." Her hand lay heavy on Nick's shoulder, and she pinched him to make her point.

The room grew quiet, no one daring to contradict Lady Cupps-Foster and certainly no one wished to approach Nick. He could hear the rustle of the ladies' skirts, the snapping of his sister's fan as well as Lady Marsh whispering furiously to Lord Marsh.

Jem tried once more to sit up. She squirmed in his arms and tried to push him away.

Nick stood in one fluid motion, bringing the struggling Jem to her feet as well. Pulling her to him, he laid one arm about her waist, staring at Lord Marsh as if daring the man to intrude.

Lady Marsh gasped at Nick's actions—the woman looked as if she might faint herself.

"Dear God," Aunt Maisy said under her breath.

Arabella muttered something in a rude tone, which elicited another gasp from Lady Marsh.

The thought crossed Nick's mind that the ducal coach sat

just outside. He could simply throw Jem over his shoulder and run as he should have in Bermuda. He was a powerful duke. Would anyone stop him? He stole a glance at Lord Marsh whose nostrils flared with mounting anger, to the earl's son, Lord Malden, who looked as if he would come at Nick with his fists. They would *try* to stop him.

"No eye-patch." Jem whispered, spitting like an outraged cat. "A disguise. A ruse. To hide *those*." She tried to pull away.

"You find them ghastly?" he said quietly, using the words Lord Corbett flung at him that night.

Before Jem could answer, Lady Marsh mustered her courage and came to her niece's side, pretending nothing had happened out of the ordinary. "I told you to eat something today, dear. Why, you've given us all quite the scare." She turned to Nick. "I'm so sorry, Your Grace. I think my niece must excuse herself." She inclined her head.

"I'm fine," Jem said to no one in particular. She never looked away from Nick. Her fingers twitched as if she wished to slap him, which she likely did. Jem was nothing if not consistent in her temperament.

"Leave us," Nick said quietly, reluctantly dropping his arm from about Jem's waist. "All of you. We must speak in private."

"Your Grace," Lord Marsh objected, "this is quite unusual and I—"

Nick put up his hand to silence the man. "My lord I intend no insult or disrespect to you or your family, but I must speak to your niece in private. We are previously acquainted."

Lady Marsh clasped her hands to her heart as if she were about to have a fit of apoplexy.

Lord Marsh looked to Jem for confirmation.

"We are, uncle." She smoothed her skirts and shot Nick a hard look.

Lady Marsh pressed a hand against her mouth and grabbed at her husband's arm. She shook her head furiously in denial. "But, how—"

"Your Grace, perhaps I should stay." Lord Marsh's features hardened. "It is unheard of for an unwed lady of good family to—"

"Please," Jem interrupted her uncle. "Please, Uncle John."

Aunt Maisy gave Nick a pinched look before gathering her skirts and leaving the room, her back stiff with disapproval.

Arabella opened her mouth to speak.

"Not now, Bella. Please." Nick urged his sister to leave. The truth of who Jem was, indeed who her family was, would send Arabella into a fit of rage.

A look of understanding slowly spread across Malden's face as he looked at his cousin in Nick's arms. He nodded once at Nick, then he tried to take Arabella's arm, to escort her from the room.

Arabella, contrary as always, refused Malden's courtesy and marched out after Aunt Maisy.

Petra wrinkled her nose, still pondering the situation but took her mother's proffered hand and followed obediently out, her face full of questions.

Nick watched them all filter out, his eyes lingering for a moment on Petra. Had he really considered marrying her only an hour ago? Now that Jem was alive, the very idea of the match proposed by Lord Marsh seemed preposterous.

Lord Marsh remained, seemingly determined not to allow Nick to be alone with his niece. Something flickered across the man's face as he looked at Nick, but the strange emotion was gone in a thrice.

"On my honor, my lord," Nick inclined his head, pretending not to notice Jem's snort of derision at the word honor, ""he will come to no harm."

"I wish to hear what His Grace," she said mockingly making her uncle wince, "has to say."

The earl finally gave in and left the room, shutting the door quietly behind him.

Jem waited calmly until the sound of her uncle's footsteps receded, the only sign of her emotional distress the slight movement of her feet beneath her skirts. She looked as if she were preparing to flee at any moment.

"You're a bloody *duke*? *You* are Petra's suitor?" she said calmly. "Not one-eyed. Not Nick Shepherd, poor relation to the Dowager Marchioness of Cambourne. Not a fortune hunter. Do you even know the Dowager Marchioness?"

"Yes. She is a friend of the family." He reached for her.

Violently, she slapped at his hand. "Don't touch me."

"You're alive."

"Yes, I'm alive. How else did you expect to find me?" She crossed her arms and turned from him, her shoulders hunching as if she were in pain. "Although, I would wager you did not expect to find me at all."

Nick's voice broke. "I was told you had died."

She turned around her face deathly white, with no trace of the golden tan of the islands upon her cheeks. "Were you? How inconvenient for you that I am *not*. How shocked you must be. Tell me, *Your Grace*, do you often go about seducing young women under the auspices of another identity? What a delightful game. How unfortunate for me to show up during the very dinner where my uncle would likely discuss a betrothal of his daughter to you."

What else could she think? "I never meant to leave you."

He heard the pleading in his voice for understanding. Dear God, how could he tell her the truth? The whole of that truth was now even worse than he could have imagined. Not only was her father a traitor to his country, but he was the brother to the current Earl of Marsh. He wondered if

Lord Marsh knew of his brother's past and realized that he must.

She slapped at him again. "Why would *you*, a bloody duke, have anything to do with an untitled girl from Bermuda except as a game?" Her breasts heaved with emotion. "I know that some of the *ton* are so depraved that they find pleasure in toying with others. Are you so despondent over your vast fortune and status that you came to Bermuda for amusement?"

"That is not the truth of it."

"Oh, then please enlighten me," she said coldly. "I heard all of it, Nick, before I saw you in the hall that night at Sea Cliff."

Nick took a deep breath. "And what did you hear, exactly?"

"That you tried to blackmail my father with my lapse of judgment on the beach. For money. Money you clearly don't need. He died soon after. Pray tell me how my father displeased you, Your Grace, so that you would seek such revenge upon a man by ruining his daughter? Did he beat you at cards? Perhaps you just didn't like the way he tied his cravat. Surely, he must have done something terrible to earn the displeasure of the infamous Duke of Dunbar." Her voice shook.

"I was not a duke when we met and—" Nick's mind raced with a plausible excuse for his behavior in Bermuda and could find none. "Do you really think I am capable of such a thing?"

"Sport. I was an amusement, *Your Grace*. What other reason could there be?"

Nick said nothing. Relieved as he was that she did not know the truth about her father, it still broke his heart to hear her assumptions of his character. That she could think he would use her after—"

"You can offer up no other reason, I see." Her eyes welled

with tears. "Certainly, ruining a virgin in the backwater of Bermuda buys one several rounds of drinks at White's?" A caustic laugh escaped her lips. "*Ruined*. The good people of Hamilton gossiped that my father died because of my indiscretion with you. The knowledge killed him, you see."

Her words cut into him, slicing him as deeply as if she wielded a blade.

"Those same good people called me a whore behind my back. They said I was crazy, driven mad by the fact I killed my father by spreading my legs." Tears streamed down her cheeks. "And then the Corbetts—Augie—he—" she stopped, wiping furiously at her face with the back of her sleeve.

"What did they do to you?" Her appearance in London began to make sense. She ran from marriage to Augustus Corbett. "The Corbetts are why you are presumed dead." He could feel the anger, the unmitigated fury at Lord Corbett as it rolled through his body in waves. "Answer me."

"It no longer matters, does it?"

"It matters to me." He growled, taking her by the shoulders.

"It matters now only because I am here." She tried to twist out of his hold. "Well, don't worry. I won't put a damper on your plans to marry my cousin, and I release you from any obligation you may feel towards me. I'll tell everyone that we met as you passed through Hamilton on your way to the islands further south. No one will ask any more. My family knows no one in Bermuda." Her voice caught. "And no one misses me in Hamilton. I will say that you and I courted for a time but fell out. I will not," her body shook with a sob, "stand in your way of marrying Petra."

His hands slid down her arms. "There will be no match between myself and Petra, or anyone else for that matter. I want only you."

She twisted away from him. "I wish to hear not one more

word from your lying mouth. Everything about you is a lie. You are a lie." She stepped back from him, her voice trembling.

"Jem." He snatched at her, grabbing her to him and pressing her head to his chest. He took her chin in his hand, though she resisted, and forced her to look at him. Gently he pressed a kiss to the corner of her mouth.

"This is not a lie. What is between us is not a lie. I dream of you beneath me as you were on the beach." He brushed her lips with his, feeling the familiar jolt of lightning between them.

"No." She put her hands against his chest, and he allowed her to push him away. "I would not have you use me again for your own ends, whatever they may be."

Hate me or not, she belongs to me. He weighed the thought of her hatred against the thought of Jem wed to another man and quickly disregarded any noble thought of letting her go.

"You are overwrought," he said smoothly, hiding the pain of her rejection behind the mask of bored politeness that all the *ton* knew well. He deserved her wrath, her hatred.

"Yes, I believe I am, *Your Grace.*" She clasped her hands neatly before her, but her eyes looked daggers through him.

"We will speak later, when you have had time to consider our future."

"Future? I don't believe there is anything more to discuss, *Your Grace.*"

"We most assuredly do have more to discuss as you will see. Make no mistake." He left her then, her body tight and frozen like a statue. He shut the door, willing himself to move forward even as he heard her begin to weep and went to speak to Lord Marsh.

❧ 17 ❧

"**M**y lady, another gift has arrived for you."

Jemma frowned as she looked up from her tea to watch the butler lay a large box on the table next to her. A note accompanied by the Duke of Dunbar's calling card was tied to the top with a red velvet ribbon.

"Oh, do open it Jemma." Petra clapped her hands in excitement, as if it were she, and not Jemma who was the recipient.

Carefully placing down her cup and saucer, she took the box to her lap. A fortnight had passed since finding out Nick was not Nick, but Petra's cursed duke, the Devil of Dunbar, a man all of London held in respectful fear.

Nick, for she found it difficult to think of him as His Grace, had taken to sending her gifts. Thoughtful gifts. Wonderful gifts. Each gift accompanied by an envelope which when opened revealed the name *Jem* written across the top in a bold masculine hand.

The first gift brought to Marsh House was a magnificent chestnut stallion, his mane and tail threaded with red silk ribbons. A blood red rose graced the horse's bridle. The stallion was an incredibly inappropriate gift for a woman, especially an unwed girl of good family. A young boy dressed in the livery of the Dunbars' held out the note.

I would court you.

Jemma ran her fingers through the thick mane of the stallion, reveling in the horse's beauty. She stood for several moments, her heart softening, until she remembered her stallion Ajax, a gift from her father. Her horse was probably languishing in Preston Jones' stable right now, payment for one of Augie's debts. The thought strengthened her resolve. She sent the young boy and the stallion back with a note of her own.

No.

Two days later, another, even more inappropriate gift arrived. A large wooden box which when opened, revealed a brace of pistols with intricately carved ivory handles bearing Jemma's initials. This time the note read;

I would take you hunting in Scotland. The Highlands are beautiful this time of year.

She ran her fingers over the pistols, marveling at the workmanship. They must have cost Nick a small fortune. She thought of her first meeting with him and the inclination she'd had to shoot him for his arrogance. Jemma hastily scribbled a reply.

I am afraid the temptation to shoot you would be too great, Your Grace.

Now, another gift arrived.

"Do open it." Aunt Mary took a bite of a berry scone as Jemma untied the ribbon, then choked on her scone as the contents of the box were revealed. "Goodness me."

Jemma pushed aside a pile of tissue paper and lifted out a beautiful pair of doeskin riding breeches. She marveled at the softness of the leather, knowing instinctively that they would fit perfectly. Nick was ridiculously enamored of her predilection for breeches. He would know that she would only wish to ride astride, not sidesaddle as the ladies of the *ton* did

The note accompanying the breeches read;

I planned to take you riding in Hyde Park, but alas, you returned the horse.

Petra clapped her hands at the sight of the gift, barely sparing a glance at her mother, who was now fanning herself furiously.

"How very scandalous of your duke." Petra was not the least upset that the duke's affections now fell on Jemma.

"He is not my duke," Jemma snapped at her cousin. "I find his gifts to be tiresome and his pursuit of me to be folly." She set the box in front of Petra. "Have them sent back, please."

"As you will, cousin, but I do not think His Grace would have plied *me* with such luxuries." Petra covered up the breeches with tissue and carefully retied the ribbon about the box.

"Niece," Aunt Mary lay back against the tufted cushions of the couch, "whatever the cause of your falling out, surely it can be remedied. The duke is determined to win back your affection. Lord Marsh is very much in favor of the match."

"We do not suit." Jemma took a sip of her tea and dared Aunt Mary to contradict her. "At all."

Aunt Mary merely raised a brow at her tone and turned her attention to Petra.

Jemma fumed and sipped her tea. She wished Nick, *His Grace*, would just leave well enough alone. Hard enough to come to terms with the fact that she was not Jemma Manning, but Jane Emily Grantly, that the Corbetts whom she thought of as her family, cared more for her wealth than herself. She supposed she should not really be surprised that the fortune hunter who took her virtue was really a duke. Why the ruse? Why had Nick been in Bermuda?

She tried to wrap her head around the events of over a year ago, going over every detail carefully in her mind, but ended up only causing herself to either rail at Nick or lie weeping as she thought of her father. The uneasiness and confusion of her father's false identity mixed with Nick's own deception left her angry at both men, but only Nick she blamed for the disaster of that night at Sea Cliff.

⊗⊰⊗

"MISS JANE EMILY," ANNA, THE MAID, STUCK HER HEAD through the door of Jemma's bedchamber. They are waiting for you downstairs. Lady Marsh bids you to hurry or you will make the entire family late."

Jemma turned and straightened, smoothing down her skirts, wishing she could admire the beauty of the green silk taffeta, but her dread at the upcoming event cancelled out any joy she may have felt at the loveliness of the gown or the upcoming ball.

"A moment," she instructed the maid, thinking of escape and wistfully glancing at her open window and the trellis beneath it. She'd tried to plead illness to avoid the ball tonight, but Uncle John called her bluff with a visit by his own physician, who pronounced Jemma fit as a fiddle. More sternly than she'd ever seen him, Uncle John told her pointedly that he would not tolerate her further disobedience.

As she made her way down the stairs, her hand lingering against the balustrade, she thought of her father. He had never spoken again after that horrible night, but only lay in his bed, his eyes following Jemma's every movement as she mopped his brow. She sensed he wished to speak to her, but when she gave him pen and paper, he turned his face to the wall.

"No amount of gifts or platitudes can replace my father."

She felt a fresh rush of anger towards Nick and held on to it tightly. "Nick has much to answer for."

"There you are." Rowan's cheery tone floated up to her. "I worried that I would need to come up and fetch you."

Her cousin looked especially dashing tonight in his black tailored evening clothes. His dark brown hair gleamed in the candlelight and his face held a slightly impish look.

"Everyone else is already in the carriage. Mother is a bit put out with you for keeping us waiting. After all, this is an opportune time to launch Petra amongst the *ton*." He held out his arm. "Shall we?"

Jemma took his arm with little enthusiasm. "Tell everyone I have twisted my ankle coming down the stairs, won't you? I've no wish to go." Uncle John could punish her later.

Rowan clasped her to him. "You must go, Jemma. We have received a personal invitation from the Dowager Marchioness of Cambourne, a woman who rules the *ton* with an iron fist. Her invitations are most sought after and not attending would be considered a huge affront. Besides, Mother would never let you get away with it."

Jemma shot her cousin a scathing look, her anger at Nick getting the best of her. "We are only going because *he* wishes it."

"Perhaps." Rowan winked at her. "One does not deny the Duke of Dunbar."

"Maybe someone *should*." She had no problem defying the Duke of Dunbar, thinking it the least she could do after all that had happened. Whether deserved or not, she placed the blame for all that had befallen her on Nick. Her mind whispered that Nick had a reason, were she only to give him the chance to give it. "I do not care for his high-handed manner." She had no choice in attending tonight, but Nick may regret forcing her.

"Cousin, I do not think it wise to antagonize the man.

What in the world could have happened between you and the Duke of Dunbar to make you behave in such a fashion? I believe you are baiting him intentionally, an unwise course for any man, or woman."

"I do not wish to discuss it," Jemma said stiffly. "We simply courted for a time but parted badly."

She knew that Nick and Uncle John had met several times, but she didn't know what exactly had been discussed other than Nick had concocted the story that he arrived on Bermuda to explore investing in her father's salt business. Every time she tried to corner her uncle to speak to him about Nick, he seemed otherwise engaged.

"So you have said. I can't believe Uncle William never let any of us of know he was alive."

"The war." Jemma paused, sensing Rowan doubted her father's reasoning. Jemma embraced her father's tale at first, written to her in a letter she read all the way from Bermuda until the pages were torn and tattered. Her parents' marriage forced Papa's own father to disown him, so her parents fled to Bermuda. The war kept the family apart and her father was suspected dead. But Rowan's suspicions were beginning to give rise to her own.

"My mother was Irish as well." Jemma repeated the words of her father's letter to her. "Grandfather didn't approve." Her father's story was a little too pat though she was loathe to admit it.

"Yes, our grandfather was quite unforgiving in certain respects. I cannot say I miss the old man." Rowan looked at her thoughtfully and led her out to the waiting carriage.

DONATA REYNOLDS, THE DOWAGER MARCHIONESS OF Cambourne, smiled in pleasure at the swirling couples dancing across her grandson's parquet ballroom. It was so *lovely* to use the ballroom again. Only she and Miranda lived at Cambourne house as her grandson, Sutton, and his wife, Alex, did not care especially for London. Not that she blamed them, mind you, after the *incident*, but it was nice to have the ballroom used again. The room fairly glittered with candle-light and cheerful conversation.

Donata spied her granddaughter, Miranda, huddled in conversation with Lady Arabella. The two girls stood, their heads nearly touching as they conversed. Miranda looked especially lovely tonight in a pale lavender gown, covered in tiny brilliants. She sparkled like a beautiful fairy princess. The poor child should have dozens of men vying for her hand for she was stunning and possessed of an obscenely large dowry. But Miranda had no decent suitors, the fact of which made Donata quite anxious for her granddaughter's future. *In time, I hope she finds a man worthy of her affections for she deserves great happiness.*

Lady Arabella pointed to someone amongst the dancers, her dark head bobbing with agitation and her lips curling with dislike as she showed Miranda the object of her wrath.

I wonder who she's found wanting this evening? Donata loved Nick's sister dearly but Arabella was a bit of a *challenge*. Bitter with resentment over slights real and imagined, Arabella refused to allow herself an ounce of joy. It had been so since she was a child. She blamed her lack of respectable suitors on her status as the Devil of Dunbar's sister and that horrible scandal concerning her parents, but Donata thought it was far more likely that it was Arabella's austere bearing and scalding tongue kept any likely suitors at bay.

She followed the direction of Arabella's scorn to where it landed on one of the spinning couples.

A willowy girl, dressed in green silk, shot through with gold thread appeared to be the object of her dislike. Donata observed the girl, noting the careless way she flirted with her partner and the confident strides she took as she danced. The girl spun closer, and Donata spied the spray of freckles across her cheeks and the mulish slant to her chin.

The manner of the girl caused Donata to smile. *I pity the man who takes her on for she has a stubborn, reckless look. I should know, for I was once a bit reckless myself.*

The girl's dance partner was Lord Berton, a gentleman known more for his seduction of wealthy widows than the dubious military exploits he bragged of. Lord Berton was considered to be a catch, though for the life of her, Donata couldn't imagine why.

Pursing her lips in disapproval, she viewed Lord Berton with distaste. The man was a bit too *common* and she didn't like the way he combed his hair. His pomade smelled of lavender, a scent she found appealing only on ladies. She doubted he had ever held a sword.

The girl, oblivious to the deficits in Lord Berton's character, swatted him playfully on the shoulder with her fan and laughed. As Lord Berton swung her around, she sent a withering glance at Donata.

Intrigued, since she didn't know the girl and thought it unlikely to have incurred her dislike, Donata turned slightly to see who stood behind her.

The Duke of Dunbar's large form hovered just behind her right shoulder. Dressed all in black, for Donata didn't think he owned clothes in any other color, he fairly emanated a bored arrogance and power, as if he cared nothing for the opinions of those in the ballroom, which she knew was not the case. His Grace was glaring at Lord Berton, but especially at Lord Berton's partner, with undisguised displeasure. And *possession.* Donata thought His Grace looked...*jealous,* as if he would storm onto the dance floor at any moment and claim the girl in green. In all the time Donata had known the current Duke of Dunbar, which was a very long time indeed, she had never known him to show an ounce of possessiveness towards a woman.

Donata turned, holding tightly to her cane. "Good evening, Your Grace. Forgive me if I don't curtsy," she said smartly. "I might snap in half should I attempt to bend in such a manner at my age."

His Grace said nothing for a moment, as all his attention was focused on that reckless girl whirling about with Lord Berton.

Donata stamped her cane. She didn't give a fig who Nick was, she would not be ignored.

Finally he turned, a half-smile on his handsome features as he regarded her from his great height.

"Good evening, Lady Cambourne." The Duke of Dunbar bent over her outstretched hand. She saw him looking over her hand to the dance floor, his eyes following the girl in green.

Donata was relieved to see that outside of his annoyance at Lord Berton, Nick looked better than he had in months. The darkness was gone from his mismatched eyes and the sadness that seemed to linger about his shoulders since his return from Bermuda had faded. She turned to study the girl in green more closely.

Donata knew full well *why* Nick had gone to Bermuda, after all she wrote him his false letters of introduction. She also knew that he came back empty handed, saying only that the man he sought had died and the trip had been for naught.

Donata suspected he lied.

He spoke little of his time on the islands, even to Sutton, his closest friend. Nick began to drink heavily several months after his return, avoiding everyone and everything. Sutton thought that perhaps it was grief over his grandfather's death or the pressure of assuming the vast responsibilities of Dunbar.

The mantle of grief Nick wore about him was profound and spoke of a great loss. While she knew Nick missed his grandfather, Donata sensed his grieving was not for Henry. Reluctantly, and only after the urging of his aunt, Lady Cupps-Foster, and his sister, Arabella, did he begin to attend events and return to his usual haunts, though he seemed to take no joy in any of it. Sutton told her that Nick had resigned himself to marrying in order to provide Dunbar with an heir.

Donata's gaze flicked from the jealous countenance of the Duke of Dunbar to the reckless girl in green who appeared determined to annoy the most dangerous man in London.

The girl purposefully steered herself and Lord Berton closer to where Donata stood. She giggled and batted her eyes at Lord Berton as if he were the most interesting man alive.

He was not. Donata had the misfortune of conversing with Lord Berton once. The man was not especially entertaining.

The girl threw back her head, swatting Lord Berton again with her fan. She shot Nick a smug look of satisfaction.

An odd sound came from His Grace's throat.

Donata thought it sounded like a *growl*. She rather thought His Grace would leap at Lord Berton. Perhaps strangle the man. Dear Lord, Alex, her granddaughter-in-law would never throw another ball if Nick strangled someone on the parquet dance floor.

Donata stamped her cane again in agitation. When His Grace's attention did not immediately turn her way, she whacked his shin.

His Grace scowled. "That hurt."

"Balderdash. You are built like a great oak. I have the ruined chairs to prove it. Who is she?" Donata countered.

The duke shot her a look that would have withered a lesser mortal.

Donata was not one to be quelled by an irritated male and certainly not His Grace whom she had known since he was a lad. "Use your scowl on someone who truly believes you to be the Devil, *Nicholas*." Addressing him by his given name she beat her cane on the floor in order to make her point. "You will have to do better should you wish to frighten *me*."

A whisper of a smile crossed his lips. "Truly, my lady, there are many more of the *ton* afraid of *you* than the Devil of Dunbar." He bowed, the shaggy locks of his hair hiding his face. "I stand down. I know when I am beaten."

"Well?" Donata was not one to be put off by apology. "Answer my question, scamp."

"I don't know what you mean." Nick's eyes flicked back to Lord Berton's dance partner, his gaze hungry on the girl as it followed her about the room.

"Mmph." Donata gripped her cane, not caring to be thwarted in her curiosity and considered swatting His Grace again. "Don't be obtuse, Nicholas, it doesn't suit you."

The dance ended and the girl allowed herself to be led off the floor by Lord Berton. She laughed loudly as he said something in her ear and pretended to muffle her outburst with one gloved hand.

Donata rolled her eyes at the girl's theatrics, for clearly she acted purely for Nick's benefit. Lord Berton had the wit of a boiled turnip.

The girl lifted her chin in Nick's direction, the challenge in her eyes clear.

His Grace made another disturbing noise.

Goodness. He is growling, rather like a wild animal.

"I fear for Lord Berton," Donata said blithely.

"You should." Nick nodded to her. "My lady, I beg your leave. There is something that requires my attention."

"Indeed there is." Donata said more to herself than Nick as he moved away to follow Lord Berton and the girl.

"What in the world is wrong with Nick tonight? He reminds me of an angry bear who hasn't had a bite to eat all winter. Lady Tomlinson is quite put out that he's left her on her own."

Donata smiled at the arrival of her grandson, Sutton, bearing two cups of punch. She lifted her cheek for his kiss, inhaling the smell of cinnamon that always clung to him. "I believe his interest in Lady Tomlinson waned some time ago."

A group of women to Donata's left openly admired Sutton, ogling him as if he were a great plate of sweets. They giggled behind their fans, one of them daring to inch closer.

Lifting one eyebrow in an imperious manner, Donata stamped her cane and glared at the group. *Trollops.* Her grandson's allure was legendary amongst the ladies of the *ton*, but he was a married man now, a very *happily* married man.

The group of women quieted, one or two blushing at having been caught leering at the Marquess of Cambourne by his fearful grandmother.

Sutton, incredibly, was oblivious to being fawned over. Handing a glass of punch to Donata with a beautiful smile, he held his cup aloft in a toast and took a sip. His angelic features contorted immediately as if he'd bitten into a rotten apple. "Do you think Alex gave Cook the recipe for this?" He looked down at the punch in his cup. "It's quite awful."

"There's no spirits in it." Donata smiled. "It's for the young ladies."

"A waste of punch then. Good Lord this is terrible." He handed off his cup to a passing servant and took a glass of wine from the man in one smooth motion.

"Mmm." Sutton took a large sip. "Much better."

"Sutton? Who is she?" Donata lifted a gloved hand to point at the girl towed through the crowd by Lord Berton as Nick trailed the pair at a discreet distance.

"I don't know her name, though she came with Lord Marsh. She's his niece I believe, grew up in the islands, though I can't seem to recall which one. You and Alex wrote the guest list, surely you recall?"

"Lord and Lady Marsh?" Donata bit her lip. "Ah, now I remember." Nick had asked specifically that Alex invite the Earl of Marsh and his family, claiming to be involved in a business venture with Lord Marsh. "How interesting."

"How so?" Sutton watched his friends stalking of Lord Berton over the top of his madeira.

"I believe something happened to Nick in Bermuda," Donata murmured, nodding towards the girl. "Her."

❦

JEMMA NODDED AUTOMATICALLY TO LORD BERTON, NOT truly listening to his incessant chatter as he led her off the dance floor. The man prattled endlessly since the moment he'd been introduced to her. Puffing out his chest, he regaled her with faintly humorous stories of his family and a vague military career. If Nick hadn't been watching, she would never have spoken to the man, let alone danced with him. But Nick *had* been watching, like some dark demon, his jealous gaze lingering on her as Lord Berton swung her about.

"How do you know the Marquess of Cambourne? Perhaps you are acquainted with his sister?" Lord Berton asked as he led her through the crowded ballroom.

Scanning the crowd for the tall form of the Duke of Dunbar, Jemma smiled and nodded, already planning how to excuse herself from Lord Berton. Where was Nick?

"Miss Grantly?" Lord Berton gave her a practiced toothy

smile. His dark blond hair was slicked back from his face, artfully curling about his ears. Light blue eyes sneaked a glance down her bodice. "Would you care for a turn about the gardens?"

She finally spied Nick's dark head a quarter of the way across the room. He frowned at her over Lord Berton's left shoulder.

Good.

It was high time the Duke of Dunbar learned she was not to be lied to and ordered about. Rationally, she knew it was childish of her to torment Nick, but her long pent up anger overrode her caution. "I would love a turn about the gardens." Jemma smiled brilliantly at Lord Berton.

Lord Berton gave her a wolfish look as they reached the far edge of the ballroom. "As you wish." He opened one of the tall French doors overlooking the gardens. "Miss Grantly." The brush of cool air wafted over her shoulders and she shivered.

"Lord Berton, I—" She could feel the press of Lord Berton's hand at her back and nearly decided to turn back except she saw Nick make a beeline towards her. Lord Berton and she had only crossed the threshold into the waiting gardens when a dark shadow loomed over them both.

"Ah. There you are." Nick appeared, his large form dwarfing Lord Berton. The mismatched eyes stood out starkly against taut lines of his face, giving him an air of menace.

Startled, Lord Berton jumped and released Jemma's arm, dropping the limb abruptly. The color drained from his cheeks. "Your Grace, a pleasure to see you this evening," he stammered.

Jemma pressed a hand to her chest, not from fear at Nick's appearance but to still the sudden, unwanted stirring of her heart. The scent of citrus and cheroot reached her nostrils and unconsciously she leaned towards him. *Damn him. He has much to answer for.* She righted herself immediately.

"I believe, Lord Berton, that you are operating under a misconception." The husky baritone addressed Lord Berton. "I wish to keep you from making an error of judgment through your own ignorance."

Heat ran up Jemma's cheeks at Nick's words. How dare he?

Lord Berton turned to Jemma, curling his lip at the sight of her cheeks. Clearly distressed to have angered the Devil of Dunbar, he bowed low, "My sincerest apologies, Your Grace. Had I known that the lady was spoken for—"

"But you do now," Nick interrupted Lord Berton's polite speech and waved him away as if Lord Berton were no more than a fly. "Good evening, Berton."

Lord Berton's eyes widened at the sight of the pewter ring on Nick's thumb. He nodded, bowed politely once more then turned away, not sparing Jemma another look. The french door shut firmly, leaving her alone with Nick.

Hushed whispers met her ears as several couples, their clandestine activities interrupted, emerged from the shadows of the garden. They gave the Devil of Dunbar and Jemma a wide berth as they made their way back inside.

Nick never even bothered to look at them.

"What did you think you were doing, Jem? Coming out to the garden with a man like Berton?" The mismatched eyes flicked over her. "I do not care to be made a fool of."

"A man such as Berton? I find him fascinating and endlessly amusing. He is also a fine dancer," she retorted, sounding not the least convincing.

Nick snorted in disbelief. "Jem, I am trying to allow you to wade through your anger at me, endless though it appears to be, but coming out to the gardens with him was unwise."

"As going out to the gardens with you once was? I am now well versed in the ways of a rake."

Nick's eyes narrowed and she thought he would lash out at her, but instead he ran his forefinger gently down her cheek. "I beg you cease this foolishness, for both our sakes. We must talk. You must *allow* us to talk."

The very touch of his finger sparked against her skin, followed by a lightning bolt through her body of intense longing. She hated him for this incessant wanting, hated herself for not being able to stop it. "I find Lord Berton and indeed any man here tonight, to be far more to my liking than *you*. You cannot stop me, should I wish to be courted by another." She poked him in the chest with her fan, determined to make her point. "There are many here who would vie to be my suitor."

Nick's hand dropped to his side as his lips compressed into a grim line. "Your charms are not *so* great," he said in a cold, flat tone, "that a man will risk his life for them. Indeed, you will not find one man amongst the *ton* willing to do so."

"What do you mean?" She gripped her fan. What *did* he mean?

Nick took her arm roughly. "The same, however is not true in reverse." His fingers bit into her flesh as he *pulled* her back into the ballroom.

Jemma attempted to shake him off, but his grip only tightened. "I beg you turn your attentions elsewhere," she spat as the meaning of his words sunk in. "I wish you to find another woman to torment."

"Do you? Let us test such a theory."

The gossips of the *ton* twittered maliciously as they watched Nick drag Jemma through the ballroom. Women murmured behind their fans. Men turned away and began to speak in loud tones. The orchestra started up again, much louder this time, as if someone had instructed them to do so.

Lord Berton stood to the left with a group of men laughing gaily as they lifted their goblets to toast each other. He caught her eye, held it, then purposefully turned away before Nick noticed.

Nick did not release her until he found Uncle John standing with Aunt Mary and Petra. He pushed Jemma towards her aunt. "Your niece is unwell. A terrible headache brought on by too much excitement."

Jemma's mouth opened to refute his claim when she felt the pinch of her aunt's fingers on her arm.

Aunt Mary was pale but composed as she faced Nick's fury. She pulled Jemma to her. "Yes, Your Grace."

Nick spun on his heel, his dark hair floating above his broad shoulders as he moved back into the crowd. A beautiful blonde, dressed in pale blue fell into step beside him, taking his arm. He did not shake her off.

"I believe I am ill, Aunt Mary," Jemma whispered, her stomach lurching at the sight of the blonde. The blonde had nothing in common with the Sinclair sisters, but the sickening feeling in Jemma's stomach was the same. "It is best I return home."

❧ 18 ❧

Jemma threw down the book in her hands—a dull romantic bit of fluff Petra lent her earlier that morning, in frustration. Since the altercation with Nick at the Marquess of Cambourne's ball, she had dreamt of the scathing setdown she would give him for his treatment of her once he arrived at her uncle's door.

His Grace did not cooperate.

"Perhaps he is busy with his companion of the other night." Jemma stood and picked up the discarded book and flounced back to the chair she'd been sitting in. Against her better judgment, she'd asked Rowan who the woman was. Rowan, his embarrassment clear, confessed Lady Tomlinson had once been the duke's mistress, though, Rowan assured her, he did not think that the case any longer.

Jemma looked at a silver tray lying atop the side table. Earlier the tray had held a small display of chocolate tarts but was now empty.

Not even a crumb left. Aunt Mary will be horrified.

"Hello niece." Lord Marsh quietly entered the drawing room.

"Uncle." Jemma sat up and picked up the discarded tome. She wished she could magically wave the empty tart tray away as well.

"I see you've enjoyed Mrs. Livingstone's chocolate tarts." He nodded at the tray.

"I've had a bit of a sweet tooth lately, Uncle."

"Indeed." Uncle John moved to the window as if to admire the lovely view of the Marsh House gardens. He clasped his hands behind his back and cleared his throat.

"His Grace has offered for you."

⚜

JOHN, LORD MARSH, HAD BEEN DREADING THIS confrontation with Jane Emily for weeks. He wished she could be more even tempered, as his daughter was, but he supposed that given all she had gone through, her anger was warranted. Her anger was simply directed at the wrong man.

William's letter to John, and the contents of the packet brought with Jane Emily from Bermuda, told the story of a life filled with lies and regret. And treason. John felt the shame of his brother's sins deep in his bones. The wrath of the Dunbar family had filled William with fear until his last breath.

As it did John.

But the Devil of Dunbar did not come to Marsh house immediately upon Jane Emily's arrival as John supposed he might, which meant one thing. The duke did not *know* the identity of William's family—yet. The logical solution to avoid future destruction, in John's mind, was to marry Petra to the duke. The man would not destroy his wife's family. John thought it a most prudent and intelligent decision.

Until, the Duke of Dunbar saw Jane Emily.

The last piece of the puzzle that was his brother William's

life came together for John the moment he saw the way His Grace looked at her. Bravely, he did not try to hide anything from the duke, instead, depending on the affection the man clearly felt for Jane Emily. His Grace did not seem surprised by John's identity, nor did he condemn John for trying to protect his family. He simply made it clear that Jane Emily, or *Jem* as the duke referred to her, would be his wife. He wished to give her time to come to terms with her anger and come to him willingly.

But Jane Emily, obstinate and still angry, refused to be courted by the duke.

"How kind of him," his niece said in a brittle tone, her voice raising an octave. "But I'm afraid the duke and I don't suit. At all. I shall have to refuse his generous offer for me."

John wanted to tell her just how generous His Grace was in forgiving the Marsh family of so much, but the duke made John swear to *never* tell Jane Emily the truth about her father. No one must ever know.

"You misunderstand, niece." Her uncle's hands clenched and unclenched behind his back, not wishing to battle her. "His Grace has offered for you and as your guardian, I have accepted."

John heard the sharp intake of her breath. Why must she be so difficult? It was clear she and the duke *did* suit.

"You would force me?"

"I doubt you would be miserable as a duchess, Jane Emily, nor do I doubt you would be unhappy with His Grace. He's enlightened me, you see, on your previous relationship." John felt the blush rise up on his cheeks just thinking about his most recent conversation with the duke. Horrified, John listened while His Grace made it clear that Jane Emily had been ruined, and quite thoroughly, by His Grace.

"Our previous relationship?" Jane Emily's voice shook.

Uncle John ignored her question. She *would* marry the

duke. Even if he didn't guess that Jane Emily was in love with the man, he would still have her marry him. She was no longer a maid. Her father committed treason and the duke knew about it. He did not turn to look at her as he spoke. Instead, he tried to focus on his rose bushes in the garden as he looked out the window. "You *will* marry His Grace."

"I will *not* marry him." She sounded as if she were choking on a meat pie. "He cannot force this upon me. I will not do it."

"Yes." John unclasped his hands to place his palms on the window sill, feeling a bit of peeling paint and wishing William were here so he could shake him senseless for all the mess he'd laid at John's door. "His Grace told me you would refuse. He is waiting for you in the conservatory."

※

Jemma flew down the hall, her heels clicking on the gleaming wooden floors, insides churning, her cheeks flaming with embarrassment.

I will never be able to face my uncle over a meal again.

She flung open the thick oak doors of the conservatory to find Nick calmly sitting at the family piano. His fingers picked at the keys, and Jemma caught the bit of a melody she couldn't name. The sunlight streaming through the large paneled windows caused the red in his hair to shine like copper.

He didn't turn as she entered.

"You bastard." Jemma stood, her entire body shaking, her fists clenched so tightly she feared her nails would make her palms bleed. "You told my uncle. Did you also tell him you killed my father?"

"There you are." Nick cut off the rest of her heated speech neatly. "I wondered whether you would walk or *race* down the hall to confront me. A pity you returned the pistols, I imagine you could make good use of them today." He spun about on the piano bench, his hair swinging about his massive shoulders. Shadows hung beneath the mismatched eyes, and stubble shown across his cheeks.

"I learned to play as a child. Hours upon hours with Monsieur Dubois, who slapped my fingers with a ruler when I hit a sour note. My grandmother thought learning the piano would soften me. Care to play a duet?" The joking note in his voice did not match the hard set of his lips.

"Bastard."

He shrugged. "Perhaps, later." Nick stood, peering down at her from his great height. His glance lingered on the line of her bodice.

"Stop looking at me like that," she snapped though she felt the familiar tingle of her skin at his nearness.

"Like what?" He lifted a brow. "As if you were a chocolate tart?"

The words brought back a wealth of memories of the first time he touched her, so long ago on Governor Lord Corbett's terrace. A shudder of longing ran through her. "Stop staring down my bodice. It's unseemly."

"I don't think so. I've missed those delicious little goodies. Your nipples are the most delightful shade of pink." The whiskey of his voice seemed to seep into her skin, curling her toes inside her slippers.

The nipples in question stood up immediately at being recognized.

"I see they've missed me as well." He gave her a sensual, smug look. A wave of hair fell down over his cheek and he shook it back.

A languid feeling came over Jemma, though she tried mightily to maintain her outrage. Her nipples were hard and tight, aching where they stretched under the cotton of her chemise. A honeyed heaviness slid down her stomach to pool between her thighs. "My uncle tells me you offered for me. I have refused."

"Have you? Another man has a hold on your affections? I find that unlikely." He placed his palm against her stomach.

"Yes," Jemma retorted, moving away. Her skin felt as if it were on fire beneath her gown. "I find your surprise odd, given that you have warned every man in London away from me."

A dark brow rose in question. "I have?"

"My dinner companions won't converse with me. I stand alone during every dance. Please do not pretend you are not the cause. Perhaps I will go abroad."

Nick moved forward swiftly to grip her upper arms. Pushing her roughly against the wall, he pressed her against him. "No. You won't."

Even through the layers of her gown, Jemma could feel Nick's arousal, hard and thick against her. She closed her eyes and inhaled the scent that was all Nick, citrus and cheroot mixed with a purely primal smell that was him. She wished to rub herself against him like a cat, put her skin next to his. Touch the planes of his stomach. "I will."

"Clearly," Nick bent and nipped at her bottom lip, "you are not convinced of the desirability of our match." A hand fumbled under her skirt, to run leisurely up her leg and pause briefly at her garter before reaching further.

Her body relaxed into his, what little fight she had left in her fading away in the face of Nick's onslaught. She grabbed at his hair.

"Yes." The husky whisper urged her as a ripping sound reached her ears.

"Useless." He impatiently tore through the layers of petticoats.

Jemma moaned softly, giving no resistance. What would

be the point? She wanted this. She wanted him. "Oh God Nick," she panted as his fingers pushed inside her.

"So wet, for me." He rubbed his thumb against the most sensitive part of her, eliciting a cry of want from her lips. "Only me," Nick said roughly into the nape of her neck. "No one else." He toyed with her, his fingers gliding against her, the ring he wore on his thumb, cool against her flesh.

Jemma clutched at his shoulders, pushing against the pressure of his moving fingers. "No," she gasped, knowing it was a question, finding that when the moment came, she could not lie to him about that. "No one else. There is no one else."

A feral sound came from Nick. His fingers moved against her tender flesh as she pushed herself against his hand. Just as her body tightened, he stopped and pulled away, leaving her shaken and unsatisfied.

"Damn you." She slapped at him, and then gasped as he entered her in one hard thrust, rocking her body back against the wall. "Oh." Jemma's body slid deliciously down the length of him. "Nick."

He kissed her fiercely, his mouth capturing hers even as one arm reached underneath her bottom. A low growl escaped his lips. "Wrap your legs around me."

She did as he bade her, sliding her legs up against his hips, pulling him into her with each thrust.

His mouth trailed up her neck. "Yes, Jem." He groaned. "Like that." He thrust deeper inside her, the force knocking a picture from its peg to shatter on the floor.

Jemma clung to him, a wild thing with no thought other than the pleasure of their joining. How she missed him, longed for him, how lonely she had been without Nick.

"As you can see," his breath came in a gasp, "you are wrong. We are completely suited to each other." He put one palm against the wall to steady his body as he ravaged her.

Her fingers grabbed at his shoulder, urging him on. "Harder." She moaned, feeling half crazed at being with Nick, and her impending release. How many nights had she lain in bed, wanting him? Hating him?

"Yes." He pulled back and forced himself further inside, swiveling his hips in the most delicious manner.

"Oh God, please." How could she have forgotten what this felt like?

The ache, the agonizing, delicious ache, seemed to go on and on until Jemma thought it would never burst, and then suddenly it did, making her cry out.

"Shush, love." He pressed his mouth over hers as he slowed, moving in time with the trembling that rocked her body. "Again." He twisted his hips.

Jemma tried to catch her breath. "Stop," she panted. "It's too much." She felt her body clench and tighten around him once more.

"You love me," the dark voice murmured in her ear. "Say it."

A tear ran down her cheek, even as she mouthed the words, and her body shattered, yet again, into a million pieces.

Nick buried his head in her neck, saying her name over and over as he climaxed, spilling himself into her as her body throbbed around him.

The room grew quiet except for the sound of she and Nick panting, trying to catch their breath. Their joining, so primal and violent, left them both shaken. Her legs dangled wantonly on either side of him and she closed her eyes, unable to look at him.

"Is it that unbearable to love me?" he said softly, pressing a kiss to her cheek.

"Yes." The sadness she felt threatened to overwhelm her. Loving Nick betrayed her father. "I wish I did not care for you." She thought of Bermuda, of Sea Cliff, forever lost to her. Her father dead because of Nick, and she still didn't know *why*.

"Again? Still you wish to deny us both."

"I want you to go away, leave me and my family in peace. My father is dead, my life gone because of you."

"Shut up," Nick said quietly. "Shut up. Were your life in Bermuda the idyll you profess it to be, you would not be here, but on that cursed island."

Jemma's temper flared at the truth of his words. The illusion of her life in Bermuda hung over her until she felt she would collapse with the weight of it. He was right, and well she knew it, but her damnable pride made her speak before thinking.

"You wish to marry me, then so be it. I understand that most marriages of the *ton* are simply conveniences. I shall flirt and dance and flit about. I will *cuckold* you at the first opportunity. Thanks to you," she sneered, anger making her reckless. "I enjoy thoroughly the pleasures of the bedroom. You've taught me to be a most competent whore."

Nick released her so abruptly she toppled to the floor. He righted his clothing, his fingers flying angrily over the buttons, nearly tearing them loose.

"If you wish to continue to lament your life in Bermuda and blame me, so be it. I am an expert in holding on to the past and have paid a dear price for it. You wish to hear the truth? Your father committed *treason*, he was a *traitor*, to his family and the Crown. That's why I was in Bermuda, to find the man who allowed the suspicion of his deceitful act," he spat out the words, "to fall on *my* family. Your precious Sea Cliff was bought with blood money. Because of the," his voice caught, "*affection* I hold you in, I did not take him to hang."

Jemma slid her back against the wall, shaking her head. She clutched at her skirt, pulling the cotton up against her as if the gown would protect her from Nick's words. "Liar. My father would never do such a thing." Her throat went dry as she tried to swallow.

"Yes, your father would never be *duplicitous* in any way, would he? Why else would an honest man change his name and allow his family to think him dead? Are you really so naïve, Jem?" Nick smiled unpleasantly. "Why else be in league with a man like Corbett?"

"You are one to talk about duplicity, aren't you?" Jemma snarled back at him, her mind refusing to believe his words even though she sensed the truth in them. "Though given your true identity, I would wish to pretend to be someone else as well."

Nick's entire body moved as if she'd slapped him. He staggered back at her words.

Jemma pressed her advantage. "I'm told the Countess of Durry made the sign of the cross as she met you." She took deep gulps of air, no longer mindful of her words or the damage they would inflict. "That grown men flee your company at White's. Petra lived in terror that she would have to marry you, comparing herself to a *sacrificial lamb*. I think it must have been your eyes. After all, what woman wants to be reminded every morning," she pointed to his face, her hand shaking, "that she's married to the Devil?" She said the last bit triumphantly.

Nick shuddered once then went very still. Wincing as if in pain, he closed his eyes against her for several moments. When at last his eyes opened it was to regard her blandly, without a flicker of emotion.

The brief spurt of satisfaction she felt shriveled into nothingness.

"I am the Duke of Dunbar," he said in an icy, clipped tone, "and my cursed line stretches back to Henry Tudor. I am more wealthy and powerful than you can possibly imagine. No one in London, or in all of England would dare cross me.

That your miserable father did and stayed hidden for so long is a testament to your family's true nature. Rats do tend to go to ground when being hunted."

Jemma clasped her knees tightly. She opened her mouth to speak, perhaps defend herself, but closed her mouth at seeing the cold fury on Nick's face. For the first time, Jemma saw the man others feared.

"You *will* marry me and bear my children. You will not behave as a whore unless it is in our bedroom. Should you defy me or seek to play me false, I will destroy you and your family. The entire nest of rats."

She glanced up, barely recognizing Nick or the words he spoke. What had she been thinking to say such awful things to him? She wished to wound him and she had, brutally, so much so that he would likely never forgive her.

"If any other man is *stupid* enough to try to claim you, I will snap his neck with my own hands. Do you understand, Jane Emily?"

Jane Emily. The use of her given name proved to her the depth of the pain she caused him.

"You think me unkind? Damned? You have no idea." Nick's lips curled into a sneer. "Get up, you look like a bawdy house slut."

Jemma clutched her hands to her stomach. "Nick, please, I didn't mean—"

"But you *did*. I saw it in your face." He looked towards the door. "I hear someone coming, likely your uncle."

Jemma tried to scramble to her feet and failed. She could do nothing but sit against the wall stupidly, her chest heaving with emotion and shock.

The door to the conservatory flew open.

"Jane Emily? The maid heard something shatter and I—" Her uncle's confused glance took in her disheveled clothing as she sat on the floor and the flush on her cheeks. A large chunk of her hair had fallen from its pins and now lay between her breasts.

"If you did not believe I ruined her before, believe it now." Nick spoke calmly in a snide, patrician tone. "My solicitor will call on you, Lord Marsh, tomorrow morning. Due to the circumstances of my," Nick paused, "*discussion* with your niece, we should post the banns without delay."

Mortified, Jemma turned away from her uncle. Her eyes welled with tears. *Did I really think hurting Nick would make me feel better? Because it hasn't. This is far worse than anything I could have imagined. Worse than Uncle John seeing me here like this.*

"Oh, I almost forgot." The whiskey voice remained calm. "I will send a seamstress tomorrow to fit Jane Emily for her trousseau."

"Your Grace, perhaps—" Uncle John started to say, barely glancing at her.

Nick raised his hand, the ring on his thumb winking in a stream of sunlight from the large conservatory windows. "I insist, Lord Marsh." Nick brushed an imaginary piece of lint from his forearm. "On the marriage *and* the trousseau." He turned back to her uncle all civility gone from his tone as he said, "The Devils of Dunbar keep what they claim."

Nick's words had the desired effect. Her uncle did not contradict him again nor offer any other resistance. "All shall be as you wish, Your Grace."

Jemma looked down in her lap, horrified at the mess she's wrought.

"Good day, Lord Marsh." Nick nodded to her uncle. He never looked at her again.

Wishing she could take back every awful word she had thrown at him, Jemma watched Nick's tall form leave the conservatory. As soon as she thought him gone, she promptly burst into a fit of weeping, burying her head in her lap.

"Come, stop your crying." Uncle John patted her

awkwardly on her shoulder. "I shall turn my back while you —" he waved his hand at her and turned around. "Be quick about it, we don't want a servant to hear. It would be disastrous were your aunt to get wind of this. The scandal would send her to bed for *weeks*. Thank goodness she took Petra shopping. I would never be able to explain *this*."

Jemma struggled to her feet. Hands shaking, she adjusted her bodice and her skirts and attempted to tuck her stray hair back into the bun at the base of her neck. Perching cautiously on the edge of the couch, Jemma cleared her throat to signal her uncle she was presentable.

Uncle John briefly glanced at her before striding to the sidebar. Pouring a scotch for himself and a sherry for her he walked back over to where she sat on the sofa. "Here." He thrust the glass of sherry at her. "Not many have survived the wrath of the duke and lived to tell the tale." Uncle John gave a slight, sad smile. "I assume your discussion with the duke was," Uncle John's ears pinked considerably, "mutual?"

"Yes," Jemma whispered, wiping her eyes with the edge of her skirt, humiliated to the very core of her being. Uncle John, however, seemed to be handling the situation much better than she.

"We will speak of this once and never again. I should have told you sooner, but I hoped I would have no need, and His Grace begged me not to. How I wish you had just simply forgiven the duke and been happy. I should have known that was impossible, you are not the kind of girl who would blindly follow my instructions and ask for no explanation. Have you realized yet that your anger is misdirected?" Uncle John took a sip of his drink and sat down beside her.

"You know?" She looked her uncle in the eye, not believing that he could have kept such a secret from her.

Uncle John didn't flinch. "I knew before His Grace did. I

knew after I read that damn packet of letters you came to me with. William gave up all of his secrets in the end."

"It's true, isn't it?" Jemma choked. "My father did those things, didn't he?"

"Drink." He helped lift the glass to her lips. "Your aunt says that sherry is good for a sudden shock."

"You're," Jemma took a large swallow of the sherry and immediately coughed, "taking this all rather well, Uncle John."

"I've had time to grow used to the truth, as awful as it is. William stole the letters from the Duke of Dunbar, the current duke's grandfather," he explained, "and sold them for a small fortune, though I suspect that Corbett put him up to it. William confessed everything to me in a letter he wrote as he fell ill." Her uncle looked at her. "He was ill for months before the Devil of Dunbar found him and suspected he was dying. I loved my brother but William was a weak man. He committed treason. Men died." Uncle John shook his head sadly. "He wished to marry your mother and father disowned him for it. But what did William expect?" Uncle John shook his head sadly. "Maureen was a servant at this very house."

Her surprise must have shown, for her uncle reached out and patted her hand. "Do not worry, no one need ever know. That secret is safe as well."

Another lie unveiled. Jemma's stomach twisted into knots. Her mother was a servant? She'd been told her whole life that Mama was from a good Irish family, that the marriage was objected to on the grounds her mother was Catholic. "I fear, Uncle John, that I may not be able to handle much more honesty."

"But, you will." Her uncle wrinkled his brow and drained his glass. "You and I know the truth, and no one else, except the Duke of Dunbar. Your marriage, though you fight against it, ensures that the Tremaine family will never seek to make the truth public. Never harm us."

"I am to be a sacrifice to save our family?" She sucked at her sherry, hoping the liquid would chase away the sudden sense of bitterness she tasted on her tongue.

"Really Jemma? Petra was to be the sacrifice," Uncle John stated with a bit of irony, his voice calm. "But then you fainted at his feet. Your poor aunt was horrified and worried that we had offended him beyond repair." Uncle John took another sip. "Had he wished to, His Grace could have brought your father back to London in chains. I doubt seriously that the Crown would have stopped him even if he wished to hang William. But something changed in his plans for revenge."

Sliding the sherry around her mouth with her tongue, she still felt the press of Nick's lips against her own. "Me. How convenient then, that he's ruined me, for all our sakes."

"Niece." Uncle John took her hand in his. "His Grace has told me of his time in Bermuda. I was given to believe that you have feelings for him as I know he does for you. He did not leave you willingly."

"What—"

"It is his story to tell, and not mine. Suffice it to say niece that if you will just put aside your anger and pride, you will find yourself to be that rarest of things amongst the *ton*. A love match."

Remembering the pain in Nick's face as she lashed out at him, tears welled up in her eyes. "What have I done?" She put her head in her hands as a sob caught in her throat.

"Angered a very dangerous, very powerful man. He loves you though, so that is something."

❧ 19 ❧

Lady Arabella Tremaine sipped her lukewarm tea and wished to be anywhere but at the Ladies Society for Orphans. Miranda, curse her, should be here suffering as well, but she'd begged off today's tea in order to attend some boring, dry lecture. Miranda simply adored lectures about ancient dead people who Arabella could have cared less about.

The hostess for today's gossip mongering masquerading as an event to raise funds for parentless children was none other than Lady Tomlinson. Lady Tomlinson, bless her, wasn't known for her kindness towards others, and certainly not orphaned children, but as the wife of the wealthy, highly respected, and elderly Lord Tomlinson, she was expected to show her support. The one thing Lady Tomlinson *was* known for was being the onetime paramour of Arabella's brother, Nick.

Most young ladies of Arabella's age would be overcome with shock at such knowledge. But Arabella was no typical young lady. She was the sister of the Duke of Dunbar. Her brother had been a topic of gossip since their mother screamed upon seeing Nick's eyes. Nick had continued to endear himself to the *ton* by running wild at Eton. Society still called he, Sutton and Lord Kilmare the "Wickeds." Then, of course, there was the "accidental" death of her parents. The *ton* simply adored treason and suicide, especially when served up in a London town home complete with screaming servants and blood splattered walls.

Arabella glanced around the room and spied a nice over-stuffed couch hidden partially behind a palm where she could sip her tea in peace.

It wasn't as if she didn't care about orphans, she did. She donated loads of money to various causes but didn't actually take part in any of the social niceties that went along with them. She detested ladies luncheons, having nothing to say to the vapid women of the *ton,* many of whom remembered her parents, as evidenced by the way they addressed Arabella with a look of spiteful pity in their eyes. Besides, she was in no mood for company, having had another row with her brother over his determination to marry that girl. Dear God, Arabella almost preferred Lady Petra to her cousin, Jane Emily.

"More tea?"

Arabella smiled politely to the servant. "No, thank you." She took another sip. *Ugh.* Tepid and lacking a bit of taste. The tiny cakes being served even looked bland and dry, certainly she couldn't hope to choke one of those down. She should have gone to the lecture with Miranda, at least they had decent tea at the Royal Exposition.

An older woman, her hair a faded red laced with gray, walked slowly past Arabella and stopped, nodding politely. "May I join you?"

Arabella tilted her head. "Of course, though you won't be able to hear the proceedings from here. Lady Tomlinson will be taking the small podium up there." She pointed to a small stand at the other end of the room.

"Oh, I've already made my donation and I'm just waiting for my daughter to collect me. She's an avid supporter of the orphans." The woman said in a dry tone, "Are you, my lady?"

"I try to be supportive of all those in need. It is my duty," she replied politely, the practiced words slipping off her tongue with ease. She couldn't place the woman beside her. Had they met before?

"A pretty speech." The woman smiled wryly and munched on one of the cakes. "My, this is very," the woman hesitated, "light."

Arabella smiled over her teacup, beginning to enjoy her new companion. "Have we met? I am Lady Arabella Tremaine." She inclined her head and waited for the inevitable gasp as the woman realized who Arabella was.

"It is my great pleasure to meet you. I am Lady Corbett. My daughter, Dorthea Jennings is just there," she nodded towards a plump redhead in violet. She took another sip of her tea and wrinkled her nose. "Is this the usual way that tea is prepared? I've been gone from London for such a long time, but I don't remember it tasting this way."

"I don't make tea," Arabella shot back. "I've absolutely loads of servants to do that sort of thing." It amused her to say shocking things to people, something she and Nick had in common.

Ignoring Arabella's rudeness, Lady Corbett gave a soft chuckle. "Forgive me, as I said, I've not been to London in ages and my daughter resides in Yorkshire, but you are related to the Duke of Dunbar? Perhaps his granddaughter? I heard he was at the Cambourne ball. I'm sorry to have missed him."

"My grandfather passed away last year, Lady Corbett. It was my brother who attended the Cambourne ball. He is the current duke."

The color drained from Lady Corbett's face. Her teacup rattled against its flowered saucer. "Your brother?" She blinked rapidly.

Arabella tried to keep the polite smile on her face. Apparently, Lady Corbett *was* familiar with Nick. "Yes, my brother." Arabella tried to keep her tone bland waiting for Lady Corbett to give her a horrified look and suddenly pretend she needed to find her daughter.

Lady Corbett blinked once more, then took a deep breath. "I beg your pardon, Lady Arabella. Please accept my deepest sympathies on the death of your grandfather." An embarrassed laugh escaped her lips. "I just assumed. I knew your mother, you see, we were friends." She fanned herself and looked away. "It did not seem so long ago. Why, I'm quite embarrassed to have reminded you of your grandfather's passing. I fear my only excuse is I have traveled much of late, and it has me feeling a bit rattled."

A spurt of sympathy welled up inside of her for the woman, quite an unfamiliar feeling for Arabella. She did not suffer fools gladly, but the poor woman looked as if she would faint, for her face was deathly pale. "So you knew my mother? Where did you say you were from?" Arabella signaled a servant to bring more tea. Perhaps she should also ask for some smelling salts.

"Bermuda." Lady Corbett's lips were pulled into a thin, taut line.

"Bermuda?" Arabella lifted a brow, attempting to keep the distaste out of her voice, lest Lady Corbett think it was meant for her. "What an odd coincidence. My brother has betrothed himself to a girl from Bermuda." She thought of those long months when Nick's endless, horrible grieving for someone named Jem had Arabella and Aunt Maisy fearing he would drink himself to death. Her brother was finally past his grief when *she* showed up again and quite alive. Mysteriously.

Her brother told her that he and Jemma had courted briefly in Bermuda and fell out over something too ridiculous to name. He later tried to find her and was told she'd died. Nothing about her brother's story rang true for Arabella, and it made her all the more suspicious of Jemma. Nick was hiding something from her.

"Perhaps I know your brother's betrothed?" Lady Corbett said quietly. "Bermuda is really a string of islands, and not so large as all of that. We only have one truly large city, Hamilton, where I reside. It is the capitol. My husband is governor." A wan smile crossed her lips. "At any rate, we all know each other."

Arabella thought it all sounded rather provincial and not at all interesting. "I'm not sure which island, and I daresay I didn't realize there was more than one. She's only ever mentioned Bermuda. Her name is Jane Emily Grantly. Her family calls her Jemma. She is the niece of the Earl of Marsh. After her father passed away, she came to stay with her uncle. I believe her father was in trade of some sort, though I'm not sure what. I'm afraid I knew nothing about Bermuda until she became betrothed to my brother." Arabella looked hungrily at the plate of small sandwiches a passing servant laid on the table before her. She was starving. The watercress looked particularly tasty. "Do you know her?"

Lady Corbett's left eye twitched. "Jane Emily Grantly?" Her hands shaking, she set down her teacup with a clatter.

"Lady Corbett?" Arabella thought the woman had to be ill. Probably all the traveling back and forth from Yorkshire. Arabella detested Yorkshire. Everything was dark and dank and smelled of the moors. "Should I ask for your daughter?" Raising her hand, Arabella waved back the servant who'd brought the sandwiches.

"No." Lady Corbett lightly touched Arabella's arm. "No."

She cleared her throat. "I'm just a bit shocked. I need to collect my thoughts."

Arabella lowered her hand and nodded for the young servant girl to leave them alone. The skin on the back of her neck began to prickle, and she had the distinct impression Lady Corbett was going to tell her something she didn't wish to hear.

"You see, my lady," Lady Corbett said in a rush, her voice quaking, "I know Jane Emily. Quite well as it turns out."

Arabella swallowed and regarded the woman patiently. "How do you know her my lady?"

Lady Corbett turned to Arabella. "She is betrothed to my son."

❦ 20 ❧

"Miss Grantly," Jacobs, the Marsh's butler intoned, "you have a visitor." He held out a silver tray.

Dear God, she hoped it wasn't the dressmaker again. She'd been pricked and poked with enough pins within the last fortnight to last her a lifetime. The woman usually made an appointment, but her last visit was not planned. Jemma's betrothed kept adding to her trousseau. Nick, as it turned out, could be more thorough in the dressing of a woman than a lady's maid. She wished to warn him of his highhandedness, but he avoided her, neither attempting to see or speak to her since that day in the conservatory. All communication for her came through Uncle John.

I caused this. I asked for this.

Her father's deceit would be with her always, but at least she no longer woke up every day feeling as if a stone sat on her chest. She thought if she waited, perhaps a bit longer, Nick would make the first move and try to see her. As the weeks dragged on though, it was becoming clearer that if she wished to speak to her future husband before their wedding, she would need to extend the olive branch first.

Sighing, she took the card, expecting to see the dressmaker's name but instead her eyes flew to the Dunbar coat of arms. Beneath, in perfect gold script read *Lady Arabella Tremaine*.

Petra looked up from her embroidery. "Oh dear, is it the dressmaker again? I don't believe I've ever seen so many fittings and so many gowns. I wonder that you'll be able to wear them all."

Jemma's mouth went dry. "No, not the dressmaker, though for once I wish it was." Nick's sister did not bother to disguise her dislike for Jemma, so there was little likelihood that Arabella was paying a social call.

Petra laughed. "I've never seen such an assortment of gowns and underthings. I still can't believe you are to marry the Duke of Dunbar. I wish you had told me of your prior relationship as I pattered on about him."

"He called himself Viscount Lindley when I met him," Jemma said lying automatically, using Nick's former title. Her uncle explained to the family that Jemma, living in Bermuda, would not know of the death of Nick's grandfather, and thus not know Nick by his current title. It was the simplest way to explain why Jemma remained silent as Petra spoke of the duke.

"Yes," Petra shot her a look of sympathy, "and all that time you thought he didn't care and he thought you were dead." Petra was a rather hopeless romantic. "But you have found each other again."

"Indeed we have." Could she pretend not to be home for her future sister-in-law?

"My lady?" Jacobs, with a servant's intuitiveness, said, "Shall I say you are not at home? Perhaps abed with a headache?"

Petra put down her embroidery hoop with a frown and marched over to Jemma, her skirts swinging. Snatching the note out of Jemma's hand, her eyes widened in panic as she saw who called upon her cousin.

"Good Lord. Lady Arabella." The blood left Petra's face. "Why is she here?"

"I'm here." Lady Arabella waltzed in, pausing only to wave Horace away. "To speak to my brother's betrothed." She said the last with particular distaste, her full lips pursing as if she sucked on a lemon. "Your presence." She glared at Petra. "Is not required."

Lady Arabella sauntered over to the sofa facing Jemma. "Be useful," she said over her shoulder to Petra who stood still clutching the calling card in one hand, shocked into silence by Arabella's intrusion. "Send for tea." She flounced down across from Jemma, her dark eyes glittering with dislike.

Jemma wondered what on earth Arabella wanted. They'd been re-introduced, of course at the Cambourne ball, but barely spoke, Arabella's attitude one of chilling indifference. If the two women did see each other in public, Arabella made a point of avoiding Jemma. Invitations from Aunt Mary for luncheon or tea were returned with curt regrets, followed by much hand wringing from her aunt. Jemma wondered that Nick's own aunt didn't take Arabella in hand and teach her better manners. Truth be told, Jemma did not care for Arabella either, finding her to be so bitter she could likely turn wine to vinegar.

Arabella's eyes, such a dark brown they were nearly black, looked Jemma over from head to toe. Her lips curled in disdain as if Jemma were wanting in some way. Hair, a shade darker than her brother's but with the same red glints, was pulled back severely from the thin oval of her face and twisted into two large braided hoops over each ear. Bits of topaz dangled from each ear, complementing the coffee colored gown she wore. She looked privileged and elegant, though the gown and hairstyle would better suit a woman twice Arabella's age.

"Well?" Arabella said, addressing Petra while keeping her eyes firmly on Jemma. "I'm quite parched. Do get on with it. Surely you can ask for tea to be sent?" Arabella tapped her foot in irritation.

Petra stood frozen, her mouth still slightly agape. She looked like a mouse paralyzed upon being discovered by a cat.

"I knew the Devils of Dunbar were infamous for many things, but I did not think rudeness one of them," Jemma said curtly to Arabella. "Do not speak to my cousin in such a way."

Lady Arabella favored Jemma with a taut smile that could have curdled milk. "Would you please," she addressed Petra, "leave us and send for tea."

"Of course." Petra fairly raced from the room, nearly upending a cluster of figures on a table in her haste to get away.

A satisfied smirk crossed Arabella's lips. "It boggles the mind that Nick would even have considered her. What little backbone she has would have been destroyed by my brother within a week, and myself the following."

"I'm thrilled, Lady Arabella," she kept her tone mild, "that you have graced me with a visit. I know how busy you must be as evidenced by the number of times you've refused my aunt's invitations to tea."

"So you are the girl from Bermuda."

"Clearly. I believe that has been established."

"Yes." Arabella raised a brow. "The traitor's daughter. From Bermuda." She lay back against the plump cushions of the sofa as if they were discussing the latest fashions.

Jemma tried not to let her surprise show on her face and

kept her breathing normal, even though inside her stomach shifted so forcefully she thought she'd be ill all over her aunt's favorite sofa. How could Arabella know the truth? She clasped her hands calmly in her lap and ignored Arabella's little speech.

"Do you have something you wish to discuss?" Jemma asked pointedly as a maid brought in tea, setting the tray down gently between Jemma and Arabella. "Or is there more? I'll pour if it will hurry you along."

Arabella's eyes narrowed. "My, my, Nick did say you have a bit of a temper. *Jem.*"

Jem. His nickname for her, and one she did not think he would use in front of his sister or anyone else for that matter.

"Do I?" Jemma reached over to the steaming teakettle and poured for Arabella, then herself. "Sugar? I'm *certain* you could use a bit of sweetening. For your tea, of course." Jemma had absolutely no intention of cowering in front of this rude, mean spirited girl, nor did she dare give credence to Arabella's words about Jemma's father.

A small hissing noise came from Arabella's lips and she blinked twice. "You would not be so smug were your father rotting in chains and your precious family branded traitors."

Jemma forced herself to remain calm to Arabella's baiting. "I've a busy day, Lady Arabella, I've a wedding to plan and a trousseau being readied. I pray you—"

"I've heard the whole of it. I know the truth," Arabella declared.

"Indeed?" Jemma sipped her tea, the heat of the brew on her tongue helping to steady her. If Arabella knew, what was to stop anyone else knowing?

"Yes. All of it." Arabella brought the teacup to her lips and inhaled the subtle aroma. "*Jem.*"

Nick's name for her coming from his sister unnerved her. "My name is Jane Emily. Forgive me, Lady Arabella, while I find our discussion most entertaining, I fear I must cut our conversation short." Why would Nick tell his sister when he swore to her uncle to tell no one?

Arabella didn't budge. "My brother calls you that, doesn't he?" She leaned forward, her eyes narrowed into slits. "*Jem.*" Arabella's resentment seeped through her words, filling the drawing room with a horrible dark bitterness.

What did Arabella want, exactly? A confession? A confirmation that Jemma's father was a traitor? If Arabella did not leave soon, Jemma would leap across the table between them and perhaps pelt her future sister-in-law with sugar cubes until Arabella ran screaming from the room.

"*Jem,*" she said again. "I heard him say your name every evening, weeping, as he sought to drown his grief over you in a bottle of fine Irish whisky. But then, here you are," she waved her hand, "miraculously alive and returned to my brother, the *wealthy* duke."

Arabella's words cut into Jemma like tiny swords, each nipping at enough of her flesh to leave her bleeding but still aware. She had never allowed herself to truly imagine how news of her death affected those she cared for, and certainly she did not contemplate Nick's reaction, but the knowledge that he'd wept over her, broke Jemma's heart. The words she'd said to him in the conservatory made all the more vile by the fact that he had mourned her so deeply. She walked through every day wishing she had not spoken such horrible things to him. Over the last weeks she'd had much time to consider the past *and* the future. Prideful and foolish she may be, but she loved Nick. She hoped he would at least allow her to tell him so.

Jemma's hand shook slightly, and she immediately set her cup down on the tray.

"More tea?" Arabella widened her eyes innocently, clearly enjoying Jemma's discomfort.

"Does the duke know you are here?" Jemma said softly.

The triumphant look in Arabella's eyes faded a bit, and she looked away for a moment.

"I thought not," Jemma said, her voice neutral.

"I came to ask you something." Nick's sister put down her cup next to Jemma's. Arabella's eyes, sharp like bits of brown glass, stared Jemma down and her voice took on the same whiskey filtered tone of her brother's. "You already have a betrothed, do you not? Why come to my brother under false pretenses? Have you not had enough of the Dunbar wealth that you must follow my brother to England to claim more?"

The reference to Augie made Jemma's heart skip a beat. How in God's name could Arabella know about Augie? A chill crawled up her spine. *Why would Nick tell Arabella such a thing?* "Did His Grace tell you this incredible fable?"

Arabella gave a small shrug as if what they discussed were of no consequence. "Perhaps. I'm not sure you are even free to marry my brother. Surely, if you were betrothed to another man, that man would have a prior claim."

She thought of Augie as he slapped her to the floor at Sea Cliff, of his gambling debts, of his greed for everything she owned. She thought of the Corbetts' betrayal of her father and of her. She wondered if they had taken Sea Cliff for themselves and found she didn't care, she cared only for Nick and what was left of the Marsh family. She would never return to Bermuda.

Poor manners though it was, it was time for Arabella to leave, whether she wished it or not. Jemma stood, looking down her nose at her future sister-in-law and used her most haughty demeanor. She would not allow this woman, nor anyone else, to harm her family. Nick may not love her any longer, nor ever forgive her, but Jemma was still betrothed to him.

"I'll be sure and let His Grace know how much I enjoyed our visit, Lady Arabella."

"I am not done speaking to you," Arabella sneered.

"Yes, but I am quite done speaking to you, *Arabella*."

Arabella drew in her breath sharply. Her nostrils flared with outrage.

"I've had quite enough of you for today, your reputation is well earned." Jemma stood and regarded the woman who was now almost hissing like a trapped cobra on Aunt Mary's sofa. "You do not frighten me, *Arabella*. You may be the sister of a duke," her voice was even, "but I will be a *duchess*. I will not be subjected to your foul temperament. Nor do you have leave to speak to me so."

Arabella shot off the sofa, her hands curled into fists at her sides. An ugly, mean look crossed over her beautiful features. "Make no mistake, I know what you are." She made a choking sound. "You are nothing but the daughter of a *traitor*, by all rights you should be in rags begging in the streets. You lived well for years because of *my* family. My parents are dead because of you." Her voice shook with rage. "You are the daughter of a *servant*. A *maid*. And *you* think you are good enough to marry a *duke*?"

Jemma placed both hands across her waist. Dear God, she would be ill. Had her uncle told Nick about her mother? He must have for how else could Arabella know such a thing?

"Did I not tell you, *Jem*, the Devils of Dunbar know everything?" Arabella smiled gleefully at her. "I will spend every moment dissuading my brother from this marriage. Every moment." Her head shook, and her earbobs swung against the length of her neck.

Jemma stepped back carefully lest she trip on the rug and embarrass herself in front of this viper. She reached behind to grab at a tasseled cord to summon the butler, pulling so forcefully she thought she might tear the ringer from the ceiling.

Jacobs immediately appeared at the door. His knowing glance flitted over Arabella before looking directly at Jemma, belaying his concern at her evident distress. "Miss Grantly?"

"Please show Lady Arabella out. She's feeling ill and must return home immediately." Would Arabella contradict her? She thought not.

"Yes. I've developed a sudden headache." Arabella gathered her gloves and stood to face Jemma, tilting forward so that their noses nearly touched. "I wish you had stayed dead," she snarled before sailing past Jacobs and through the drawing room doors.

"Is there anything I can bring you Miss Grantly?" Jacobs inquired politely.

Jemma didn't answer, she couldn't. Her temples throbbed with Arabella's horrible words. She must speak to Nick and end this foolish stalemate.

The butler nodded and began to shut the drawing room doors.

"Jacobs."

The doors swung open again, and the butler's head immediately reappeared. "My lady?"

"Bring me pen and paper. I need to send a message to His Grace immediately."

❧ 2 1 ❧

Jemma paced back and forth for the thousandth time, counting the number of roses adorning the rug beneath her feet. Tugging her dressing gown tighter, she shivered in the damp coldness of the room. England was so bloody frigid compared to Bermuda. Her uncle assured her that over time she would acclimate to the difference in temperature, but Jemma thought she would be forever cold.

A light rain rattled against the window and the sky had gone gray and dark with the coming storm.

Jemma moved before the roaring fire in the hearth, holding out her hands to chase the chill from her fingers. Two days. It had been two long days since she'd sent a note to Nick, asking to speak with him privately. She thought he would reply immediately, perhaps show up demanding to see her at the door of the Marsh town home. When he didn't come right away, she tried to keep herself busy, reading books she had little interest in, pretending to care which gown Petra would wear to Lady Dobson's ball and glancing at the door every five minutes in hopes that a message from Nick would arrive. Dinner came and went and still there was no messenger, no word.

She retired early.

After a sleepless night in which she repeated to herself over and over what she would say to Nick, she'd finally given up, rising from her bed to see the day had turned cold and gray. In spite of the weather, she'd walked around the garden, endlessly, thinking of her meeting with Arabella. Had Nick suddenly changed his mind about their marriage and had yet to inform her uncle? She could still see him moving through the crowd at the Cambourne ball and the blonde who trailed him, attaching herself to his tall form.

The longer she waited, the more muddled her thinking became until she now found herself wishing she'd simply appeared at Nick's home. The sight of her on his front steps might force him to speak to her, or he might have her refused at the door. Arabella would certainly deny her entrance. Nick had been very angry the last time she'd seen him, and rightly so.

"Bloody arrogant man. He wishes to make me suffer."

"Well, you deserve to, but then, any pain I cause you comes back to me ten times over."

Jemma jumped, stumbling back over the leg of a wing-back chair. The husky voice seemed to emanate from her armoire.

"Goodness, Jem." A shadowy form came forward. "How you became adept at weaponry given your propensity for tripping constantly amazes me." The shadowy form revealed itself as that of the Duke of Dunbar, wet and dripping water all over her floor.

"Nick?" Jemma clutched her dressing gown closer, wondering if she had fallen asleep and Nick's appearance in her bedroom was a dream.

"You are so very lucky another man's name did not cross

your lips. It would be bad for all concerned." He shook himself like some giant wet dog, his coat spilling droplets of water all over the rug as he made his way to the fire.

Although his tone was light, Jemma did not miss the underlying threat in his words. "There is no other man, and well you know it," Jemma countered, her pulse quickening at the sight of the large man standing in her chambers. "Keep your voice down lest you awaken the entire house."

"True," came the husky voice. "If any other man had come near you, I would already have committed murder."

"I am in a murderous mood myself, as it happens, should the reverse be true." The blonde she spied trailing Nick the night of the Cambourne ball flashed before her eyes again for the thousandth time.

Nick stilled and looked at her. "Agreed. Although I find the thought of you challenging Lady Tomlinson to a duel over me to be highly erotic. You'd best her, of course."

"Lady Tomlinson would not stand a chance." She lifted her chin.

Nick shook out his coat and laid it before the fire to dry. He moved to hold out his hands towards the flames, blocking every bit of the fire's warmth with his body.

"You've no call to be jealous. I've not touched another woman since Bermuda. I want no one but you."

Jemma shivered again from the note of possessiveness in his words. How like Nick to speak to her so bluntly. Instinctively she knew he spoke the truth. Unsure of how to proceed, she said tartly, "Move Nick. It is like a giant tree blocking the warmth of the sun. I'm freezing. The cold of London, I fear, is something I shall never grow accustomed to."

He complied, stepping to the side.

Jemma sighed in pleasure as the warmth of the fire hit her

skin. She could sense him watching her, waiting for her to say more.

"This is most inappropriate, to visit a lady in her bedchamber. I am outraged at your impropriety," she murmured, watching the play of the fire against his features. "How did you get in?"

"I'm a witch, remember?" he said somberly. "I made myself magically appear at your request." He wiggled his fingers as if casting a spell.

"You are not a witch, nor are you cursed." She bit her lip. "I am sorry for the words I spoke. I was angry, I was——"

"Trellis."

She shook her head at the word. "What?"

He nodded towards the window. "Trellis. Didn't think it would hold me, but it did." He grinned, clearly not wishing to accept her apology yet. "Not sure it will on the climb down. What a ruckus that will cause if I fall."

"Yes, rather like the giant and the beanstalk. My windows are locked." She made her way to an overstuffed chair before the fire. She sat, shifting just enough so that her wrapper slipped down one shoulder exposing it and the top of a breast.

Nick's eyes flickered to her bared flesh, then back to her face. "Locks? Easily picked. I should speak to your uncle about the security of his home. It is quite poor. The rosebush barely put up a fight as I climbed." The ring on his thumb caught the flames of the fire and winked at her.

Her thoughts were neither on the trellis nor the abused rosebushes. Shamefully, all she could think of was Nick and the intensity of their joining in the conservatory. Her intentions to clear the air regarding her family and Arabella's knowledge of the past receded from the allure of the Devil of Dunbar.

"I've wondered," she said casually, "what the ring is that you wear."

Nick shrugged. "Surely you've heard the stories by now?" He turned his thumb towards her. "The damned one wears it."

"You are not damned, Nick." It made her heart hurt to have him think such a thing. How many people had mocked him or shriveled from him in fear because of that story? A rush of protectiveness for him came over her even as she acknowledged that he had little need of her protection, or did he?

"We must talk." His lips curved upward. "Then I will permit you to take liberties with me."

She looked away, wondering why she was so transparent. *Because I love him, and well, he knows it.*

"No more anger between us, Jem. I cannot bear it."

The pain and longing in his words echoed her own feelings. "No more anger, Nick." She held out her arms.

"I did not leave you in Bermuda of my own accord. I would never have left you to face all of that alone had I been given a choice." The husky words, spoken with so much feeling, warmed her more than the fire. "I would never harm your family or hurt them. Surely you know this?"

Jemma nodded, her arms still open to him, the tears welling in her eyes. "I do. I am a reckless, foolish girl from Bermuda who does not place the blame for the past at your feet."

"Your friend Wren, sent by Corbett, jumped me after I left your father's study. I wasn't paying attention, you see, I was—"

"Worried for me." Her hands fell to her lap.

"Well," he gave her a sad half-smile, "I hadn't meant for you to see me, I meant to confront your father and leave. But actually I was looking up at the windows, trying to figure out which one was yours."

"Whatever for?"

"I planned to kidnap you and take you with me."

"Kidnap me?" Jemma said in surprise.

"I did not think that after eavesdropping in the hall you would come willingly, thinking I was a cad and a blackmailer." He shrugged. "At any rate, Corbett paid the ship's captain to throw me to the sharks once the ship was far enough out and there was no risk to my body washing back to Bermuda." He came forward and knelt at her feet. "Once the captain saw my eyes," his voice trailed off, "he knew who I was."

"And that you were worth more alive than dead to him," Jemma finished.

Nick placed his hands on her knees. "Yes. But Henry, my grandfather died. I couldn't get back to Bermuda, to you. I couldn't—"

"Rescue me." Jemma laced her hands through the dark mass of his hair, still damp from his climb up the trellis.

"I sent one of my men, Hotchkins, to bring you back, because I couldn't leave London." The deep baritone lowered to a tortured whisper. "He was told you were dead. When I received Hotchkin's letter, I—" He swallowed. "I thought you were lost to me. That I had destroyed the thing I love most." Nick looked up at her. "I think the worst was the knowledge that you died thinking I used you and discarded you after that day on the beach. My heart—"

"Stop." A tear ran down Jemma's cheek. She pressed a kiss to the top of his head. "I did not die. I am here. I will never leave you." Her throat felt raw. "My uncle told me everything. My parents. The treason. He was my father, and I loved him, but he was a weak man, Nick. He lived a life he didn't deserve."

"I never wished for you to know."

Jemma cupped his face. "I was to be your revenge, wasn't I?"

Nick closed his eyes for a moment, refusing to look at her. "In the beginning." His eyes fluttered open, one blue, one brown, both filled with remorse and regret. And painful honestly.

She fell apart completely then, as much from the emotion of the moment as the relief that the telling of the horrible tale was over. For so long she had cursed him, loved him and wondered what possessed him to come to Bermuda. Now she knew. Corbett cost she and Nick dearly. She wept bitterly as he stood and gently lifted her from the chair.

"My entire life has been a lie." Her chest shook with the force of her tears. "All of it."

"But we are not, Jem. We are not a lie." He held her close to his heart and whispered nonsense words of comfort into her ear, gently rocking her until she settled.

"Nick." His name came out as a hiccup. She ran a fingertip over his nose, stopping at the bump. "You will have to tell me how this break happened. Her hand fell to his stomach, and she felt the muscles contract under her palm. "And of the scars you bear." Her voice grew fierce. "I will not allow anyone to harm you again."

A wry smile crossed his lips. "I accept your protection. I've no doubt that should I require it, you will rescue me." He moved and the chair wobbled to one side. "Another poorly made chair. I don't understand why I cannot find a sturdy chair in all of London." He paused and cupped her face in his hands. "No more tears, Jem, not for the past and especially not the sins our parents have visited upon us."

She nodded as he wiped a tear from her cheek.

"There is one more thing." A large hand clasped hers. "You know of my reputation, my family's past. We are cursed and most of my ancestors, particularly those that bear my affliction, have come to a bad end. The last Devil of Dunbar went raving mad, clawing at her face and tearing at her clothes."

"Do you seek to dissuade me?"

"Perhaps, warn," he murmured in her ear, the tip of his tongue circling the outer edges of her lobe.

Jemma shivered at the press of his lips against her neck. She moved her hand further down his stomach until it lay between his legs. She could feel his arousal beneath her fingertips. "I don't believe that you are damned and cursed." Her hand tightened and Nick's chest rumbled with a soft growl. "I see I will have to convince you of the suitability of our match."

"You are making an excellent start." He pushed up against her. "Remember, I once told you that this was the wanting."

"Yes, the wanting. I don't believe it will ever go away."

"God, I sincerely hope not." Nick jumped as she gently squeezed the hardening bulge beneath her hand.

"I will not be parted again." She whispered against his ear, loving the way he tightened beneath her.

"You'd best mean it." His mouth fell forcefully against hers, urging her lips apart until their tongues intertwined. "Wanton. I knew you would wish to take liberties with me." He pulled her up and held her in his arms.

Playfully, Jemma swung her legs to and fro. "I suppose I am."

๑๕๕๑

Joy, that most elusive of emotions, coursed through Nick's veins. He marveled that only this girl, over all the women he'd known, ever evoked that feeling in him. He thanked whatever entity, God or the Devil, allowed him a second chance.

"We really mustn't." She swatted at him as he carried her to the bed. "You cannot possibly mean to take advantage of me in my uncle's home? Again?"

She smelled of lemons and sunshine and a chocolate. He spied the empty tray near the bed. A plate sprinkled with crumbs lay on it next to a small pot of tea. "Of course I do even though you've already had your bedtime snack." He nodded towards the tray, feeling the heat of her body beneath the wrapper.

"I should lock the door," Jemma said primly. "I do not wish for my maid to walk in unannounced. The sight of the Duke of Dunbar in a state of undress would cause Anna to scream the house down."

Nick tossed her atop the coverlet, and she bounced against the down mattress, hand pressed against her mouth as she stifled a giggle.

The dressing gown fell open, and her long slender legs parted, giving Nick a view of the delicacy that awaited him. "A prudent thought." Nick quickly turned the lock then approached the bed, pausing only to shed his shirt. He tossed the fine lawn on the floor to be followed by his boots.

Another giggle, this time seductive, floated up from the feather mattress.

Nick put one knee on the bed and splayed his hand across her stomach, marveling at the warmth of her skin beneath the silk. "Finally, I will have you in a bed."

"You will have me always, in a bed or not." Her hands ran up his arms.

"I will make you happy." He crawled onto the bed, ignoring the creaking springs, and hovered on all fours above her. He bent his head to trail his tongue up her neck to the tender flesh below her ear. "I swear it. In fact, I will begin the task immediately." He nipped at her earlobe.

Grabbing the waist of her dressing gown, he tore the belt

open to expose her nightgown. The fabric of the nightgown was so sheer he saw clearly the dark tips of her breasts and crevice between her thighs. "This garment," he tried, and failed to untie the ribbon holding her nightgown together with one hand, "is in my opinion," he tore the fragile cotton in frustration, "completely unnecessary."

"How should I explain that to my maid?" Jem gasped, watching him toss the remains of her nightgown to the floor.

"Shoddy workmanship," he muttered, ignoring her.

"Yes, the same as the bed and the chair. You are plagued, Your Grace, with mediocre craftsman. That may be the true curse you are under."

He ran his hand down the swath of flesh gleaming on the bed before him. "Lovely." He pressed a kiss to the valley between her breasts and made his way to a pale pink nipple. Nick gently sucked the peak into his waiting mouth.

Jem arched beneath him like a cat, a soft moan escaping her parted lips. She wound her fingers into his hair, pulling him closer to her breast. "Nick."

His fingers found the wet, silkiness between her thighs. Rubbing one finger against her, he lightly stroked the tender flesh, delighting in the way her body tightened in response.

"I am a lucky man." His mouth left her nipple, instead circling the tip with his tongue. "I will become exhausted in my attempts to satisfy you."

Jem pounded a fist against his shoulder in mock indignation. "Bloody, arrogant, *duke*," she panted, her legs splaying wider. She reached for the buttons of his trousers.

Dear God, he would not be able to take much more of her questing fingers. The seams of his breeches were about to burst. He rolled to the side and off the bed abruptly, leaving the bed shaking.

Jem bounced about on the mattress. "Lord Nick, do you

mean to make me seasick?" One hand languidly reached out to him.

Nick jerked at his trousers, wondering if he would need to instruct his tailor to leave a bit more room in the future. Lust for his wife would keep him from sitting a horse properly, and it was undignified for a duke to go around with split seams. A thought occurred to him. "You will have your own suite of rooms, next to mine but you will sleep with me, in *my* bed. Unfashionable though it may be."

"I shall wear breeches to ride," Jem slid her glorious legs against the coverlet, "under my skirts. I do not care to ride sidesaddle." She looked at him with defiance. "Unfashionable though *that* may be."

"I do as I wish." Nick climbed into bed next to her, turning her body so that she lay partially on her side, partially on her stomach. "And so shall my duchess." He ran his lips down her spine, all the way to the crack of her buttocks. "You have a most lovely arse."

Jem moved her backside against his lips. "Mmm."

"You will breakfast with me every day." He moved her top leg forward and pressed a finger inside her warm wetness. "And dine with me at night."

"Oh," Jem panted. "I will have," she pushed against his questing finger, "back that stallion." Her breathing came in soft gasps as he thrust another finger inside her. "He—was lovely."

"Lovely." He wrapped his arm under her neck and brought her face back to his for a lingering kiss.

She groaned again. "I wish to name him Cyclops, in memory of a former beau."

Nick nosed the nape of her neck. He lifted her leg higher, baring more of her to his purpose. His fingers moved in and out slowly, wishing to draw out her pleasure.

Slowly, he eased his fingers out to replace them with the

tip of his arousal. "A former beau? And you wish to name your horse for him?" He entered her, slowly, easing into the tightness of her, reveling in the sensation of her body grasping his.

"Oh. Yes." Her breath caught. "I was quite fond of him."

He held on to her hip, pushed into her fully, his swollen arousal forcing her to widen for him. Unhurried, he pulled back and deliberately thrust again, this time harder, to bury himself fully.

She cried out his name and turned her face into the pillow.

"God." He gritted his teeth and thrust into her again and again with a slow, measured stroke.

"Please, Nick," Jem whimpered, pushing back with each thrust. "I want you so badly."

Her words roused him more. All thoughts of his pledge to be gentle fled. Reaching down between her legs, he stroked the taut nub as he moved roughly to satisfy them both.

Jem's breath came in quiet gasps as she matched his rhythm. She grabbed his hip, holding him tight against her.

"You are bound to me," he whispered to her.

"Yes." Her nails bit into his thigh as her body grew taut like a bow.

He felt the peak between his fingers begin to pulse. "I love you," Nick breathed into her ear.

They climaxed simultaneously, their bodies locked together in one long expression of pleasure. The bed beneath them creaked and bounced against the wall as Nick buried his face in her neck, trying not to cry out his release.

After, he didn't leave her, but stayed inside of her, their limbs twisted about each other's on the bed. Whispering his love for her, he rained kisses down the freckles across her cheeks and into the dampness of her hair. He wished never to leave this bed, not tonight, not ever.

Reluctantly he let her go and she immediately turned to

snuggle next to him, her chin propped up on his chest. Her fingers ran across his torso, lightly twisting and pulling at the hair until she found one of his nipples. The tip of her finger circled round and round as if she were thinking.

"What do you wish to ask me?"

"Reading my mind again. I find that most distressful that I am like an open book to you."

He wished he could see her freckles in the flickering light of the candle. He wanted to count them. "You look like a child about to beg for a sweet."

"I'm not good at begging." At Nick's raised brow she said, "At least not for sweets. I wanted to ask, and you must not laugh."

"I promise to remain solemn and serious." He kissed the tip of her nose, thinking how precious to him she was.

"Do you really have an estate called The Egg?"

Nick held back the laughter that rumbled in his chest, lest he shake the rafters. "Do you not find that a most mysterious and foreboding name for the Devil of Dunbar's seat? Now he did laugh, turning his head as his shoulders shook.

"So it is true." Jem wound a bit of his chest hair around her finger and pulled.

"Ow."

"You promised not to laugh." She looked across his chest and her brow wrinkled. "You are very hairy."

"That bothers you?" He sincerely hoped not. Some women were horrified by an expanse of male chest and swooned upon seeing a man's bared arms. He glanced at Jem. She didn't look the least horrified—in fact, she rolled her eyes.

"Don't be an idiot, Nick. I was simply making an observation." She tentatively stuck out her tongue and touched it to his nipple.

His manhood, exhausted from its previous exertions, immediately came to life at the touch of her tongue.

"Tell me how it is that your ancestral estate came by a ridiculous name. I did not believe Petra when she told me." She flicked out her tongue again and watched for his reaction.

"Stop doing that, else you'll never hear the tale."

Jem smiled innocently at him. "Continue."

Nick cleared his throat, attempting to ignore the hand roaming towards his waist. "My ancestor, the first duke, was an English bastard who was gifted land, a days ride from the border in Scotland. The area was remote and inhospitable, owing to the fact he was a bastard. The town there still bears our name."

"Get to The Egg, Nick." She stretched, rubbing her body against his.

He rubbed back and continued with his story. "The keep and the surrounding wall were made of dark, almost black rock. The first duke's given name was Robyn. He was a redhead."

Jem tugged at a curl of Nick's hair, rubbing it between her fingers. "Mmm. I see. Go on."

"Robyn Tremaine possessed a large army, a very fierce army, but he was known as much for being a leader of men as he was being wise in his dealings with the Tudor's. He protected Henry Tudor's interests well and the king granted Robyn many favors. So many favors in fact, that Henry's court whispered that Robyn's influence was more than wisdom."

"The Devil's work." Jem's fingers moved to trace the outline of Nick's ribs. "The start of the curse."

Trying to focus on the story at hand he said, "Henry was guardian to a young woman, thought to be a witch. She was promised to another, but Tremaine wanted her. Henry elevated him to duke so that he would be of proper station to marry the witch. She was a countess in her own right, you see."

"He married her to be made duke?"

"No." Nick brought her wandering fingertips to his lips, kissing them gently. "Theirs was a great love match. I have her eyes."

Jem looked up at him intently. "No wonder they thought her a witch." Her hand moved lower and encircled his hardened arousal. "But," she squeezed gently, and Nick sucked in his breath, "you still have not explained why your family seat is called 'The Egg.'"

He turned suddenly, rolling her onto her back. "Robyn tore down the old keep and built his bride a beautiful house made of brilliant white stone." He held her hands to her side and made his way down her stomach with his mouth and tongue. Dear God, would they ever leave the bedroom once married? Nick thought not.

"And?" Jemma's voice dropped an octave, and she arched her back as his breath fluttered between her thighs.

"And," he nipped at the inside of her thigh, "the house is so white, and it sits amid the dark rock of the cliffs. I suppose it rather looks like an egg in a nest, and well," he kissed the downy softness of her womanhood and heard her moan, "the court mocked Robyn behind his back by calling it The Egg and the name stuck."

"Oh." Jem said as he hooked her leg over his shoulder and took that most delicate, sensitive part of her into his mouth.

"Yes, indeed," he breathed against her.

And they ceased talking.

HOURS LATER JEMMA, HALF ASLEEP, WATCHED NICK DRESS in preparation for his climb back down the trellis. She hoped the lattice would hold. They had talked and made love at intervals all night, and Jemma thought she would likely sleep past noon. A delicious ache filled her as she watched him climb back out the window and blow her a kiss. Drowsily, she thought of Arabella's accusations. She'd completely forgotten to ask why he'd told his sister about Jemma's parents, but possibly he did in his grief and anger. What did it matter anymore, she thought as her eyes closed, and she snuggled under the covers. The past was the past, and she and Nick had the future together.

"Lady Arabella! Over here!"

Rowan turned as he heard the name, immediately searching the crowds that roamed Bond Street for a glimpse of that cantankerous female.

"Rowan! Do watch yourself. You almost stepped in a puddle." Lady Mary Marsh frowned at her son. "You'll ruin those boots."

"Sorry." He scanned the crowd and finally spied her, looking like a sparrow in a group of brightly colored birds. As usual, Arabella was clothed in a variation of dull, muted brown, which failed to hide her stern beauty. She was engaged in a somewhat animated conversation with a plump, older woman and a young man. Rowan's eyes narrowed as he took in the gentleman who politely nodded and brought Arabella's gloved hand to his lips. He didn't look familiar, nor did the woman.

"Oh look at these lovely confections." Lady Mary clapped her hands at the hats displayed in the milliner's window.

Rowan gave his mother a weak smile. His cousin's wedding to the Duke of Dunbar would be taking place within a fortnight, and Lady Mary had no wish to look provincial. She'd spent a small fortune on her gown and had now turned her attention to a hat befitting the aunt of a duchess. His attention returned to Arabella.

Arabella stepped back from the pair and shook her head in refusal. The woman took Arabella's hand and spoke to her urgently. The young man just looked annoyed.

"Mother." Rowan turned to his mother. "Do you see Lady Arabella just down there?"

His mother didn't turn from the window. "Please, I beg of you, do not tell me you've grown fond of Lady Arabella. One Dunbar in the family is quite enough."

The gentleman lightly touched Arabella on the arm as if making a plea of some sort.

"Don't be ridiculous." Rowan didn't turn away from Arabella and her companions. There wasn't anything remotely sinister about the pair, but something seemed *off*. "I'm just curious. The lady looks vaguely familiar," he lied. "I believe I danced with her daughter at some affair recently and would like to know the daughter's name." His mother would not be able to resist the thought of adding another young lady to her list of potential brides for Rowan in case a match with Lady Gwendolyn White didn't pan out.

She took the bait and turned around, squinting her eyes. "I don't believe I know her. Where did say you met?" His mother shook her head and returned her attention to the hats on display in the milliner's window. "Perhaps you should go over and inquire after her daughter."

"Splendid idea." Rowan doubted she could make out the woman properly and took a step, meaning to interrupt the three when Arabella opened her reticule and pulled out a slip of paper, handing it reluctantly to the woman.

Patting Arabella's arm, the woman seemed to say something soothing while the gentleman doffed his hat before the pair both turned and disappeared into the crowds on Bond Street.

Once the pair was gone, Arabella bit her lip and looked down at her feet, giving a great shrug of her shoulders as if coming to a decision, and not one she was completely happy about. Looking up from her feet, she spied Rowan. A red flush stole up to stain her neck and cheeks, guilt stamped plainly across her lovely features. Her mouth opened slightly in surprise, then closed firmly as she composed herself. A scowl twisted on her lips and she looked down her nose at Rowan as if daring him to approach her. She gave him one last scathing look before stepping into her waiting carriage.

As he watched the coach bearing the Dunbar coat of arms become lost in the congestion of Bond Street, Rowan was struck again with the feeling that something wasn't right. What was Arabella guilty of?

◔◕◔

"COME." NICK ANSWERED THE KNOCK AT HIS STUDY DOOR. A mass of papers lay across his desk, various notes, bills and other business of the enormous Dunbar empire. Even with two secretaries at his disposal, a team of solicitors and several property managers, the task of seeing to all things Dunbar was a daunting one. His eyes fell to a bill from the dressmaker, all for a vast assortment of frilly female undergarments. "None of them will last long," he said out loud, thinking of the demise of his future wife's bedroom attire.

"Who will not last long?" Arabella sauntered into the room, her lips compressed into a grim tight line as if she were about to announce a death or some other awful occurrence. "I see she is already costing you a king's ransom." She nodded towards the stack of receipts. "I assumed as much. She is determined to bankrupt you."

Nick neatened the stack of bills, laying the dressmaker bill atop the others, preparing himself for the confrontation his sister longed for. He loved Bella dearly, and the two had been close their entire lives. They went together to Grandfather, a matched pair of orphaned Dunbars after the scandalous death of Nick's parents. He still remembered the nursemaid hired by his grandfather prying Bella's hand from his own upon their arrival so that she could be given a bath. Bella had screamed in agony at the separation from her brother, throwing herself at the ground to wrap her arms about Nick's ankles.

Arabella viewed the world with uncommon bitterness even though her very station in life gave her much to be grateful for. She set herself apart from others, adopting a stern, closed off attitude to protect herself from the gossipmongers who baited her after the alleged treason of their father. Later, she learned to use the infamy of the the family name to protect herself, wrapping the wealth and power that came from being the granddaughter of the Duke of Dunbar around herself like a security blanket. She blamed her lack of suitors on the treasonous taint of their father and Nick's own reputation, never once acknowledging her own waspish behavior terrified any man who might pursue her. Even her outrageously large dowry didn't help. He doubted his sister would ever marry, for who would wish to marry such a shrew?

"You assumed what? That I am delighted to provide for my future wife?" Nick countered. "Then you are correct. It is a pleasure."

Bella flounced down on the leather chair before his desk. Nick expected her to dislike the idea of his marrying anyone, save Lady Miranda, her dearest and only friend. But, her outright dislike of Jem had lately turned to outright hatred.

He allowed his sister a time for adjustment, but that time was over. Her rudeness towards Jem and her family had become tiresome. Just the other evening, at the opera, Bella refused to acknowledge Jem at all, though the entire family shared a box. Jem, bless her, acted as if her future sister-in-law hadn't just cut her dead in public. She'd only squeezed Nick's shoulder and leaned into him, murmuring it was of no import.

Nick disagreed.

He was rather close to throttling his sister, or banishing her, which he truly didn't wish to do. Aunt Maisy told him Bella would come around in time, but Nick wasn't so sure. Bella stayed mired in her own world, blind to the fact that her brother was happy, truly happy, for the first time in his life.

"She will spend the entire Dunbar fortune," Bella snapped as she sat back in the chair, bracing herself against the arms as if in an effort to keep herself in place. "Do not make the mistake of opening an account for her."

"We've plenty to spare, Bella. It will take more than my lifetime to spend all that is in the Dunbar coffers. Why do you begrudge me the joy of gifting my betrothed?"

Arabella shot him an ugly look, reminding Nick of their mother, Charlotte. A most unwelcome comparison.

"I do not begrudge you, I begrudge your betrothed." Bella drummed her fingertips against the arm of the chair. "Why do you wish to marry her? She allowed you to think she was dead. After all, that does not speak well of her character."

"As I said previously, we parted on poor terms and realizing my error, I sought her out to make amends. I was given incorrect information that she was dead. She did not know I was looking for her. How could she?" He didn't care to continue the ruse he and Lord Marsh had concocted, but there was little else Nick could do. Arabella would be unforgiving of Jem's true identity and might lash out, harming the entire Marsh family. Nick could not allow that. "Why do you dislike her so?"

"If she did not want you in Bermuda, then why does she want you now? I think she is after your fortune and protection."

"So, my own charms are not enough to induce a woman to love me?" His fingers tightened on the desk.

"Love?" Arabella snorted. "You think she loves you?" she continued, ignoring the coldness in his voice. "She has the look of a gold digger, one who would seduce a man out of his fortune. Did she tell you she's with child? Good Lord, it's probably not even yours."

Nick turned his palms to press against the cool oak of the desk lest he slap his sister, something he had never done. "Careful, Bella."

Bella leaned forward, her chest heaving with fury. "Really, Nick, there's whore's aplenty in London, why must you have this *whore*?" She questioned vehemently. "The daughter of an Irish servant and a traitor," Bella hissed under her breath. "How could you, Nick? How could you?"

Nick saw red the moment his sister used the word 'whore' in reference to Jem. He barely heard anything else his sister said, his anger so great he was afraid he would do Arabella bodily harm. Instead, he slapped the top of the desk with his open palms, causing the carefully sorted piles of paper to flutter like a flock of birds to the floor. "Enough," he bellowed.

Bella fell back into the chair in front of him, the color leaving her face. "Nick, you must listen—"

"You," he slowly stood and came around the side of the desk to face her, "will shut up. Do not dare to utter another word about Jem in my presence."

Bella's eyes grew wide. "You must—"

Nick leaned over and grabbed his sister's elbow, pulling her out of the chair, not caring if he hurt her. "I must what?

How I regret ever allowing you to comfort me while I grieved for the woman I *love*."

"She was not worth your grief, nor is she worth your love. She—"

"Silence!" He shook her, his nose nearly touching hers.

Bella's nostrils flared, but she stayed silent.

He let go of her arm, pushing her away. "Listen well, sister. I tire of your unceasing litany of hatred for my future wife. That you cannot understand the feeling that lies between Jem and myself tells me how deep rooted your own misery must be. You will not insult her again."

Bella fisted her hands at her sides but did not look away from his anger. "She is a charlatan."

Nick turned and beat his fist upon the desk, this time causing a frog shaped paperweight to slide to the floor with a dull thump. *Why must Bella be so difficult?*

"You'd best reconcile yourself now, sister, to Jem." Nick grit his teeth, trying to regain control of his emotions. "She will be my duchess, the mother of the Dunbar heir and your blood kin. If you do not treat Jem with the respect due her, you will find yourself shipped off on an extended trip to one of our lesser country estates. Perhaps Twinings?"

That threat hit home. His sister sucked in her breath with shock. "Twinings is cold and dark and in *Wales*. You would not dare. Aunt Maisy would object, not to mention *me*. You can't be serious." She waited for him to gainsay her and when he did not, she said, "Dear God you *are* serious. Has she that much power over you then? She tells you to send me away, and you will do it? What lies does she tell you about me to drive a wedge between us?" A short, ugly laugh came from his sister's mouth. "I should have expected as much from *her*."

"Jem has said nothing to me about you, Bella." Nick watched his sister carefully. "Never in action or word has she maligned you to me, though it appears you have not offered her the same courtesy."

"I cannot believe you truly mean to marry her, that you cannot see what she is. How can you do this to your family?"

"Stop behaving like a spoiled child, Bella. I tire of your tantrums. You just do not wish to be alone and unmarried with no family of your own. I am not of the same mind." He pressed his fingers to his temples, exhausted from battling his sister.

"You will see that I am right." Bella turned on her heel, flinging open the study door so forcefully the knob bounced against the opposite wall. Skirts swirling about her ankles, Bella stormed out, her heels angrily clicking against the tile of the hall.

Nick watched her leave, wondering if he actually *would* have to send her to Wales.

He bent to pick up the scattered papers strewn across the floor of the study. As he carefully put them back in order and placed the frog paperweight in its place on his desk, he glanced at the clock hanging over the mantle, determined to push the argument with his sister aside. Jem would be going for the final fitting of her wedding gown, and if he didn't hurry, he'd miss her.

"**I** am ridiculously happy," Jemma informed the butterfly hovering over a spray of roses bushes in her uncle's garden. Humming a merry tune, she gave the butterfly a last look and languidly strolled down the stone path, pausing to chat with a nest of robins in the elm tree above her head. She was delirious with happiness. Drunk with joy. She wished to burst into song like the birds around her.

Her wedding to the infamous Devil of Dunbar would take place in just a few days in the very garden she now stood, much to the dismay of Lady Marsh and Lady Cupps-Foster. Lady Cupps-Foster implored her nephew to change his mind, insisting that the wedding of a duke, especially a Dunbar, should be a much more grand affair.

Nick stood his ground. Only the Marsh family, the Cambournes and Nick's friend, the Earl of Kilmaire, in addition to the Dunbars would attend. Lord Kilmaire had arrived only last night for his stay in London and Jemma had yet to meet him.

Jemma agreed with Nick. She'd no wish to parade herself in front of the *ton* so that they could pick apart and gossip over every aspect of her wedding. She'd no desire to hear their breathy comments as she walked up the aisle. The *ton,* Jemma thought, had no idea what the future would hold with the Duchess of Dunbar in their midst. She loved Nick and had made a solemn oath to use her new influence and power to ensure her husband and future children would never suffer that malicious pack of fools. In that, she had allies, the Marchioness of Cambourne and the Dowager Marchioness.

"I love him and he loves me," she told the tiny wren perched on the edge of a stone birdbath.

Nick was her dearest friend. Her lover. Her companion. He took her to shoot at an exclusive gentleman's club, scandalizing the titled men who frequented that establishment. Striding in with Nick, her wooden box of pistols carried by a footman, she winked at Lord Derby and his son as she took her place next to them. Nick laughed at their discomfort while she bested Lord Derby's every shot.

He took her riding nearly every day in the park. She rode astride, looking down her nose at any who would question her. None did, of course for Nick hovered next to her, daring anyone to challenge his future duchess. She loved him all the more for allowing her to be who she was.

After their ride, Nick would throw down a blanket, and she and Nick would picnic on the thick grass while Anna acted as chaperone on a bench nearby. They spoke of many things, but mostly of his life before their meeting in Bermuda. The Devil of Dunbar entrusted her with himself and his secrets, a gift that reminded Jemma a bit of Pandora's box. She did not take his trust in her lightly.

As she held his hand tightly to her heart while he spoke of his past, she sought to comfort the dark, complicated man she adored. While outwardly mysterious and feared for his reputation and sharp wit in the *ton*, Nick was a different man with those close to him. Rowan especially embraced Nick, often accompanying him to White's to play cards with Lord Cambourne. They dined often with the marquess and his family, and Jemma delighted in the friendship of Lady Miranda, feeling especially proud that the Dowager Marchioness approved of her.

Arabella remained absent from all gatherings, usually pleading a headache. Jemma did not miss her though she knew his sister's continued absence pained Nick.

"I hope he likes the dress," she whispered to a ladybug, thinking of her wedding gown, the last fitting of which was today. The cream-colored gown, shot with brilliants, was meant to be a recreation of the dress she wore the night they met at Lord Corbett's. Jemma giggled. "I can't very well march down the aisle in breeches, can I? Though I suspect Nick would like that."

"I would indeed. I adore you in breeches." Nick stole up behind her and pressed a kiss to her neck.

"Oh." Jemma tripped over a stone at the feel of his lips. She hadn't heard him sneak up on her. "Bloody hell, Nick. How is it possible for such a big man to be so quiet? Stop appearing unannounced."

He caught her deftly by the elbow and pulled her close, kissing her soundly.

"I beg you, Jem, to watch where you walk." Nick looked down on her from his great height, the blue and brown of his mismatched eyes twinkling at her in mischief. "I want you in full command of your limbs for our honeymoon. In fact, I insist upon it. I assume you were so enthralled with thoughts of the vast array of liberties you can take with me once we are wed, that you didn't hear me stalking you."

"You are most full of yourself, Your Grace," Jemma said primly. "I am an innocent girl. I was thinking of the flowers that will grace my bride's bouquet."

"Yes, I forgot your innocence." He pinched her bottom.

Jemma wiggled further into his arms. "Stop that," she chided, looking towards the windows of her uncle's house hopeful no one could see Nick in the garden. "I was thinking of my wedding gown, I've the final fitting today. I cannot wait to wear it for you."

"I cannot wait to take you out of it." He leaned over to press his lips to hers again. "Come let us seek the shelter of yonder bushes lest Lady Marsh find me here."

"Must we obey my aunt?" Jemma said. Aunt Mary declared that she and Nick not see each other for the week before their nuptials, and so Nick resorted to sneaking into the garden every morning. Unfortunately, due to the preparations for the wedding, the garden would be full of tradesmen by teatime today, and Jemma doubted she would see Nick again until he took her arm before the minister.

"Your aunt is very clear that I not see the bride before the wedding, and you are fortunate she has not noticed me sneaking into her garden. Were she to catch us, I fear she would be most unforgiving." He shook his head. "With the manner in which she argues her opinion, Lady Marsh should have been a barrister. It is only for these last two days, love, whilst the tradesmen set up the bower."

"I am beginning to regret agreeing to a garden wedding. Is Lord Kilmaire settled? I'm not sure why he chose to find a town home to let rather than stay at Dunbar house. We will be gone on our honeymoon after all. It would be no bother."

"Colin is looking for a bride." Nick winked. "His chances are slim enough with his reputation. I fear my notoriety, were he to stay with us, would lessen his chances even more. Besides, Colin is a bit of a loner. He's used to living on a large estate by himself. I think he wishes the privacy. He's constantly scribbling notes on bits of paper, though I'm not sure what he uses them for."

"Perhaps he's a writer of sorts or keeps a journal." Jemma

thought Lord Kilmaire sounded as mysterious as Nick himself. "And what does his 'reputation' consist of?" She inhaled the warm male scent of Nick and felt the familiar pool of honey between her thighs. Could anyone see them from the house if they were to disappear behind the lion shaped topiary?

"That is a tale for later." He must have seen her assessing the topiary for he said, "Yes, love, they would certainly see us. We must wait." He cupped her face in his hands, gently pulling her to him with a brush of his lips against hers. "Then we shall be off to the Continent, alone, just the two of us."

Jemma hugged him tight, smiling into his coat. Nick couldn't truly read minds, for if he did, he would certainly know that this would be a wedding trip for three.

"What are you about Jem?" Nick pressed a kiss to the top of her head, sensing she had a secret.

"A wedding gift." She leaned back and brushed a bit of lint off his shoulder, trying to sound nonchalant, lest he guess at her news. "A surprise." While she didn't dare ask anyone, Jemma thought her suspicions correct.

Nick gave her a sideways glance but didn't press her for more. He took her hand in his and proceeded to meander through her uncle's glorious garden, careful to stay out of sight of the house. Every now and then, she would squeeze his fingers tightly and Nick would squeeze back.

"Miss Grantly," Anna called from the back door of the Marsh home. "Are you still out there? Your aunt and cousin have come down. The carriage is waiting."

Jemma could see the red of her maid's hair as the woman put a hand over her eyes to see into the garden.

Nick pressed a kiss to her forehead.

"I don't want you to go," she whispered, suddenly feeling desolate that she would not see him for the next two days.

"Don't be silly. I must see Colin settled."

"Settled? I suspect that the settling will involve a bottle of whisky shared between the Earl of Kilmaire, the Marquess of Cambourne and my cousin. Try not to fleece Rowan of his fortune over cards, please?"

Nick chuckled softly. "Why do you insist that I must cheat at cards? Rowan is a terrible card player and never bets much. Dice is his game. And as for the whisky, I doubt Lord Kilmaire will overindulge. Colin becomes drunk after drinking a teacup full unless his tolerance has changed. And what shall you do?"

"I shall stay in my room tonight with a book, mooning over you." She tried to look demure. "As a dutiful betrothed would for her future husband, though I will miss a visit from my lover."

Nick laughed, and then quickly covered his mouth lest the maid hear him. He had been crawling up the trellis to her room several times each week. "I am just happy that the trellis has remained sturdy. I should applaud the gardener for his construction, perhaps he can pass his knowledge on to the makers of chairs in London."

"Miss?" Anna was now walking down the path.

"I hate to disappoint you, Your Grace, but the trellis has been repaired several times." At Nick's look of surprise, Jemma continued, "I caught Rowan telling the gardener to reinforce it. He's known the entire time and never said a word."

"Your cousin has been consciously aiding your ruination at my hands?" Nick said in mock horror.

"Indeed." She kissed his hand.

"Well, then perhaps I will let him win at cards tonight." Nick nuzzled her neck. "I love you."

"And I you." She lifted her head for a kiss. "Go on. Enjoy yourself. Pray be quiet as you leave so that Anna doesn't see you."

Nick raised her arm to press a kiss to her wrist. "Soon."

She watched his tall form disappear behind the hedges leading to the stables, feeling a bit bereft at his leaving.

"Silly," she muttered. "That I should already miss him. I wonder if Cook has any of those delicious tarts leftover from last night. A bit of chocolate would be most welcome." She waved to Anna who was rapidly approaching.

"I'm here, Anna. Do I have time to change?"

The maid cast a searching look about the garden, frowning as she did so. "I could have sworn I heard the duke." She regarded Jemma with disapproval.

"Don't be silly." Jemma smiled to herself. "You know we aren't to see each other until the wedding."

❧

"I THINK THE GOWN FITS YOU BEAUTIFULLY." PETRA, HER arm linked with Jemma's hugged her tightly. The pair strolled down a path in the park, the watchful coach bearing Aunt Mary and Uncle John close by, but out of hearing.

Jemma enjoyed her cousin's enthusiasm. "Madame Fontaine is an excellent seamstress. I think the duke will be very pleased when he sees me."

Petra laughed. "Pleased is not the word for it, cousin. The *ton* is scandalized by the duke's adoration of you. It's quite unheard of." Petra smiled broadly and gave Jemma another squeeze. "I hope to someday find a gentleman who looks at me the way His Grace looks at you. I quite like him and cannot believe I ever feared him."

"I have no doubt you will find your match," Jemma said to Petra as she turned to wave at her aunt and uncle. She watched as Uncle John tugged on a stray curl that escaped her aunt's coiffure. The gesture caused an instant ache in her for Nick.

"Oh look, there's Lord Bennett." Petra waved at a hand-some young man riding a coffee colored horse that drew aside her parents' carriage. The young man greeted Lord and Lady Marsh warmly before looking over his shoulder at Petra. "I think I'll just say hello. I'll be right back."

Jemma nodded, knowing that Petra favored Lord Bennett. At least for the moment. She moved farther along the path to inspect a particularly lovely bloom, careful to keep within hearing of her aunt and uncle. The name of the flower escaped her. Certainly, it wasn't a rose.

"My lady?" A young boy ran out of the bramble and wood of the park to stand before her. The boy was panting with exertion and sweat beaded his upper lip. "I'm to tell Jem that His Grace wishes you to find him." The boy's voice shook. "You're to follow the path of peonies, my lady."

Peonies. That's what the flowers were called.

More importantly, Nick had found her in the park. Perhaps he had changed his mind about obeying her aunt's restrictions. Was he even now hiding in the thick wood before her?

"My lady?" The boy looked up at her. "I'm to lead you to him."

Jemma slid a glance towards her family and Lord Bennett. "Only for a moment. His Grace should know better." But she was glad he did not for she longed to see Nick again.

The boy nodded nervously and started down a small trail leading into the wood. Beckoning Jemma with one hand he urged her. "He waits."

Jemma gave her aunt and uncle one last glance before following the boy. The trail twisted from the main path as the boy led her deeper into a wooded thicket. She turned around but could no longer see her uncle's carriage nor hear Petra's tinkling laugh as her cousin flirted with Lord Bennett.

"Where is the duke?" she said to the boy, leaning forward to catch the back of his coat.

The boy twisted out of her hands and ran further ahead before disappearing into a large thicket.

"Why I'm right here." A voice came from behind her just as a sweet-smelling cloth came over her mouth and nose. Jemma struggled against the arms holding her and turned her head trying to get away from the cloth, but the man held the fabric firmly against her nose.

She struggled, realizing too late that the message did not come from Nick. Twisting and turning, she tried to gasp at fresh air even as the lids of her eyes threatened to close. All strength left her body, and she slid into the arms of the man holding her. She felt herself sag against him as he lifted her, limp as a rag doll. Bleary eyed she tried to focus on her surroundings, the wood around her fading, but not enough that she didn't recognize the face that hovered above hers.

Augie smiled down at her. "Hello, Jemma."

❧ 24 ❧

Rowan walked up the steps of the Dunbar town house, pausing only to rap at the door with his walking stick. As he waited for the door to open, a carriage bearing the Cambourne coat of arms pulled up. A footman opened a shiny black door to help the stunningly beautiful occupant, Lady Miranda, sister of the Marquess of Cambourne, exit the carriage.

Rowan bowed politely to her as the Cambourne footman escorted her up the steps. The smell of lavender and honey preceded Lady Miranda, a light feminine scent that instantly caused Rowan to smile in appreciation. Rowan had met Lady Miranda several times and even led her into dinner once at the Marquess of Cambourne's. Not only was she beautiful, but pleasant and clever to boot, being knowledgeable on a variety of subjects. He could not countenance that the sweet woman who stood next to him waiting for entrance was the closest friend of the ill-tempered Lady Arabella.

"Good day, Lord Malden." She addressed him by his courtesy title, her dark green eyes were friendly as she waited for her footman to rap sharply on the door. "I assume you have been invited so that my brother and his friends can best you at cards?"

"Undoubtedly." Rowan gave a shrug. "But they will have a tough time doing so as I am a terrible card player and aware of my failing, thus I do not gamble much. I fear they will be sorely disappointed as they will win only enough from me to purchase a tart from a street vendor."

Lady Miranda laughed, a light airy sound that reminded Rowan of tinkling bells. Why this woman remained unwed mystified him. He'd heard the gossip of course but refused to believe Lady Miranda capable of such a thing.

An elderly butler opened the door, his lips twisting in annoyance as he spied Rowan, then he turned to Lady Miranda and his face softened.

"Lady Miranda, welcome. Lady Arabella will be down in a moment. Please come in."

The butler turned to Rowan pursing his lips. "Lord Malden, His Grace awaits you in the study."

Handing her cloak to a waiting servant, Miranda raised a carefully plucked brow at Rowan. "Ignore Peabody. He has an aversion to new people."

A rustle of skirts caught Rowan's attention. He turned to see Lady Arabella coming down the grand staircase. Her face was soft and light with no trace of her usual stern manner, allowing Rowan and anyone else who saw her to see how lovely she really was. Beautiful in fact. His heart skipped a beat. And good God, she was actually *smiling*

But not at him.

"Hello Miranda. I've tea waiting in the drawing room. I thought we'd indulge in one of Cook's scones before we—" Arabella's forehead wrinkled in consternation as she noticed Rowan standing just inside the door. Grimacing in annoyance at his appearance, her entire demeanor changed. "What are *you* doing here?" The irritated words echoed in the foyer.

Shaking out her somber, pewter colored skirts, Lady Arabella flounced down the remaining steps. "Don't tell me my brother has invited *you?*" She rolled her eyes, sounding as if His Grace were half mad at inviting Rowan to the house.

"Bella." Lady Miranda smoothed down her skirts and shot Rowan a look under her lashes. "Of course he was invited, else he would not be here." Her tone was soothing and even. "Don't be foolish."

"Lady Arabella." Rowan bowed. *Rude, waspish woman.* He tried to keep his tone polite and failed. "How lovely to see you." Sarcasm dripped from every word. It was incredibly poor manners to speak so to the sister of a duke, but Lady Arabella exasperated Rowan to no end. Why couldn't the woman at least be courteous, like Lady Miranda?

Lady Arabella immediately stiffened at Rowan's tone, her eyes narrowing. Turning her back to him as if he were beneath her notice, she headed into the drawing room. "Come, Miranda."

Lady Miranda walked past Rowan and said quietly under her breath, "Very good, Lord Malden. Arabella does not suffer fools. Do not give up."

Lady Arabella turned as she entered the drawing room, glaring at Rowan over her friend's shoulder.

"Enjoy your tea." He winked at Lady Arabella and was satisfied to see her flinch at his forwardness. *Good.* He hoped she was annoyed beyond words.

"This way, my lord," Peabody intoned, motioning Rowan to follow him down a long hallway lit by a perfect line of wall sconces. The hall was decorated with small Roman busts and several large portraits of men and women in a variety of fashions. The Devils of Dunbar, he surmised, noting that several of the people in the portraits bore mismatched eyes, much like the duke.

Rowan stopped, his attention riveted on a particularly

large portrait, a painting so tall it took up nearly the entire wall. A big man, dressed as if he meant to go to battle, leaned against an apple tree. The man's hands lay on the hilt of a large broadsword and a battle-axe lay near his feet. The man's hair shown a dark auburn as did his goatee. An L-shaped white house sat in the distance, and Rowan could just make out a woman and several children who seemed to be walking across the expanse of lawn towards the man. Something about the commanding, fierce way in which the man stood reminded Rowan of the current duke.

"The first Duke of Dunbar, Robyn Tremaine," Peabody informed him. "His Grace favors him."

"Indeed." Rowan walked past the painting and deeper into the house, marveling at the number of doors and the size of the Dunbar town home.

Peabody paused before a dark paneled door. He rapped his knuckles against the wood, and not waiting for instruction, threw open the door. "Lord Malden."

The three men in the room all looked up at Rowan at the same time. A bottle of whisky sat on the table before them along with a pair of dice.

"Peabody," the Marquess of Cambourne welcomed the butler. "I'm starving. Can you see about a tray of—" he looked at the duke who shrugged carelessly. "Something? Cakes? Some roast left over from last night?"

"We had pheasant," the deep baritone of the duke informed him.

"Very well, pheasant." Cambourne shook his head. "Really Nick, one would expect a much more robust repast than *pheasant* at a duke's home. Perhaps a meat pie?" He looked at Peabody hopefully.

Rowan smiled, feeling instantly at ease. He liked the scandalous marquess, having met Cambourne at White's for the first time while in the company of the duke. At the time, he'd been curious about Cambourne's reputed dragon tattoo, which the *ton* twittered about endlessly, especially the ladies. Rowan had yet to meet a female who was immune to Cambourne's charms, but the man was notoriously faithful to his wife.

Another man sat between Cambourne and an empty seat, which Rowan took to be his. The man's coloring was fair, his dark blond hair standing out clearly between the darker heads of Cambourne and the duke. He gestured to the space beside him. A scar, starkly white and puckered ran the length of the left side of the man's face.

There was no mistaking this man's identity as the *ton* gossiped about him as well. Rowan often heard him referred to as *cursed*. If the rumors were true, his mother had given him that awful scar. The Earl of Kilmaire.

"Malden." The duke welcomed him with a broad smile. "Sit man." A crystal glass full of whisky immediately appeared in his hand. "I believe you know Cambourne."

Rowan nodded in greeting to the marquess. "A pleasure to see you again, my lord."

"Cam." Cambourne lifted his glass to Rowan in toast. "My friends call me Cam."

Kilmaire gave a short laugh. "Or Satan Reynolds. I'm rather disappointed I don't have such a frightening nickname. I find it quite unfair. After all, I look much more dangerous," he ran a fingertip down the scar, "than you. I had to tolerate the incessant chatter at Lord Swit's dinner last night. His wife and her friends lamenting over your angelic good looks nearly made me ill before dessert was served."

Cambourne glared at his friend. "Do shut up, Colin."

"I am Kilmaire." He completely disregarded Cambourne's annoyance. "Do you possess a scandalous past or perhaps a terrifying nickname? One must if you are to sit at this table."

The dark eyes twinkled. "All the ones referring to Old Scratch are taken, so we'll need to come up with something else."

"He does not. Malden is my betrothed's cousin." The duke rolled the dice. "You have been so kind, Malden, in your attention to your father's garden, particularly the trellis, I thought we would start with dice tonight."

Rowan tried not to look too surprised that the duke had found him out.

His Grace lifted his glass in a silent toast to Rowan, nodding as he did so.

"It is a shame that you lack a shocking distinction, but there is still time," Kilmaire continued, speaking to Rowan as he took up the dice. "There are plenty of wicked things in London." The scar gleamed a stark white against his lightly tanned skin as he quirked his lips. "So perhaps you will cause a scandal and thus receive a nickname. You are in the right company, after all, for such to happen."

"So, I am given to understand." Rowan chuckled, taking his seat. His mother, of course, knew all the gossip. Horrified to the core that her son would spend the evening carousing with a trio that the *ton* referred to as The Wickeds sent her to her bed early. "I was an ill-mannered child so perhaps I just need a bit more time to do something dreadful."

Kilmaire burst into laughter, handing Rowan the dice. "I believe it's your turn, Malden."

❦ 25 ❦

Jemma was running, running across the bluff behind Sea Cliff, trying to get away from Augie. Her dress was torn, and she kept tripping over rocks in her path, lamenting as she lost her shoe. Desperate to find Nick, she called for him over and over to find her. Then Augie appeared, standing over her, grabbing her by the elbow. Terrified, she tried to push him away but her arms wouldn't move.

"I see you are finally waking up. Goodness, I feared he'd put too much on the cloth and you were dead. That wouldn't do us any good now would it?"

The lids of Jemma's eyes felt as if they were weighted and her temples ached. Struggling to open her eyes, she made to rub them and found her hands firmly bound at her sides. She tried to speak but something foul tasting had been shoved into her mouth. Terror gripped her as she remembered the trail at the park. The man's voice.

Augie.

Struggling against the ropes at her wrists, she blinked in an effort to clear her vision.

"That won't do you any good, I've tied them extra tight." A voice mocked, a voice she recognized.

Slowly, and with much effort, she opened her eyes. A dimly lit room greeted her along with a fetid odor as if there were rotting fish nearby. A lone candle sat on a small table next to what Jemma took to be a bed but more resembled a large, lumpy mattress covered by a filthy looking coverlet. Peeling wallpaper hung from one corner, though the room was too dark for her to make out the pattern. She heard the tinkling of a piano somewhere below her as a woman began singing off-key in a raspy voice. The aroma of sour wine reached her nostrils as the sound of a woman's skirts came from behind her.

"You were so busy thinking about *that man*," the wine-laden whisper said, "that you followed that boy without question. Lord, you are like a bitch in heat and stupid as well." Lady Corbett rounded the chair in which Jemma sat.

Jemma struggled more fiercely against her bindings. My God, Lady Corbett and Augie were both in here, in London.

The Governor's wife, resplendent in a plum colored taffeta gown shot through with silver threads, looked as if she were about to attend the opera or perhaps a ball, rather than participating in abduction.

Curling her lip, Lady Corbett peered down at Jemma. "So blind to your lust for that man, I could have told you to hop a ship to the Indies and you'd do it if you thought he awaited you. George will be so distressed to find out that the Devil of Dunbar still lives. He was so very certain that he was dead."

She paced back and forth in front of Jemma as if attempting to solve a difficult problem. The black jet earrings hanging from her ears whipped against her neck as she shook her head. "Of course, the knowledge that he failed may just give George that final fit of apoplexy. One can only hope."

Still surprised by Lady Corbett's appearance, Jemma

tried to make sense of the woman before her. All her life, Lady Corbett had been motherly, meddling and if Jemma were honest, a bit of a dimwit. Certainly, Jemma had been hurt to know the Corbetts' affections were less for her than for Sea Cliff, but she never suspected they were this desperate.

Jemma tried to spit the gag out of her mouth and failed.

"Oh, do stop wiggling around, Jane Emily." Lady Corbett stopped pacing and stared at her. "You'll wear yourself out and not have the energy for your upcoming nuptials."

Jemma shut her eyes, willing herself to wake up from this terrible dream. She'd always considered Lady Corbett to be no more than a nuisance and Augie a weak-willed gambler who coveted her father's estate. After what happened in Hamilton, she thought them capable of many things, but kidnapping?

"You were always so full of sass. It's unfortunate you couldn't have been more like my darling Dorthea. She did what she was told, even though it meant marrying a second son, but I had a plan for her, just as I have for you. Peter's elder brother is consumptive and won't last too many more winters and my Dorthea will be a Countess." Lady Corbett placed a finger against her chin. "That will be lovely."

The matter of fact way in which Lady Corbett spoke of her husband's fate and that of her son-in-law's brother chilled Jemma to the bone. *How could I have known her my entire life and not suspect her true nature?*

Lady Corbett continued to pace back and forth across the scarred wooden floor of the room, her fingers flying around as she spoke, whether to herself or Jemma, Jemma wasn't sure.

"I suppose we'll have to keep you bound and gagged all the way back to Bermuda. I've already told the minister that you're simple and have fits. That you may pose a danger to yourself and others. I'm sure he won't find it surprising that you can't recite your vows. I've paid him enough not to care, at any rate."

Bermuda. My God, she means to take me to Bermuda?

Fear, the likes of which Jemma had never known, shot through her. She struggled madly, feeling the bite of the ropes into her wrists. Wet warmth seeped across her skin as blood coursed from the wounds.

Lady Corbett stopped and leaned over, her eyes wild. "Stupid, headstrong girl. I've told you that it's quite useless." Curling tendrils of faded red hair spilled about the side of Lady Corbett's cheeks and forehead, the tiny hairs standing on end, giving her the look of an agitated bird. "All of Hamilton was quite shocked at your death. Quite shocked. None, more than Lord Corbett and myself. Why, we searched everywhere for you as did everyone on the island. What a dirty, nasty, trick you played on us. We mourned, we Corbetts." She snickered. "But we mourned the loss of Sea Cliff even more. We were so close." She shook her head sadly, and then she straightened, a hard look coming into her eyes. "It was Tally, wasn't it?"

Jemma shook her head vehemently in denial.

"Don't lie, dear. That maid of yours, Mercy? She wasn't smart enough to assist you, nor was Mrs. Stanhope. No, it must have been Tally. He likely absconded with the account books as well. We haven't been able to find them."

Tally would never allow the Corbetts to force her to marry Augie. If they succeeded in taking her to Bermuda, Tally would be there.

"I see what you're thinking, dear girl. That Mr. O'Dell will assist you again." Her voice hardened. "But he is no longer in Hamilton. Gone and no one knows where. Possibly my husband had him killed and forgot to tell me."

Jemma's heart sank. She prayed with all her might that Tally was alive and safe.

"It's of no matter, at any rate, for you will still marry my darling son. Now, I realize you've been behaving like a trollop, dear, but I think marriage to Augie will cure you."

Jemma tried desperately to spit the gag out of her mouth and began to retch.

"Now stop that or you shan't be able to breathe." At Jemma's continued gasping, she sighed. "You are probably thirsty." Lady Corbett changed her demeanor to one of motherly concern. "I would prefer you be conscious for your wedding, of course, that will make it so much easier. Now, don't you dare make a sound, or I'll have to give you more ether." She pointed to a small brown bottle on the table. "Though I sincerely doubt it would matter if you do scream. I can't imagine anyone would come to your aid in this house. I'm told screams are quite common." The gag was pulled back and a cup of tepid water was pressed to Jemma's lips.

Jemma gulped the water greedily, ignoring the tinny taste. She took a deep breath. "No one in Hamilton will believe—"

"Oh my! Do you really assume I will let you actually speak to anyone in Bermuda?" Lady Corbett made an awful braying sound. "Really? Oh, my, no. I'll tell them all that we found you, living in the streets here in London like a beggar when we came to visit Dorthea. Augie and I were shocked. Just shocked. You lost your mind, dear, after William died, and stowed aboard a ship bound for England. No one will question me when I lock you in your room, permanently, for your own safety of course."

Jemma swallowed. "You can't be serious," she whispered. "Listen to me, if you want Sea Cliff, take it. I don't want it." A sob escaped her. "The estate is tainted, bought with blood money." Her heart beat rapidly in her chest. If only she could persuade Lady Corbett to let her go. "I'll sign it over. It will be yours."

"But we can't, dear. Not without you. The estate only goes

to you as a dowry, otherwise it will revert to the Crown. William," she made a clucking sound with her tongue, "made certain that no one but *you* would have Sea Cliff. We didn't realize, of course, until *after*."

"After what?" Jemma shook her head fiercely. "It doesn't matter. I don't want it. I'll write out that I want the estate to be yours. Just untie me and I'll write out a letter," she said eagerly. "We can go directly to the Meechum & Sons, my father's solicitors."

"Poor William," Lady Corbett continued as if Jemma hadn't spoken. "If he had just done as we asked and married you to Augie, none of this," she threw her arms wide, "would have happened. He'd still be alive. But you decided to fuck that man. That devil."

Jemma recoiled in shock at the foul words coming from Lady Corbett's mouth. She'd never even heard the woman raise her voice before, much less curse.

"I came to England prepared to beg Dorthea to assist me. Possibly sell a jewel or two that Peter's given her. George's family is near destitute themselves and weren't any help." She peered at Jemma with a maniacal smile on her lips. "I can't tell you how surprised I was to find Dunbar alive and well. I nearly choked on my tea. Thank goodness Lady Arabella was there to console me."

"Lady Arabella?" Jemma whispered, her stomach falling.

"Oh, my yes. That dear girl was an enormous help. She does hate you *so*." Lady Corbett's eyes lit up. "So much that she couldn't wait to tell us where your uncle lived and what hour you typically walked in the park. I explained everything to her. That you are addled and betrothed to Augie, so you couldn't possibly marry her brother. I told her of your humble origins, what with your mother a chambermaid and all." Lady Corbett tapped her temple. "Oh, and I may have mentioned that your father betrayed the Crown and allowed her family to shoulder the blame. Why after hearing that, Lady Arabella fairly jumped at the chance to reunite you and Augie."

Jemma shuddered against the chair. *I never expected that the Corbetts would come to London, never spared a thought that I would see them again. Foolishly I thought they would forget about me. Who would have guessed that Lady Corbett would cross paths with the one person whose hate for me matches their own?*

"How," she choked, "did you come to know Lady Arabella?"

The woman before her giggled and twirled about. "Oh, it was because of the orphans you see. Dorthea does love to take care of strays and such. I must say, I managed to keep from fainting, first after finding out that man was still alive and then you as well. My goodness, I thought I would have a fit of apoplexy just like poor George, but when I calmed myself and considered it, I realized my coming to London and finding you was God's providence."

Jem. That's what my brother calls you. Only Arabella could have given the Corbetts that name, the name that only Nick used for her. How Arabella must despise her to assist the Corbetts.

"Wake up." Lady Corbett smacked the open palm of her hand against Jemma's cheek.

Her eyes immediately snapped open, the pain beating away the last of the fogginess from her brain. Tears welled in her eyes and threatened to spill down her cheeks. *She is insane; perhaps she's always been. How could I not see that?*

"William did *love* his teacakes." Lady Corbett fluttered about the room discarding the previous conversation. "He couldn't wait to eat them, the cakes I made *especially* for him." She laughed maniacally, dancing a bit on her toes. "Teacakes. That's what you get when you marry a *servant*, a little Irish *slut*, instead of a lady." Lady Corbett shrugged. "I never did care for your mother, Jane Emily. She thought too much of herself. What a relief that she died in childbirth. *She* loved my teacakes as well. George and I were delighted when she expired."

What the woman implied was so evil Jemma could barely form the thought, let alone the words. Her mind refused to consider the possibility, it was so *horrific* that her parents' dearest friends had not been their friends at all. She had to know. "What are you saying?"

"Haven't you been listening?" Lady Corbett fisted her hand and hit Jemma again, this time across the nose. "See what you made me do? I'll have to tell the minister you became violent and I had to subdue you."

Jemma saw stars for an instant before a flood of something warm and wet spurted from her nose. Her entire face ached. Drops of blood dotted the lap of her gown. "Did you kill—" She choked, the words to horrifying to say a loud.

Lady Corbett rolled her eyes in exasperation. "Well, of course I *did*. Haven't you been listening? They both *loved* my teacakes.

❦

THE EARL OF MARSH SLID UP AGAINST THE LEATHER SQUABS of his carriage as the Marsh coachman took a sharp turn in his haste to reach Dunbar House. John pounded the top of his cane against the roof. "It'll do us no good if the coach overturns in your haste."

The coach slowed, but only slightly.

John placed one hand on the window frame and hung on for dear life as his coachman navigated the busy London streets. His stomach flip-flopped as much from the ride as from the news he had for the duke. How do you tell the Devil of Dunbar that his bride has gone missing while in *your* care?

The coach slowed to a halt and John fairly leapt out to

land on the steps to the duke's town home. When Jane Emily disappeared from sight at the park, they'd all assumed she'd merely wandered off the path, after all, the lass had been wandering about dreamy-eyed for the last few weeks since she and the duke had come to an understanding. Still, Jane Emily was not a silly girl, and not without skills. He knew for a fact that His Grace took her shooting often, something John did not share with his wife. Certainly, she would not be so foolish as to allow herself to be set upon and taken. But, apparently, she *had*.

Impatiently, he pounded on the door, worry for his niece causing him to disregard all politeness.

"Yes?" A slightly pompous, elderly butler greeted him.

John barely spared the man a glance. "I am Lord Marsh. Where is His Grace?" he said loudly into the hall. "I must speak to him immediately. It is a matter of the utmost urgency regarding my niece, Jane Emily."

The butler's eyes widened at hearing Jane Emily's name. "Of course, my lord, this way."

John followed closely behind the butler through the length of the Dunbar hallway, marveling that the older man could move so swiftly.

The butler stopped before a pair of large wooden doors from which the sound of revelry could be heard. He rapped once, and then opened the doors.

Four men lounged on several enormous, overstuffed chairs. John recognized all of them, especially his son Rowan, who sat up immediately as his father entered, a cheroot dangling from his fingers.

The duke had been telling a joke, or so it appeared from the look of laughter in the group's eyes, but he stopped mid sentence when he saw John. Instantly, the look of amusement fled from the duke's face, and the odd eyes narrowed danger-ously. "What is it?"

John swallowed. He had forgotten how menacing His Grace could be for the duke had been kindness itself to the Marsh family since the betrothal, but the man he looked at now was not the laughing dinner guest who bantered with his niece and complimented his wife's table. There was a reason the *ton* feared him.

"What is it?" The whiskey-laden voice said again.

"She's gone," John choked out. "Jane Emily. She's disappeared."

※

Nick thought for a moment he had misheard the earl, and so he had asked the question again. He heard a buzzing noise in his ears and a sickening feeling crawled across his chest. "What?"

Lord Marsh wobbled to a free chair and sat. "We've looked everywhere, Your Grace." The earl pressed a handkerchief to his brow, clearly distraught. "After visiting the dressmakers, we stopped for tea. We were in the park. She—"

"When?" Nick strived to keep his voice calm. He told himself to breathe. But that horrible darkness that had visited him when he thought Jem was dead reappeared, threatening to choke him.

"Not more than an hour or so. I've men still searching for her, walking through the bramble and the wood." He shook his head. "Lord Bennett rode over to speak to Lady Marsh and myself. Jane Emily and Petra were strolling the path before us, well within our sight." He shook his head. "Petra wished to say hello to Bennett and left her cousin on the path. Jane Emily was following a trail of peonies. The park was full of people." His hands twisted over his cane. "We looked away only for an instant. Only an instant." His voice broke. "Why would anyone take Jane Emily?"

Rowan stood and walked over to stand behind his father, laying his hand on Lord Marsh's shoulder in an attempt to comfort the older man. "Your Grace—" Rowan started.

Nick forced himself to breathe. The tips of his fingers went cold and his heart beat erratically. Bits of conversations ran through his mind at lightening speed, one in particular standing out. A conversation he should have paid closer attention to, but she'd made him *so* angry.

"Peabody."

The butler immediately stood at attention. "Your Grace, what do you require?"

"My sister. Has she returned?" Nick's body was taut. *Arabella*. Every instinct screamed aloud that his sister had something to do with Jem's disappearance.

"Yes, Your Grace. I believe she and Lady Miranda arrived home a short time ago. They are in the drawing room with several dozen boxes of hats. A moment." Peabody whirled and disappeared, moving with unusual speed for a man so old.

Lord Marsh looked to Nick, anxiety etched across his features. "You must find her. Please," he implored. "She is all I have left of my brother. I love her as if she were my own."

"Yes, Your Grace?" Arabella came through the doorway and gave her brother an impudent lift of her chin in response to his summons. She calmly clasped her hands before her and waited.

Miranda followed, a question on her lovely face. She nodded briefly to her brother and Rowan, hesitating for a moment at the sight of Colin.

Nick watched Arabella closely—she looked a bit smug and exceedingly proud of herself. He doubted it was over a stylish new hat she'd bought.

"What has happened, Your Grace?" Arabella clasped her hands tighter, but her face remained bland, her tone a polite inquiry.

"My cousin has gone missing," Rowan said roughly. "She has disappeared."

Arabella's right hand twitched and she quickly hid it in her skirts.

Nick saw the slight movement. That's when he knew.

"I beg you all, leave us," he hissed, barely able to stop himself from rushing towards Arabella and shaking her.

Colin stood, his eyes on Nick but only nodded his head. "We'll wait in the drawing room." He made his way over to Miranda, hesitated, then took her elbow.

"Whatever you need." Cam squeezed his shoulder.

Lord Marsh stood and allowed Rowan to lead him to the door.

A flicker of fear crossed his sister's features as the group exited the room, but then she composed herself. "Has Jane Emily finally run off?" She smiled sweetly, ignoring the outraged gasp of Rowan who had not quite cleared the room. "I did warn you Nick."

"I saw her just this morning." Nick kept his eyes on Arabella. "I know we aren't supposed to see each other before the wedding, but I snuck into the garden. She said she had a surprise for me." He saw Rowan move back into the room out of the corner of his eye.

"Well, she most certainly did, brother." Arabella shot him a look of concern, but there was something else in her gaze. *Triumph*. "Though I'm not surprised in the least that she's left you."

"Leave?" Rowan sputtered, looking at Arabella with disdain. "How dare you. My cousin would never do such a thing."

"Of course, *you* would defend her," Arabella hissed. "Lord knows, your family is *nothing* if not *honorable*."

Nick felt the blood leave his face. "Rowan, shut the door." How horrible it was to watch someone you loved betray you for his or her own ends. How had Bella found out? How could she possibly know?

"What have you done?" Nick said to Arabella before turning to Rowan. "Stay. Sit. If only to keep me from throttling my sister."

Settling into a nearby chair, Rowan regarded Nick with confusion. "As you wish, Your Grace."

A vein pulsed in Arabella's temple as her hands fluttered out and landed on the top of a paisley patterned sofa. She wavered a bit, hearing the ferocity of his tone but stood firm.

Nick set his glass down on the table before him and stood to face his sister.

She lifted her head bravely, but after one look at Nick's face, her gaze fell to her hands and she clung to the back of the sofa.

"She is a charlatan," his sister said under her breath, the tremor in her voice apparent. "She has played you false."

"Liar." Rowan nearly jumped out of his chair, but Nick's raised hand stayed him.

"I never told you, Bella," he said softly, "that Jem *had* a suitor in Bermuda. Earlier today, when we argued, you mentioned such, and you made reference to Jem's mother, which I also never told you about. Then there is the matter of our family's honor. I believe you called my intended's father a *traitor*."

Rowan made a gasp of surprise. "What are you talking about?" His voice shook. "Why would you say such a—" His mouth shut tightly as he looked at Nick expectantly.

Arabella had gone deathly pale. Her lips parted slightly as she watched him approach her. She blinked, her pupils dilated with fear, no longer triumphant.

"Tell me, sister, how you came to learn those things about my future wife." He kept his tone intentionally light, hoping he would not shake his beloved sister to death in front of Rowan. "What did you do?"

"Nothing." Arabella's voice shook and her eyes welled with tears. "I've set things to right, that's all I've done. She was already promised to another man, Nick. And after what that family," she said, pointing at Rowan, "has done to ours, I cannot even countenance your desire to marry her. She is unworthy of your affections."

Rowan rose, about to defend the Marsh family when Nick turned on him violently. "Sit."

Rowan nodded and sat. His fingers clutched at the arms of the chair. The look in his eyes as he watched Arabella was murderous.

"*She* told me everything. All the things you kept from me, brother." Arabella's voice shook. "*She* just wanted to return Jane Emily to her proper place, her *home*, with the man she is promised to. I did this for you, to keep you from making a terrible mistake." Arabella's chest heaved with emotion. "That you will regret."

"You thought to make this choice for me? You have no idea what you have done." He thundered at her and lurched forward.

Arabella cowered before him, her hands shielding her face as if Nick would strike her. "I only wanted to save you from making a mistake," she said, arguing back. "I do not mean her to come to harm."

"You meant nothing *but* harm." His heart beat wildly in his chest.

"I saw them," Rowan said quietly from his spot in the chair, looking directly at Arabella. "And I saw *you*. I wondered why you behaved so oddly."

Arabella shook her head wildly. "You know nothing. Preposterous."

"Where?" Nick turned to Rowan so fiercely his friend

shrank back in into the chair. The Corbetts. It had to be. There was no one else in all the world who wished Jem harm.

"On Bond Street." Rowan sat up. "A little over a week ago. A woman with faded red hair and a slender gentleman, much younger, with brown hair." He looked at Nick. "Who are they?"

"The reason your cousin fled Bermuda," Nick hissed, not bothering to hide the disgust in his voice as he turned to Arabella. "I cannot bear the sight of you. If anything happens to Jem, *anything,* you will spend the rest of your days at Twinings where you can wallow in your bitterness till your heart's content. Do you hear me, Arabella?" He was yelling now and didn't care who heard him. Arabella had given Jem over to the Corbetts. Nick thought quickly, for every moment would count.

Bermuda. They would try to take her to Bermuda so they could claim that damned estate.

"Get from my *sight!*" He bellowed at his sister.

The door to the study burst open to reveal Cam, Colin and Miranda, with Peabody hovering in the background. They'd been listening at the door and doubtless heard every word that was said.

Nick never looked away from his sister, whose face had collapsed into sheer terror as tears ran down her cheeks. "Cam, please take my sister to your home and keep her there until arrangements can be made for her immediate departure to Wales. She will be leaving London."

"Nick." Arabella sobbed. "Please. I beg you."

"If *any* harm has come to Jem, *sister*, your banishment will be permanent." He turned away, unable to bear the sight of his sister for one more moment. His heart ached with misery over her deceit.

"I'm sorry. Please—" Arabella wailed. She tried to pluck at his coat sleeves. "Don't send me away."

"Get her from my sight," he growled over his shoulder. "I wish her far away from me."

Miranda stepped forward and Arabella immediately turned to hide her face in her friend's shoulder. "Come, Bella. You're to come home with me until things are sorted out with Jemma. We'll send for your things." She wrapped her arm about Arabella's shaking shoulders. "I'll take care of her, Your Grace," Miranda murmured as she led Arabella away.

Cam gave him a stricken look. "Are you sure, Nick?" He shot a look through the doorway where the sounds of Arabella's sobbing could still be heard. "Wales?"

"I trust you to make the arrangements, Cam. And I trust," he nodded to the doors, "in your and Miranda's utmost discretion."

"Of course." Worry furrowed his friend's brow.

His mind was racing over where the Corbetts could have taken Jem. He had underestimated them and their lust for Sea Cliff, yet again. Nick's solicitor, Hotchkins had finally left Bermuda several months ago, after buying up all of Augie Corbett's markers and calling them due, effectively bankrupting the family. After that, Lord Corbett's health had failed, and Nick thought the Corbetts would fade into the past. He'd not considered Lady Corbett a threat, but apparently her greed for Sea Cliff and its wealth was equal to Lord Corbett's. Happy, for the first time in his life, he'd let his guard down and that viper and her son were in London.

"My father knows, doesn't he?" Rowan looked as if he'd been punched. "About Jemma. About the treason."

"Yes." He clasped his friend on the shoulder to stop him from peppering him with questions. "Not now. Later. I promise."

Rowan nodded. "We must find her."

"If they mean to take her back to Bermuda, they'll need a ship," Colin surmised.

Nick nodded in agreement. "Lady Corbett and her son must know I would come for her, which means leaving England immediately for Bermuda. I doubt they'd try for another port, neither of them know England well enough." He thought rapidly. "Cam, please send someone to Yorkshire to watch the household of Dorthea Jennings, just in case they try to go there. And Augustus Corbett is a gambler, perhaps someone has played cards or diced with him during his visit."

Cam nodded. "I'll check the usual establishments myself. Should I find anything, I'll send word here." He turned swiftly, shouting commands to Peabody to bring several young boys from the stables and scullery to serve as messengers.

"Thank you." Nick braced himself for the worst. Would Augie try to marry her here or wait until they were aboard ship? If Corbett touched Jem, Nick would tear the man apart with his bare hands.

Colin poured a whisky and pushed it into Nick's hand. "How many of the ships sitting at the wharf are yours, and how many are bound to New York or Bermuda? There can only be a handful that are due to leave this time of year." He motioned to the glass of whisky. "Drink up, man. We'll find her."

Nick downed the glass in two swallows, allowing the warmth of the whisky to fill him before speaking. "There are only three and two of them are mine. I doubt Corbett and his mother have any idea that I own a fleet of ships, let alone that they've likely booked passage on one."

"Won't they be surprised, then?" Colin nodded grimly, gripping a cheroot, between his teeth and putting a match to it. "I'll have the carriage brought round." Colin reached into the inside of his coat and pulled out a wicked looking knife and shot Rowan a look. "You've a weapon, Malden?"

Rowan's eyes widened slightly at the sight of the knife.

"No." He nodded towards the blade. "You carry that around with you?"

"I'm Irish. Or at least partially. We're a suspicious lot." He shrugged and pushed the knife back inside the pocket of his coat. "Besides, London is a dangerous place."

Nick drew a large knife and two pistols from his desk drawer. He slid the knife into his boot and held one pistol out to Rowan. "You're coming, aren't you?"

"Of course." Rowan took the pistol, his face hard. "I expect you will tell me the particulars regarding treason and kidnapping on our way to the wharf."

Nick nodded and strode through the open study door, Colin and Rowan on his heels. "I'll tell you everything, once Jem is safe."

❧ 26 ❧

Jemma kicked out with her foot as hard as she could, satisfied to hear a grunt of pain as she caught Lady Corbett in the shin. The chair moved forward with the force of her efforts. *She killed my father. She killed my mother.* The words thundered in her head. Jemma kicked out again, unmindful of her own safety, not caring about anything but injuring the vile woman who stood before her.

"You little bitch." Lady Corbett's hands went around Jemma's neck, her thumbs digging into the tender flesh. "I'm glad I killed William. He would have been nothing without me. *I* told George about the bloody packet. *Me.* I knew the value of that document and the small fortune its contents would bring." She sprayed Jemma with bits of spittle as she spoke. "I thought William meant for *us* to be together and I could leave George, but instead he set up that Irish chambermaid as the lady of Sea Cliff. Your father grew rich while George squandered our share, and I could do *nothing*. Then I saw another way to finally have what was due me—Sea Cliff, and you ruined it!" She tightened her fingers.

Jemma couldn't breathe. She kicked and twisted, trying to

break Lady Corbett's hold, but to no avail. Spots danced before her eyes as she gasped for air.

"Mother." The door flew open.

Jemma struggled to turn her head and speak as Augie appeared before her. His clothes were rumpled and his cravat was loose, the ends fluttering about his neck. The dark hair of his head stood up in spikes as if he'd been raking his hands through it. "What do you think you're doing?" His eyes held a hunted look.

Shocked at her son's sudden entrance, Lady Corbett's grip loosened. "Augustus. Where have you been?"

Coughing, she gulped in the fetid air as Lady Corbett's hands fell from her neck. "Augie," she implored. "Please untie me. Please help me."

Augie snorted, his eyes filled with distaste as he looked down at her. "Surely, you jest. Why would I help you? You are the cause of all my ills."

Lady Corbett danced around her son. "Where is the minister?" A beatific smile crossed her features as she leaned to look behind Augie. "I can't wait for all of Bermuda to see you married. Once we have Sea Cliff, perhaps produce a child just in case someone tries to challenge our claim, you can throw her from the rocks." Her face fell as she realized Augie was alone. "But where is he? Did you instruct him to meet us onboard? That's very clever of you, dear one. He can serve as a witness once we reach Bermuda."

Jemma tried to kick out again with her heel and missed.

"A child? Marry?" Augie's lips quirked into a sad smile. "I'm sorry to disappoint you, Mother, but there's been a change in plans." His lips curled into a cruel sneer. "I fear your scheme has little chance for success. I stopped at White's for a drink after finding a minister willing to perform the ceremony, and the place was rife with gossip over the Devil of Dunbar's incredible lust." He gestured at Jemma.

"For *her*. The *ton* is incredulous. You led me to believe that the duke was only marrying her out of a misguided sense of duty. I decided to stay for one more hand of cards when who should appear but the Marquess of Cambourne, the duke's closest friend. Do you know who he was looking for Mother? Me. I am fortunate that he didn't see me as I ran for the door."

Lady Corbett's mouth gaped open like a fish. "Darling—" she tried to stroke Augie's arm.

Augie shrugged off his mother. "I've no desire to perish at the hands of the Devil of Dunbar. You see, I've heard the things he's done. He'll come for her. If I were to be stupid enough to marry her, he would widow her in a thrice."

"But—" Lady Corbett sputtered. "We have a plan. She is your betrothed."

"Betrothed?" His fingers fluttered to Jemma. "Why would I want that man's leavings when there are other ways I can take my pound of flesh? Ways in which it is far less likely I'll be killed."

"No." Lady Corbett shook her head as if trying to dislodge something. "No, that is *not* what we discussed." She sidled over to Augie and ran a plump finger down his cheek adoringly. "My dear boy, this is the only way. You know that. We leave on the evening tide."

Augie swatted his mother's caress away. "Nothing would make me marry that *trollop*."

Jemma winced at the vehemence in his tone.

He truly hates me. He probably always has.

"I promise," she pleaded, hoping she could make him see sense, "I won't allow Nick to hurt you if you let me go. In fact," she bargained, "if you release me now, I'll hail a hack and go back to my uncle's and say I simply got lost. *Please*."

Augie snorted in derision. "Let you go? But you're the perfect distraction. He won't even know until it's too late."

Shaking her head at the riddle in his words, she tried again. "He'll find you unless you release me."

"Shut up." The plump, be-ringed hand of Lady Corbett shot out across Jemma's cheek. "But, our debts, Augie," Lady Corbett cajoled, her hands held up in supplication. "We are ruined. You *must* marry her."

"I'm not going back to Bermuda, Mother. I've no desire to return to be mocked by the whole of the islands for marrying her. Nor do I wish to spend my days watching Father drool while a servant feeds him breakfast. It will take all of Sea Cliff's wealth to make the Corbetts whole again. There are much easier ways to become wealthy if one knows where to look."

"Augustus, you don't know what you are saying." Lady Corbett tried to take her son's arm, clutching at his coat and ignoring his attempts to pull away. "It's been our dream."

"No, Mother. Sea Cliff is *your* dream. Since I was a lad, you've harped about that bloody estate and pushed me into courting *her*." Augie turned to Jemma. "I never wished to marry you. *Ever*. You have always treated me as your eager lapdog." He gave a sharp laugh.

Jemma swallowed. "I am sorry, Augie, if you feel I've mistreated you." Her voice cracked. "You were my dearest childhood friend, for the sake of that friendship, please untie me. I'll make sure His Grace rewards you."

How can I persuade him to help me?

"I've no doubt I'll be getting money from the duke, but it won't be in the way in which *you* think," he mocked. "You overestimate my affection for you. You always have."

Her shoulders slumped in frustration. He was going to leave her to the mercy of his mother. She tried again to loosen the ropes at her wrists.

"But I've waited so long, so very long." Lady Corbett wailed as she wobbled from side to side in distress. Her faded red hair spilled free of its pins, whirling about her shoulders in a cloud. "You must marry her or I won't have Sea Cliff and we'll be destitute." Lady Corbett fell to the floor at her son's feet. "What am I to do if you don't marry her?"

"If you are smart, and I know you are, Mother, you'll dispose of this little problem and leave tonight. You said your goodbyes to Dorthea yesterday, and she is blissfully headed back to Yorkshire with no idea of your machinations. I'll visit her later and tell her I've decided to stay on. She'll welcome me. Tell everyone I was accosted on the streets of London and killed. My debts will likely be wiped clean out of pity for you and Father. I'll send you money as soon as my future plans come to fruition."

Lady Corbett pounded the floor in frustration. "I've done this all for you, Augustus!"

Augie stepped over his mother and made his way to the door. "You've done this all for *you*."

A great sigh of resignation escaped Lady Corbett and her eyes, red-rimmed and watery, looked up at her son with uncertainty. "But how shall I—"

"Look, Mother," Augie peered down at her cheerfully, "you're going to have to tidy up things yourself." He straightened and lay something on the bed. "Then you need to get on that ship bound for Bermuda. I promise I'll contact you later."

Gasping in horror, Jemma saw that Augie had placed a pistol on the filthy coverlet.

"I've loaded it for you. No one will even hear the gunshot. Not here in this disgusting brothel. You must take care of this before he finds her, Mother. Besides, everyone already assumes she's dead, you may be able to convince the magistrate to hand you and Father Sea Cliff . You just need to try harder." Augie leaned over and pressed a kiss to the top of his mother's head. "Goodbye, Mother."

"Augie, please." Jemma implored. "Don't do this."

"Farewell Jemma." He sidestepped around her, pausing only to shoot her a scathing glance over his shoulder before shutting the door behind him.

Her gaze turned to the pile of skirts, sobbing on the floor. Lady Corbett pulled at her hair and pounded at the floorboards.

Jemma twisted her arm to pick madly at the knot above her wrist, fear making her fingers sweat and become slippery against the rope. *She'll kill me here in this room, and Nick won't know what's become of me.*

The end of the primed pistol stared at her from the bed.

Frantically she tugged at the ropes and felt one of the knots loosen, and her eyes flew to the heap of weeping silk in front of her.

Suddenly, as if she knew Jemma was watching, Lady Corbett stopped her weeping, wiping at her tears with the hem of her skirt. She rolled to the side like a plump turtle and struggled to get to her feet. Finally, she stood, unsteady and sluggish, swatting madly at her cheeks and muttering.

"He's right of course. I must clean up this mess. Oh, how things have gotten mucked up." A stream of snot ran out of one nostril and her complexion was a mottled red. "You've mucked up things." She pointed a finger at Jemma.

"You don't want to do this. I'll sign over Sea Cliff to you. I've told you I don't want it." What could she do to convince Lady Corbett? "I can't go back to Bermuda, you know that. I don't wish to go back. The town knows I'm a fallen woman," she said in a rush as her eyes welled with tears. "No one will welcome me, so you see I don't need Sea Cliff." At the hardness of Lady Corbett's eyes, she whispered, "You were like a mother to me." Did she sound convincing?

"Shut up," Lady Corbett hissed, her fingers running over the coverlet towards the pistol. "You were *never* like a daughter to me. I never cared for you. How could I? Your mother cleaned chamber pots." Her face contorted in disgust. "You have always just been a means to an end. Had you married Augie like a good girl, I would have tolerated you, perhaps for years, before I made you eat my teacakes."

Jemma could feel the knot of the rope giving way and thought she could free her wrist. Gritting her teeth, she tried not to make a sound as the pain of the rope bit further into her skin.

"If you bring me a solicitor, I'll sign over Sea Cliff to you straightaway." She stalled for time. "I know where the account books are hidden," she lied, wondering for a moment if Tally had written to Uncle John where they were and thought he had. "I'll never return to Bermuda. I'll stay dead."

Lady Corbett gave a snort, "You'll stay dead all right. Quite dead." Her hands curled around the pistol. "Now that I think on this, I believe Augustus is correct. I *can* convince the magistrate in Hamilton that your original betrothal agreement entitles me to Sea Cliff. After all, it is what dear, departed William would have wanted. The estate would never go to auction. I am still the Governor's wife. She swiveled around, the pistol clutched firmly in her hand. "I shall pretend you are a wild pig or some other dumb animal. I've never shot a pistol before, but at this range I shouldn't miss." Squinting at Jemma, she clucked her tongue. "Just look at those freckles. *Hideous.* You never listened to me about wearing a hat or the lemon juice. Well, I suppose it hardly matters now."

Jemma's hand came free and she swung straight up with all her might to catch Lady Corbett on the shoulder. The chair, still bound to Jemma's other wrist swiveled against Lady Corbett's skirts, catching her on her thigh.

The Governor's wife stumbled, grunting in pain and

surprise, but she did not go down. The pistol swung about wildly in her hand. "You little bitch."

The chair, still tethered to Jemma, slid to the floor. Heaving with exertion, she lay on her side, kicking and pulling in a futile attempt to get away from the bore of the pistol. "Please, Lady Corbett. I am with child." Her hand reached out and tried to grab at Lady Corbett's ankle.

Lady Corbett stepped out of range of her questing hand. "All the more reason then," she pointed the pistol at Jemma's chest, "to dispose of you both at once."

I will not lay here like a wounded animal and allow her to shoot me.

Pointless though it was, she continued to attempt to free her other wrist. The cock of the pistol echoed in the room. "No." She closed her eyes, thinking of Nick.

27

Nick surveyed the three ships from where he stood, assured that the harbormaster would allow none of them to leave port without his express permission. He had searched two of them personally. Colin and Rowan were now searching the third, but Nick doubted they would find anything. The Corbetts were aboard none of them, though he did find a seedy man of the cloth, torn bible in hand, attempting to escape unseen from the deck of one of the ships bound for Bermuda. A silk purse was found in his pocket. After questioning the minister, Nick knew only that Augustus Corbett had hired him to perform a marriage ceremony on board ship. After assuring himself that the man did not know where Jem was, Nick released him.

His sixth sense insisted stubbornly that Jem was here amongst the dilapidated buildings on the dock. "Where are you love?" He'd never been more terrified in all his life.

The feather light touch of a small hand against his coin purse startled Nick out of his thoughts. Immediately, he reached out to grab his would be assailant.

"Ow. Lemme go." A grimy-faced boy, no more than nine

or ten and dressed in rags wiggled on the end of Nick's hand like a fish on a hook.

"Trying to rob me? Don't you know who I am?" Nick snarled, shaking the boy.

The boy screamed for his friends as he caught a good look at Nick's eyes. "The Devil's got me! Help! Help!"

A group of equally dirty lads, watching from the far dock, scattered, running into dark corners and alleys like cockroaches, abandoning their friend without a backward glance.

"Let me go. I beg you." The pickpocket kicked, his legs swinging wildly in his attempts to get away. "Oh, God. I didn't know it was you. Let me go Devil."

"Yes, I'm the Devil." Nick warmed to the task. He did not intend to hurt the boy, but the thought occurred to him that the lad might be of service in finding Jem. The boy 's profession, that of a pickpocket, meant he noticed everyone on the docks. "Now if you wish to leave with your soul intact, you'll do me a small favor." He lowered his voice to a growl.

The boy nodded enthusiastically. "Anything. Whatever you want. Just don't send me to hell. Don't take my soul."

Nick smiled, confident he'd be obeyed. "I am looking for a woman. Likely about your mother's age." He peered into the lad's face.

"I've got no mum." The boy apologized sadly, suddenly looking bewildered. "She died last winter from the consumption."

"Neither do I," Nick said lightly, feeling a surge of pity for the small thief.

The boy cocked his head and some of the fear left his eyes. "Did she die of the consumption too?" Then he bit his lip. "Beggin' your pardon, but I didn't think the Devil had a mum."

"You've been misinformed." He shook the boy again. "An older woman then. Her hair is a faded red, like a copper pot that's been used poorly, and she looks as if she's eaten one too many tarts."

"I think I seen her." He smiled, showing several missing teeth. Nodding eagerly, he said, "I know I've seen her."

The boy was in dire need of a bath, it was all Nick could do not to drop the lad and cover his nose. "You're not lying, are you?" Nick raised a brow. "We'll leave for hell right now if you are. What is your name?"

"Teddy Mac. And, I'd not lie to the Devil of Dunbar." The boy's eyes, a light blue, regarded Nick solemnly. "If I was to lie, you'd find me again," the boy reasoned. "I've heard—"

Nick shook his head in irritation. "Never mind that. What about the woman with red hair, Teddy Mac?" The boy *had* seen Lady Corbett, Nick was sure of it.

"Do you mean to take her to Hell?" Teddy Mac no longer seemed terrified, merely curious. "She's not a nice lady, that's why I'm askin'."

"I grow weary of this conversation." He peered at the little thief. "Would you rather we head down to the flames, Teddy Mac?"

The boy shook his head, swallowing so hard his Adam's apple bobbed up and down. "Miss Devine, she owns the house over there." He pointed to a large three-story building with peeling gray paint and a general air of neglect. The sound of piano playing met Nick's ears just as a couple of sailors stumbled out of the establishment, slapping each other on the shoulder.

"Sometimes, if I run an errand for her, Miss Devine feeds me a bit of meat pie or sausage in the kitchen. It's warm and the ladies that live there sometimes bring me a sweet." He swallowed again. "They was talking about a lady who came to Miss Devine and rented a room. Miss Devine thought the lady wished one of the girls to come to her room, but it wasn't like that."

"What was it like?" Nick murmured as he studied the brothel.

"She just wanted the room. The girls were talking that maybe the red-haired lady might want to consort with a sailor or such—"

"Do you even know what that word means?" Nick queried.

"—And that's why she wanted the room. The girls said the red-haired lady called them all whores. Leggy Lucy said there weren't no man who'd want to consort with that woman."

"Indeed?" Jem was in that brothel with Lady Corbett and Augie. Nick would bet his life on it.

Slowly he eased his hold on Teddy Mac but still held tight to the lad's shirt. "I'll give you my purse if you find out which room the red-haired lady rents."

"Your purse?" The boy's face took on a look of wonderment. "All of it? And you won't damn me? Won't take my soul?"

"What would I do with a pickpocket's soul?" Nick scoffed, letting go of Teddy Mac. "Show me," he commanded, "and I'll not only give you my purse but a place to sleep and plenty to eat." Peabody would find a spot at Dunbar House for the boy. He could work in the stables or sweep up the soot from the fireplace. Anything would be better than waiting to be hung for stealing a gentleman's purse.

"Truly?" the boy said, astonishment visible under the layers of grime that coated his face.

"You have my oath." Nick glanced at the wharf, but there was no sign of Colin or Rowan. "Once you show me, you're to come back out here and wait until you see a golden-haired man with a scar on his face. You tell him where I've gone, and you'll sleep with a full belly tonight."

Teddy Mac nodded in agreement as one small, filthy hand pulled at Nick's sleeve and led him into Miss Devine's.

"I LOVED YOUR FATHER."

Jemma's breath came in shallow gasps as she opened her eyes. A rat scurried under the bed and through a hole in the wall. The piano player downstairs played in earnest while the drunken laughter of men and women floated up through the floorboards. "I didn't suspect." She kept her voice soothing, hoping that she could still possibly talk some sense into Lady Corbett. She looked at the gun held loosely in the woman's fingers. *If I could just get my other hand free.*

"Yes," Lady Corbett said, her face wrinkling mournfully. "I thought William a delightful man. Just delightful. That was why I had to get rid of your mother," she said with conviction. "I thought William would turn to me, you see, and we could dispose of that toad, George. But he didn't turn to me."

Footsteps sounded in the hallway outside the door. Even with the noise from downstairs, Jemma could clearly make out the heavy tread of a large man. *Nick.* It had to be Nick. She kept her eyes on Lady Corbett and the pistol. The Governor's wife seemed lost in her memories of the past and didn't appear to hear the footsteps coming towards the room.

"My father spoke fondly of you, and often. He held you in high regard." She choked out the words. *Please, let it be Nick.*

The footsteps came closer.

"Did he?" Lady Corbett smiled. "Well, then I suppose I should have made those cakes for George rather than your father." The pistol dangled from her hand, and she aimed it directly at Jemma's heart. Lady Corbett regarded her with unabashed glee. "But I'm still going to shoot you, you little tart."

The door shuddered and broke on its hinges, bursting open in a spray of splinters and peeling paint. A dark shadow hovered in the hall.

Startled, Lady Corbett dropped the pistol and the weapon slid across the floor.

Jemma immediately stretched her fingers to reach the pistol, wanting to scream with fear and frustration when she couldn't quite reach it.

"If you're looking for one of Miss Devine's girls," Lady Corbett addressed the large form blocking the doorway, "you've got the wrong room. The only whore in here isn't for sale."

"I'll thank you not to call the future Duchess of Dunbar a whore," a gravelly voice replied matter-of-factly.

Jemma nearly shook with relief. *Nick. It was Nick.*

From her place on the floor, Jemma watched as Lady Corbett sidled over to Nick, giving him a flirtatious smile. "Well, if it isn't my erstwhile house guest, Mr. Shepherd, or should I say Your Grace?" Lady Corbett stepped over the pistol until it was hidden beneath her skirts.

"Jem? Are you all right?" He never once looked away from Lady Corbett.

"I'm fine." Her words faltered as Lady Corbett suddenly bent at the waist. "A pistol, she has a pistol."

Lady Corbett lifted her head and smiled slyly at Nick. She was still smiling as Nick's fist made contact with the side of her head. Her plump frame lifted up for a moment, then collapsed into a heap on the floor.

Nick stepped over Lady Corbett as if she were a bit of trash and came to Jemma's side. "Jem. Thank God." He turned to free her from the chair, growling at the sight of her bloodied wrists. A large hand cupped her face as he pulled her to stand next to him. "Jem."

"I found you to be an insolent houseguest, Mr. Shepherd.

You never *did* write that introduction for Dorthea to the Dowager Marchioness of Cambourne," Lady Corbett spat. "And I so wanted to have tea with her." She shoved herself against the bed for support as she came to her feet. Her hand shook as she pointed the pistol at Nick.

"Nick." Jemma said softly in warning.

He calmly turned towards Lady Corbett with not a shred of fear. "Do you really think you can shoot *me*?"

"I shall." Lady Corbett shook her head back and forth, swatting at her cheek as if a fly tormented her. "I will. You deserve it," she cried as Nick reached for the gun. "But maybe I'll just shoot her instead." She turned the weapon towards Jemma.

The pistol went off, sounding like a thunderclap in the small room

"No!" Nick cried out as a burst of pure fire licked against Jemma's shoulder and she fell, the rough wood of the floor scrapping against her cheek. The pain was intense, as if someone had pushed a hot poker into her shoulder. The room swam about her and she grabbed at her shoulder, staring at amazement at her bloodied fingers.

An unearthly growl erupted beside her along with the sound of kindling being broken. Rowan's shouts reached her ears as Nick's worried face swam before her eyes.

"Jem."

28

Jemma opened her eyes and recognized the top of her canopied bed. She was in her own room at the Marsh home. Snatches of a terrible dream filled her head. Lady Corbett and Augie had kidnapped her and were going to take her back to Bermuda. She took a deep breath and tried to sit up, falling back against the pillow at the burst of pain emanating from her shoulder.

"Stop moving, Jem. You'll open the wound and it will start to bleed anew." Nick lounged on a chair next to the bed, his shirt unbuttoned, and his clothing rumpled. The chair creaked under his large form, and Jemma doubted the piece would ever be the same. Nick's cheeks were dark with stubble. More so than usual.

"You," her mouth was dry, "need to shave."

"Indeed." He stood and came over to the bed, taking her hand in his.

Jemma licked her lips, wincing as her tongue ran over the split at the corner of her mouth. "You should not be in my bedchamber," she choked. "My aunt—"

"Has come to terms with my lack of propriety. I insisted

that I be here when you woke, not patiently sitting at home, waiting for Lady Marsh to send word to me of your recovery. Ridiculous after what has occurred. Nor was I content to wait in a guest room." He pressed her hand to his lips. "Your aunt strenuously objected, of course, but I ignored her. I believe the last thing she did was to scream for the smelling salts." The full lips twisted into a wry smile. "I've ordered them all away, including the doctor, who has promised me absolute discretion. How do you feel?"

"My shoulder hurts." Carefully she leaned forward as Nick pushed another pillow behind her.

"It should. That bitch shot you." Nick sounded worried and annoyed at the same time. He ran a finger lightly down her face, carefully avoiding the bruise on her cheek. "You need to rest. We're to be married as soon as you can stand, and your face has healed. Thank goodness your nose isn't broken." His very tone implied there could be no objection.

"What happened?" She looked behind him to the small table next to her bed where a pitcher of water sat.

"Thirsty?" He stood at her nod and poured a glass of water. He held the glass to her lips. As the cool liquid slid down her throat, panic filled her. Her hand flew down to cup her stomach.

"Jem, everything is fine. You are both fine." He took the glass from her lips. "Thankfully the doctor did not make *that* proclamation until after your aunt had left the room." The mismatched eyes twinkled with mirth. "Dr. Martin wasn't sure whether to tell me or not. I assured him of the child's paternity."

She closed her eyes and said a grateful prayer. "Lady Corbett killed my father, Nick. She poisoned him. And my mother." She opened her eyes and tried to blink back the tears threatening to fall. "Teacakes. She poisoned the teacakes." Her hands clutched the coverlet. "She said she loved him and he should have married her," the words came out in a rush, "and that it was she, and not Lord Corbett, who told my father about your grandfather's papers."

"You need not ever worry about Lady Corbett again, my love. She slipped on the stairs as she tried to flee. Broke her neck." Nick spoke lightly. "A shame. I would have liked her to stand trial for her crimes." He waited, watching her to see if she would question him further.

Remembering the strange popping sound she'd heard after the pistol discharged, Jemma had serious doubts that Lady Corbett fell down the stairs on her own. She'd been in London long enough to hear the rumors even before she knew Nick and the Duke of Dunbar were one and the same. Loving Nick meant accepting who he was. Instead of pondering her future husband's less savory activities she said, "How would she have known about those documents?"

Nick kissed the tip of her nose, appearing relieved she would not question him further about the means of Lady Corbett's death.

"She was an acquaintance of my mother's, prior to her marriage to Corbett. I found out several months ago." Nick pursed his lips in thought. "Mother was more of a drunkard than my father, oddly enough. She just hid it much better than he. She must have stumbled on her knowledge of those papers by accident, probably while going through grandfather's desk looking for spare coin. My parents were deeply in debt, and when my grandfather cut them off, I suppose she became desperate. She must have told Lady Corbett at some point, possibly thinking to enlist her aid in stealing them, but the Corbetts outsmarted her." He slid further onto the bed, ignoring Jemma's protests. "Not difficult. My mother was a bit of a dimwit."

"I'm wounded," she said pointedly as Nick stretched out

his legs on the bed next to her. "You could delay my recovery."

He leaned his head against hers and took her hand, careful not to jostle her wounded shoulder. "Shush. You do not really wish to get away," the husky voice whispered against her temple.

"No. I do not," she assured him, sinking against the warmth of his body, remembering the first time he'd said such to her.

They lay together quietly for some time before Jemma said, "What of Arabella?"

"My sister," Nick's voice became brittle, "will be residing at Twinings, our estate in Wales, until the babe is born. She left this morning with Aunt Maisy. I haven't yet decided whether or not I will allow her to come back to London, and I certainly do not wish her at our wedding with your shoulder still bandaged and she the cause."

Jemma did not care if she ever saw Arabella again, but Nick loved his sister. "I will not be the cause of your estrangement. I think Arabella believes she was acting in your best interests, Nick." Miranda had told Jemma much about Arabella, and regardless of her machinations, Jemma felt some empathy for her soon to be sister-in-law.

He snorted. "You are kind, my love, far kinder than I would be were the situation reversed. Bella needs to learn a lesson, perhaps Twinings will give her the education she lacks. Wales is very stark and cold, much like Bella. She will either accept recent events and forgive the past, or she will live out her days alone." Nick's tone did not brook further discussion. "Sleep, Jem," he murmured. "I'll not leave you. Not tonight. Not ever."

Jemma closed her eyes again, letting the warmth of Nick's body seep through her own. Rain began to patter against the window panes, the gentle rhythm lulling her into sleep. She thought of all the things that had transpired, how revenge had turned to love, a great love.

Her love.

Bermuda was her past, and as much as she missed some of her friends there, she had no wish to return. She would ask Nick tomorrow to find Tally. Uncle John likely knew his whereabouts. If possible, she would gladly sign Sea Cliff over to him. After all, he had saved her life. How surprised he would be to find himself a wealthy man. Sea Cliff and all its inhabitants would be safe with him. He was an honest man. A good man. Not a gambler. Jemma tensed next to Nick, where he snored softly at her side.

"Nick." She shook him awake, hating the fear in her voice. "Where is Augie?"

EPILOGUE

Lady Arabella settled herself in the Dunbar coach and told herself not to cry.

Twinings. He's sending me to Twinings.

The estate was rarely used, in fact it was little more than a hunting cottage. She would be alone except for servants and one decrepit, eccentric cousin thirty years her senior. Not even her aunt would be there to comfort her.

"Arabella, I insist you buck up." Lady Cupps-Foster settled in across the coach and sat back against the fine leather squabs. "One must learn to accept one's fate." She smoothed down her skirts. "Particularly when one is to blame for that ill –fated turn."

"I *am* bucking up," Arabella snapped. "How do you expect me to behave? He's sending me to Wales."

"Well, he's forcing *me* to escort you. And I'll stay with you. At least until you are settled." Aunt Maisy pursed her lips. "My dear, Nick will forgive you." She looked out the window. "Eventually." She frowned. "I should speak to Peabody. Two of those footmen do not look appropriately clean shaven, and their livery looks rumpled."

"How long do you think eventually is?"

"Well." Aunt Maisy turned from her assessment of the Dunbar footmen. "Let me see," she put a gloved finger to her lips, "your actions *did* nearly get his betrothed killed, so I would not expect he'll forgive you anytime soon. It may take years before he allows you to come home."

Arabella pulled at a loose thread on her skirt. "No, I don't suppose he will allow me home for some time. And I didn't mean for her to be hurt. I only wished her gone. How could he marry her? The daughter of a traitor. The traitor that—"

"Listen to me, niece," Aunt Maisy snapped, her eyes hard. "I love you dearly, so I say this for your own good. Best you make peace now. Nick loves that girl, *truly* loves her. I thought never to see such a thing. He will keep you in Twinings forever if you do not see some sense. And I've no desire to visit you there."

Arabella felt as if she'd been slapped. A great gulp of air escaped her lungs, and she sat back in surprise at Aunt Maisy's tone.

Her aunt hesitated a moment before reaching over to pat Arabella on the knee. "You must open your heart and move past all the ills done to you, real or imagined, for the path you are on now leads only to loneliness and disappointment. I beg you, give Nick some time, then make your apologies, sincerely, and he will forgive you."

"And what of her?"

Aunt Maisy brow wrinkled as she mulled the question. "She is not to blame for the sins of her father, just as you are not to blame for yours. I loved my brother, Phillip, but he was a wastrel, without an ounce of sense. Your mother was worse. I've no doubt that things would have ended badly for them even without the assistance of the Marsh family. There may come a time when you will choose happiness over the honor of those who do not deserve it."

Arabella looked askance. "I have never heard you speak thus."

"Then perhaps," Aunt Maisy settled the rug about her lap and feet, "'tis time I did."

Arabella opened her mouth to speak and gainsay her, but Aunt Maisy had shut her eyes, her hands in her lap. The streets of London passed by the window, the coach gaining speed as they headed out of the city. She pressed her forehead to the cool glass of the window, thinking on her aunt's words and shut her eyes as they headed to Wales.

❦

Thank you for reading Nick and Jemma's story. If you enjoyed Devil of a Duke I would greatly appreciate you leaving a review.

Keep reading more of the Wicked's....

Devil of a Duke (Book 2)

My Wicked Earl (Book 3)

Wickedly Yours (Book 4)

Tall, Dark & Wicked (Book 5)

Still Wicked (Book 6)

Wicked Again (Book 7)

ABOUT THE AUTHOR

Kathleen Ayers has been a hopeful romantic since the tender age of fourteen when she first purchased a copy of Sweet Savage Love at a garage sale while her mother was looking at antique animal planters. Since then she's read hundreds of historical romances and fallen in love dozens of times. In particular she adores handsome, slightly damaged men with a wicked sense of humor. On paper, of course.

Kathleen lives in Houston with her husband, a college-aged son who pops in to have his laundry done and two very spoiled dogs.

Sign up for Kathleen's newsletter:
www.kathleenayers.com

Like Kathleen on Facebook
www.facebook.com/kayersauthor

Join Kathleen's Facebook Group
Historically Hot with Kathleen Ayers

Follow Kathleen on Bookbub
bookbub.com/authors/kathleen-ayers

Made in the USA
Middletown, DE
02 February 2024